UNSUITABLE

SAMANTHA TOWLE

OTHER CONTEMPORARY NOVELS BY SAMANTHA TOWLE

Sacking the Quarterback (BookShots Flames) with James Patterson

The Ending I Want

When I Was Yours

Trouble

REVVED SERIES
Revved
Revived

THE STORM SERIES
The Mighty Storm
Wethering the Storm
Taming the Storm
The Storm

PARANORMAL ROMANCES BY SAMANTHA TOWLE

The Bringer

THE ALEXANDRA JONES SERIES
First Bitten
Original Sin

Copyright © 2016 by Samantha Towle
All rights reserved.

Visit my website at www.samanthatowle.co.uk
Cover Designer: Najla Qamber Designs
Editor and Interior Designer: Jovana Shirley,
Unforeseen Editing, www.unforeseenediting.com

No part of this book may be reproduced or transmitted in any form or by any means, electronic or mechanical, including photocopying, recording, or by any information storage and retrieval system without the written permission of the author, except for the use of brief quotations in a book review.

This book is a work of fiction. Names, characters, places, and incidents either are products of the author's imagination or are used fictitiously. Any resemblance to actual persons, living or dead, events, or locales is entirely coincidental.

ISBN-13: 978-1537734811

*This one is for my Wether Girls.
Your support and daily laughs (and hot men pics!) are
invaluable to me.*

SEVEN YEARS AGO

W˥ˢʳᴱ ᴀᴍ I?

What's happening?

Pain everywhere...

Then, I remember.

No.

I force my eyes open.

I can't see. It's dark. My sight is blurred. Blood. I can feel it running down into my eye.

I can't see anything.

I can't see *her*.

Holding my breath, I listen...waiting for a sound to tell me where she is.

Nothing.

I try to say her name, but it hurts.

It hurts so much.

My lungs are burning...my stomach is on fire...I'm bleeding...

I have to move. Get help.

I reach my hand out, but all I feel is the damp earth I'm lying on.

I inch my fingers around, trying to find something to hold on to, to help me up, but there's nothing.

Forcing my eyes open, I blink rapidly, trying to clear my vision, but it doesn't work.

I rub the back of my hand over my eyes, clearing them of the blood and tears, and finally, I can see.

I turn my head to the side.

She's there.

And she's not moving. Her once-pretty pink dress is now covered in blood and dirt, and it's pushed up, exposing her.

No.

I grit my teeth hard, rage tearing through me.

I drag myself over to her. Pain screams in my body. I press a weak hand to my stomach.

My hand is slick against my shirt.

Wet. So wet. And cold.

I'm bleeding badly. But that doesn't matter. I just have to get to her. I have to know she's okay.

She has to be okay.

I'm coming, baby. Just hold on.

I reach her.

Her eyes are open. And blank.

"No…baby…no." Pure anger tears through me, and I cry out a primal sound.

I collapse beside her. "I'm…s-sorry." I pull her dress down, covering her up.

My vision blurs again.

My heart is slowing down.

It hurts to breathe, and when I do, it's like I'm taking in water.

I'm dying.

I close my eyes and reach out for her hand. Taking hold, I curl my fingers around hers.

Footsteps. Heavy footsteps are treading through the undergrowth.

Then, I hear a snuffle.

An animal. A dog maybe?

"Help…" I croak, trying to expel my voice as loud as I can. But, even to my own ears, it's not enough.

UNSUITABLE

There's no response.

Using all the strength I have left, I force my voice out. "Help!"

The footsteps stop.

"Is someone there?" a male voice says.

Yes. "Help...*please*..."

The footsteps start up again, moving quicker, coming closer.

I hear the rustling of leaves from the bushes surrounding us and then, "Jesus Christ!"

Thank God.

The man lands on his knees next to me. A dog licks my face.

"Hank, stop it. I just gotta tie my dog up. I'll be right back."

"No! Don't...go. Help...her...please," I gargle, blood flooding my throat, as I panic.

He moves away, but he returns a second later. "I'm back. Try not to speak."

Ignoring him, I say, "Help...her."

Maybe she's not really gone.

He can try to revive her...do CPR...

I feel him move over me to get to her. "Honey...can you hear me?"

I force my eyes open, turning my head.

He's checking her neck for a pulse.

Why didn't I do that?

Those seconds watching him, waiting...feel like hours.

His expression drops, his eyes closing, with a sad-sounding breath.

And it confirms what I knew was already true.

She's gone.

My heart rips open and bleeds out with the rest of me.

"Is she..."

"Try not to talk. Just hold on for me, yeah? Can you do that? I'm calling an ambulance right now." He's on his phone. "Yes, it's an emergency. Be quick, please. Two kids...one, she's not moving. I don't think...there's no pulse. The other one, he's alive...talking, but there's blood everywhere...so much blood..."

PROLOGUE

DAISY
EIGHTEEN MONTHS AGO

"TELL ME AGAIN, where were you last night?"

I look at the detective sitting across the table from me. My palms are clammy. I knot my fingers together in my lap.

Why do I have to tell him again? Did he not believe me the first time I told him?

"After I left work, I went straight home, and my boyfriend, Jason, came over. He was with me all night. Ask him; he'll tell you."

"My colleague spoke with Jason a few minutes ago." The detective leans forward. Placing his forearms on the table, he links his hands together. "He told us that he wasn't with you last night."

"*What?*" The word leaves my mouth in a breathless rush.

"Jason told my colleague that he was with his brother and friends, playing cards, at his house all evening and that he didn't see you at all last night."

"I-I...what? I don't understand..." My eyes are frantically searching the room. Confusion and panic are racing through my mind and body. "I don't understand. Why would Jason say that?"

The detective gives me a steady look, saying nothing.

I lick my lips. My mouth is dry as I try to speak, "Jason is lying. I was with him at my place all night."

"Can anyone corroborate that?" the detective asks.

Jesse.

No…he stayed out last night at his friend Justin's house. It was just Jason and me in the house.

Oh God.

"No." I moisten my lips again. "But I'm telling you the truth, I swear." I stare steadily into the eyes of the detective, trying to convey that my words are the truth.

But I know it's fruitless. He thinks I did it.

I swallow hard, fighting to hold in my rising panic. "You think it was me. You think I stole the jewelry. But you're wrong. It wasn't me," I state emphatically.

The detective leans back in his seat. "What am I supposed to think, Daisy? It was your key card that was used to gain access to the store after it was closed, the same card that was still in your possession when we picked you up. You know that cancels out the alarm trigger. You know how to turn the camera equipment off. You know exactly where the high-end pieces of jewelry are—"

"But I didn't take them! Why would I?"

"You've been raising your brother alone, you're behind on your rent, and you have bills to pay and outstanding credit cards. People have stolen for less."

"But I didn't steal the jewelry! I would never! I'm not a thief! I-I don't know how my card was used. Maybe…maybe it was copied." I'm clutching at straws because not one thing about this is making a shred of sense to me.

The detective is shaking his head at me.

"Yes," I argue, "maybe someone stole it and then put it back."

UNSUITABLE

"Who, Daisy?" He leans forward. "Who would have done that?"

My brain scrambles. Then, it clings to the only other person in my house with me last night.

"Jason." My voice is shaking, tears thickening my words. "Jason lied and said he wasn't with me when he was. He could have taken the key card, and—"

"But how could he have committed the robbery when you said he was with you?"

He's right. I drive my fingers into my hair, scratching at my scalp.

I'm hit with a thought.

"Maybe...maybe Jason gave it to someone." I'm panting now, breathless, frightened.

I can see the detective retracting from me. I'm losing him. He thinks I did it. He thinks I stole the jewelry from the store. My place of work. The job I love.

"Maybe Jason gave it to someone and then put it back in my bag before I knew it was gone."

"It's a good theory, Daisy." The detective nods. "And we have looked into your boyfriend, Jason Doyle. A few years ago, he was locked up for stealing a car. He also has some juvenile shoplifting offenses on his record, and of course, we know who his brother is—"

"That's it! Damien!" I cry. "It could have been Damien and Jason in on it together! I know Damien's a bad guy. I've heard things about him—"

"We're well aware of the type of man that Damien Doyle is," the detective cuts me off. "Robbery is just one of the many things that he's had his slippery fingers in over the years, but we've never been able to tie anything to him. No one ever gives him up." He runs his hand over his chin, scratching at the stubble on it. "Look, Daisy, if you give me something, then I can help you. Maybe you didn't want to do this, and you were forced into it. Maybe the sound of the money was just too good to pass up. Give me the name of the person or persons who helped you do this, and tell me where the items are now. Then, I can help you."

He wants me to say it was Damien and that I was a part of this robbery.

But, if I do that, it would be a lie. I don't know for sure who did the robbery. I know, in my gut, that Jason took the key card, but I can't prove it. And, if I say it was Damien, then I'd be admitting to something that I didn't do.

I'd go to jail.

Shaking my head, I drive my fingers into my hair again, pulling at it, my eyes staring down at the table.

I have nothing to give him because I don't know anything, except my own truth.

And I'm not a liar.

Oh God. I can't believe this is happening.

Lifting my eyes, I catch sight of the clock on the wall. It's three fifteen. School will be finishing soon.

"My brother, Jesse. He'll be leaving school soon. I need to be home for him. He'll worry if I'm not there."

"Don't worry. Jesse is being taken care of."

What does he mean, Jesse is being taken care of?

I part my dry lips to ask him when the door opens. A policeman in uniform is standing there.

The detective rises from his seat. "I'll be back in a minute," he tells me.

I watch him through the glass pane in the door as he talks to the uniformed officer. Their expressions don't give away anything as to what they're talking about.

My heart is thundering in my chest. I've never felt fear like this.

The door opens. The detective comes back in with the uniformed officer following behind him.

The detective takes his seat in front of me while the officer remains standing. "Daisy, while you've been here, officers have been searching your apartment…and they've found one of the items of the stolen jewelry."

UNSUITABLE

No.

This can't be happening.

"I didn't steal anything!" I cry, getting to my feet. "I didn't do this!"

The uniformed officer moves quickly, and before I know it, I'm being restrained, my hands behind my back. I struggle to get free, begging him to let me go.

Then, I hear the voice of the detective saying, "Daisy May Smith, I am arresting you on suspicion of theft. You do not have to say anything, but it may harm your defense if you do not mention when questioned something which you later rely on in court. Anything you do say may be given in evidence."

Oh Jesus. I'm being arrested. For a crime I didn't commit.

A holy terror, unlike anything I've ever felt before, seeps into every part of my body.

ONE

PRESENT DAY

I STARE AT MY REFLECTION in the small mirror.

My long brown hair is tied back into a ponytail. Face clean, free of makeup. I glance down at my clothes. Jeans and a baby-blue T-shirt. Black ballet flats on my feet.

The clothes and shoes that I wore when I came to prison.

The jeans and T-shirt are a little loose on me. I knew I'd lost weight in here. Daily use of the gym and stress will shed pounds off a girl. Not that I was heavy to begin with. I look too thin. I could do with putting some weight back on.

"You ready?"

Turning from my reflection, I look at Officer Roman standing in the doorway. "I'm ready."

So ready.

I have never been more ready for anything in my life.

One last look around, and with nothing to take with me, I leave the cell I spent my last night in and follow her down the corridors.

I was moved to a release cell last night, so I didn't spend my last night in the cell where I'd spent the past eighteen months. Not that I'm upset about it. Quite the opposite.

I'm frigging ecstatic.

I'm being released.

Eighteen months, I've dreamed of this moment. Counted down the minutes, hours, days…praying I would be released on parole after serving eighteen months of the three-year sentence I'd been given.

Being out on parole means I'll be living under conditions set by my probation officer, but at least I won't be here.

I'm getting out of this hellhole.

I'm holding the relief back, keeping it restrained.

I won't let myself feel anything until I'm out of here and back in the real world.

A world where I get my life back. A world where I can get back to the only person who has ever mattered to me.

My brother, Jesse.

I say my brother, but he's my kid. When I was sixteen and Jesse was six, our drug-addicted, waste-of-space mother bailed on us, disappearing with all the money we'd had and leaving me alone to raise him. But I'd been raising him since he was a baby because all my mother cared about was herself, drugs, and whomever she was screwing at that time.

When she left, I quit school and got a job, working in a factory, to get money to feed and clothe Jesse and pay our rent and bills. Not glamorous but it helped. Just barely. We scraped by. I'd buy the cheap food and go to the supermarket just before closing time, so I could get the reduced food, like dented tins because the price had been dropped on them. Sometimes, they would get dented on purpose. I'd shop in secondhand stores for clothes. I did everything I could to make sure the money would stretch.

It was hard, but I always made sure that Jesse was okay. He came first.

He always comes first.

UNSUITABLE

I worked at the factory for a year, but I got laid off when they had a cut in the work force. It was last in, first out. I was the last one hired, so I was the first to be out of a job.

It got hard until I found another job. I didn't have savings because there was never any spare money to save.

I applied for jobs but wouldn't get them because I didn't have any qualifications. I received state benefits, and I still cashed in Jesse's child benefit that came through for my mother—yes, I would forge her signature—but it wasn't enough for both of us. And I couldn't exactly tell the benefit people that I needed more money because, if they knew that my mother had left, they would have taken Jesse away. And I couldn't lose him.

It got really tough for a time. There were days when I would go without food so that Jesse could eat.

I could have asked my best friend, Cece, for help, but I had to do it alone. Jesse was my responsibility.

Then, luck came on my side, and I got a part-time job, stacking shelves at the local supermarket. A week later, I got a part-time waitressing job. The waitressing was in the evenings, and I hated leaving Jesse, but Cece would look after him while I was working.

I did those jobs for six months, all the while still applying for full-time work. Finally, I landed a job in this upscale jewelry store. I could hardly believe I'd gotten the job. I mean, the interview had gone well, but I was uneducated, and the place was nice. For some reason, the manager had seen something in me and given me the job.

It was the best...and worst thing that ever happened to me.

The best part was the money. I was being paid more than both of my part-time jobs combined. I was learning a trade in the jewelry business, and it meant I could be home every night for Jesse.

Little did I know, four years later, I'd be framed for stealing hundreds of thousands of pounds' worth of jewelry from the store and that I would go to prison for it.

That I would lose everything.

Lose Jesse.

My kid. My family.

I want him back.

I will get him back.

Eighteen months without seeing or speaking to him, it's killed me.

Our communication was only via letters. Well, I say *communication*, but it wasn't exactly that. I wrote to him. He never once wrote back.

He's angry.

Because I wouldn't let him come visit me while I was in there.

He thought I'd abandoned him.

Truth was, I couldn't bear the thought of him seeing me in there. And I didn't want him coming to this place.

I wouldn't let anyone visit me. Not even Cece.

So, I haven't seen or spoken to anyone I love in eighteen months.

My heart pounding, I continue to follow Officer Roman. I wait while she unlocks the gate, and then she takes me through, heading toward the reception area.

I haven't seen this part of the prison since I arrived here.

I look out through the window. My heart pounds with equal measures of nerves and excitement.

I'm getting out of here. I'm getting my life back.

The life that was stolen from me.

Officer Kendall hands me a plastic carrier bag. "The things you came in with," she tells me.

Opening the bag, I look inside.

UNSUITABLE

My old phone that no longer works, a used lip gloss, my purse. I pick my purse out and open it. Inside is a twenty pound note.

I have twenty pounds to my name.

Sigh.

I spy my old house keys in the bottom of the carrier bag. I touch my fingers to them. The keys to my old home. The home I no longer have.

Tears prick my eyes. I blink them back.

"You okay, Daisy?" Officer Roman asks me.

Swallowing past my emotions, I nod my head and drop my purse back into the carrier bag.

"You know where you're going from here?" she asks me.

"Yep." I look at her. "I go straight to London Probation Service to see my probation officer..." I stall, trying to recall his name.

"Toby Willis," she fills in for me. "Toby will determine the terms of your release and give you details of the hostel where you'll be staying."

"You mean, I'm not staying at the Ritz?"

I give her a look of mock-horror, and she laughs.

"Come on, comedian, let's get you out of here."

The officer inside the reception room buzzes us through. I follow behind Officer Roman as she leads me to the door that will take me out of here.

I watch, my heart hammering in my chest, as the final door opens.

I'm free.

I take in a deep breath. A lungful of free air.

I know it sounds stupid, but the air just feels better out here. Cleaner, fresher. Better than the air I was breathing behind those high walls that kept me prisoner for so long.

I take my first step toward freedom.

"I don't want to see you in here ever again." Officer Roman's voice comes from behind me.

I glance back at her. "You won't ever see me again; that's a promise."

A smile works its way onto her hard mouth. "Good. And good luck, Daisy. I hope everything works out for you."

Yeah, me, too.

I give her a nod and then face forward. Another deep breath, and I step out onto the street.

The door closes behind me with a clunk. I hear the lock turn, shutting me out.

For a moment, I panic.

I literally don't know what to do. I've spent so long being told what to do that I feel like I don't know my own thoughts in this moment.

I look up and down the street. People are milling around.

A figure across the street catches my eye, and I can't help the smile that breaks out on my face.

Cece.

"Ce?" I say, suddenly choked with emotion at the sight of her.

"Mayday!" She smiles big.

Hearing her call me by the nickname that Jesse gave me when he was little fills me with an ache so deep that I fear it'll never leave.

Cece pushes off the car she was leaning against and comes bounding toward me. Her dark brown waves, now streaked with purple, are dancing around her face, her big brown eyes wide with happiness.

The wind is knocked out of me as Cece collides with me, wrapping her arms tight around me, hugging me hard.

She smells like home.

God, I've missed her.

"I missed you," she whispers.

I hear the emotion in her voice. It makes my chest constrict and my eyes sting.

UNSUITABLE

Dropping the carrier bag to the ground, I hug her back. "I missed you, too, Ce." I swallow back tears. "What are you doing here?"

"Nice to see you, too." She chuckles.

"I mean"—I lean back to look into her face—"I thought you'd be at work."

"Monday's my day off now. But, even if it weren't, did you really think I wouldn't be here, waiting for you?" She smiles warmly. "It's been too long. I hate that you wouldn't let me come visit you." A frown puckers her brow.

I exhale a breath. "I know, but it was better that way, Ce. I didn't want you seeing me while I was in that place."

And I couldn't spend my time counting down the days to her visits. I needed to just focus on counting down the days to my release.

"And you knew I didn't agree. It didn't matter to me—"

"I know," I cut her off. My voice comes out sharp, so I soften it. "But *I* needed it to be that way."

She stares at me for a long moment. "Yeah, well, you leave again, and I'm coming with. You got me?"

I give her a tight smile. "I got you. But I'm not going anywhere."

And I mean that. I'm never falling prey to anyone ever again.

She smiles. "You look good," she tells me. "You sure you've been in prison and not just at a fitness camp?" She gives a comical tilt of her head.

"Funny." I give her a light jab to the shoulder. "I used the gym every day. Not much else to do in there." Well, apart from reading, watching TV, and doing the cleaning job I had.

"Well, you totally have the whole Lara Croft thing going on now." She reaches over my shoulder, giving my ponytail a tug.

"I love the purple." I gesture to her hair.

"It was blue last week." She grins.

Cece is always changing her hair color. It comes with the territory. She's a hairdresser—or I should say, hairstylist. She works at this really cool upscale salon in London.

Releasing her hands from my arms, she grabs my hand. "Come, let's get you out of here."

I scoop my carrier bag up from the ground and let her lead me across the road, toward her car.

I've just buckled up in the passenger seat when she turns to me, biting her lip, with a nervous look in her eyes.

"I did something…that I hope you'll be cool with."

"Depends. The last surprise someone gave me landed me in prison." I give her a deadpan look.

Her lips lift into a half-smile. "How long are you going to play that card?"

"Forever. I think I've earned it."

"True." She nods.

"So, this thing?"

"I got us a place."

My eyes widen in surprise. "You moved out of your mum and dad's?"

"It was time. And you need somewhere to live. My gran left me a good chunk of money when she died, so I put it to good use and invested it in an apartment."

Shame covers me. "I'm sorry I wasn't there for the funeral."

She waves me off. "I know you would have been there if you could. Anyway, I got us this apartment in Sutton. It's nice. Three bedrooms. Not far from where Jesse is living, so you can be close to him."

"Three bedrooms?" I stare at her.

"Yeah, a bedroom for you, one for me, and one for Jesse when he comes back home."

A lump forms in my throat.

I can't believe what she's done for me.

UNSUITABLE

She got this apartment to help me. She knows this is what I need to get Jesse back. It's not like I can apply for custody of Jesse without a stable home. I was expecting to be in a hostel to start with until I got on my feet, and it would have taken me ages to sort out a place.

"Have you…" I bite my lip. "Have you seen Jesse recently?"

She exhales, and I know the answer. "I went to see him yesterday."

Jesse has been living in a group home since I was put in prison.

I know what those places are like. I've been worried sick about him every moment I've been away from him, praying to God to keep him safe until I could get back to him.

Cece promised to check in on him regularly, and she's kept me updated on his progress.

"How is he?"

"He's doing okay."

"Did you…" I swallow past the ache. I know full well the answer to my question, yet I have to ask it anyway. "He knew I was getting out today?"

"Yeah." Her voice is quieter now. "He's just confused at the moment, Mayday. But he'll come around. He loves you."

My eyes lower. "I let him down."

"No, you didn't." The force in her tone brings my stare to her. "You met and trusted a guy you thought was nice, but he turned out to be the biggest fucker in the history of all fuckers. It was not your fault. I swear, if I ever get my hands on that bastard, I'm gonna rip his balls clear off, douse them in petrol, set them on fire, and make him watch them burn."

"That's quite the visual."

"Thank you. I do paint a good picture." She grins at me. "And I'll feel awesome after I sort out that stain on society."

"I just want to forget he ever existed. My sole focus is on getting Jesse back."

She reaches over and takes my hand in hers, squeezing. "You're gonna get him back. I have no doubt. All the good stuff starts right now."

The tears that I was holding back win the battle, and one escapes.

"Don't you bloody cry, Daisy May, or you'll have me crying, and I'm not wearing waterproof mascara. So, what do you say about the apartment?"

I brush the tear away with the back of my hand. "I say it's awesome, but—"

"No *buts*, Mayday. Just say yes, you're moving in with me."

I give her a look for cutting me off. "The *but* is, I'll have to check with my probation officer to make sure it's okay. They've already arranged for me to stay in a hostel."

"Uh-uh. No way is my girl staying in some skanky hostel for ex-convicts—no offense." Her face blanches when she realizes what she just said. "Because you're not an ex-con, Daisy. Well, technically, you are, but you aren't, and—"

"Ce, it's fine." I laugh. "I am an ex-con. It's just the way it is."

Daisy Smith, ex-con.

That brand will stay with me until the day I die.

My life is completely different now to how it was before I went inside. There's nothing I can do about that. But I can do something about my future.

I can make sure that I never let myself be fooled by a man again.

And I can damn well make sure that I build a better life for Jesse and me.

UNSUITABLE

Better than what we had before.

I'm not smart. I don't have a degree. But I'm a hard worker.

All I need is for someone to take a chance on me and give me the opportunity to give Jesse everything he should have had...everything he deserves.

The kid was dealt a shit hand. At least I had our mum around when I was growing up—not that she was much use even then—but her drug habit worsened after Jesse was born. I think our dad dying was the catalyst.

Our dad was barely around as it was. An addict himself, he was out on one of his benders and injected himself with some bad heroin—not that there's such a thing as good heroin. One minute, he was there, and the next, he was gone. And so was she. She was there physically—well, not all the time—but she checked out mentally. So, when she left, it wasn't exactly a hardship.

I had Jesse, and that was all I cared about.

"I have to go check in with my probation officer now," I tell Cece. "So, I'll ask him about moving in with you and see what he says."

"Cool. We'll go see him and tell him that you're coming home with me today." She gives me a petulant smile.

I shake my head, laughing. When Cece has something set in her head, there's no dissuading her. It's one of the many things I love about her. That, and her fierce loyalty.

She turns on the engine, and the radio in her car comes on. Drake's "Hold On, We're Going Home" bleeds out of the car speakers.

I let out a humorless laugh and meet Cece's eyes. "You have this playing on purpose?"

A small smile plays on her lips. "Maybe."

I let out another laugh. But I don't really feel it. Because I'm not going home. Not really. Home is where Jesse is, and I can't be with him because I made a mistake. I trusted the wrong person, and it cost me my brother and eighteen months of my life.

I rest my head back against the seat and stare out the passenger window, letting out a sigh.

"Hey…you okay?" Cece's voice is soft.

I turn my head to look at her. "Yeah"—I smile—"I'm good. And thanks for…everything. I don't know what I'd do without you."

She reaches over and squeezes my hand. "You'll never have to find out."

TWO

SITTING IN THE EMPTY waiting room on the first floor of the probation service office, waiting to see my assigned probation officer, Toby Willis, I stare out the window and look at the busy London area.

Everything looks the same but different.

Or maybe it's just me that's different.

Cece wanted to come in with me, but I told her to go grab a coffee instead of being stuck in the waiting room until I was done. I told her that I'd meet her back at the car in an hour.

That was half an hour ago, and I still haven't been called in to see him.

As I think it, a guy appears in the open doorway. Looks to be in his mid-thirties. Shaved hair—like literally not a hair is to be found on his head—and he's wearing a black pinstriped suit that looks like it's seen better days.

"Daisy Smith? I'm Toby Willis. Do you want to come through?"

I get to my feet and follow him down the corridor and into his office. I take the seat at his desk as he shuts the door behind us.

He comes around the desk and takes his seat. "Sorry I was late for our appointment. I got stuck in a meeting I couldn't get out of."

"It's fine." I smile. "I'm used to waiting around, and it's not like I have anyplace to be."

He lifts his eyes to mine. They're blue and kind-looking. Actually, now that I think about it, his whole face looks kind. In stark contrast with his harsh-looking bald head.

He smiles. "Well, let's hope we can change that for you." He turns to his computer and taps some keys. Then, he reaches over and grabs a file.

I see my name written on the top.

He opens the file, looking through some of the papers. "So"—he looks up at me—"I won't keep you here long. Really, all we need to do is have you look over the terms of your release and have you sign the license that signals your release. Then, we'll discuss housing options and employment possibilities."

"Can I start with the housing options?" I ask.

Leaning back in his chair, he gives me a nod, giving me the go-ahead.

"I know I'm supposed to move into a hostel. But my best friend has a three-bedroom apartment in Sutton, South London, and she's asked me to live with her. If that's okay with you."

"Your friend, she doesn't have a criminal record?"

"God, no." I laugh quickly. "She's a hairstylist. Never been in trouble in her life."

But then again, neither had I until I was stitched up for theft.

I hold my tongue on that one. No point in protesting my innocence anymore. That ship sailed a long time ago.

"Then, I don't see a problem with it. So long as I have the address and your friend's details, then it's fine."

"Thank you." I breathe a sigh of relief. I didn't want to say it to Cece, but the thought of living in a hostel…it felt like I would be going back into a form of prison. "Do you want the address now? I have it. Cece wrote it down for me."

UNSUITABLE

"Sure."

From my jeans pocket, I get the piece of paper with my new address on it and hand it over. He takes it from me and puts it inside my file.

"Here are the terms of your release. You have to adhere to these rules for the remainder of your sentence." He hands over the sheet of paper. "Read them carefully, and then sign at the bottom. Know that you don't have to sign, but the terms will still be legally binding."

"Okay." I give him a weak smile.

I read over the terms. They say what I expected them to…that if I am found breaking the law in any way, then I'll be back inside to serve out the remainder of my sentence.

That's never going to happen, so it's a moot point. But I'll sign anyway. Picking up the pen from his desk, I etch my name on the dotted line at the bottom and then hand it back to him.

He slots it in my file and rests his arms on top of it, his hands clasped together. "Have you put any thought into what you want to do now that you've been released?"

"Get a job. Get my brother back."

His eyes dim a little at that, and it's like rocks are dropping in my stomach.

"Daisy," he breathes out. "I read through your case file extensively, so I am familiar with your family circumstances. And I know your desire to get custody of your brother…but please take into note that it will be a lengthy process. You will have to prove to social services that you have your life back in order. A life that can accommodate your brother. That you can offer him stability."

"I gave him all of that before." My voice is toneless.

"And then you broke the law. You stole from your employer. An employer you had worked for, for four years. Those people trusted you. You have to show *me* and social services that you can be trusted again."

I can't explain how hard it is to know that you didn't do what everyone believes you did and watch them judge your character based on that. Watch them control your life, take away your family. It's painful and frustrating and heartbreaking.

Curling my fingers into my palm, I press my nails into my soft skin, letting the bite of pain keep my emotions in check.

So, instead of saying everything I want to say—the truth—I hold those words in and say what he wants to hear, "I can do that. I can be trusted again. All I want is to get Jesse back, and I will do whatever is necessary to prove that I'm worthy to have him back with me."

That seems to appease him, and he smiles. "Good. Well, the first thing we can start with, now knowing that you have a stable home to live in, is employment. I have a job lined up for you."

"You do?" My brows lift in surprise.

"Yes. We run schemes with employers who are willing to take on people who have recently been released from prison." He stares at his screen, reading from it. "The position is working as a maid. The owners have a livery and stable business on their estate. You wouldn't be expected to be involved in any of that. Just cleaning duties within the main house itself. The hours are eight thirty until six with an hour lunch break. Pay is seven pounds an hour."

I quickly try to do the math in my head.

About sixty pounds a day. Just short of three hundred pounds a week. I can pay Cece rent and contribute toward bills.

This is going to be my new start. I have a good feeling about this.

"That sounds great. Thank you so much." Honestly, I'd shovel horseshit if it meant I could earn money and be one step closer to getting Jesse back. "When do I start?"

"Tomorrow."

UNSUITABLE

"Tomorrow? I didn't expect it to be so soon. Not that I'm complaining," I'm quick to add.

"Here, we think it's good to get people back into work as quickly as possible, Daisy. Get them into a solid, stable routine. A mind left to sit is a mind likely to wander."

Nodding, I agree with him.

He smiles again. "Good. Well, the job is in Westcott, in Surrey, at the Matis Estate. You need to ask for Mr. Matis when you arrive. And assuming you don't have a car"—I shake my head in response—"you can get a train there, no problem."

Shit, train fare expenses. I'll have to factor that in. I can get a railcard and make it a bit cheaper. Or better still, I can look into the buses, see if one goes from Sutton to Westcott.

"You will be paid weekly, so your first payment will be at the end of this week," Toby says. "How are you fixed financially?"

I swallow down, lowering my gaze, my face reddening with shame. "I, um…have twenty pounds to my name."

I feel embarrassed to admit this. I know he's probably heard this a thousand times before, but it doesn't make it any easier to say.

"How are you fixed for clothes?"

"Um…I have my old clothes." I lift my eyes to him. "My friend, Cece, who I'm going to live with, boxed up all my stuff and kept it in storage for me while I was inside."

"She sounds like a good friend."

"She is." I smile.

"Well, you are going to need money to get you to and from your job and also for food for this first week, so I'll grant you a small loan to get you through this week."

"That would be great. Thank you so much."

My gratitude is real here.

I mean, I hate taking charity from people, but he said this would be a loan, which means I'll have to pay it back.

That, I can live with. It means my savings plan might have to wait a short while, but that's just the way it is.

"Right, well, I'll arrange that for you now. So, aside from that, we're done here." He presses his hands to the desk. "I'll need to see you once a week for the next four weeks. I'll arrange with your employer for you to leave early on that day, so you don't need to worry about that. Then, after that, I'll need to see you once a fortnight for the second and third month from your release. And, as long as everything is satisfactory and going well, then we'll go down to once a month. I will come do a visit at your home in around ten days. Actually, we'll pencil that in while you're here." He turns back to his computer, tapping on the keys. "Okay…as you'll be working and I don't want to keep taking you away from your job, how does a week from Saturday sound? The morning?"

"I can do that." I smile.

"Good." He taps the keys again and then turns to face me. "Right, let's get this loan sorted for you."

THREE

CECE TURNS THE CAR down into a cul-de-sac. At the end of it is an apartment building.

"Here we are." Cece pulls into an allotted parking space and turns the engine off.

Through the windscreen, I glance up at the four-story-high apartment building. It looks really nice. More than I could have hoped for.

Just as we exit the car, the heavens open, so we dash for the building.

Cece opens the main door with a key. "If we have visitors, they have to be buzzed in," she tells me.

I like that. It's safe.

We take the stairs up to the second floor where our apartment is.

Cece unlocks the door, letting me inside first.

The first thing I see is the *Welcome Home* banner hanging from the ceiling in the hallway. I turn, smiling.

"Welcome home!" she says, throwing her hands skyward.

"You're a total geek." I laugh.

I walk down the hallway, toward the first door, and find myself in the living room. I take in the beige-painted walls and the furnishings. A big brown leather sofa with fluffy cushions and a matching chair. Glass coffee table. Flat screen TV sitting on a maple oak cabinet.

Turning, I see Cece standing in the doorway.

"It's amazing, Ce. Did you do all of this?"

She comes over and sits on the arm of the chair. "My dad did the decorating, and Mum helped me pick out the sofa, but the rest was me."

"How long have you been here?" I run my hand along the soft leather of the sofa.

"I moved in a month ago. It gave me time to get it nice for you and Jesse."

Jesse.

The reminder that he's not here with us slices through me.

I know the pain shows on my face because Cece comes over and puts her arm around my shoulders. "Come on, let's go see your bedroom."

I follow her out of the living room and down the hallway.

"Bathroom's there." She points to a closed door. "And the kitchen's through here."

I poke my head through the open door to find a modest-sized kitchen with white gloss cabinets and a small white breakfast table with four black leather chairs.

"Nice," I say.

"Only the best for us," she informs me. "And this one is your room."

I follow Cece into a medium-sized bedroom, complete with a double bed, pale pink duvet cover, nightstand, wardrobe, white walls, and a dressing table in the corner.

"I didn't do much to it. Thought you'd want to put your own stamp on it."

"It's perfect," I say.

That's when I spy a gift box sitting on the nightstand. I walk over and pick it up. I turn back to Cece.

"It's your welcome-home present. It's not much."

UNSUITABLE

Sitting down on the edge of the bed, I pull the lid off the gift box. Inside is a mobile phone.

I lift my eyes to hers. "You didn't have to…"

She sits on the bed beside me. "You need a phone, so you can ring Jesse. It's only a prepaid. I put some credit on it for you—"

"Cece…it's too much. The apartment…the phone."

"Bullshit." The harsh tone in her voice brings my eyes to hers. "It's the least I can do. You've had the worst time, and there wasn't a fucking thing I could do to help you. The apartment and the phone, I can do, so let me do them."

My eyes water. I bite my lip and give her a silent nod.

"Good." She gets to her feet and crosses the room. "I brought all your things from storage. Your clothes and shoes are in here." She taps the wardrobe that she's standing beside. "The other stuff, I wasn't sure what to do with, so I left it boxed. It's in here, up on the shelf."

"Thank you."

"Stop thanking me." She gives me a soft smile. "Now, do you wanna order in, or I can cook?"

"Pancakes?"

Cece makes the best pancakes ever.

Her smile widens. "Pancakes, it is."

Stuffed from the mound of pancakes that Cece made for me, I head to bed early. My body clock is still on prison time. It will be for a while, I imagine.

But, now that I'm in bed, I can't sleep. My eyes are wide open, and I'm staring at the shadows on the ceiling.

I keep expecting to hear the clanging of turning locks and the endless sounds of crying and wailing that echoed throughout the prison at night.

I turn the lamp on and sit on the edge of my bed. Pushing to my feet, I walk over to the wardrobe, open the door, and stare at my clothes hanging in there.

Cece washed and ironed them, and then she hung them up, all ready for me.

Honestly, I couldn't have wished for a better friend.

I reach up and get one of the boxes down from the shelf.

I sit on the carpeted floor. Legs crossed, I open the box.

Sitting on top of the stuff is my old iPod. I try to turn it on, but it's dead. I search through the box and find the charger. I go over and plug it in, charging it so that I can use it tomorrow.

I go and sit back down at the box.

There's a picture frame, upturned. I know which picture it is. The one of me and Jesse that used to sit on the mantel at our old apartment. It was taken when I was sixteen and Jesse was six. It wasn't long after Mum left.

Picking it up, I turn it over and stare at it.

Cece and I took Jesse out for the day to Brighton. We took the train there. We were so lucky with the weather, as it was glorious that day. We spent most of the day on the beach, eating the picnic we'd packed and messing around in the water. It was a great day.

Just as we were heading back to get our train home, Cece stopped us at the railing that overlooked the beach and took the picture.

My arm is around Jesse, as he's tucked into my side. We're smiling. The beach, sea, and sky are in the backdrop.

We look happy.

We were happy.

"I'll fix this, Jesse," I whisper to the photo. "I'll get you back home, I promise."

I don't realize I'm crying until a tear drips onto the glass of the frame.

UNSUITABLE

Drying my face with my hand, I get to my feet. Taking the frame with me, I climb back into bed and hold the picture tight to my chest.

FOUR

I WAKE EARLY, my body still set to the prison clock. It takes me a moment to remember that I'm no longer there, trapped in that prison cell. I'm safe in my own room, in my new home.

I'm free.

For a few moments, I let that soak in.

I can eat breakfast when I want. Shower when I want. Shower alone, without twenty other women there.

Relief fills me.

I turn over in bed, and something digs in my side.

I realize it's the picture of Jesse and me. I fell asleep holding it.

Picking it up, I look at it one last time before putting it up on my nightstand.

I push the covers back and get out of bed, loving the feel of the carpet beneath my feet instead of the cold concrete that used to be waiting for me every morning while in prison.

Closing my eyes, I dig my toes into the fibers.

Heaven.

I might be feeling good right now, but a restless energy is starting to burn inside me.

I need to exercise. My body is used to it now from all the hours spent in the prison gym.

I could go for a run. It's hours before I have to be at my new job.

Decision made, I push to my feet and grab my old running shorts, tank top, and trainers from the wardrobe. I get my old iPod and earphones. Putting the earphones in, I put the iPod in the pocket of the shorts.

I let myself out of my silent apartment and out of the building. The air is cool and crisp. The street is quiet.

I push my key into my pocket and get my music going. The sound of Christina Aguilera's "Fighter" fills my ears.

Ready to burn off this unspent energy, I take off, starting in a slow jog, onto the main street. Then, I quickly pick up pace. I make note of where I'm going and the street names, not knowing this area very well. I don't want to get lost and be late to work on my first day.

The freedom to run outside doesn't go unnoticed by me. I relish the feel of the cold breeze whipping on my face and at my legs. I take in the sight of people setting off for work early.

I'm back in the real world. And it feels good. Damn good.

I run for an hour, feeling like I could run for another, but I need to get back to have breakfast and get ready for work.

When I let myself in the apartment, I hear the TV on in the kitchen.

Cece must be up.

"Hey." I smile, seeing her sitting at the table, nursing a cup of coffee.

She smiles. "Coffee's in the pot," she tells me.

I grab a glass first and fill it with cold water from the tap before downing it.

"You go for a run?" Cece asks, eyeing my trainers.

Nodding, I lean back against the counter.

"The Daisy I knew would have broken out in a rash at the thought of going for a run." She gives a cheeky grin.

UNSUITABLE

"The old Daisy is gone," I tell her, putting down the glass. I turn and get a cup from the cupboard. I pour myself a coffee before adding milk to it that I got from the fridge.

"I kinda liked the old Daisy," Cece says softly.

I take a seat across from her. "The old Daisy was weak and gullible." My tone is harsher than I meant it to be.

Cece's eyes darken. "You were never weak or gullible. You're the smartest, strongest, bravest person I've ever known."

I let out a sharp laugh before I take a sip of my coffee. "I was never smart, Ce. If I had been, then I wouldn't have fallen for Jason's bullshit."

"I hate what that bastard has done to you."

"*Did.* And it'll never happen again."

"'Cause you're Lara Croft now?"

Cece grins, and I can't help but smile.

"No," I say, forcing the smile from my face. "Because I learned my lesson. I won't make the same mistake twice."

"And the running?"

"It makes me feel better. Exercise isn't a bad thing; it's actually a good thing, you know."

"I'll take your word for it." She grimaces.

Laughing, I shake my head at her.

After having some breakfast, I head off to take a shower and get ready for my new job.

After I'm finished showering, Ce jumps in after me.

I go back to my room where I blow-dry my long hair and fasten it up into a makeshift bun. I grab the makeup that Cece bought for me. I apply eyeliner and mascara on my eyes and a little gloss on my lips.

I put on my old white bra and knickers along with the black trousers and white shirt that I used to wear for work at the jewelry store. The trousers hang off me, and the shirt is loose.

Even though Cece washed all my clothes for me after getting them out of storage, wearing them now feels wrong. They're from my old life. A life I no longer have.

As soon as I can afford it, I'll buy some new clothes.

I stand and look at myself in the mirror.

I look exactly like I used to before all of this happened, except thinner and older.

I definitely look older.

Sadness overwhelms me, and I want to cry, but I refuse to.

I've cried enough to last me a lifetime. No more.

I focus on the now. New job. Get Jesse back.

Sucking it up, I grab my bag and put my iPod in it. Then, I let myself out of my room.

I pop my head round Cece's half-opened door. "I'm off to work."

God, it feels good to say that.

Even if I am only a glorified cleaner, I don't care.

I have a job.

Cece is sitting at her dressing table, applying makeup, with a bath towel wrapped around her. "You look nice." She smiles at me in the mirror before turning to face me.

"I look like crap," I tell her, grinning.

"Shut up," she chastises. "You're gonna knock 'em dead at your new job."

"I don't want to kill them. I just got out of prison. I'm not looking to go back."

"Funny." She rolls her eyes at me. "Isn't it early to be setting off? I thought you started at half past eight."

"I do, but it's a fifteen-minute walk to the train station, forty-five minutes on the train, and according to Toby's instructions, a twenty-minute walk from the station to the Matis Estate."

"I can drop you at the train station, if you want? I don't have to be at work until ten."

"Nah, it's fine." I wave her off. "You're not dressed, and I fancy the walk."

"If you're sure."

"I'm sure." I smile at her. "I'll see you tonight."

"Takeaway and a bottle of wine to celebrate your first day?"

"Sounds perfect."

Giving her a wave, I head off. I stop off in the kitchen to grab a banana, a Dairylea Snack Box, and a bottle of water from the fridge for my lunch. I put them in my bag and leave the apartment.

FIVE

I REACH THE TRAIN STATION in good time and buy my ticket at the booth. I'm not waiting long before my train pulls in.

I get an empty seat by the window and get out my iPod. Putting my earphones in, I turn the music on and let Muse take me into another world for a while.

It seems like no time at all, and the train is pulling in at my station.

I put my iPod in my bag and get up from my seat.

I get off the train, and using the route instructions Toby gave me, I walk out of the station and onto the main road. Then, I turn off and make my way down a quiet country road.

It feels like I've been walking for ages, just endless fields and trees, before I see a high brick wall in the distance.

It reminds me of the wall that surrounded the prison.

Shudder.

I reach the high wall and keep going until I come upon huge wrought iron gates. On the wall to my right is a bronze placard with the words *Matis Estate* engraved in black lettering on it.

I've made it! And with time to spare. Let's hope my early show earns me some brownie points with my new employer.

Okay, so how do I get in this place?

Glancing around, I notice an intercom and keypad on the opposite wall of the placard. I press the call button and wait, and then out of nowhere, I feel a sudden bout of nerves.

A minute later, I hear a crackle on the line, and then a deep male voice says, "Yes?"

My skin breaks out in goose bumps. I don't know if it's because of the sexy-sounding voice coming out of the speaker or because I'm nervous.

"Hi." My voice is squeaky. I clear my throat and try again. I lean closer to the speaker. "My name is Daisy Smith. I'm, um, starting work here today as a maid."

The line crackles again and then disconnects.

A few seconds later, I hear a loud clang, and the gates begin to slowly open.

When the gap is big enough for me to fit through, I slip in and head down the gravel driveway. Trees line my right side, and open fields are to my left with roped off paddocks surrounding scatterings of horses. The driveway is long and winding.

Finally, it opens out onto a paved courtyard with a manicured lawn to the left, and the house is straight across from me.

And what a house it is.

I've never seen a house this big in real life.

It's beautiful. Brown sandstone bricks. Two-stories high with attic windows. Triple garage to my right.

It's a house that people like me dream of living in but, in reality, will only ever get to clean.

Taking a deep breath, I walk up the two small steps and onto the covered porch, and I ring the doorbell.

I hear the chime as I take a step back and wait.

Heavy footsteps approach, and then the door swings open.

Oh, fuck.

UNSUITABLE

Those are the first words that enter my head when I see the guy standing on the other side of the door because he is an oh-fuck kind of guy.

He's tall. I'm five foot five, and this guy towers over me. He looks to be around my age, maybe a few years older. He's wearing navy-blue trousers and a white shirt. The top button is open, the sleeves rolled up.

He's built. Not bodybuilder bulky, but he clearly works out.

He has a deep scar on his chin and one cutting through his eyebrow, which is pulled toward the other in a frown. Roman nose. High cheekbones. Jaw like a razor. His hair is dark brown, collar-length, and swept back off his face. He looks like he hasn't shaved in days. Everything about him shouldn't work, but it does.

It *really* does.

There's something strangely compelling about him.

Compelling enough to have me staring.

I'm staring.

Flushing, I push a few loose strands of hair behind my ear as my eyes sweep the floor.

"Hi." I clear my throat as I lift my eyes back to him.

He's staring at me blankly. No smile or friendly look. His brows are still drawn together, and that's when I finally notice his eyes.

They're black. Hard and cold.

I force a smile onto my face. "My name is Daisy Smith. I'm starting work here today as a maid."

The frown deepens. "You said that already." His voice is as hard as his eyes. It sounded much sexier on the intercom. Maybe he's not the guy I spoke to.

"I did?"

"At the gate. On the intercom."

He's the guy.

"Oh, right. Of course."

And I feel like a prize idiot.

Great first impression I'm making here.
Come on, Daisy, you can do better than this.

I hook my thumb under the strap of my bag and meet his eyes again, forcing another smile. "I was told to ask for Mr. Matis—"

"I'm Kastor Matis."

Kastor.

Unusual name. Suits him.

"My friends call me Kas. My employees call me Mr. Matis."

Guess I know which category I fall into.

He's still staring right at me with those cold eyes of his. I decide that they remind me of coal. Hard and unyielding.

"Okay, Mr. Matis, it is. Matis…is that Greek?" I tip my head to the side in question.

A flash of surprise enters his eyes.

Yes, I've been in prison, and I might be a glorified cleaner, but I'm not completely thick.

He moistens his lips, and that's when I notice his upper lip is fuller than his lower. The kind of lip you suck on. Not that I'm going to be sucking on his lips anytime *ever*.

"It is," is his brittle answer.

And then an awkward silence envelops us.

I hate silences.

I'm scrambling for something to say but come up with nothing, wondering if he's ever going to let me in the house.

As if reading my mind, he abruptly steps back and holds the door. I take that as my cue to go inside.

I step gingerly inside the huge entryway.

It's ginormous. The whole of Cece's and my apartment could probably fit in here.

It's beautiful though. The floor beneath my feet is marble. The staircase is sweeping and goes off to both sides.

UNSUITABLE

He shuts the heavy door behind me. The bang echoes memories of the sound of my cell door banging shut behind me.

My heart sets off like a racehorse in my chest.

I feel trapped. Beads of sweat break out on my skin.

You're okay, Daisy. You're just in a house.

I squeeze my eyes shut and force a deep breath.

When I open my eyes, Kastor Matis is standing right in front of me, watching me with curiosity…and something else.

Anger.

He's staring at me like the crazy bitches in prison used to stare at me. Like they wanted to stab me with a blunt instrument at any given moment.

My insides tighten, my Spidey sense going on full alert.

If it weren't for the terms of my release forcing me to be here, then I'd be turning around and hightailing it back out of the door.

But I have to be here. And I need this job. So, I suppress the feelings and suck it up.

"So, where should I start? Do you have a schedule that you'd like me to follow?" I'm making this shit up on the fly because, honestly, I don't know what the hell I'm talking about. I just need to fill this horrific silence between the good-looking bastard and myself.

"Do you have cleaning experience?" he bites out.

I swear, it's like he's spitting at me every time he speaks.

I'm taking that it's because I've been in prison. But if he has a problem with ex-cons, then why the hell did he hire one?

And I'm assuming he should already know my level of cleaning experience. *Wouldn't Toby have filled him in?*

"Some. I had a cleaning job in, um…prison." The shame prickles my skin, like it always does when I say that word. "My duties were to clean the library and rec area—

recreational area," I correct. "Also, I mopped hallways and—"

"I don't need a rundown of your time in prison," he cuts me off.

Okay...

My cheeks sting with embarrassment—and, if I'm honest, anger.

This guy is a bit of an arsehole.

Biting my lip, I bind my hands together to stop myself from…I dunno…punching him in his handsome face.

Wanker.

"Sorry. I guess I misunderstood. I thought you wanted to know my cleaning experience."

Again, he says nothing, just does that unnerving staring thing.

I fidget.

Clear my throat.

Avert my eyes.

Then, I try to change tack. "You have a beautiful home." I cast my eyes around the spacious hallway.

"It's not mine."

That brings my eyes back to him, and…yep, he's still staring. Well, *staring* is being kind. He's glaring.

"Who's—"

"It's my parents' house. I live here and run the estate for them."

"Where—"

"Away," he cuts me off again. "I'll show you the rest of the house."

He turns on his heel and strides away.

SIX

THE TOUR OF THE HOUSE takes a while. The place is like a cavern.

I'm actually worried that I, alone, won't be able to keep this place clean.

There are a lot of rooms.

Downstairs, there's a library—yes, a library. A gym. An indoor swimming pool, which Mr. Matis told me he has a guy who comes in to clean it. His office. The biggest kitchen I've ever seen in my life with a separate utility room, which is where all the cleaning products are kept. A huge dining room, complete with a sixteen-seater dining table. I guess the Matises entertain often. A living room, which looks like it's barely used. And a sitting room, which hosts a huge TV and looks like it gets used more often.

Upstairs are six bedrooms, each with their own bathroom. Kas's bedroom is at the side of the house, overlooking the paddocks. He has a private balcony, and the view from it is gorgeous. There's also a separate bathroom that hosts the biggest bathtub I've ever seen in my life.

I need to work out which rooms get used the most and clean them regularly.

He also gives me a uniform to wear while I work, which means I won't ruin my own clothes. It's just a short-sleeved, knee-length plain black housekeeping dress with a white collar and cuffs, and he's given me two, which is good, as I'll have one to wash against.

I'll change into it once we're done here.

We're back downstairs and in his office now.

He had a few employee forms for me to fill in with my address and that kind of thing.

Shit, it's asking for my bank details to pay my wages into.

I press the pen to my lip. "Um, Mr. Matis…I don't have a bank account."

He looks from his phone, which he was just staring at, to me, his eyes sharp.

I shift with discomfort under his laser stare. "I, um, don't remember the details of my old bank account, as I haven't used it in eighteen months. I'm not even sure the account is still open or if the bank closed it down."

"Find out."

"Okay. I'll call the bank—"

"Make the call on your own time, not mine."

Yes, sir.

I nod my head and finish filling the forms out.

I hand them and the pen back to him. He doesn't even bother to look at them. Just opens a drawer on his desk and shoves them inside.

"So, I guess I should get to work." I start to rise from my chair.

"One more thing."

His voice halts me, and I put my butt back in the seat.

He sits forward, putting his elbows on the desk, and stares at me with those unyielding black eyes of his. "There are things of value in this house, but I'm guessing you already know that."

I do?

"And I know the temptation might be great, but I have to ask you to try not to steal anything. I'd hate to have to send you back to prison."

UNSUITABLE

What. The. Hell?

I feel like he just slapped me. My cheeks sting with humiliation.

God, I hate that this stuck-up bastard can affect me in this way. I've known him for, what? An hour, and I despise the fucker already.

If I didn't need this job as badly as I do and if assault wouldn't land me straight back in prison, then I'd kick him right where it hurt—which would probably be his wallet because I'm pretty sure nothing else would penetrate his rhino skin.

My fingers curl into my palms, and I let the sting of pain ground me.

Come on, Daisy. You've heard…had worse than this. He's just a stuck-up arsehole who clearly needs to get laid.

Says she who hasn't had sex in…well, forever.

"Yes, Mr. Matis," I grit out the words.

Really, what else could I have said?

Try to defend my honor? I almost laugh out loud at that absurd thought.

I tried doing that in a court of law, and it didn't work out so well for me.

And this jumped-up prick believes I'm a thief because that's what the law told him.

It doesn't matter to him if I'm innocent or not.

I'm poor and a criminal; therefore, I'm beneath him.

I'm beneath everyone.

I'm branded for life.

I was always poor. Now, I have the criminal tag to go with it.

Well, aren't I a perfect catch?

God, I hate Jason fucking Doyle. He ruined my life.

But I know I'm not a thief, and that's all that matters.

Or that's what I tell myself.

But I figure, if I say it enough, then I'll start to believe it one day.

Kas's head is tilted, his jaw tight but his eyes appraising, like he was expecting more.

Almost like he was expecting…retaliation.

Why would he think I'd retaliate?

Because I've been in prison; therefore, I'm a thug.

God, I'm so fucking done here.

This guy is the biggest of all arses. I just want to get my job done.

The thing that's bothering me most is that he hired me, knowing I have a criminal record. *Why do that if he wants to be a complete tool to me?*

Maybe he gets off on it—belittling people.

Well, he can do what he wants, say what he wants.

Because I don't care what he thinks of me. I just care that he pays my wages at the end of every week.

"We're done here," he says blandly, like he's suddenly bored.

And I take leave before he can say anything else shitty to me.

SEVEN

AFTER CHANGING into my work outfit, which surprisingly fits me, I get to work. I figure I'll begin downstairs. So, I make a start on the kitchen.

By the time one o'clock rolls around, every surface in the kitchen is shining. The oven is sparkling, inside and out, and the floor is so clean that you could eat your dinner off it.

Speaking of eating, my stomach is rumbling.

I wash up my hands and grab my bag from where I left it hanging in the coat closet in the hallway. Then, I head outside to the back garden as the sun has made a rare appearance, and I'm determined to enjoy it while it's here.

I do a little wandering around the huge back garden where it's clear that it's been lovingly cared for. A lot of hard work has gone into this garden.

I can't see Kas-hole—*see what I did there?*—getting his hands dirty with gardening, so I'm guessing he has a gardener. Unless his parents do the gardening.

I wonder when they'll be back. Hopefully, they're nicer than their son.

But then, if they raised that miserable twat...I shouldn't hold out much hope.

It's such a shame he's a wanker because he's really good-looking. Shame his personality spoils what could have been a perfect person.

I spy a bench by a colorful shrubby, so I decide to sit there.

I take out my phone and check it.

There's just one text from Cece, sent a few hours ago. Not surprising, as she's the only person who has my number—well, aside from Kas-hole and my probation officer.

How's your first day going?

I type back.

My new boss is a wanker. But, aside from that, good. The house is beautiful.

She replies back instantly.

Do I need to kick his arse?

I chuckle at that.

Nah, it's nothing I can't handle. You on your lunch break?

Yeah, just about to head back in though. Catch you tonight. Love ya.

Love ya, too.

I keep my phone in my hand, and I go to the only other contact I have in there. I press Call and put the phone to my ear. I wait, listening while it rings.

It goes to voice mail. "Hi, you've reached Anne Burgess, Department of Social Services. Leave your name and number, and I'll call you back."

UNSUITABLE

Disappointed that I won't get to talk to her, I wait for the beep. "Hi, Anne, it's Daisy Smith. I'm just calling to let you know that I was released yesterday. I was hoping we could get together to talk…about Jesse. I'm hoping I can see him soon. If you could call me back on"—I rattle off my number—"I'd really appreciate it. Thanks."

I hang up and put my phone back in my bag.

Hopefully, she'll call me back soon.

Anne is Jesse's social worker. Over the last eighteen months, I've kept in regular contact with her, regarding Jesse. She knows my keenness at getting Jesse back home with me. Anytime I ever tried to broach getting custody of Jesse, she'd always tell me that it was something we'd need to discuss after my release.

Well, I'm released now, and I want to talk about it. I also want to see my brother.

Determined not to let the frustration I feel overtake me, I reach inside my bag and get my lunch out.

I have this sudden feeling of being watched, but when I look around, I don't see anyone.

Weird.

I open my Dairylea Snack Box and start eating.

I enjoy sitting in peace and just eating my lunch, but I'm done in fifteen minutes, leaving me with just over half an hour left to kill.

I put my empty wrappers back in my bag and dust off the crumbs from my dress. I decide to take a walk around the estate and check out the paddocks and stables.

I hang my bag on my shoulder and set off walking across the garden. I hit the garden path and follow it. It curves along the garden and then leads me out through an archway.

I stop on the other side of the archway and look around.

This place is massive.

Far off to my left and straight ahead is the wall that surrounds this place. It disappears off into a forest of trees.

I can't even imagine how long it took to build that wall—or the cost alone. Although it's not like they couldn't afford it.

To my right are the stables. The paddocks are to my left and ahead. They cover a lot of the area. Horses are dotted around in each one.

I start to wander toward the paddocks. As I near, I see a guy who looks to be fixing one of the fences that keeps the horses in.

As if sensing my approach, he lifts his head.

I smile. "Hi." I lift my hand in a wave.

He waves back. Smiling, he stands.

Nice smile. He's good-looking. Sandy-blond hair that's cut short. Tan skin. Looks to be around my age. Seems friendly.

Complete opposite of Kastor Matis.

But, as much as I hate to admit it, Kas is better-looking. This guy is a pretty boy. Kas is a man in all sense of the word. Even if he is a complete dickhead.

"You're new," he says when I reach him. He has the most delicious Australian accent I've ever heard. Well, the only Australian accents I've ever heard have been on the telly. "And you can't be a horse owner, as I know all the owners, and we haven't had a new horse in recently."

"I'm the new maid, and you're Australian."

Duh.

Dumb, Daisy. So dumb.

"You got me." He chuckles, lifting his hands in surrender. "Cooper Knight, native of Adelaide." He drops his hands and puts one out to shake mine.

Reaching out, I slip my hand into his. "Daisy Smith, native of London."

He squeezes my hand and grins. "I heard we had a new maid starting."

UNSUITABLE

I wonder what else he heard.

But he's not looking at me like I'm a piece of trash, so maybe he doesn't know where the last place was that I had to call home.

Weirdly, he's actually looking at me with a spark of interest.

He releases my hand and rests his arms on the fence, linking his fingers. "So, how are you finding it so far?"

"It's…okay."

"Why don't I believe you?" There's an impish grin on his handsome face.

"Because I've met Kastor Matis." The words are out before I can stop them.

I slap my hand over my mouth, and he laughs loudly.

"He been giving you a hard time?"

"Mmhmm," I murmur, dropping my hand.

"Yeah, he can be a tough nut to crack. But Kas isn't a bad guy, not really. He just likes people to think he is. Just stay out of his way, and you'll be fine. Mr. and Mrs. Matis are awesome. You'll love 'em."

"Where are they?" I ask him, relieved that he didn't think I was being a bitch about Kas.

Bitching about my boss to the other employees on the first day isn't the best thing to do.

"They have a place in Greece. Mr. Matis has family there, so they spend half of the year there and the other half here. Kas runs the place for them."

"How long have you worked here?" I ask.

"Six years. The Matises hired me soon after they bought the place."

Six years. Maybe he's older than I initially thought.

"Where did they live before here?" I realize how nosy I'm being. "Sorry, I sound really nosy."

"Don't ask, don't find out, right?" He gives me a reassuring smile. "They moved up here from London. Mr. Matis was big in the banking industry—stocks and that sorta stuff. Made a lot of money. Think he and Mrs. Matis wanted out of the city, so they moved here for the peace and quiet. And it's a good investment, a place like this."

"How many others work here?" I ask, looking around.

"Well, there's me, of course. I'm the stable manager. Ellie and Peter are trainers. Mack and Tash are my stable hands. They're all off on lunch at the moment, but you'll meet 'em soon. Then, we have Dom, who's the gardener. It's his day off today, but he'll be back in tomorrow. And that's it."

"What happened to the maid who worked here before me?"

Cooper's expression drops a little. "Tania. She left...well, I say *left*, but she upped and disappeared on us about two months ago."

"She disappeared?" I frown.

He nods. "One minute, she was here. The next, gone. When I asked Kas about her, he just shut me down."

"Weird," I muse. "Had she been in prison?"

He gives me a surprised look, and I instantly blanch.
Shit.

"No, not that I know of. Why'd you ask?"
Because I'm an idiot.

"Um...I don't know. Just with her running off..." I give an awkward shrug.

I guess I just assumed that, because of what Toby said, the Matises are employers who are willing to take on people who just recently got out of prison.

Knowing I'm the first leaves me feeling a bit weird.

"Nah, Tania was a good girl. No way she was mixed up in bad stuff."

Yeah, because girls who go to prison are mixed up in bad stuff. And they're definitely not good girls. Right?

The knowledge of how Cooper's opinion of me would instantly change once he knew the truth about me leaves me feeling a little sick.

UNSUITABLE

I don't know why because I should be used to this by now.

I guess my recent encounters with Kastor Matis have left me feeling a little raw. More than I want to admit.

Cooper leans closer, lowering his voice. "I know Tash thought that Tania and Kas were…you know…" He gives a knowing look before leaning back. "I couldn't see it myself, but if Tash was right and they were bumping uglies and it didn't work out…maybe he gave her the push. Or maybe it has nothing to do with Kas, and Tania just went back home."

"Home?"

"She was from Poland."

"Oh, right."

For some reason, I'm having visions of a tall blonde beauty and Kas liking her a lot.

But not little old jailbird Daisy.

Not that I give two shits about what Kas-hole thinks of me.

"Tash tried ringing Tania's mobile after we found out she'd left, but it was out of service."

"How long did Tania work here?" I ask.

"About six months."

Feeling a bit strange about this conversation as a whole and knowing it must be time for me to get back to work, I reach into my bag for my phone and check the time.

Yep, five minutes before I have to be back to work. I don't want to be late and give Kas-hole another reason to be shitty to me.

"Well…I should get back." I gesture to my phone before dropping it back in my bag. "It was nice meeting you, Cooper." I take a step away.

"You, too. Hey, before you go," he calls me back. "Do you ride?" He tips his head back at the horse grazing behind him.

"No." I shake my head.

"Well, if you want to learn, let me know. I'll give you some lessons on the house. Perks of working here." He smiles, and it's a friendly smile.

I decide on the spot that I like Cooper. He might think jailbirds are bad news, and in most cases, he's not wrong, so I can't blame him for thinking that.

"That'd be great. Thanks. But maybe not in this dress." I wrinkle up my nose, nodding down at my uniform.

"No." He chuckles. "Unless you want to ride sidesaddle, that is."

"How very old-fashioned of you."

"I'm an old-fashioned kinda guy." He winks.

Usually, I hate winks, but he can totally pull it off. And I'm a little rusty here…but is he flirting with me?

"I'm serious. If you want a lesson, let me know, and we'll arrange something."

I smile. "I will do that. See you later."

"Sooner, I hope."

Okay, I totally smile like a girl at that one.

He's charming. And it's nice to be charmed after Kashole's mean ways this morning.

Not that I'd take Cooper up on any offer, aside from the free riding lesson.

Men are a no-go area for me. Jason burned me for life.

Smiling, I swivel on my toes and walk back to the house, feeling a little lighter than when I first left it.

Out of nowhere, a feeling creeps up my spine. That sense again of being watched.

I lift my head, seeing no one.

I glance back over my shoulder, but Cooper is back to work on the fence.

I look back ahead, staring up at Kas's bedroom window, but no one's there.

Weird.

I swear, I'm going mad.

UNSUITABLE

    Shaking off the feeling, I pick up my pace and head back through the archway before getting back to work.

EIGHT

IT'S MY SECOND DAY at work, and I'm walking quickly down the lane, heading for the Matis Estate, because it's raining like a bitch. I don't have an umbrella with me, but I'm wearing my raincoat with the hood up, keeping my hair dry.

I'm not far from the gates when I hear a car coming up fast behind me.

Glancing back, I see a petrol-guzzling four-by-four approaching. A gust of wind blows my hood back off my head. I scramble to pull it back up, but before I can—

Splash!

Mothereffing effer!

I stop in shock, muddy water dripping down my face.

The bastard hit a puddle at the side of the road and gave me a muddy-water drenching.

I grit my teeth together. "Wanker, bastard, thoughtless twat of a four-by-four driver!" I seethe to myself, stomping my foot.

I drag my hand down my face, clearing away the muddy water.

Can this day get any worse?

And it's barely even started.

I still haven't had a call back from Anne, which is stressing me out.

I weirdly overslept this morning, meaning I didn't do my run, and I nearly missed my train. It was only light drizzling when I got on the train. Then, I had to stand the whole journey here, as there were no seats, because, apparently, the world and his wife were using the train this morning. I stepped off in Westcott, and the heavens opened, the sky raining down like it was preparing for the Great Flood.

I hadn't brought an umbrella with me because I thought I'd be okay with my raincoat. And I was doing okay until four-by-four dickhead soaked me through to the bone.

Okay, so, evidently, my day can get worse because when I zero my eyes in on the taillights of the four-by-four, I see that it's slowing and turning into the Matis Estate.

I growl. I actually growl and pick up my pace, heading for the car, which is stationary, waiting for the gates to open.

With the windows blacked out, I can't see inside, but I don't care because I'm mad. I'm soaked and mad. Not a good combination.

Reaching the car, I rap my knuckles on the passenger window. "Hey, buddy," I say in a pissy tone. "You just soaked me back there! Watch where you're going next time. And *I'm sorry I just drenched you* would've been goo—" The words die on my tongue when the window rolls down, and I see who's in the car.

"Mr. Matis."

Shit. Shit. Shit.

He already hates me. And, now, I've just banged on his car window and yelled at him.

I'm so fired.

His black eyes move over me. I see a flicker of humor in them.

He's laughing at me.

Bastard.

UNSUITABLE

"Daisy. Good morning. Or maybe not, as the case might be for you."

I bite my tongue so hard that I draw blood, tasting metallic in my mouth.

I'm gonna…I'm gonna…

Walk away.

It's either that or punch him in the throat, and I don't think punching my boss would be a good idea. It'd be my fast pass back to prison.

And I really don't want that.

Jesse. Think about Jesse.

Jaw locked, I swivel on my toe and walk through the open gates.

I'm speed-walking, sticking to the edge to keep out of the way of his car for when he drives past me.

My hands are balled into fists. And I honestly feel like I could cry.

I like to think of myself as strong and capable. But, right now, I just feel torn up with emotions.

I miss my brother. I hate my boss. I'm soaked, and I'm about to start my period. So, yeah, I'm feeling a tad emotional.

I hear his car roll up behind me, and it drives straight past me, just like I expected him to.

Because it'd be too courteous to offer to drive me the rest of the way.

Arsehole.

Gritting my teeth, I stomp the rest of the way to the house, my trainers squelching. All the while, I imagine strangling Kas-hole with my bare hands.

As I approach the house, I see the front door is open, and Kas-hole is standing there, looking all dry in his dark blue jeans and V-neck jumper.

He looks hot—as much as I hate to admit it.

I hate that he's a good-looking bastard.

Jaw clenched, hands balled at my sides, I come to stop in the porchway.

"Dry off before coming inside." He holds out a towel to me. "I don't want you dripping all over the floor."

Um…what?

I stare at him in shock.

He blankly stares back at me and gestures for me to take the towel.

Argh! I hate this guy!

I have to stop myself from reminding him that, if I make a mess, I'll be the one who cleans it up anyway.

Ignoring him, I drop my bag to the floor and pull off my trainers. Barefoot on the cold floor sends shivers running up my legs. Unzipping my raincoat, I yank it off and drop it on the floor by my bag. Leaving me in just my wet dress.

Shivering and not looking him in the eyes, I reach out and pull the towel from his still-outstretched hand. I bring the towel to my face, patting it dry. Then, I run it over my arms and bare legs, drying them off. Reaching back, I tug my hairband out. Gathering up my hair, I squeeze the water out of it and then rub the towel over it.

When I'm done, I make the mistake of looking at Kas.

He's staring right at me.

But, for once, he's not looking at me with distaste.

The look in his eyes…it's intense.

I can't remember anyone ever looking at me like this before. I feel like he's stripping me bare.

A tug of need pulls at my lower belly, surprising the hell out of me.

And I suddenly don't feel so cold anymore.

His stare is heating me up from the inside out.

What the hell is this?

How can I be feeling…whatever I'm currently feeling for him? I hate him.

UNSUITABLE

But, apparently, my body missed the memo on that one because she seems to quite like him at the moment.

"Mr. Matis..." I whisper his name, not sure why or what I hope to achieve by doing so. I'm beyond surprised at how breathy my voice sounds.

And it's the sound of my voice that seems to bring him back to life. I watch as his expression shuts down. His brows draw together in a frown of disdain, and without a word, he turns on his heel and strides away.

Okay. What the effing hell was that all about?

I'm putting it down to me not having had sex in a really long time. My body and hormones just saw *man* and got confused for a moment.

That definitely will not happen again.

On a sigh, I bend and pick my raincoat up before shaking the water off it. I pick my shoes up and walk into the house, shutting the door behind me.

I head straight for the utility room and hang my coat over the clothes airer. I put my trainers into the dryer.

My dress and underwear are soaked. But there's nothing I can do. I don't have anything to change into. I'll just have to wear them and hope they dry while I work.

First though, I need to sort my hair out.

Taking my bag with me, I head to the downstairs bathroom. Locking myself inside, I stare in the mirror.

I look like a drowned rat.

I get my hairbrush out and brush the knots out. Then, I tie it up into a messy bun. Stashing my hairbrush back in my bag, I unlock the door and let myself out.

My feet slam to a halt when I see Kas standing on the other side of it.

"I brought you something to wear." He gestures to my wet dress and then holds out a red polo shirt and a pair of jodhpurs. The polo shirt has *Matis Estate* embroidered on the right breast.

"The polo's a large, but the jodhpurs should fit you. It was all we had left in stock."

I'm so stunned by his kindness that it takes me a moment to speak.

"Thank you." I take the clothes from him and look up into his eyes.

He gives me a sharp nod, and then he turns and walks away.

I've just turned back into the bathroom when his voice pulls me back. I turn to see that he's stopped at the end of the hallway, and he is half-turned back to me.

"I'm sorry for drenching you earlier."

My jaw hits the floor in shock. "I-it's okay."

Without another word, he disappears around the corner, leaving me standing there, stunned.

NINE

I'M ON MY KNEES, scrubbing the bathtub in the main bathroom, when my right boob starts to vibrate.

I decided to keep my phone on me in case Anne called, and as these tight-as-hell jodhpurs don't have any pockets, I had to stash my phone in my bra, hence the vibrating boob.

Reaching in my top, I pull my phone out, seeing Anne's name on the caller display.

My heart starts to beat a little faster as I connect the call. "Hello?"

"Hi, Daisy. It's Anne from Social Services."

"Hi. Thanks so much for calling me back."

"Sorry I'm a bit late in returning your call. I wasn't in the office yesterday, and I'm just catching up on messages."

"No problem at all. I understand."

"So, your release came through."

"Yes." I smile.

"Good. I am pleased for you."

"Thank you. Anne…I wanted to talk to you about Jesse. What do I need to do to start the process of applying for custody? And when can I see him?"

"Well, first things first, you and I need to have a chat."

"About?" My tone is edgy. I just can't help it.

"Just about your circumstances now—"

"I have a place to live. My best friend's apartment. I'm living with her, paying rent." Not that Cece will talk to me about paying rent, but I will be giving her money as soon as I get paid. "It's a really nice place in Sutton, and it has three bedrooms. One is for Jesse. I have a job. I'm a maid at a big estate house in Surrey. So, I'm in a really good position to care for Jesse now, and I really—"

"That's wonderful, Daisy," she cuts me off. "I am so pleased that everything is coming together for you. I'd love to see your new place. So, how about I come to visit? We can have a chat and go from there."

I slump back onto my haunches, disappointed, knowing that I'm not going to see Jesse anytime soon.

"Sounds great," I say, trying to inject enthusiasm into my voice that just isn't there.

"Fabulous. Now, looking at my calendar, I'm free on Friday at five p.m."

"I work until six, and it takes me just over an hour to get home."

"Oh, well, how about I come at six? You could ask your employer if you can leave an hour early. I'm sure if you explain your reason for needing the time, your employer will be understanding."

Kas understanding? Ha. Not likely.

However, he was nice to me earlier, bringing me the clothes and apologizing. Maybe his hard shell is softening toward me.

There might just be some kindness in him.

"I'll ask and let you know."

"Fabulous. Speak soon."

Hanging up my phone, I stash it back in my bra.

She wants to come to my place at six, which means I'll need to leave at four. It takes me an hour and twenty minutes with the train journey and the walks to and from the train stations. And I'll need to shower before she arrives, so I don't stink of cleaning products.

UNSUITABLE

That means I'll have to ask Kas if I can leave two hours early.

I dread the thought.

But knowing I have no choice but to ask—because this is about Jesse, and he's all that matters—I push to my feet, which are still bare.

I make my way out of the bathroom and pad down the carpeted stairs, heading for Kas's office. Nerves are tumbling around in my stomach.

Come on, Daisy. The worst he can say is no.

And be an arsehole about it.

Sucking it up, I lift my chin and march toward his office. I reach his office door and knock on it.

"What?" he barks from the other side.

Okay…that isn't a good start.

Reaching for the handle, I turn it and let myself in his office before closing the door behind me.

I turn to face him, and he's leaning back in his chair, arms on the rests, staring at me with those coal-black eyes of his.

My stomach flips, and I suddenly feel queasy. I bind my hands together in front of me.

His eyes follow the movement and then shoot back up to my face. "Are you just going to stand there all day, or are you going to tell me what you want?"

I guess the nice clothes-bringing-and-apologizing Kas is gone, and Kas-hole is back.

I swallow nervously. "Mr. Matis, I know this is only my second day working here, and I really do hate to ask…but I was wondering, if I came in an hour early on Friday and worked through my lunch, would it be possible for me to leave at four instead of six?"

"No." He sits forward in his seat and turns the chair to his computer.

Bolts of frustration and anger fly around me, buzzing like bees in my head. I'm not normally quick to temper, but this guy makes me want to scream my head off.

Dropping my hands to my sides, I curl my fingers into my palms. "Mr. Matis, I wouldn't ask if it wasn't important—"

"And what's so important that you have to leave work? A hair appointment? Nail appointment?" His eyes drag over me. "But then, looking at you, I'd say it's neither of those things. So, what is so important that you have to leave work early?"

Mother...effer.

I take a step back, affronted. "I'm sorry, but have I done something to give you the impression that I deserve to be talked to like this? I know I've been in prison, but that doesn't give you the right to judge me for it. You don't even know me." Even as I say the words, I know how ineffectual they are because they sound weak to my own ears.

Fire lights his eyes. The look in them makes me want to take a step back.

He looks like a scary-arse fire-breathing dragon.

He leans forward, pressing his hands to the desk. His voice is so low that I feel the temperature in the room drop. "Trust me," he seethes, "that's not what I'm judging you on."

What?

"God, you're a—" I bite my lip to stop the words from coming out.

"I'm a what, Daisy?" Then, he smirks.

The bastard smirks.

I have a vision of wiping that smirk off using the chair he's sitting on.

I've never been one for violence, but this guy just brings it out of me.

Closing my eyes, I blow out a calming breath, wishing I were anywhere but here.

UNSUITABLE

Why does this guy hate me so much?

"Unless you're a magician or you've figured out the theory of time travel, I'm still going to be sitting here when you open your eyes."

Argh! I want to throttle him!

Going back inside for murder is looking pretty appealing right now.

Two days, and I want to kill my boss already. This is not good. I need to get a handle on this and find a way to deal with his Kas-hole-ness.

He's just a man. A man whose opinion of me doesn't matter.

All I need from him is the paycheck at the end of every week.

I can do this. I've handled worse.

I open my eyes, and his smug, handsome face is there, staring back at me.

I force the brightest smile I can onto my lips. "It's not you I'm trying to wish away. Sorry to have wasted your time. I'll get back to work now."

I turn for the door, but his deep voice stops me. "You haven't told me why you needed the time off."

Blowing out a breath, I turn my eyes his way. "I had an appointment with my brother's social worker to discuss me getting custody of him. But it doesn't matter now."

I yank open the door and walk through it before he can throw another barb at me.

I run up the stairs, anger and frustration and a bunch of other emotions burning through me.

I get in the bathroom, grab a folded up towel off the shelf, press it to my face, and scream into it.

I hate him!

Hate! Him!

I've never had such an instant deep-seated hatred for another human being as I do with Kastor Matis.

Don't get me wrong; I hate Jason. *God, how I hate that bastard.* He is the reason I went to prison.

But Kas…he's just so fucking…mean. And heartless.

He's…Kas-hole.

I pull the towel away from my face and take in some deep breaths.

When I feel a little calmer, I put the towel back on the shelf. Then, I perch my bum on the edge of the bathtub, curling my fingers around it, and I let my head hang.

I've got to call back Anne and tell her that I can't make the appointment, thus delaying things further with Jesse.

What if she can't see me again for ages? Or she takes me not making the appointment as a bad thing, thinking I'm unreliable?

I really need to make a good impression, and I can't do that when I can't even make the first appointment she's tried to make with me.

Tears sting my eyes.

Life is so unfair. After everything I've been through, I just figured I was due a break.

Apparently not.

I press the heels of my hands to my eyes to curb the tears in them, and I blow out a breath.

When I feel a little more under control of my emotions, I pull my hands away from my eyes, lifting my head, and my heart nearly leaps out of my chest when I see Kas standing in the doorway.

"I'm sorry." I jump to my feet. "I was just getting back to work."

His voice stops me. "You can have the time off on Friday."

Not only am I shocked by his words, but by the sound of his voice as well. It sounds gentle. I've never heard him speak that way before. Not even when he apologized earlier.

"Thank you," I whisper, looking up into his face.

UNSUITABLE

His eyes meet mine. There's a flicker of something...compassion maybe? But it's gone as quickly as it arrived.

"But I want you in at seven thirty on Friday and for you to work during your lunch to make up the time."

"Of course."

"And, Daisy?"

"Yes?"

"Don't take personal calls on my time again. You do, and I will fire you." With that, he turns and leaves.

What?

Did he know...that I took Anne's call?

How?

I glance around the bathroom, suddenly feeling very uneasy. A shudder rolls through me.

Then, I force myself to get back to work, so as not to rock the boat.

TEN

I INPUT THE CODE into the keypad and wait for the gates to open.

It's so quiet. Well, it's always quiet around here, but it seems especially quiet. That could have something to do with it being seven thirty a.m.

It's Friday, and I'm in early, as promised, so I can leave to make my appointment with Anne.

I haven't seen Kas at all this week. He hasn't been here when I have been. I asked Cooper where he was, and he said Kas would do this from time to time, disappearing during the day, which got me wondering where he might go.

Maybe he's got a girlfriend.

I get this weird feeling in my chest at the thought.

Shaking it off, I walk through the gates and up the drive. I veer off the driveway when I reach the paddocks.

"Hey, Butterscotch."

Butterscotch is fast becoming one of my favorite horses. She's a palomino. No, I haven't suddenly gotten all horsey. Cooper told me.

I've been hanging out at the paddocks on my lunch hour.

I met Ellie, Peter, Mack, and Tash. They were all lovely. Ellie, especially so. She seemed really friendly. She invited me to go to the pub for lunch with them the next time they go.

It was nice to be asked. To be included in something so normal as going to the pub for lunch with my work colleagues.

But, in the back of my mind, I couldn't help but wonder if they would still invite me if they knew I'd just gotten out of prison.

The other thing that's been bugging me is that, clearly, Kas hasn't told anyone that I was in prison. If I'm being honest, I thought he would've.

But I'm not complaining. It's nice not to be judged at my place of work. So, if Kas is keeping his mouth zipped about my past, then so am I.

I met Dom, the gardener, as well. He's a really nice guy. After my little disagreement with Kas on my second day, I was outside, sitting on my favorite bench and having my lunch, when he came over to introduce himself.

"I brought you treats," I tell Butterscotch. Reaching into my bag, I pull out two of the four apples I brought with me.

Danger, Butterscotch's paddock pal, spies me with the apples and comes trotting over. He's a big-ass horse. Black as night. Gorgeous.

"Don't worry. I didn't forget about you, Danger." I reach out and feed him an apple.

As I turn my head, something in my peripheral catches my eye.

And that something has me turning fully around.

Kas is standing on his balcony. And, when I say *standing on his balcony*, I mean, he's up on the stone railing.

Standing there, hands on his hips, face turned up to the morning sun.

He's wearing black running shorts and a black T-shirt.

He looks like a god.

A mean god.

UNSUITABLE

He moves down to sit on the edge of the railing, legs dangling. Then, he slides his butt off, putting his feet on the outer ledge, keeping ahold of the railing with his hands, so he's standing on the wrong side of it. The not-so-safe side.

My heart starts to beat faster. My eyes are glued to him.

I watch as he casts another glance skyward. Then, without hesitation, he moves down into a crouch. One hand still on the railing, he slightly leans forward.

And jumps.

Noise pops in my ears, and I realize it's my own voice screaming, "No!"

Then, I'm running toward him, my heart in my throat the whole time.

He's going to die.
Oh my God, he's going to die, and I don't know CPR!
Why didn't I learn CPR?
And why the hell did he just jump?

My mind is going a million miles a minute as I sprint toward him, my bag banging against my side.

And I watch in fascinated horror as Kas hits the grass, landing on his feet in an almost catlike way. The motion takes him down to a forward roll, and he's back up on his feet in seconds.

What the... bloody fuck?

And I'm still running.

Kas turns his head, seeing me, and his stare brings my feet skidding to a stop.

There's about thirty feet between us.

He watches me for a long moment, no hint of emotion on his face.

Then, the fucker grins.

He actually grins. And then he takes off running across the paddocks, heading for the forest at the back of the estate.

Me? I'm shaking like a leaf, my heart going ten to the dozen.

What the hell was that?

Trying to catch my breath, I put my hands on my hips and look up at the balcony. It's about a twenty-foot drop, and he just jumped it, like it was nothing.

I'm just...I can't believe he did that.

I need a coffee.

Well, a stiff drink would probably be nice, but as I can't have that, I'll go for a hit of caffeine.

Still feeling a little wobbly, I head around the house and let myself in the open front door. I hang my bag and coat up in the coat closet and make my way to the kitchen.

I see an envelope on the counter with my name on it. Picking it up, I open it and see money and my payslip inside.

It's my wages. Not a full week, as I've only worked four days after starting on Tuesday, but it's my first pay.

Weirdly, I get a little lump in my throat.

My boss might be an arse, but I have a paying job. Later on, I'll be seeing Anne, and I will be one step closer to getting Jesse back.

Smiling, I fold the envelope up and put it in the pocket of my dress.

I work the fancy coffee machine they have and start brewing coffee, figuring Kas might want some when he gets back.

Because I sure as hell need some after that.

I pour myself a coffee and set about filling the dishwasher with Kas's dinner plate and pans from last night. I set the dishwasher going and start cleaning down the stove, which he made a mess of, drinking my coffee while I work.

I've finished my coffee, and I'm just rinsing out my cup, thinking I'll tackle Kas's office while he's still out. Then, the back door opens, and the man appears, like I conjured him up.

UNSUITABLE

His hair is uncharacteristically ruffled up. A sheen of sweat is covering his skin, his damp T-shirt clinging to his body. The muscles on his arms are...wow, and his legs...sweet Jesus, they're really toned.

Honestly, he's never looked hotter.

I have this sudden image of going over to him. Getting down on my knees. Kissing my way up those legs, then pulling his running shorts down, and—

"Coffee?" I squeak out, quickly turning away, so he can't see that I'm blushing.

What the hell is wrong with me? I don't even like this guy.

He's mean, and he jumps off his balcony, nearly giving his employee a heart attack.

"Coffee would be good. Thanks."

I grab a cup from the cupboard and pour him out a coffee.

"Milk?" I ask.

"No. Just black."

I hand the cup over to him and step back, leaning against the counter.

"I forgot you were coming in early today." His voice is low.

Is that why you did your crazy jump? Because you thought you were alone?

Then, I tense up, hoping he's not going to change his mind about me leaving early.

I meet his steady gaze. "I hope it's not a problem?"

"It's not a problem." He looks away from me to the door. "I'm going to take a shower." He walks away, taking his coffee with him.

And I just can't help myself. "What was that before? You jumping off the balcony?"

There, I said it.

I had to, or it would have bugged me all day.

He stops. I can see the clear line of tension across his shoulders.

He stands there for so long that I think he isn't going to say anything.

"Parkour," he says without turning around.

Parkour?

Then, he walks away without another word.

The moment he's out of sight, I get my phone out of my pocket, bring up Google, type in *parkour*, and hit Search.

ELEVEN

TURNS OUT THAT *PARKOUR*—or *freerunning*, as it's also called—is the art of moving rapidly through an area, usually an urban area. The *traceur*, which is the correct term for a person who practices parkour, moves around or over obstacles by running, jumping, and climbing them.

I got all that off the Internet.

After I finished reading up on it, I was feeling kind of fascinated. I saw there was a whole bunch of videos online. But I didn't want Kas to catch me on my phone, so I had to wait until I left work.

The moment I was out of there, I was back on Google, and I watched videos the whole walk to the station and on the train journey home.

I can't believe that Kas does parkour. Not because he's not fit—because he clearly is—but because...well, it's really cool, and he's such an uptight, miserable bugger.

But, clearly, there's this whole other side to him that I know nothing about.

And it kind of makes me curious.

I didn't see Kas for the rest of the day. When he came down from his shower, he holed himself up in his office, and I left him to it.

I knocked on his door at four to let him know that I was leaving, and he barked at me from the other side, so I hightailed it out of there.

And, now, I'm home, and I'm awaiting Anne's arrival.

I'm all showered and ready, wearing my best *mum* clothes. I've gone for a calf-length powder-blue dress. It's an old dress, but it's nice, respectable. It has capped sleeves and a cute belt around the waist. My hair is tied back in a braid. I also put on a light dusting of makeup.

I'm good to go.

Cece is working until eight, so I've got the place to myself.

The good biscuits are set out on a plate on the coffee table in the living room. Tea is in the pot, and coffee is in the carafe on a tray. Cups are ready along with milk in a jug and sugar cubes in the pot.

I'm ready to show Anne that I've changed.

Even though I haven't changed. Not really. Deep down, I'm the same person I've always been. Just a little less trusting than I used to be.

But Anne sees what she's read on paper. She sees me as a thief and ex-con. A woman who kept the fact that her mother had run off and abandoned her kids a secret.

Social Services doesn't see the good in my reasons. They don't care that I worked my arse off to keep a roof over Jesse's head and to put food in his belly. That, every single day, I made sure he knew how much he was loved.

Social Services doesn't care about any of that.

All they see is a liar. A thief. And a criminal.

All because of Jason.

But I'm not going to go there. Today is going to be a good day.

I'm not going to think about that piece of shit.

I'm going to get Jesse back.

UNSUITABLE

I'm going to show Anne the real Daisy—the responsible, reliable Daisy, who loves her brother like he's her own kid. *He is my kid.* And I will do anything for him.

The doorbell rings, and a tremor of nerves runs through me. Standing from the sofa, I smooth my trembling hands down my dress and walk to the front door.

Pulling open the door, I see a woman on the other side. Looks to be in her fifties. Plump. Shoulder-length curly black hair. Kind face.

"Anne?" I've spoken to Anne many times on the phone, but I have never actually met her in person.

"Yes. And you must be Daisy. You and Jesse have the exact same eye color. Lovely." She smiles.

Jesse and I both have amber eyes with flecks of hazel in them. In certain lights, it looks almost gold. It's a fairly unusual eye color, one that we inherited from our dad.

It's one of the things that I actually like about myself.

"Come in." I smile, stepping back to let her in.

I shut the door and lead her straight into the living room. She takes a seat on the sofa, putting her huge bag on the floor next to her. I take a seat in the armchair across from her.

"Lovely place you have here."

"Would you like a tour?" I offer.

"Tea first, if that's okay." She smiles. "I haven't had a cuppa since lunch, and I'm dying for one."

Smiling, I reach over and pour tea in a cup. "Milk and sugar?"

"Just milk, please."

I pour the milk in, stir with the teaspoon, and hand it over to her. I pour myself a coffee, adding milk.

"Help yourself to biscuits," I tell her.

She sips her tea. "Oh, lovely cup of tea," she tells me.

I've always been told I make good tea even though I never drink it myself. I don't know what I do when it comes to making tea that makes it taste so good. I guess I just have the tea touch.

I smile and sip my own coffee.

She puts her cup down on the table and reaches into her bag, pulling out a green folder. It has Jesse's name on the front.

My heart beats just that little bit faster.

"So, how have you been finding things since you got out?" Anne asks me.

"Really good." I smile, putting my own cup down on the table. "It's nice, not having to shower with twenty other women." *Oh God, did I actually just say that?* "I mean, it's fine. Like I never left. Of course, it was a little strange at first—you know, being free—but living with Cece has really helped. She's such a rock for me. And starting my new job, of course, has helped." *Stop talking. Stop talking now.*

"How is the job going?"

I'm so nervous that I'm actually starting to sweat.

"Really great." *Aside from my bipolar boss.* "I'm really enjoying it."

"You're working at"—she pulls a sheet of paper from the folder and looks at it—"the Matis Estate, as a maid."

"That's right." I clasp my hands together in my lap.

I don't want to talk about my job. I want to talk about Jesse. But I need to let her take the lead here.

"I just had my first payday today actually." I smile.

She lifts her kind eyes to mine. "That's great, Daisy. I'm really pleased that things are coming together for you."

"Me, too." I smile, probably too enthusiastically, but I'm just feeling nervous and jittery.

"Can I ask...how is Jesse? I know, the last time we spoke—well, not the last time; the time before, when I was still in prison—you said he was doing well. Getting his grades back up."

When I got put away, Jesse went off the rails for a while. He'd always been a good boy, a sweet boy, and done great in school. But he started acting up in school. Letting his grades slip.

He hadn't acted up like that when dad died or when mum disappeared on us. But he did when I left.

That was hard to take, knowing what I had unwittingly let happen, how it had affected him so badly.

I know it was because I was all he had left.

"He's still doing well. His grades are almost back up to where they were. His teachers are pleased with his progress. He recently started playing football. Him and some of the boys he lives with have a team. Tim Marshall, the head of the boys group home, is the coach. They've been competing in some local tournaments."

"That's so great. I would love to watch them play sometime."

She doesn't say anything to that, and her nonaction drops like rocks in my stomach.

There's this awful pause…and it makes my eyes burn and my stomach sink lower.

"I'm not getting him back, am I?"

She looks me straight in the eyes. "It's not a no, Daisy."

"But it's not a yes."

"I can see how well you're doing here. And how hard you're trying to make a good life for yourself and Jesse. But you've only been out of prison for four days, and you're out on parole. It would be irresponsible of me to put Jesse back in your care under the current circumstances. But that being said, we can reassess in six months and see where we're at."

Six months.

I feel like I'm dying on the inside.

Tears are fighting at my eyes. My lower lip trembles. I bite down on it.

"Daisy, the ultimate goal here is to have Jesse back with his family, and that's you. But I need to make sure that the environment I put him back into is a stable one. You need time to acclimate to life on the outside. And this will give you time to get your finances steady, get your life in a good place, and get you ready for Jesse's return."

"Am I..." My voice breaks, so I clear my throat and blink back the tears. "Will I be able to see him?"

"Absolutely. I have talked to Jesse, and he is willing to see you."

"He's still angry with me?"

She presses her lips together. "The anger has simmered. It's more like he's harboring resentment, but I have no doubt that, once the two of you start spending time together, he'll come around in no time."

"When can I see him?"

"I was thinking next Saturday. So long as Jesse is okay with it, I see no problem with you picking him up at nine a.m. and spending the day together. He'll need to be back at five for dinner. But, aside from that, the day will be yours to do with as you wish."

"Thank you," I tell her.

She picks up her cup and takes a large gulp of tea before putting it back on the table. "Well, I must get off. My husband will have dinner waiting on the table for me."

I stand at the same time as she does.

"Oh, before I forget, here's the address to where Jesse is living. I'll call the home on Monday to let them and Jesse know that you'll be coming."

She hands me a piece of paper, which I look at before folding it up into my hand.

I walk her to the door, opening it. "Thank you for coming to see me," I tell her.

She puts her hand on my arm. "Try not to feel too disheartened, Daisy. Just try to remember that you and I are both working toward the same goal—doing what's best for Jesse."

I want to tell her that I am what's best for him. Not living in that boys home with a bunch of strangers, but being here with his family.

Of course I say nothing. I just smile and nod my head.

"We'll talk soon." She steps through the door. "And have a lovely time with Jesse next Saturday. Call me on the Monday after to let me know how it went."

"I'll call on my lunch break."

"Perfect. Chat then."

I watch her walk away and then shut the door.

I lean back against it, once again fighting tears in my eyes.

I'm not getting him back.

But I am going to see him in just over a week. That's a good thing. I know it is, but I just want him back here with me.

Fucking Jason! He ruined my life.

But more so, I'm angry with myself for being so gullible and stupid. For not seeing when I was being played.

I hear my phone beep in the living room. I go to retrieve my phone and see a text from Cece.

> *Is she still there? I've finished work early, but I can hang around here if you need more time.*

I decide not to text but to call her back.

"Hey," she says.

The sound of her voice breaks my resolve, and a sob slips out. I press my fist to my mouth.

"Dais, what happened?" she asks, concerned.

Lowering my hand, my voice trembling, I say, "I'm not getting Jesse back. Well, not anytime soon."

"Oh, Dais…"

"I have to prove to them that I'm responsible enough to care for him and that I'm not going to end up back in prison."

"You were already all of those things. Fucking Jason!" she seethes. "I swear to God, when I find that little bastard,

I'm gonna kill him. Hang him up by his balls and chop his cock off."

Her anger for Jason soothes me a little. Cece has never been shy about vocalizing it. I know she wonders why I don't get mad like she does. But I know that losing my shit over Jason isn't going to help me get back those eighteen months. And it sure as hell isn't going to help me get Jesse back.

"If you chopped his cock off, wouldn't the rope just keep slipping off his balls?"

"Nope, because I'd tie it so tight that the circulation in his ball sack would be cut off, and then his balls would just shrivel up and die."

"But wouldn't they just fall off, and then he'd be free?"

"Maybe. But at least he'd be cock- and ball-less."

That makes me laugh. "You always manage to make me feel better, Ce."

"I am the queen of comedy."

"That, you are."

"So, what else did Anne say?"

"She said I could see Jesse. A week from tomorrow."

"That's great news."

"It is. I just…" My smile fades away, seeping into the sadness.

"I know. You want him home. I want him home, too. Look, I'm leaving work now. I'll pick up a bottle of wine on the way home. So, I'll see you in twenty."

"Thanks, Ce. See you soon." I hang up the phone and rest my head back against the sofa.

I can't believe I was so stupid to think that, if I dressed nice and fed her tea and biscuits, then she'd let me have Jesse back.

I mean, I wasn't expecting to get him tomorrow, but…six months…

God, I'm so fucking dumb.

UNSUITABLE

I should have known that nothing is ever that easy for me. I have to fight for everything in this life.

Another sob breaks free, and this time, I don't stop it. I just let the tears flow.

TWELVE

EARPHONES IN, I'm listening to OneRepublic's "Wherever I Go." I get the cleaning products, bucket, and mop, and I hook the vacuum cleaner under my arm. I drag it along the floor, heading toward the gym.

I haven't seen Kas since I arrived an hour ago, and his office door is closed, so I figure he's in there.

I really need to clean his office, but I'm not in the mood to be growled at, so I'll wait until he emerges, and then I'll set about cleaning in there. But, in the meantime, I'll give the gym a good going-over.

When I reach the door, my hands are full, so I press down on the handle with the back of my hand and push the door open with my butt. I back into the room, pulling the vacuum through. I put the cleaning stuff down, pivot on the spot, and stall at the sight of Kas and another guy fighting. Well, when I say *fighting*, I'm guessing they're sparring.

A large mat is laid out on the gym floor. Kas and the other guy are barefoot, both bare-chested, wearing only shorts. Their hands are wrapped, like fighters. Kas's hair is tied back with a hair tie. I've never seen his hair like this before. It looks good...hot.

He has his back to me, so I can see the defined muscles there along with his broad shoulders. Sweat is trickling down his back.

Holy hell.

I pull the earphones from my ears, riveted.

I should leave. I will leave.

Now would be a good time, as neither of them has noticed me.

Okay, Daisy, grab your stuff and go.

I'm just about to turn away and make my exit when the guy that Kas is sparring with catches my eye and smiles.

He lifts a hand to Kas, stopping him. His eyes come back to me. "Hey," he says. Smiling again, he gives me a chin lift.

Kas's head turns so fast that I'm surprised he didn't break his neck.

The moment his eyes hit me, something that looks an awful lot like panic enters his eyes. But it's gone quickly, replaced with anger.

Yanking his eyes from me, he walks past his sparring partner—well, more like, he stomps—and heads over to the edge of the mat. He picks up a T-shirt from the floor and yanks it on, his movements rough and jerky.

Then, he turns to me. Pissed off doesn't even cover the look on his face right now.

I brace myself for a tongue-lashing.

"You need to learn to fucking knock," he snaps at me.

That takes me back a step.

That's the first time I've ever heard him swear. And I really don't like that it was directed at me. All I did was walk in a room, for God's sake.

"I'm sorry. I didn't realize anyone was in here."

"Well, if you'd knocked, then you would've."

My eyes flicker uncomfortably to the other guy in the room, who is surprisingly frowning at Kas.

UNSUITABLE

At least I'm not the only one who thinks he's acting like a total dickhead right now.

"Point taken. But please don't swear at me again. I'm your employee, not a dog."

His hands grip his hips, his face tightening with anger. "I'm fully aware of just exactly who you are. And, just so you know, I would never tell a dog to fuck off. I happen to like dogs."

He might as well have just belted the backs of my legs.

Arsehole!

Rage and hurt and a hundred other emotions burn through me. And it's worse because someone else is here to hear him talk to me this way.

My cheeks burn with embarrassment.

I'm about to tell him to go fuck himself and walk out of here when his sparring partner says, "Chill the fuck out, Kas."

I lift my eyes to see the guy walking toward me, wearing a kind smile on his face.

He stops in front of me. "I'm Jude, a friend of Kas's." He puts his hand out for me to shake.

Kas has friends?

I glance down at Jude's hand and then lift my eyes back to his face.

I'm desperately trying to keep my eyes off his bare chest. He has a really nice chest and arms and…well, he's the first guy I've seen semi-naked in a really long time.

And he's fit.

Seriously fit.

Ripped to hell with some ink on his bicep that goes over his shoulder. His skin is the color of milk chocolate. His black hair is shaved close. He's a few inches shorter than Kas. About six foot, I'd say. And he has the most amazingly vivid green eyes, a total contrast to his hair and skin color.

"Daisy." I take his hand and shake it.

"Oh, *you're* Daisy." Releasing my hand, he glances back at Kas.

Kas frowns at him, giving a slight shake of his head, and Jude laughs.

Um, what?

And he's heard of me. What the hell is that supposed to mean? And what was the frown and head shake all about?

Jude brings his eyes back to me. "Ignore Kas. He's just pissed off because I was beating his arse."

Kas scoffs, causing Jude to grin at me.

He has a really nice smile.

Honestly, if I were butter, I'd melt right now.

"And, here I was, thinking I was the eternal cause of his grumpiness."

"Nah, don't take it personally. Kas is just a miserable bastard ninety percent of the time."

"What about the other ten percent?"

"He's usually sleeping."

Jude grins, and I giggle.

"I am still here," Kas growls as he walks over to us.

Jude winks at me, making me smile again.

"Were you boxing?" I ask Jude as Kas comes to a stop beside him.

"MMA," Kas answers, forcing my eyes to his. "Mixed—"

"Martial arts," I finish.

"You like MMA?" Jude asks.

"It's okay." I shrug before flicking another glance at Kas, who is frowning at me. I swear, sometimes, he almost looks like he's in pain when he's looking at me.

"We'll be done in here in an hour," Kas says to me, his tone hard. "Clean my office now. It's about time you did it."

I have to stop myself from saying, *The reason I've never cleaned it is because you're always in there!*

I repress a sigh and say, "Fine."

UNSUITABLE

Turning, I pick up my bucket and cleaning supplies and hook the vacuum under my arm.

"You need a hand?" Jude asks from behind me.

I glance back at him, ignoring Kas's stare on me. "I'm good, but thanks."

"It was nice meeting you, Daisy."

"You, too."

I start to walk to the door. Surprise has me nearly tripping over myself when Kas quickly moves past me and holds the door open for me.

Okay...

"Thanks," I utter.

"How did your meeting go?" Kas asks in a low voice, bringing me to a shocked stop.

I really don't get this guy. One minute, he's Kas-hole, being a total dick to me. The next, he's Kas-nice, asking how my meeting went.

His mood swings are really starting to give me whiplash.

I turn to him to find that his eyes are soft and fixed on me. A stark contrast from the way he was looking at me mere seconds ago.

I give him a sad smile. "Not as well as I had hoped. But thank you again for letting me have the time off. I do appreciate it."

Hand still on the door, Kas lifts a shoulder, shrugging off my comment.

We stare at each other for a long second. I feel a tension start to rise in the air between us. His eyes darken and flicker to life. I see his hand tighten around the door. My own breathing is coming in faster. My skin prickles to life under his intense gaze.

Then, as if coming back to his senses, he steps back, holding the door open wider. I walk through it.

"I'm sorry things didn't work out for you." Kas's soft words touch my back.

I glance back at him. "Yeah, me, too."

Then, he's just staring at me again. There's no warmth in his eyes this time, but there is definitely something. Almost like an invisible thread attaching us.

Then, I watch as his face shuts down. He gives me a sharp nod and releases the door, letting it close.

I stand, staring at the closed door.

Who is this guy?

Letting out a sigh, I turn to walk away, but one of the cleaning sprays slips from my hand.

"For eff's sake," I mutter.

I bend down to pick it up, and that's when I hear my name being said from behind the door.

Of course, I have to listen in.

"So, that's Daisy."

"Mmhmm," Kas answers.

"She seems nice. Hot, too. You didn't mention that."

"Why would I?"

Hang on...was that Kas saying he thinks I'm hot in a roundabout way?

"So, you actually admit you think she's hot?" Jude sounds really surprised by this admission.

Kas sighs. "Of course I think she's hot. A man would have to be fucking blind not to see that she is."

Wow. He thinks I'm hot.

I steadfastly ignore the thrill that runs through me at the knowledge.

"And?"

"And what?"

"And what are you gonna do about it?"

"I'm going to do absolutely nothing about it."

"Come on, Kas." Jude's tone is teasing, coaxing.

"She works for me. End of story."

There's a long pause.

Then, I hear Jude say, "Well, if you're not gonna ask her out...then I will."

UNSUITABLE

"Jude…" Kas's tone is like a warning.

Interesting.

Um, hold up…I'm not bothered that Kas is pissed off at the thought of Jude asking me out.

Am I?

"What? You're not gonna ask her out," Jude counters. "She's hot as fuck, and she seems like a really cool girl."

"You don't know her." His tone is really harsh and blunt.

Wow. Okay. That hurt.

"That's the point of asking her out, dickface. You know, so I can get to know her."

"Not happening. Daisy is off-limits to you." Kas's voice sounds like a growl.

Um, what?

Jude laughs. "Off-limits? To just me or everyone?"

There's a pause, and then Jude laughs again. "You so wanna bang her."

"Jesus Christ! Will you just shut the fuck up about Daisy?" Kas bites.

"Hey, no need to get all testy, man. But be real for a sec. This is the first time in all the years I've known you that I've seen you get all bent out of shape over a chick. That's gotta mean something."

"It means nothing."

"Come on…"

"Seriously, Jude," Kas snaps. "Just fucking drop it, will you?"

There's a long silence.

Then, I hear Jude say, "Consider it dropped. We sparring again?"

"Yeah."

Jude chuckles. "Come on then, pretty boy. Give me your best shot."

Knowing their conversation about me is over, I move away from the door.

I walk down the hallway in a daze, not really sure what to do with what I just heard.

Kas likes me. Well, he thinks I'm hot.

So does Jude, but that's neither here nor there.

But Kas…he's such a prick to me, like all the time. If I fancy someone, then I tend to be nice to them.

I'm so bloody confused right now.

"Daisy?"

My eyes snap up, my insides jumping like I've just been caught doing something wrong.

It's Cooper.

"Hey." I paste on a smile.

"Hey. Everything okay?"

I nod my head.

"I was just coming to grab some milk. We ran out, and I'm dying for a cuppa."

"Sure. You want me to grab it for you?"

"Looks like you've got your hands full." He nods at the stuff I'm carrying. "How about I help you with this stuff, and then we can get the milk together?"

"Sure," I say, smiling, as I hand over the bucket to him, my thoughts about Kas momentarily forgotten.

THIRTEEN

I'M NERVOUS.

Scared and beyond terrified of how Jesse is going to be when I see him.

God, I wonder what he looks like now. I haven't seen him in so long, not since the day I was sentenced in court.

"You ready?" Cece's soft voice comes from beside me.

We're sitting in Cece's car, across the street from where Jesse lives. She offered to drop me off before she heads to work.

"No." I shake my head. "I don't know if I can do this, Ce."

I've wanted to see Jesse so badly since my release, but now that I'm so close to it happening, I'm sick with nerves.

She places her hand over mine, gripping it. "There's no need to be afraid. It's just Jesse—that sweet kid you raised, who adores you."

"Not anymore. He hates me."

"No, he doesn't. He's fourteen and angry, and he has a massive chip on his shoulder because he convinced himself that you'd left him. He knows, deep down, that it isn't true. He just needs to see you. I think, once he sees you and you guys start talking, things will be okay."

I look at the surety in her eyes and try to feel it myself.

"Yeah, you're right." I force a smile. "Thanks for the lift." I lean over and kiss her cheek. "Have a good day at work. See you at home later."

"Have a great day," she calls as I climb out of the car. "And tell our boy I said hi."

"Will do." I give her a thumbs-up and then shut the door.

I watch her car pull away, and then I cross the street to the boys home where Jesse lives.

Walking up the steps to the front door, my legs are trembling. I take a deep breath and lift a shaking hand to ring the doorbell.

I wait, my leg jigging on the spot.

Through the frosted glass, I see someone approaching the door. Then, the door opens, revealing a man with light-brown hair, who looks to be in his early thirties.

"Hi, I'm Daisy Smith, Jesse's sister. I was told to ask for Tim Marshall."

"I'm Tim." He smiles. "It's nice to finally meet you, Daisy. I've heard a lot about you."

He has?

That must mean that Jesse has talked about me.

It's just what I needed to ease my nerves and lift my spirits a little.

"Come in," he tells me.

I step inside. Tim closes the door behind me.

It's quiet in the house, and I wonder where the rest of the boys who live here are.

As if reading my mind, Tim says, "The house is empty—aside from Jesse, of course. The boys have gone out for ice cream with Jenna, who works here with me," he explains. "We thought it'd be nice to give you and Jesse some space."

"Thank you." I smile, but it feels awkward and clumsy on my lips. My hands are shaking. My head feels like it's

UNSUITABLE

about to explode. I bind my hands together in front of me, trying to ease the trembling.

"Jesse's just in the living room."

"Okay. Thanks."

"You can breathe." He gives me a gentle smile.

I laugh softly, exhaling.

"I know how nervous you must be feeling right now. But, trust me when I say, it's going to be okay. Jesse will never admit this, but he's just as nervous to see you."

"He is?" I hate to think that Jesse is feeling nervous, but knowing that I'm not alone in this and that he does actually want to see me helps.

"Don't tell him I told you this, but he was up at six thirty this morning. He showered and is wearing his nicest clothes. For a kid who I have to put a bomb under to get him out of bed for school every morning and practically hose him down in the garden to get him to wash…well, it says a lot."

"Yeah." I smile, but his words also hit me. Telling me just how much Jesse has changed.

The Jesse I knew was always up and out of bed early. And he loved taking baths.

I've missed so many changes in his life.

Tim walks down the short hallway. Stopping at a door, he opens it. "Jesse…Daisy's here."

I follow inside behind Tim.

And there he is, the sole reason I get out of bed every morning.

Love floods me. Tears prick my eyes. I feel like I've been smothered in happiness and punched in the chest with a fistful of pain, all at the same time.

The boy I knew looks like a young man. Even sitting, I can see how tall he is. His legs are so long. And he looks so much like Dad. He must have grown about two feet in the last eighteen months.

His hair is different. He always liked to wear his hair short. But, now, his dark brown hair is all grown out, curling around his ears. His jeans are black with a chain fixed on the pocket, linking to his belt that has a skull on the front of it. His T-shirt is black with a band on the front that I'm not familiar with. He looks a world away from the boy I left.

And the way he's looking at me…

It's the exact same way he looked at me the last time I saw him.

Hurt mixed with disappointment. And loss. So much loss.

Pain curls like a fist around my heart and squeezes tight.

Jesse sits forward in his seat, his eyes never leaving mine.

"Hi," I say softly, my voice not offering much.

He stares blankly at me.

"Why don't you sit down? I'll make us a drink. Tea or coffee? Or something cold?" Tim asks me.

Taking a seat across from Jesse, I answer Tim, "Coffee would be great. Thanks."

"Jesse?" Tim asks.

Jesse doesn't answer. He just shakes his head.

"Right. Well, I won't be long."

I watch Tim leave the room.

When I look back, Jesse is still staring at me.

The tension in the air is unnerving.

It makes me sick to my stomach to know the size of the wedge between us.

This is a kid who would talk nonstop to me. A kid who I could sit in perfect silence with and always feel at ease.

Now, it's almost like sitting with a stranger.

But a stranger I love very much.

My mouth is dry, so I lick my lips before speaking, "You look…so grown-up."

UNSUITABLE

I watch as his eyes shut down. Shutting me out.

He's looking at me like Kas looks at me.

Like he hates me.

Pain spikes me in the gut.

"Yeah, well, it's been eighteen months. I'm not just gonna stop growing 'cause you haven't been around."

"I know. I'm sorry—"

"Save it 'cause I don't want to hear it." He turns his face away, looking in the direction of the TV. Leaning back, he stretches his long legs out, folding his arms over his chest.

I fight back the tears burning my eyes and take a deep breath. "So...how have you been?" I ask.

He sighs and drags his eyes from the TV and back to me. "You want to make small talk, Daisy? Really?"

Daisy. He always called me Mayday.

Another spike of pain hits me—this time, in the chest. I rub at the ache. "I just want to talk to you, Jesse."

"Okay, let's talk." He swivels around in his seat, hands pressed to his thighs. He looks like he's roaring for a fight. "How was your time in prison? You learn any new tricks? How long you staying around for? Or should I expect another visit from the cops sometime soon, telling me that you're going back inside?"

"I-I'm not going back, Jesse. I'm here to stay."

He lets out a bitter laugh. It hurts to hear.

"Like Mum and Dad?"

"Jesse, please...I'm not like them. You know this. Deep down, you know this. I've missed you so much. I just want—"

"I don't give a shit what you want!" he yells, jumping to his feet. "As far as I'm concerned, you don't exist anymore!"

Pain punches me square in the chest. I push to my feet. "Jesse, please. Y-you don't mean that."

He laughs bitterly. "Yeah, I do."

"So, why see me today? Why let me come?"

He steps closer. "So, I could do to you what you did to me. You left me, Daisy. You fucking left me on my own. And, now, I'm leaving you. I never want to see you again. Do you hear me? As far as I'm concerned, I don't have a sister. You're as dead to me as Mum and Dad are."

I feel like I've been shot.

Tears fill my eyes. I can't help them or stop them from running down my cheeks.

Regret flickers in his eyes, but he quickly shuts it down. "I want you to leave." His voice is low.

"Je-Jesse, please." I press the heels of my hands to my cheeks to ebb the flow of tears.

"I said, go!"

His anger hits and shakes my body.

I stumble back, moving for the door.

When I reach it, I turn back. Putting strength in my spine and my voice, I say, "I know you don't want to hear this, but I'm saying it anyway. I'm going now because you asked me to, and I'm respecting your wishes. But I love you, kiddo. I will *always* love you. I need you to know that I'm not going anywhere. I'm here to stay. Never again will I leave you. I will do nothing to risk ever being taken away again. I swear that to you."

I press my hand to my chest. "I let you down, and it will never happen again. I'm going to prove to you that I mean every word. And I'm going to keep coming back every Saturday and knocking on your door until you decide to let me back in. I won't give up on you—ever."

"Yeah, well, good luck with that," he mutters before turning his back on me.

Pain clamps a strong arm over my chest.

It takes everything in me to pull that door open and walk out of it, leaving him standing there.

FOURTEEN

ALCOHOL.

The. Best. Invention. Ever.

Wait...was it invented? Or was it just made?

I don't know.

And, really, who gives a shit?

Not me—that's who.

All I give a shit about is that it makes the hurt go away.

Away...away...away.

A few drinks...okay, well, more than a few but less than a lot, and I'm no longer hurting over what Jesse said.

Jesse.

See? Even thinking his name doesn't hurt like it did an hour ago.

Hurt be gone because Daisy Smith is pain-free!
And it's the best feeling ever!

I mean, why haven't I been drinking all along? I've been feeling shitty for years, and all that time, I could have been drinking the shitty feelings away.

Alcohol—the cure to all my problems.

And, speaking of alcohol...I have some serious drinking time to make up for, considering I've never really drank.

You know, with trying to be a responsible adult and a parent to the kid under my care.

You know, the kid who hates me.

He hates me.

A pain pierces my heart.

No more pain!

More alcohol needed ASAP!

I down the last of my—*what am I drinking?* Honestly, I have no clue. But it tastes good. Well, actually, it tastes like shite. But it makes me feel better.

I let out a giggle.

The bartender glances at me.

Ah, the bartender. The bringer of goodness.

He's cute, too.

A bit too clean-looking for my liking but still cute.

Not that I'm interested in men.

Men are bastards.

Wanker bastards.

Every single one of them.

Well, all the men I've known, which isn't many. But whatever.

Smiling, I push my empty glass toward the cute bartender. "I'll have another of whatever that was."

That actually comes out like, "I'll s'have 'nother of whatsever tat twas."

But it's all good. I'm drunk, and drunk is awesome!

Cute Bartender leans his forearms on the bar. His shirtsleeves are rolled up. He has nice arms.

Not as nice as Kas's arms though. Kas's arms are all strong-looking and muscly. And his skin is so lovely. Lickable. I would totally lick Kas's arms.

And other parts of him.

Um, hold the effing phone. Why am I thinking about Kas in a sexual way?

He's another wanker-bastard man. The biggest of wanker-bastard men.

And I don't like him. At all.

UNSUITABLE

"You sure another drink is a good idea?" Cute Bartender asks me.

I rest my elbows on the bar and place my chin on my fists. It slips off.

I snort-giggle.

Then, I put my chin in the palm of my hand. It's steadier.

Is it just me, or is the room starting to spin?

"'Tis the best idea I've had in a long time." I give him a big smile.

God, my lips feel weird. Numb.

But numb is good!

Numb means no pain.

Cute Bartender smiles at me. "How about I get you a coffee instead?"

"Um..." I screw my face up. "Will the coffee be Irish?"

He chuckles and shakes his head.

"Then, no siree. I want the alcohol. Lots of alcohol!" I sweep my arms out.

"I think the last thing you need is more alcohol."

"Alcohol is the only thing I need."

"Why?" He smiles, bemused.

"Because"—I smile big—"alcohol equals happy."

"And why aren't you happy?"

"Who said I wasn't happy?"

"When a pretty girl like you tells me that alcohol equals happy, then she's telling me that she's not happy when she's sober."

Oh.

My smiles slips, and then my alcohol-induced loose lips just start yapping, "So, maybe I'm not happy when I'm sober. That doesn't mean anything. Lots of people need alcohol to feel happy. Sure, they're probably alcoholics, but I'm thinking I should try that out because nothing else is working for me. I try so hard, and I still manage to fuck everything up. My brother hates me. Actually really hates me." I press my hand to the pain in my chest that's trying to force its way back. "He wishes I were dead," I whisper that last part.

"I'm sure he doesn't wish you were dead."

I look him in the eye. "Oh, he does. He told me so himself, like an hour ago. But the thing is, I don't blame him. I kinda hate me. I mean, I let him down. The only person in the world who truly matters to me, and I failed him. He's right to hate me. I'm a fucking fuckup. I mean, even my boss hates me. And whose boss actually hates them?"

"I'm pretty sure my boss doesn't like me." Cute Bartender chuckles.

"Ah, see?" I point at him, like he just told me the cure for cancer. "You said your boss doesn't like you. My boss effing *hates* me! I mean, like can't-stand-the-sight-of-me hates me. And, sure, he's a massive dickhead. But he does think I'm hot, so there is that. I mean, he thinks I'm hot, but he hates me. How fucking weird is that? And, really, what does that say about me? Hot but annoying as fuck—that's what that says. Everyone hates me. Well, except for Cece, but she has to like me by default because we've known each other forever. Honestly, I don't know what I've done to deserve her as a friend because I think I deserve to be hated. I'm an idiot. An actual twatting idiot."

I feel wetness on my cheeks, and I realize I'm crying. I press the heels of my hands to my cheeks.

"Hey now, I don't think you're a twatting idiot." Cute Bartender hands me a napkin.

"You don't know me." I sniffle, drying my eyes. "Trust me, if you did, you'd think I was a twatting idiot."

"Well, how about I get you a coffee? We can sober you up, and then I can get to know the sober you."

"Okay." I give him a grateful nod, wiping my eyes because those damn tears keep coming.

UNSUITABLE

"You stay right there, and I'll be back with that coffee," Cute Bartender tells me.

I watch him walk away. Taking a deep breath, I wipe my eyes again. Screwing up the napkin, I toss it on the bar.

Ugh, I'm such a fuckup.

I lay my arms on the bar and rest my head on them.

I should call Cece and let her know that Jesse hates me.

Reaching for my bag on the stool next to me, I rake through it, searching for my phone. My fingers find and curl around it. Pulling it out, I unlock the screen.

Bloody thing is all blurry.

I blink, trying to clear my eyes.

I go to my Contacts, all four of them.

Jesus, I'm pathetic.

That makes me snort-cry.

I wipe at my eyes as I press Cece's number. I put the phone to my ear and wait.

It seems to ring for ages.

Then, the line connects, and a male voice says, "Daisy?"

Um, what?

I pull the phone from my ear and look at the screen.

Oh, holy mother of crap.

Kas.

I dialed Kas's number instead of Cece's.

Crappity crap!

I can hear him yelling my name down the phone.

I tentatively put the phone to my ear.

"Hey, Mr. Matis." I try to sound normal. Of course, I slur the words.

"Daisy"—his voice is like stone—"are you drunk?"

"No!" I shake my head, like he can see me. "Of course I'm not!" And, of course, that also comes out slurred. I clear my throat and try to focus on my words. "I'm not drunk. I'm just happy! Happy! Happy! Happy! This is my happy voice!"

"Jesus fucking Christ," he sighs. "Where are you?"

I don't think I've convinced him of my soberness.

Shit.

"Where am I?"

"Yes, Daisy. Where the fuck are you right now?" He talks to me like I'm a small child.

"There's no need to swear, *Mr. Matis*. And I'm in a bar."

"Which bar?"

"Dunno." I shrug.

"Daisy..." His voice is a low warning.

"Okay!" I try to think if I saw the name when I came in, but I don't remember. I just remember seeing the place and realizing it sold alcohol, so I just went straight on in. I glance around the bar, seeing nothing. "Um...there's nothing. I mean, there are chairs and tables and a bar and alcohol...lots of alcohol." I giggle. "I've had some amazing drinks. You'd love it here. Well, probably not. But maybe you should have a drink. It might loosen you up a bit because you are kind of uptight. You should come and drink with me! We can get drunk together!"

"You sound like you've had more than enough already."

"Ugh! You sound like the cute bartender."

"Cute bartender?"

"Yep. He's lovely. He's been giving me lots of drinks. And he has really nice arms. They're not as nice as your arms though. Your arms are the best. Really muscular. And your skin reminds me of caramel—oh, I'm hungry now. I could just eat—"

"Daisy—"

"A Cadbury Caramel. And the cute bartender is sweet. He's gone to get me a coffee, and then we're going to get to know one another."

"What do you mean, you're going to get to know one another?" His voice is like granite.

UNSUITABLE

"I dunno. But he's nice. You're nice sometimes—well, rarely." I snort. "I mean, you act like a Kas-hole pretty much *all* the time. But you're nice sometimes, and it's nice when you are nice, you know what I mean? Because there's only Ce who's nice to me. But the cute bartender is nice. So, yeah, that's cool. Did I tell you that my baby brother hates me?" I laugh, but I hear the pain in my voice loud and clear. "He's like my kid. I raised him, and he actually hates me. More than you do, I think. Unless you wish I were dead 'cause he wishes I were dead. So, if you wish I were dead, then you probably hate me more."

I pause to take a breath. Instead, a sob falls from my mouth.

"Shit...Daisy..." Kas's voice is softer than I've ever heard it.

I feel that softness touch me. It touches that pain in my chest and soothes it a little.

"Tell me where you are." His voice is still gentle, but this time, I don't feel better. I feel something break deep inside me.

I hold that crack together. But more tears track down my face. I grab that screwed up napkin and wipe my face again.

Then, I see Cute Bartender coming back with my coffee, so I pretend all is okay, and I force a big smile at him.

"Daisy?" Kas says my name, a little sterner this time.

"I'm still here. Just wait a sec." Keeping the phone to my ear, I move the mouthpiece away from my mouth, and I speak to the bartender, "I meant to call my friend, Cece, but I somehow called my boss—you know, the one who hates me. Well, he wants to know which bar I'm in, but I'm not sure what this bar's called, and I thought you would know. Do you know?"

Dur! Of course he knows, dummy.

Cute Bartender chuckles as he puts the cup of coffee down in front of me. "The Nelson."

I move the mouthpiece back to my mouth. "I'm in The Nelson," I repeat to Kas.

"And where exactly is The Nelson?" He sounds really pissed off.

This is the Kas I know. I feel more comfortable that he's being pissy with me. It's weird when he's nice.

I tip the mouthpiece away again. "He wants to know whereabouts The Nelson is? He sounds really pissed off," I whisper-giggle.

"I am really pissed off," Kas growls in my ear.

"You're really bloody grumpy, you know that?" I tell Kas.

"Yeah, and you're a monumental pain in my arse," he fires back.

"We're in Camden," Cute Bartender tells me.

But I only half-hear what he said because I'm too focused on what Kas just said, and it's ignited a fire in my belly.

"Um, I'm a pain in your arse? Er, hello, Mr. Pot Kettle Black! You're mean to me every single day! Like, *every* day! And not just marginally mean. You're, like, high-level mean! Meanest of the highest level ever! I've never had someone be so horrible to me as you are. So, if anyone is a pain in the arse, then it's you!"

My rant over, the line goes deathly silent.

Shit.

I just reamed out my boss over the phone. I drunk-dialed him and yelled at him and called him a pain in the arse.

Fuck.

"Am I...fired?" I ask quietly.

"Tell me exactly where the fuck this bar is." His voice is low, deadly.

I'm so fired.

UNSUITABLE

"Camden." I wince.

"Stay exactly where you are. I'm coming to get you."

"You are?" That takes me aback. It probably shouldn't, as he's been asking where I am for the last few minutes. I guess I just never thought he'd put himself out for me.

"I might be a Kas-hole—as you put it"—*Shit! I can't believe I called him a Kas-hole to his face*—"but I'm not the kind of arsehole who would leave a vulnerable, drunk girl in a bar alone."

"I'm not alone. I'm with the cute bartender—"

"Exactly. Stay right where you are. Don't fucking move, Daisy. And tell that bartender, if he puts a hand on you, I'll rip it off."

Okay...

Is it weird that I found that totally hot?

"Kas..."

"What?" he snaps.

"What if I need the toilet? I'll have to move—"

"I said, stay the fuck put. I'll be there soon." Then, he hangs the phone up on me.

Moving the phone from my ear, I stare at it, bewildered.

"Um...he's coming to get me," I tell the cute bartender as I lower my phone to the bar. "He said something about ripping your hand off. And...I think I might be fired."

"Daisy."

I feel a hand touch my shoulder.

I lift my head from my arms, which are resting on the bar, and I look up into the gorgeous face of Kastor Matis.

I was expecting him to look angry. Surprisingly, he looks relieved.

"Did I fall asleep?" I ask him.

I remember talking to the bartender after I spoke to Kas. Then, I laid my head down, as I suddenly felt tired, and then…nothing.

"Are you okay?" Kas asks, concern clear in his voice.

I run a self-conscious hand over my hair. I can only imagine what I look like.

"I'm fine." I nod.

"Come on, let's get you home."

He offers me his hand. I grab my bag and then take his hand. He helps me from the stool. I expect him to drop my hand, but he doesn't. He keeps a firm hold of it as he leads me through the bar.

I glance around, seeing the bartender a little further down the bar, serving a couple of people. He lifts a hand to me. I smile, embarrassed that I fell asleep in a bar.

Jesus. What a complete wanker I am.

I stumble a little on my feet, and Kas catches me by the waist, pulling me close to his side.

"Okay?" he asks softly.

"Mmhmm."

His arm stays around me all the way out of the bar and to his car. He helps me into his car. I have to admit to feeling a little bereft when his arm leaves my waist.

I'm putting my liking him touching me down to the amount of alcohol I consumed.

I put my seat belt on and snuggle down into the leather seat of his car. I shut my eyes.

His car door opens, and then I hear him climb in before the door shuts.

The engine turns on. Warm air blows on me, and Green Day's "Boulevard of Broken Dreams" is playing softly in the background.

I feel the car start to move.

"Where am I taking you?" he asks.

"Home," I murmur.

UNSUITABLE

I hear him laugh softly.

I've never heard Kas laugh before. It's a really nice sound. Like a balm to ease all pain.

"I've never heard you laugh before," I whisper my thoughts. "It's a beautiful sound. You should laugh more."

He's silent, saying nothing.

Worrying I've somehow managed to piss him off again, I utter, "I'm sorry."

"For saying I have a nice laugh? Or for the drunk dial?"

I can't read anything from his tone. So, I peek open an eye and look at him.

His eyes are fixed on the road ahead, but there's a soft curl to his lips, which isn't usually there.

Warmth spreads across my chest.

I close my peeking eye, feeling relieved but exhausted. "The last one," I whisper.

There's silence again. But it doesn't feel uncomfortable this time.

It feels... *serene*.

Not a word I thought I would ever use with Kas.

Heaviness weighs on my body. The heat and song and motion of the car—and if I'm being honest, the scent of Kas—are lulling me to sleep, and I don't bother to fight it.

"Thank you," I murmur to him.

There's a long pause.

I feel sleep start to claim me.

Then, I hear his softly spoken words just before everything goes black, "I'm the last person you should be thanking."

FIFTEEN

SHEETS ARE TANGLED around my legs. My mouth feels like the inside of a toilet. And my head is kicking a steady beat.

Groaning, I force my sticky eyes open. After a few blinks to clear them, my stare is met with a ceiling that doesn't look like mine.

It's not my ceiling.

Sharply turning my head, ignoring the pain it causes, I see that I'm not in my bedroom. It looks familiar, but I'm not sure...

Where in the hell am I?

I quickly sit up, my head going woozy. I press my hand to my head as panic makes my heart beat hard. Then, I realize that the bed I'm sitting in is the bed in one of the guest rooms at the Matis Estate.

What the hell am I doing here?

And then it all comes flooding back to me, like a bad movie.

Ah...fuck.

I saw Jesse yesterday, and he told me that he hated me. I press the heel of my hand to my chest, pushing against the pain that pierces it.

After Jesse, I found my way into a bar.

Got drunk. Cute Bartender. Drunk-dialing Kas. Him coming to the bar to get me. Putting me in his car. Falling asleep...

Why did he bring me here? Why didn't he take me home? What time is it?

My eyes swing to the clock on the nightstand, catching on a glass of water sitting by it.

Seven thirty a.m.

As in, seven thirty a.m. on Sunday morning?

Shit!

Cece!

She'll be worried sick. I didn't call her, like I said I would, and I was out all night.

Ripping the bedsheet off me, I jump out of bed, looking for my bag, but it's nowhere to be seen.

But I do see my dress from yesterday hanging over the back of the chair at the dressing table, and my shoes are on the floor by it.

I glance down at myself to find that I'm wearing a black Kasabian T-shirt that hits the backs of my thighs.

It must be Kas's T-shirt.

That means he...

Oh dear God.

He undressed me and changed my clothes. I still have my bra and knickers on.

Thank God.

I yank the T-shirt off, getting a lungful of Kas's scent as it passes over my face. I grab my dress and pull it on. Then, I quickly make the bed.

I grab the glass of water and down it. Taking the glass with me, I grab my shoes and the T-shirt, so I can put it in the laundry.

I let myself out of the bedroom and into the quiet hall.

Heart thumping, clutching my shoes and Kas's T-shirt to my chest, I make my way downstairs.

I glance at his office door, which is closed.

UNSUITABLE

I have to talk to Kas. First, to thank him for looking out for me. Then, to ask if I still have a job. And, if I don't, then beg him to give me my job back.

I'm not averse to begging in this instance.

I've screwed up so bad.

It won't look good for me if Toby finds out that I've been sacked for getting drunk and behaving like a complete idiot.

And it will look even worse to Anne. It could set me even further back with Jesse.

Not that Jesse and I could get any further back. He wants nothing to do with me.

But I need to prove to him that I'm here to stay. And *here to stay* means, I need this job.

Taking a deep breath, I head for the kitchen to put the T-shirt in the laundry basket. Then, I'll go to his office and face the Kas-wrath.

I push open the kitchen door, and my heart falls out of my chest when I see Kas sitting at the kitchen table, staring down at his phone, an empty plate and a cup sitting in front of him.

He's wearing jeans and a fitted T-shirt that shows off the lines of his body. His hair is a little messier than usual, one side tucked behind his ear.

He looks good. But then he always looks good. I hate that.

His eyes lift from his phone to me.

His look cuts right through me.

"Hey," I say, swallowing past my nerves.

"Hi." There's no tone to his response, giving me nothing as to what he's thinking.

I move slowly toward him through the kitchen. His eyes stay trained on me the whole time.

I slip into the seat across from him. I put the empty glass on the table, my shoes on the floor next to me, and hold his T-shirt in my lap.

I don't really know where to start, what to go with. My eyes drift around the room and then hook onto my bag, which is sitting on the counter.

I really need to ring Cece, but I need to speak to him first.

But he beats me to it. "Your phone kept ringing and ringing. I didn't want to wake you. I figured it must be important, whoever was calling, so I answered it for you. It was your friend, Cece. She was worried that she hadn't heard from you. I told her that you were here, you were safe, and you'd be home in the morning."

He spoke to Cece. Oh my God.

Well, at least she wasn't left worrying about me all night. But that is going to be one hell of an interesting conversation I'll have with her later.

"Thank you," I say. Then, I can't help but ask, "Why didn't you take me home?"

He pins me with a stare that has me squirming in my chair. "Because I didn't know where you lived. You passed out before telling me."

"My address is on your employee records," I challenge.

"Which are here."

Oh. Yeah.

"How did I get to bed?"

He gives me a look that clearly states he thinks I'm dumb. "I carried you."

"I was that out of it, huh?"

"Yeah. I don't think a bomb going off would've woken you up."

"Sorry."

"Don't be. It was funny, listening to you snore."

"I don't snore!" I say, aghast.

His lips curl up into a stunning smile, and he laughs.

A memory of me telling him yesterday that he had a beautiful laugh and that he should laugh more slips into my mind.

UNSUITABLE

"Do I really snore?" I ask him.

He grins and nods. "Like a pig."

I like that he's smiling, so I don't fight him on it. "Must've been the alcohol because I don't snore normally."

"Hmm...yeah, must've been."

I can hear the laughter in his voice. It makes my heart swell.

I curl my fingers around his T-shirt and then remember waking up in it.

My face flushes. "Did you, um..." I bite my lip. "Undress me?" I wince on the words.

There's a long silence.

I peek up through my lashes at him.

And I would be lying if I said that I didn't see the flash of heat in his eyes. Or that I wasn't affected by that flash of heat.

"I thought you'd be more comfortable in my T-shirt. But don't worry, Daisy. I was the perfect gentleman. I barely looked at all."

"But you did look a little."

Oh my God. Did I actually just say that?

I want to die in my seat, but I force myself to hold steady and keep his gaze.

Kas's expression doesn't falter. Not even a flicker.

Then, his lip curls a little at the corner.

I'd like to say that I'm unaffected by that as well, but I'm totally not.

I'm squirming, and I'm hot in places that haven't been hot in a very long time.

"Well, thank you for taking care of me," I manage to say. "And for the loan of the T-shirt. I'll wash it."

He lifts a shoulder in a half-shrug. "Would you like some coffee? Something to eat?" he offers as he gets up from his seat, taking his plate and cup along with my empty water glass.

I nearly fall off my chair in shock. "Um…coffee would be great. Thank you."

I watch him pour us each a coffee. Then, he adds milk to mine. I didn't even realize that he knew how I took my coffee.

He puts my drink down in front of me and then sits back in his seat across from me, holding his drink in his hand. "You should eat something. I'm guessing you have the hangover from hell?"

I watch him take a sip of his coffee.

"I've felt better." I offer a small smile. "But I don't think I can manage anything at the moment."

I curl my hands around my cup and lift it to my mouth, taking a small sip.

God, it tastes good. He makes damn good coffee.

I put the cup down, keeping my hands around it. I look him in the eye.

He's already watching me. The look in his eyes seems curious. Like I'm a puzzle that he can't figure out.

I wonder if my eyes reflect the same. Because I honestly cannot figure him out.

He exudes this harsh exterior, but beneath all of that is a guy who will get in his car and drive to London to pick up his drunk employee, bring her back to his home, and take care of her.

Warmth spreads across my chest.

"I'm really sorry about yesterday. Calling you when I was drunk. The things I said…" I briefly close my eyes in embarrassment as the words flood back to me. "Passing out in your car. You having to take care of me. I am so, so sorry. And I know I acted like a complete idiot, and I deserve to be fired, but I really, really need this job." I lean forward, putting my arms on the table, and I clasp my hands together. "And, I swear to you, what happened yesterday will never happen again. Never, ever."

"Why did you go out to a bar alone and get drunk?"

UNSUITABLE

His question throws me.

"Um…because, I'm stupid."

"You're far from stupid, Daisy. Although getting that drunk while alone in a bar was a pretty stupid thing to do."

"There was a compliment in there, right?" I smile, and his lip twitches.

But his face quickly goes back to serious. "Anything could've happened to you. You get that, right?"

He was…concerned about me?

Well, color me surprised.

"Yes. It was stupid. I was just—"

"Trying to numb the pain."

That shoots my eyebrows up. I knew Kas was smart, but I never took him for perceptive. Especially when it comes to me. Honestly, I thought he was ignorant to everything having to do with Daisy Smith.

"You said something about your brother last night…" he adds, letting his words hang.

So, apparently, he's not *that* ignorant.

Sadness prickles my skin at his mention of Jesse.

But I'm also taken aback that he wants to talk to me about this.

I really need to keep my job, and if telling him about this stuff means I will have a job at the end of it, then so be it.

"I went to see him yesterday. It didn't go well."

"Why not?"

I blow out a breath. "He blames me for him being in foster care, and he's right to. I was all he had left in the world, and when I went to prison, he got taken into care."

"Where are your parents?"

"Our dad is dead. Our mother is…gone. When I was sixteen, she ran off with her drug-dealer boyfriend. I guess she didn't want to be a mother anymore. Jesse was only six. I knew, if Social Services found out she was gone, they'd take him away.

"I'd been practically raising Jesse since he was a baby since our mother cared about drugs more than us. She'd always used drugs. She had somehow managed to stay clean while she was pregnant with Jesse; maybe she cared a little more back then. But, after our dad died, that seemed to tip her over the edge. I'd just finished doing my exams when she disappeared on us. So, I did what I had to. I got a job. It was hard in the beginning, but we managed. Things got easier when I got the job at the jewelry store, as I was earning more money."

"The jewelry store you stole from?"

I let out a humorless laugh and say in a droll tone, "Yeah, the jewelry store that I stole from."

"So, why did you do it? You had everything to lose. Why risk it?"

I stare into his face, weighing my options. Tell the truth or the truth that everyone believes.

I know he won't believe me, but I decide to go with the truth.

"I didn't risk anything. I loved that job. I didn't steal from those people. What I did do was make a huge error by trusting someone."

His expression hasn't changed. It's blank and unreadable, like always.

I wait, expecting him to tell me that he doesn't believe me.

So, I'm surprised when he says, "Trusting whom?"

"A man." I let out a bitter laugh. "Well, I wouldn't call him a man because a man wouldn't do what he did to me." I wrap my hands around the cup again, needing its warmth. I stare down into the coffee as I continue to talk, "My boyfriend, Jason—well, now, ex-boyfriend. We'd been together for about four months. He seemed like a good guy. A decent guy. I wasn't so keen on his family...especially his brother. I'd heard things about them...not so great things...but Jason was good to me. I'd never had someone be good to me before. And he was good with Jesse. So, I trusted him. And he stabbed me in the back. I don't know for sure exactly how it happened…but I know I went to prison because of Jason and, if I'm guessing correctly, his brother, Damien."

I see Kas's body stiffen, and I feel a tension rise in the air, like static electricity covering my skin.

I lift my eyes to his, and I'm startled by the anger I see in them.

I've seen Kas angry, but this…this is a whole new level of anger that I've never seen before.

I flinch inside, unsure of whether that anger is directed at me or not.

I wonder if I should keep talking, but I figure I can't make this any worse. I need this job, so I take a deep breath and continue on, "The night of the robbery, Jason was staying at my place. Jesse was staying the night at his friend's house. I only ever let Jason stay over when Jesse was staying out." I don't know why I tell Kas that, but it feels important to me that he knows that I always put Jesse first.

"I think, while I was sleeping, that Jason gave my access key to Damien. You know, I said I'd heard things about him. Well, those things were that Damien was trouble, into bad shit—carjacking, robbery, and the like. I think he used my access key, let himself in, somehow disconnected the CCTV inside the shop, and robbed it.

"Then, he brought my key card back to Jason. He put it back in my bag. Damien also gave him a piece of the stolen jewelry, which Jason so conveniently planted in my apartment. And, when the police came searching my place, there it was.

"Jason also told the police that he wasn't with me at all that night. That he spent the night playing cards with his brother and friends and hadn't seen me. I couldn't prove otherwise. I had no witnesses to prove he'd been with me all night, so I was screwed. Basically, I was set up.

"The police charged me with theft. I was put in prison until my trial. I was given a court-appointed lawyer because I had no money to pay for my own, and I'm pretty sure my lawyer had only just gotten his law degree. I didn't stand a chance. I was found guilty and sent to prison for three years. I served eighteen months and was released on parole. And here I am.

"I lost everything…Jesse…my job, my home…my freedom…because of *him*."

I lift my eyes back to Kas, not really sure what to expect.

But there's nothing. His expression is blank, his eyes devoid of any emotion.

Disappointment slams into me.

That disappointment quickly turns to panic when he stands abruptly. My fearful eyes follow him up.

"Get your things," he tells me. "I'll take you home."

I rise slowly, my heart banging against my rib cage. "Mr. Matis…please…I—"

"You still have your job, Daisy." He walks past me, heading for the door. "And you can call me Kas from now on."

His words from the first day I met him come back to me. *"My friends call me Kas."*

I guess he believes me.

I'm surprised at how much that matters to me. How much his opinion actually counts. To know that me just saying the words once to him was enough when a jury full of people didn't believe me.

I blink back the tears threatening me and swallow back the Texas-sized lump in my throat. Then, I grab my shoes and bag and quickly follow after him.

SIXTEEN

KAS.

I step off the platform and onto the walkway, exiting the station, surprised to see his car sitting there.

Is he waiting on me?

Surely not.

Unsure as to why he's here, I make my way down the ramp.

Should I go over to his car or just pretend I haven't seen him?

I don't want to go over if he's waiting here for someone else, and then I'll have to walk away…looking like a loser.

And why is this such a big decision?

For God's sake, Daisy, just go over and say hello. Then, walk away if he doesn't offer you a ride—which, more than likely, he won't.

I step off the walkway and onto the street. His car is parked right in front of me.

Our eyes meet through the passenger window.

I ignore the way my heart rate spikes from having his eyes on mine.

He rolls down the passenger window. I walk toward his car.

"Daisy," he says my name low.

That's it. He says my name, and a shiver of delight runs through me—which is ridiculous.

Totally ridiculous.

Just because he was kind to me yesterday and believed me when I told him that I was innocent, not the thief he'd thought I was, doesn't mean anything's changed.

Does it?

He's still my boss. And he still doesn't like me very much.

And I don't like him.

Right?

"Hi, Kas." It feels weird, saying his name. I nervously tuck a stray strand of hair behind my ear. "What are you doing here? I mean…you're here…and you're not normally here, at the train station."

Jesus…Daisy.

Kas laughs at my rambling.

His third laugh.

I made him laugh.

Yes, I'm glowing. And, yes, I'm counting his laughs.

It's just so rare that I hear him laugh, and I like the way it makes me feel when he does, so I'm counting.

"I was nearby, running an errand," he tells me. "I saw your train pull in. Thought I'd give you a ride. Save you from walking."

Holy…wow.

The Kas of last week would never have thought to stop and give me a ride. Here is a guy who drove past me in the rain and splashed me with a puddle.

It's a dry, sunny day, and he's here, offering to drive me into work.

I might faint.

"Okay. Well, thank you. I appreciate it."

He gives a gentle nod of his head in response, causing his hair to fall in his eyes. He brushes it back with his fingers, tucking his hair behind his ear. The sun catches on the strands, making it appear lighter than it is.

I wonder if his hair is as soft as it looks.

UNSITABLE

He's sporting stubble today as well. It looks good on him. Makes him even more rugged and handsome.

God...he's good-looking...

"Daisy?"

"Mmhmm?"

"Are you gonna get in the car, or are you just going to stand there, staring at me all day?"

And...there he is.

My face flushes bright red. "Oh, um...yeah, of course." I fumble, reaching for the handle. I pull open the door and slide onto the leather seat.

I can't believe I was staring at him.

For God's sake, Daisy, stop mooning over him. Sure, he was nice yesterday and is being nice today, but it doesn't mean anything.

Honestly, I'm starting to think that I prefer Kas-hole better. At least I knew where I stood with him. Kas-nice...confuses the crap out of me.

I put my bag in the footwell and put my seat belt on.

Kas starts the engine. Radiohead's "Creep" comes on the stereo.

"How are you feeling?" he asks me, pulling away from the station.

He wants to know how I'm feeling?

"Much better. Thanks." I glance at him. "I know I've said it already, but I just wanted to say again how sorry I am for what happened this weekend."

"It's fine, Daisy."

I curl my fingers into my lap, listening to Thom Yorke's haunting voice.

"I love this song," I tell him.

He nods.

Okay...

"How was the rest of your weekend?" I ask, trying for something different.

"Okay."

"What did you do?"

He glances at me. The look in his eyes is almost searching, and for some reason, it has me holding my breath.

He slides his eyes away from me and back to the road, and I suck in a much-needed breath.

"I went out for a ride."

"On a horse?"

His lip twitches. "Yes, Daisy, on a horse."

"I didn't know you rode."

"I do run a stable."

"I know. I mean, I've not seen you ride. I just thought…I don't know. I don't ride. Cooper offered to teach me, but I don't think I'd be any good."

"Cooper offered to teach you?"

I feel Kas's eyes burn through me. I bring my gaze to his. There's something simmering in his eyes that I can't quite decipher.

He yanks his stare away before I get a chance to try.

"Yes, he, um…said if I wanted to learn, he'd take me out. On my lunch hour, of course."

"I'll teach you to ride."

What?

"What?"

"You want to learn to ride. I'll teach you."

Wow…um…

"What about Cooper?"

I see his hands tighten around the steering wheel.

His eyes slide to mine, and he pins me with a look that makes me want to turn invisible.

"What about Cooper?" His tone screams pissed off.

Welp…

"Just…" I clear my suddenly dry throat. "Cooper offered first, is all, and I, um…" I trail off, licking my dry lips.

Kas's eyes flash to my mouth and then off me completely, going back to the road.

UNSUITABLE

"Cooper can't ride for shit." His voice is low.

He seems angry. For the life of me, I don't know why.

But then when does Kas ever need a reason?

"Isn't he your stable manager?"

"My parents hired him, not me." He frowns.

Okay then...

"Be ready at one, and I'll take you for a good ride."

I laugh. I can't help it.

I'm sorry, but it sounded dirty.

Or maybe I just have a dirty mind.

Kas's confused gaze swings to mine, his brow lifting in question.

"Nothing," I mutter, fluttering my hands, as I feel heat rise in my cheeks.

Kas must replay his words in his mind because, a second later, I see a light go on in his eyes.

"*Horse* ride," he clarifies.

I can hear a touch of humor in his voice, and it lifts my lips.

"I know. Sorry, it just sounded—"

"Pervy," he finishes.

"I was gonna say *dirty*, but pervy works."

I grin. His eyes come to mine, and he smiles.

Warmth erupts in my belly.

I really like it when he smiles at me. Every time he does, I feel like I've won something really special.

Jesus Christ, Daisy. Remember the last time you got all gooey-eyed over a man? It landed you in prison.

"There's some spare riding gear in the utility room," he tells me, his eyes back on the road. "It should fit you."

"Okay, thanks. Should I come to your office, or—"

"Meet me at the stables. One p.m.," he says.

"One p.m. Got it."

Kas pulls up to the gates of the estate. He presses a button on the dash, and the gates start to open.

We ride the rest of the way to his house in silence.

My stupid stomach is doing cartwheels at the thought of going out riding with Kas. My head is suffering with severe confusion as to why my stomach is so happy about it. It must be the excitement about riding a horse for the first time. It can't be anything else.

Right?

Also, I'm trying to figure out why he offered to take me riding. Why not just let Cooper take me?

I know Kas and I hit some sort of truce yesterday, but he still dislikes me.

And I still dislike him.

Right?

SEVENTEEN

DRESSED IN JODHPURS, a white Matis Estate polo shirt, and riding boots, I walk toward the stables.

Outside the stables, I see Kas with Butterscotch. He's putting her saddle on.

He's wearing a white polo shirt, similar to mine but without the logo, and these dark brown fitted trousers, not quite jodhpurs. They're tucked into black riding boots.

The guy even looks hot in riding gear. It's seriously annoying.

"Hey," I say as I approach. "Where's everyone?"

I was worried about bumping into Cooper and him seeing me getting a lesson from Kas after he already offered.

"They're on lunch," he says as he fastens the straps on Butterscotch's saddle.

I'm a little relieved to hear that.

"Am I riding Butterscotch?" I ask him.

"Yeah. She's an easy ride. Good for a first-timer."

"Hey, girl." I stroke her face. "No apples today, I'm afraid. But I'll bring you some tomorrow. The good ones since you're letting me ride you."

Kas finishes up with the saddle and looks at me. "I need to fit you up with a riding helmet."

"Okay." I follow him into the empty stable at the end where they keep all of their tack.

Look at me, getting down with the horsey lingo.

Kas pulls a helmet down from the shelf. I expect him to pass it to me to put on, but instead, he steps directly in front of me and places the helmet on my head. He's so close that I can smell the mint on his breath and the aftershave on his skin. It's distinctly spicy with a hint of cedarwood in it.

Not gonna lie. His close proximity is making my heart beat a little faster and my insides tighten up.

"It's a little big," he murmurs. He lifts the helmet from my head and reaches forward to put it back on the shelf, putting him even closer to me.

I shut my eyes as I breathe in. All I manage to do is take in a lungful of his scent.

My heart starts to beat faster.

It's been so long since I've been this close to a man. Of course my body is going into overdrive. He's hot.

But it's nothing to do with *him*.

Right?

I open my eyes, and my breath catches.

He's still close, and he's staring down at me. His eyes are fixed on mine, and they're darker than normal. And there's a flicker of something.

Interest?

Yes, definitely interest.

I know he thinks I'm hot. I heard him tell Jude.

But he has no interest in doing anything about it.

And neither do I.

In an unconscious move, I lick my dry lips.

Yeah, right, Daisy. Sure, it was unconscious.

His eyes flare, going to my mouth.

I'm not sure what to do.

Do I want him to kiss me?

Well, my body sure does.

UNSUITABLE

My mind? Not so much.

I need this job too much.

Sense has me clearing my throat and taking a small step back.

Kas blinks, as if awakening.

He grabs a helmet off the shelf and thrusts it into my hands. "This one will fit you." He pivots on his heel and walks out of the stable.

Okay then...

I put the helmet on and fasten the strap under my chin.

When I make my way back outside, I see Kas bringing Danger out of another one of the stables. Danger's already tacked up.

"You ready?" he asks me, his tone even.

"As I'll ever be." I smile.

"Do you know how to get on a horse?"

I shake my head.

Leaving Danger, he comes over to Butterscotch and beckons me over. "Okay, so put your left foot in the stirrup."

I do that.

"Now, grab ahold of the saddle with both hands."

I do as told and grip ahold of either side of the saddle.

"Now, push yourself up, and swing your other leg over as you go. Try not to kick the horse."

Okay, sounds easy.

I try to push myself up, but I get nowhere.

I try again. I only make it halfway up.

Okay, so, clearly, it's not as easy as it sounds.

I consider myself to be a pretty fit person, but bloody hell, getting on a horse is hard.

I let out a sound of frustration. I hear a low chuckle from behind me.

I glance back over my shoulder at Kas and shoot him daggers.

The bastard just smiles at me.

I narrow my eyes.

He laughs again. "I'll help you up."

He comes up behind me, and the next thing I feel are Kas's hands on my arse.

What the hell?

My eyes whip back to his. "What are you doing?"

"I'm giving you a boost up," he says.

I can hear a change in his voice; it sounds thicker.

"And you need your hands on my bum to do that?"

I'm feigning mild anger because I don't like the fact that I like the feel of his hands on my arse.

His head tips slightly to the side. "And where would you prefer me to put my hands?"

Is that a trick question?

"Um...not on my arse."

"So, how would you propose I get you on the horse?"

All the time we're talking, I'm still very aware of the fact that his hands are still on my bum. And that I'm also getting decidedly hotter and hotter and very flustered.

"I don't know." I frown. "But did you really need to grab my arse to do it?"

His eyes darken to coal. "Trust me, Daisy, if I wanted to grab your arse, I wouldn't use this as an excuse to do so. I'd just fucking do it."

Everything inside me halts.

Then, suddenly, it sparks back to life, setting my nerve endings on fire.

There's something so darkly sexual about his words. And it thrills me.

Though I'm not willing to admit that to him.

Somehow, I find my voice. "Th-that'd be sexual harassment." I curse the stammer in my words.

His eyes stay fixed on mine, and if possible, they get darker. "You're right; it would be."

He leans in closer, so there's nothing left but air between us. My belly flutters and clenches in anticipation.

UNSUITABLE

"And I would never do something like that. Unless you asked me to, of course."

Holy...

What. The. Freaking. Hell?

I'm riveted. And a little wet.

Okay, a lot wet.

His eyes yank from mine. "Now, do you want me to help you get on this horse or not? Because, aside from me going to get you a stepladder, this is the only way to get you on." His voice is back to normal, like nothing just happened.

I'm still gasping for air.

Trying to find my balance, I look away from him. "It's fine. Just give me the boost up."

I feel him give a firm shove against my bum, so I push my foot off the floor. Then, I'm up and swinging my leg over, finally seated on Butterscotch.

Bloody hell, it's high up here.

I feel a little dizzy. Or maybe that's just from my little interaction with Kas—which I've decided to pretend never happened.

"You hold the reins like this." He hands them to me, showing me how to hold them. He doesn't look me in the face once.

And I'm trying to ignore that I can still feel the heat from his hands on my bum.

Leaving me, he goes over to Danger. He picks up a helmet from the floor and pulls it on. Then, gathering up the reins of his horse, he gets on Danger with ease.

"I'll go up front," he tells me. "She'll follow on. But, if she stops for any reason, squeeze your heels into her sides."

"Won't that hurt her?"

"No." He smiles, shaking his head. "And, if you want her to stop, just pull gently on the reins."

"Okay."

He gives me a nod. Then, he says to his horse, "Move on, Danger."

The horse obeys, and as Danger moves past us, Butterscotch starts to walk, following behind them.

It's a weird feeling at first, riding on a horse, but I get used to it soon enough.

We ride in silence. The only sounds are the occasional cars driving past and the birds chirping.

Kas leads us along a path around the side of the paddocks, heading in the direction of the forest.

"You doing okay back there?" Kas asks.

I nod my head and then realize he can't see me. "Yeah, I'm doing good. Thanks."

"We can try trotting in a bit if you want?"

"Maybe," I say, not feeling wholly sure about that.

He must hear the uncertainty in my voice because I hear him chuckle.

His laugh makes my insides light up. I equally love and hate how easily his laugh so quickly affects me.

"Is Danger your horse?" I ask him, trying to distract myself from my inner turmoil.

Kas slows Danger down until we're side by side.

"He is. I got him three years ago."

"He's beautiful."

Kas nods. "He was a rescue horse. He'd been badly treated by his previous owner. It took a long time for him to trust me."

"Understandably. God, people can be complete wankers. Honestly, I just don't get people like that. I mean, who the hell could hurt a beautiful creature like him?"

"There are people who get a kick from hurting others, Daisy."

"Yeah, well, they're sick bastards, and there's clearly something missing inside them—like emotions."

"Emotions can be what drives people to hurt and maim...even kill."

"Maybe...but I don't understand those kinds of people, and I'm glad I don't."

"Wouldn't you like to hurt your ex-boyfriend for what he did to you?"

"That's different. That'd be revenge. It wasn't revenge, what Danger's owner did to him."

"No, you're right; it wasn't. But wouldn't you like to get revenge on your ex-boyfriend?"

Exhaling, I shake my head. "No. Don't get me wrong; when it all first happened, I spent many hours thinking up all the different ways I would cause him pain. But I quickly got past that when I realized it wouldn't change anything. Hurting Jason wouldn't alter what happened. Yeah, I'd probably feel better for a minute or two. But then that minute would be over, and I'd still be here, in the same situation. Revenge isn't for me. All I care about is the future, getting back what I lost."

"Jesse."

"Yeah. He's all that matters now. And I won't do anything to jeopardize getting him back."

"You're a better person than most."

"I don't think I am. I'm just a person dealing with the hand that life dealt me. It's all any of us can do."

Kas is silent for a long time. Instead of heading into the forest, he veers us along the back of the paddocks and around, heading in the direction of the stables.

"Was Butterscotch a rescue horse?" I run my fingers through her mane.

"No. My mother got her as a foal when we first moved here. She trained her."

"So, she's your mother's horse?"

"Yes."

"And she wouldn't mind me riding her?"

"No. She'd be happy that Butterscotch was getting exercise."

"When do your parents get back from Greece?" I throw out there.

He gives me a surprised look, and I know it's because he knows he never told me where they were.

"Cooper mentioned they were in Greece," I tell him.

He looks away from me. "They'll be there for another couple of months."

"I bet you miss them when they're away."

He lifts a shoulder in answer. "I'm used to them being away."

"Whereabouts are your parents from in Greece?"

His eyes slice back to mine. For a moment, I think that he's going to turn into Kas-hole and tell me to stop asking questions, but he surprises me by answering, "My mother's English. She was born in London. It's my father who is from Greece—Thessaloníki," he says the name of the city with an accent to his voice.

The sound ripples down my spine in the most delicious way.

"I've never heard of Thessa—I'm sorry." I laugh. "I have no clue how to pronounce it."

Kas chuckles. "Thes-sa-lo-ní-ki," he elongates the word for me.

"Thess-a-loníki," I echo badly.

"Close." He smiles kindly.

"Well, I've never heard of it before. I'm afraid my geographic knowledge of Greece is limited to Athens and Rhodes."

He laughs softly. "Most people's is. Thessaloníki is actually the second largest city in Greece, believe it or not. It's a beautiful place."

"Then, it's a shame more people don't know about it."

He nods, agreeing.

"Have you spent much time there?"

"A lot when I was a kid. Not so much as I got older."

"Why not?"

UNSUITABLE

His response is a slight shrug.

"Well, if I were you, I'd be there all the time and away from rainy England."

"The weather's nice today," he comments.

I glance up at the cloud-free sky. "True. Are you fluent in Greek?" I ask, looking back to him.

His eyes meet mine. "Yes."

I'm tempted to ask him to say something in Greek to me. But I somehow think that Kas isn't really the type to perform, so I hold my tongue.

We've reached the other side of the paddock now, close to the stables.

Danger picks up pace, heading for the stables, with Butterscotch trailing behind.

I hide the disappointment I feel from our ride being over. I was enjoying it. And I was actually enjoying talking with Kas. More than I ever thought I would.

We didn't get around to trotting either, but I don't comment on it.

Kas brings Danger to a stop in front of the stables and hops down from him.

I sit on Butterscotch, unsure of how to get down.

I watch as Kas takes off Danger's saddle, opens the stable door, and then removes his bridle. Danger wanders into the stable. Kas shuts the lower door behind him and slides the bolt across.

He turns and looks up at me. "You staying up there all day?" There's a definite smile on his mouth.

I bite my lip. "I don't know how to get down."

Still smiling, he walks over to me. "Take your feet out of the stirrups."

My right foot slides out fine, but my left foot is a little stuck. I give it a wiggle, but it doesn't come free.

"Here." Kas takes ahold of my leg and pulls the stirrup from my foot.

There's a layer of rubber and cloth between his hand and my leg, but I still feel his touch, like it's on my bare skin.

I start to flush hot.

"Hold on to the saddle, and slide your right leg over."

His hand leaves my foot. I look at him, unsure.

"I'll catch you," he tells me softly.

Hands gripping the top of the saddle, I slightly lean forward and bring my right leg back over Butterscotch, taking care not to kick her in the rear.

I feel Kas's hands come around my waist, guiding my feet down to the ground.

"Thank you," I whisper. A whisper is all I can manage at the feel of his hands on me.

He doesn't say anything, and he doesn't move his hands away either.

I feel him move closer. His chest brushes my back.

My heart takes off in a race against my pulse.

I can feel his soft breath blowing on my neck.

Involuntarily, I lean back into his touch, pressing my back to his chest. His grip tightens on my waist. And I shiver.

I want to kiss him.

I might not like him so much, but God, my body does right now, and my body is seemingly in charge.

I know that, if I turn around right now, I will kiss him.

Or he'll kiss me.

I won't be able to take back what happens.

But I'm not sure that I really care at this moment in time.

His hands on me, the feel of him against my back, just feels too good.

He feels like nothing I've ever had before and everything I didn't even know I wanted.

"Daisy," he softly says my name, sounding like a plea on his lips.

UNSUITABLE

It's a plea I can't ignore.

I turn slowly. His hands stay on me—one moving over my back, the other grazing over my stomach, both coming to rest on my waist.

My whole body is awake.

Like I've been in a deep sleep, and he's just touched me to life.

My eyes are on his chest. I'm afraid to lift my eyes to his. I know that, if I do, then this will all be over.

I can feel the heat of his stare on me.

He says my name again.

Inwardly, I'm panting and needy.

Outside, I'm…panting and needy.

Could I be more obvious?

His hand moves from my waist, leaving me cold. Then, his fingers slide under my chin. He unclips the helmet, removing it, and drops it to the floor beside us. Not once do his eyes leave mine.

His fingers brush back the loose strands of my hair. Finally, I lift my eyes to his.

And his are blazing. On fire. For me.

My whole body trembles from the inside out.

He infinitesimally moves in.

He's going to kiss me. Holy shit, he's going to kiss me.
And I'm going to let him.

I close my eyes in anticipation.

Then…

Ariana Grande's "Into You" blares loudly from my phone. It's set as my ringtone.

My phone is ringing.

My eyes snap open to meet Kas's, which are wide with surprise. I watch in those brief seconds as a multitude of emotions flash through his eyes. Shock, horror, regret…but the one that hits me the hardest is disgust. And the way his hands drop from me, like I just infected him with a deadly disease…it makes me feel sick.

Why is he so repulsed by the thought of touching me? Kissing me?

Because I'm the staff? Or is it because I'm just a maid? Because I'm poor? Because I've been in prison?

He thinks I'm not good enough for him…

Pain lances across my chest, and in this moment, I've never felt more worthless.

He steps back from me. One step. Two.

His hands go to his head, dragging through his hair. "Fuck," he growls. Then, his eyes are back on me. Cold and hard. "For fuck's sake, Daisy!" he snaps. "Answer your goddamn phone!"

I jump at the harshness in his voice, and I'm surprised that I actually forgot my phone was still even ringing.

I grapple to unzip the pocket on the back of the jodhpurs where I stashed my phone. As I pull it out, it stops ringing. I stare down at the screen, seeing the missed call. I don't recognize the number, but I do know it's a London area code.

I keep my eyes glued to my phone. I daren't look up at Kas.

I'm afraid of what I'll see if I do.

More disgust. Maybe some repulsion.

The memory makes my eyes sting.

My phone rings again in my hand, startling me. It's the same number.

I hesitate and then answer it. "Hello?"

"Daisy?"

"*Jesse?*" His name rushes out of me on a breath.

"Yeah, it's me."

"Is everything…are you okay?" My heart is hammering in my chest.

"I'm…" He hesitates. There's something in his voice. He sounds worried. "I'm in a bit of trouble."

And my heart drops to the floor. All thoughts and hurt over Kas are erased.

"I need your help, Mayday. Can you come get me?"

UNSUITABLE

He needs me. He called me Mayday.
"Tell me where you are. I'm coming now."

EIGHTEEN

"I HAVE TO GO," I tell Kas as I walk past him without looking at him.

He says my name. I ignore him and keep walking.

"Daisy." His voice is as firm as the hand that curls around my upper arm, pulling me to a stop.

"What?" I snap, spinning back to face him.

"What the hell is going on?" His brows are drawn together. He looks angry.

That makes two of us.

"I could ask you the same thing," I bite. Then, I immediately regret it. "Look...whatever. I have to go. Fire me if you need to."

Something flashes in his eyes, but I don't care enough in this moment to try to figure out what it was.

I yank my arm free from his hand, and then I'm on the move again.

I hear a growl from behind me.

"For fuck's sake, just hold up!" he yells right before he grabs my arm again, pulling me around to face him.

"I don't have time for this!" I yell back.

I see the surprise in his eyes, and it gives me sweet satisfaction.

Yeah, dickhead, I can shout, too.

"I have to go." I lower my voice. "My brother needs me, and I have to go."

"Jesse? Is he okay?"

"I don't know! That's why I need to get to him. So, let me go!"

I pull at my arm, and he lets go.

But his next words stop me.

"I'll take you to him."

He'll drive me to Jesse, but I'm not good enough to kiss? Whatever.

I need to get to Jesse, and accepting a lift from Kas will get me there quicker than me calling a cab, which I wouldn't be able to afford.

"That would be a big help. Thank you," I say the words without meeting his eyes.

He nods. "Let me just grab my car keys."

I follow Kas through the house, getting my bag from the coat closet while he gets his car keys from his office.

"Ready?" he asks, stepping back into the hall.

I nod and then follow him out to his car.

We're seated inside when he asks me where we're going.

Sighing quietly, I rest my elbow on the door and put my head in my hand. I stare out the window as Jesse's words echo in my mind after I asked him the same question.

"I'm at the mini-mart on The Broadway."

I didn't even question why he was at a supermarket and in need of my help.

I have a pretty good idea why he is there and needs my help, but I really, really don't want it to be true.

But, either way, it doesn't matter. If Jesse needs me, I'm there.

"There's a mini-mart on The Broadway in Sutton. That's where Jesse is."

I watch as Kas inputs the address into his GPS. When it's set, he puts the car in drive.

UNSUITABLE

The silence is deafening, and my mind is working overtime.

"I know what you're thinking," I say quietly.

"Do you?" He doesn't look at me.

"You think that I'm more trouble than I'm worth."

"That wasn't what I was thinking."

But he doesn't disagree that I am trouble.

He's right. I might try to keep my life clean and problem-free, but no matter how hard I try, problems always find me.

A part of me wants to ask what exactly he was thinking, but I'm too chickenshit to do so. Instead, I sit quietly and just stare out the window.

Kas pulls up outside the mini-mart twenty minutes later. It feels like it was the longest twenty minutes of my life. We didn't speak the whole way here. And I've been worrying about Jesse and what to expect when I get inside that supermarket.

"Thanks for the lift." I unclip my seat belt. "I really appreciate it."

"You seem to be saying that a lot lately."

I slide a glance at him. His expression is tight, but his lips have a soft curl to them.

"You're right. I have been. I'm sorry," I say.

"You say that a lot, too."

"You mean, sorry?"

"Yeah."

"Maybe it's because I am sorry. I don't mean to be a bother to you."

He exhales a tired sound. "You're not a bother." He turns his face to me, his eyes fixing on mine. When he speaks again, it sounds like his voice is lined with gravel, "Honestly, it's surprising to me, just what I am willing to do for you."

That takes me aback. *What does he mean by that?*

Unsure and nervous, I swallow roughly. "Well, I appreciate everything you've done for me." I tear my eyes from his and reach down to retrieve my bag from the footwell. My heart is hammering in my chest. "Once I'm done here and I've gotten Jesse back home, I'll come straight back to work, and I'll stay late to make up the time."

"You don't need to."

I don't?

That brings my eyes back to his. "I don't? But that's a whole afternoon's work." *And I need the money.* I don't say that, of course.

Kas must read the concern in my eyes because his own soften. "I'll still pay you for the full day. Just go see to your brother, Daisy."

With warmth in my heart, I curl my fingers around the door handle and open it. "Thank you so much." I blush, realizing that I'm thanking him again. "I guess I'll see you tomorrow."

"Tomorrow," he says.

I get out of the car and shut the door.

I watch as Kas drives away.

His words echo through my mind. *"Honestly, it's surprising to me, just what I am willing to do for you."*

My stomach flips and tightens. *What on earth did he mean by that?*

But, right now, I don't have the time to think about what he meant. I need to get to Jesse.

Taking a deep breath, I ready myself, and then I walk into the mini-mart.

I glance around, expecting to see Jesse. Of course, I don't.

If he did what I think he did, then he'll be in the back with the store manager.

Please don't have shoplifted, Jesse.

UNSUITABLE

I've been in here to buy groceries a few times. The tills are over to my left. There are people being served. I really don't want to go over there and ask for Jesse. I look for a security guard, but there's no one.

Then, I see a young guy filling up the shelves down the biscuit aisle. I walk over to him.

"Excuse me. I got a call from my brother, Jesse. He said he was here…" I let my words trail off, not really sure what else to say.

Something unpleasant flickers in his gaze, and then he says, "Come with me."

He puts the pack of biscuits that was in his hand back in the box and starts to walk away toward the back of the store. I follow him.

He stops by a door, swipes it with a fob, and opens it. He holds it open for me to pass through first.

"They're just in the manager's office," he says, letting the door shut behind us.

Manager's office? My stomach turns.

I follow him down the short corridor. He stops outside a door and knocks before opening it.

"The sister's here," he says to whomever's in the room. Then, he stands aside, letting me through the door.

A guy—I'd say in his late thirties—is sitting behind a desk. I'm guessing he's the store manager. A bigger guy in a security uniform is standing by the wall, and near him, Jesse is sitting in a chair.

His eyes meet mine. I see a glimmer of relief mixed with fear in them.

"Miss Smith?" the manager says, rising to his feet.

I step further into the room, closing the door behind me. "Daisy," I tell him.

"I'm Jeff, the store manager. Please take a seat." He gestures at the chair in front of his desk.

"Can you tell me what's going on here, Jeff?" I try to keep my tone even. I sit and hold my bag in my lap.

"You're Jesse's guardian?" Jeff asks me.

I glance at Jesse. His eyes are pleading.

"That's correct." I swallow back my lie, looking back to Jeff.

"Okay, well, I'm sorry to tell you, but your brother was caught shoplifting by Brett." He tips his head in the direction of the security guard who is standing by Jesse.

But I can't look at Brett, the security guard. All I can do is stare at Jesse, who's looking at everything but me. With a lump in my throat and a sick feeling in my stomach, I know this is my fault.

"I didn't call the police because I thought we could deal with this in-house."

The relief I feel at that is immense.

I pull my eyes from Jesse and look back to Jeff. "Thank you so much," I say in earnest.

"Well, after Jesse said his parents had passed away in such tragic circumstances and that he was under your guardianship…I didn't want to give the lad, or you, more grief to deal with. And I think he gets that he made a stupid mistake."

"His parents had passed away in such tragic circumstances."

One parent, and it wasn't exactly a tragic circumstance. *When did he get so good at lying?*

My eyes slide to Jesse. It surprises me that he's actually looking at me. But worry tightens my gut when I see the hint of defiance in his eyes. Almost like he's daring me to call him out for lying.

Swallowing, I look back to Jeff. "What did he steal?"

"A six-pack of Kestrel Beer."

Alcohol.

He's stealing and drinking.

Jesus Christ.

"I am so sorry." I lay my hands out in a pleading manner. "He's never done anything like this before. He's just…had a rough time of it as of late. Not that I'm making

UNSUITABLE

excuses for him because I'm not." I glance at Jesse again. Keeping my eyes on Jesse, I speak to Jeff, "You said you wanted to deal with this in-house." I look at Jeff. "What are you proposing?"

In my peripheral, I see Jesse sit up a little straighter.

"Well, the outside of the shop could do with a good clean. We lost our window cleaner a while back, and I haven't gotten around to getting a new one. So, maybe Jesse could come tomorrow after school and clean the windows, and we'll call it quits. How does that sound?"

"Perfect," I say before Jesse can say anything. Standing, I hang my bag on my shoulder. "I won't be able to accompany him, as I'm at work until six. But I'll give you my number in case you need it. If Jesse doesn't turn up, then you have my permission to call the police and report the attempted theft."

Jeff smiles at me and hands me a pad and pen. I scribble my number down and hand it back to him.

Then, I turn to Jesse. "Let's go." I give a jerk of my head, and then I turn for the door.

I hear him following behind me.

I don't speak until we're outside.

I stop abruptly and turn to him. "What the hell were you thinking?" I throw my hands up in the air.

That defiance, mixed with good old anger and resentment, flashes through his eyes. "Thought I'd join the family business."

"This isn't a joke, Jesse! You were lucky that he didn't call the cops!"

He folds his arms and frowns down at me. "Maybe I wanted him to. I've heard that prison is cushy. Might be better than where I am now."

My eyes widen, and fear bangs my heart against my chest. "You have no idea what you're talking about," I bite.

"No? Then, why don't you tell me?" he challenges.

"Because you don't need to know." I lift my eyes to his, trying to convey my feelings. "No kid needs to know what the inside of a prison is like."

His brows draw together in anger. "I'm not a kid," he grinds out.

"Yes, you are!" I snap. "You're my kid!" The words are out before I can stop them.

His eyes ignite with something that makes my stomach twist. "I'm not *your* kid!" he yells. "I don't have parents!"

Something snaps inside me, and I don't care that there are people around, listening. "Yes, you do! You have me!" I slam a hand to my chest. "On paper, I might be your sister, but I raised you, Jesse! Changed your nappies! Fed you! Clothed! Nursed you when you were sick! Read you bedtime stories! Went to all of your school plays! *I* raised you!"

"And then you fucking left me!" he roars.

The pain in his words is so apparent, and it takes me back a step, like a blade going through my chest. I can't even pull him up for swearing. In the grand scheme of things, Jesse saying a curse word is nothing.

He's hurting. Because of me.

"You...left," he whispers.

And the ache of his words only intensifies, like the blade in my chest is being twisted.

"Jesse"—I step closer to him—"you have to know that I didn't want to leave. I would have done *anything* to stay with you. *Anything.*"

His eyes flash to mine. "But you didn't though, did you, Daisy? You stole from that place, knowing what the consequences would be. Or did you just not care? Or were you that arrogant that you thought you wouldn't get caught?"

He still thinks I'm guilty. Even now. Even though I told him in person that I was innocent, he still doesn't believe me.

UNSUITABLE

I can't express the torment I feel at that.

I wrap my arms over my chest. My words come quietly. "You know me, Jesse. I'm not a thief. Deep down inside of you, you know I didn't steal that jewelry. You know I would never have done something like that."

Not meeting my eyes, he lets out a scoffing sound. It reignites something inside me.

"You can fool yourself into believing it's the truth—that I'm this thief who never cared about you—because you think it justifies your anger and your current behavior. But you know it's not the truth. You know that I would never have done *anything* to risk losing you."

His eyes come to mine. I can't get a read on them.

"Why should I believe you?" His voice is still toneless.

"Because I've never given you a reason *not* to believe me. I was there, Jesse…through everything. I never walked away. The only reason I left was because I was taken away without a choice. But I'm back now. I'm here, and I'm not going anywhere. I'll never leave. I'll never let anyone take me away again. But you have to let me in. *Please.*"

Sighing, he looks away and runs a hand through his hair. When he brings his eyes back to me, I see the hardness in them has softened.

"Why didn't you let me come see you in prison?" he asks in a low voice.

I'm transported back years. He sounds just like the boy I remember.

My heart breaks in this moment. I can't stop the tears that fill my eyes.

Biting my lip, I brush the tears away with my fingers. "Because I didn't want you coming to that place…seeing me like that. But that doesn't mean that I didn't think about you every day. The thought of you was the *only* thing that got me through those eighteen months."

I reach out a hand to touch him but pull it back, unsure of if he wants me to touch him.

His eyes are on the ground. He exhales a tired-sounding breath. "I have to go," he says softly, toeing the concrete with his shoe.

"Can I walk you home?"

He shakes his head, eyes still on the ground. "But…you can call me later, if you want?"

My heart soars, and I can't help the smile that spreads on my face. "I'd love that."

Jesse lifts his eyes to mine. He brushes his overgrown hair out of them. "Cool. Well, I guess we'll talk later then."

"Definitely."

I watch Jesse walk away with a hope in my heart that I haven't dared allow myself to feel in a very long time.

NINETEEN

FEELING HAPPIER THAN I have in forever, I hum along to the song that's been stuck in my head all morning—Gnash's "I Hate You, I Love You."

I'm happy because I called Jesse last night, and we talked for ages.

We're not fixed, not by a long shot, but we're talking, and that's more than I had this time yesterday.

Jesse said he'd call me tonight after he got done cleaning the windows at the mini-mart. I'm hoping he'll let me see him this weekend, but I'm not getting my hopes up too much. I'm just happy that I have this contact with him.

I'm currently on my way to Kas's office. I have a coffee in one hand and a bag of muffins in the other, which I got from the bakery just by the station. I don't actually know if Kas likes muffins, but I just want to thank him for yesterday. What says thank-you better than spongy goodness?

I'm choosing to forget about the fact that we almost kissed after our horse ride, and I'm also choosing to forget his reaction...the disgust.

I feel a sting of hurt in my chest.

Okay, so, clearly, I haven't forgotten entirely. But he helped me so much yesterday. Dropped everything to take me to Jesse. Let me have the afternoon off work.

So what if he thinks I'm not good enough to kiss, that I'm beneath him or whatever?

It doesn't matter. He helped me get to Jesse, and that's all I care about.

And it's a good thing that we didn't kiss. A kiss would have made things messy and possibly put my job at risk.

I need this job. Now more than ever.

Reaching Kas's office, I knock on the door.

No answer.

I wonder where he is. He's nowhere else in the house that I know of. Maybe he's out running.

Should I go look for him, so I can give them to him? Or I could just put them in his office.

Yeah, I'll put them in his office. That'll be a nice surprise for him.

Decision made, I push down on the handle of the door and let myself inside.

His office is pristine, as always. I hardly ever get to clean in here because he doesn't let me, so I can't take credit for the cleanliness.

I walk over to his desk and put the bag of muffins and coffee down on it.

I grab his Post-it notes and pen.

Kas,

Thank you for yesterday.

Daisy

Should I put a kiss?
No, that'd be too weird. Especially after yesterday.

Leaving it as it is, I pull the Post-it from the pad and stick it to the front of the muffin bag.

I've just put the pen down when a door to my left opens, and in walks Kas.

UNSUITABLE

His eyes go wide on me. He quickly slams the door shut behind him. "What are you doing in here?" His words are quick and biting.

"I was just leaving a thank-you coffee and muffins. I knocked, but there was no answer." My eyes go to the door that Kas is standing in front of, like a guard.

Has that door always been there? I don't remember seeing it before.

"Well, if there's no answer when you knock at a door, it generally means no one's there, and you come back later. It's not a fucking invitation to come on in." His tone is crass.

It pisses me off.

And I really hate it when he swears at me.

"Seriously?" My eyes drag back to him. "I have to come in rooms in this house to clean them, and they have to be empty for that to happen."

"Were you coming in here to clean?"

"No, but—"

"But what?" he snaps.

"I just wanted to say thank you." My voice rises an octave.

His eyes widen and then flash to the coffee and bag on his desk. He stares at them for a long moment.

My pulse is thrumming in my neck, and I feel hot.

Very slowly, he brings his eyes back to mine. "Well, you've said thank you, and now, you can go."

I feel stupid.

I don't know what I expected from bringing him a little thank-you gift. Maybe a smile. A, *You didn't have to.* I didn't expect him to be a wanker.

Why am I surprised?

This is who he is—Kas-hole.

Honestly, I don't know why I bothered.

Screw him.

I'm about to turn and leave, but my eyes snag on that door he's still guarding like a sentry.

Why don't I remember that door? I've been in here a handful of times before, and I don't remember it being there. And doors don't just magically appear.

I nod my head at the door. "You didn't show me that room on my tour of this place. Is it a room I need to clean?"

"No," he snaps, his tone low and dark.

Something has shifted in his expression. He still looks angry, but he also looks...uncomfortable. It's there in his eyes.

His discomfort pricks my attention because one thing Kas never is, is uncomfortable.

Arrogant? Mean? Angry? A prick? Yes, to all of those things.

But never uncomfortable.

"Okay." I take a step back. Turning, I pivot on my heel to leave.

His voice hits my back when I reach the door. "My office is off-limits to you now. I don't want you coming in here. Ever."

I stop in the open doorway and turn back to him. "Yes, Mr. Matis." I even curtsy, just to be a bitch.

He frowns. And, with darkness on his face and in his eyes, he turns away from me.

I grab the door handle and start to pull the door closed. But not before I see Kas pull a key from his pocket and put that key in the mystery door to lock it.

An hour later, I'm head in the oven, cleaning it, when I hear footsteps come in the kitchen.

UNSUITABLE

I know it's Kas by his footfalls.

How sad is that? That I know him by the sound of his steps.

Well, whatever.

I'm still pissed at him. He's a dick, and I'm ignoring him. I'm not in the mood to be yelled at again.

His presence has reignited my flame of anger, and it's turned into a raging inferno.

I continue scrubbing the oven clean, probably harder than necessary.

"Daisy," he says my name softly.

His voice is like a gentle brush of fingers over my skin, which breaks out in goose bumps.

Why does he so easily affect me?

It's annoying. He's a knobhead. A big knobhead who yells at me all the time.

Fixing steel into my spine, I ignore my traitorous skin, and I ignore him.

I hear him sigh loudly behind me.

"Daisy...earlier...I acted like a total dick. I'm...sorry."

What?

My head jerks up with my shock at his apology, and I smack it on the roof of the oven.

"Shit!" I wince. Dropping the cleaning sponge, my rubber glove–covered hand goes immediately to my head.

I pull back out of the oven, rubbing at the sore spot.

"Are you okay?" Kas's voice comes from close behind me.

"I'm fine," I huff.

"You sure?"

"I'm sure." Without looking at him, I walk over to the sink.

I yank the rubber gloves off with more force than necessary. I toss them on the side of the sink and start washing my hands.

He might have said sorry, but I'm still mad, and I think I have a right to be.

Sure, he pays my wages, but that doesn't give him the right to be an almighty tosser to me ninety percent of the time. It negates all the times he has been nice to me. And his lame-arse sorry resulted in me smacking my head. So, yeah, there's that as well.

I hear him move, and then he's standing beside me, his back leaning against the kitchen counter. He curls his hands around the edge.

I don't look at him. I stay focused on washing my hands, which are already clean. I just need something to do with my hands, or I might do something crazy, like strangle him.

"Daisy…"

I shut off the tap and grab the hand towel from the counter. Walking away, I dry my hands.

I need the distance.

I'm sick of him running hot and cold. I'm tired of being yelled at. And of him treating me with kindness one minute and then treating me like I have the plague the next.

Sure, he has come in here and apologized for, yet again, being a dickhead. Don't get me wrong; the apology is a first and a shock. But I've had enough of his dickish ways.

The silence between us stretches and drags. I've overdried my hands. Now, I'm counting the tiles on the wall.

Finally, I can't take it anymore. I toss the towel on the counter and turn around to face him. "Is there something you need me to do?"

That's it, Daisy. Keep it work-related. Don't make it personal.
Is it personal?

Kas warily eyes me. Then, he tips his head in the direction of the bag of muffins I brought him, which is now sitting on the center island.

UNSUITABLE

"You can help me eat those." His words are soft but ineffective.

"No, I'm good. Anything else?"

He stares at me, surprised and also like he's not sure what to do now.

What did he think was going to happen? That I'd fall at his feet and say, Yes, Kas! Of course I want to help you eat those muffins that I brought you and put in your office before you yelled at me.

Not likely, arsehole.

"Is there something else you need?" I push.

I'm pushing because I want to get out of here and away from him.

His brows draw together in consternation. "No."

"Okay. Well, I've got work to do, so…" I pivot on my heel and make for the door.

"Actually…"

His low tone stops me in my tracks, and I slowly turn to face him.

He pushes off the counter and walks forward, stopping by the island. The look in his eyes makes my heart bang against my rib cage. He leans his hip against the island and folds his arms over his chest. I ignore how good his arms look while stretched over that magnificent chest of his.

Magnificent chest. Have you heard me?

You dislike him, remember, Daisy?

"I changed my mind," he says. "There is something you can do for me."

I frown. "What is it?"

"You can accept my fucking apology."

I laugh.

I actually laugh.

His brows angrily crash together.

Still laughing, I say, "You really need to work on your apologies, Mr. Matis."

That makes his frown deeper.

Tired of this conversation and him, I turn and start to leave, but he stops me—this time, with a hand on my wrist.

Surprised that he got across the kitchen that quickly, I spin back and find myself staring up into his livid black eyes.

"What are you doing?" I fire at him.

But it's like he didn't hear me. "What the fuck do you want from me?" he says low and seething.

Taken aback by his words, I say, "Nothing. I don't want anything from you." Then, just like the snap of fingers, I change my mind. "Actually, I do want something from you. I want you to stop yelling at me!" It's funny I say that because I'm yelling at him right now. "I want you to stop being a wanker to me! I want you to stop running hot and cold with your moods! I want you to treat me like a human being—all the time and not just some of the time! I want—"

I don't get to finish that sentence. My words are cut off by his mouth.

Because the bastard kisses me.

He actually plants his lips on mine and kisses me.

TWENTY

HE'S KISSING ME.
Holy shit. Kas is kissing me.
He's kissing me!

It takes a fifth of a second for that shock to wear off. Then, the feel of his lips against mine registers, and all bets are off.

My free hand finds its way to his chest, fingers curling into his shirt. I part my lips on a soft moan. He takes advantage of that and slips his tongue into my mouth, kissing me deeper. And I give back as good as I get.

Kas backs me up to the wall, his mouth still firmly on mine.

His hand is gripping my wrist. He pins my arm to the wall and then pins the lower half of his body with mine, trapping me. Not that I'm looking to get away anytime soon. Or ever.

And, holy hell…he's hard. I can feel his erection digging into my stomach.

I made him hard from just a kiss.

Go, me!

The feel of him hard and pressed up against me with his tongue sweeping delicious strokes over mine has me squirming. I'm pretty sure my knickers are damp as well.

God, the man can kiss.

I could write songs about how well he can kiss.

But then that would be weird. And, also, I can't write for shit.

Kas drops my wrist and takes ahold of my face with both hands, and then he angles my head so that he can kiss me exactly how he wants to. And I have absolutely no problem with that.

I slide my hands around his back, wanting to feel him, solid and strong beneath my fingers.

His tongue sweeps over my bottom lip, making me moan and move against him.

I feel a shudder run through him, and he presses even harder against me.

"Fuck, baby," he groans before taking my mouth again.

He kisses me with more intensity, bordering on crazy.

And I match him stroke for stroke.

We're pulling on each other, both taking what we need. Basically fucking the hell out of each other's mouths.

All of him is against me, and even still, I don't feel close enough.

I want more of him. I want *all* of him.

I hook my leg around his. His hand leaves my face and slides down to my thigh. He lifts my leg higher, hooking it around his hip.

He shifts his lower body, grinding himself against me.

Right on the very spot where I need him. The spot that's begging for his touch.

His teeth graze over my bottom lip as he thrusts up against me.

"Yes, Kas," I moan.

And that's when everything changes.

Or stops. Or goes wrong.

I'm not really sure what happens. All I do know is that he's no longer moving, no longer kissing me.

He pulls back, staring at me like he doesn't even know me. Doesn't know why he's here.

UNSUITABLE

His brows draw together, and he squeezes his eyes shut. He looks like he's in pain.

A cold, sick feeling trickles into my stomach.

My hands drop from him.

His eyes flash open. The look I see in them…regret.

Fucking regret.

I feel like ice has just been poured all over me, the shards sharp and stinging against my skin.

His hand slips from my thigh, letting my leg drop to the floor. The sound of my shoe hitting the tiled floor is loud in this painful silence.

He steps back from me.

My chest hollows out.

"Kas…"

He turns on his heel and strides away, leaving me here.

What?

I sink back against the unforgiving wall.

What…just happened?

We were here and kissing, and it was amazing. I mean, he seemed to be enjoying himself. And then he…looked like he didn't even know why he was kissing me, and he walked away without a word.

I don't get it.

Or…

Maybe he just remembered exactly whom he was kissing.

Oh God.

I feel sick.

He really does think I'm beneath him.

Maybe I am.

I'm dirt-poor. Fresh out of prison. I carry more baggage than Heathrow Airport.

I'm trash.

I'm his cleaner, for God's sake!

My eyes start to sting with tears. I press the heels of my hands to them.

Kas is good-looking and rich. Yeah, he's an arsehole ninety percent of the time, but rich people get to be arseholes.

So, why in the world would a guy like him want a girl like me?

He wouldn't—clearly.

He obviously got lost in the moment. I was an easy way to spend a few minutes.

And didn't I just give it up? I would have had sex with him if he'd asked.

Jesus. I'm such a fool.

My face starts to burn with shame and embarrassment.

Don't I ever learn? Didn't I get burned enough by the last man I let close?

And to kiss him, of all people…my boss.

But then it was him that kissed me. It wasn't like I threw myself at him. He instigated it. And then he acted like a head case right after.

Total dick move.

I mean, who does that? Who kisses someone and then just walks away?

An arsehole—that's who.

Kas-hole.

Well, screw him.

I don't need his shit.

I just need this job.

I take a few gulps of air, but the air in here just feels cloggy, and all I can smell on my skin is Kas. The scent of his bloody aftershave.

Straightening my spine, I push off the wall and head toward the back door—in the exact opposite direction where Kas went.

I just need to go outside, get some fresh air. Clear my head. Figure out how to handle this monumental fuckup.

I head out back and around the side of the house, needing some quiet.

I lean against the house and rest my head back.

UNSUITABLE

Sighing, I shut my eyes. But, when I do, all that happens is that I see Kas kissing me. I remember the feel of his lips on mine, like it's happening again right now.

I want him. I hate to admit it, but it's true.

I might not like Kas, and I might want to punch him in the nutsack. But I do want him.

How screwed up is that?

But I can't have him because it would be the worst idea in the world, and he doesn't want me.

He made that fact perfectly clear when he pushed away from me, looked at me with regret, and then stalked away without a word.

I breathe through the ache of his rejection.

How am I supposed to forget the way he tastes, the way he kisses, the way he feels under my hands?

How am I supposed to see him every day after this?

I'll do it because I have no choice. He doesn't want me, but there are more important things at stake than my lusty feelings for Kastor Matis.

And it was just a kiss. One measly kiss.

Only...it didn't feel like just a kiss.

"Hey, whatcha doing out here? You avoiding work? Or just hiding out from Kas?" The sound of Cooper's chuckling voice jolts me out of my thoughts.

My eyes flash open. For a second, I panic and think he knows about what just happened in the kitchen with Kas and me, but he couldn't.

Shaking off the feeling, I push off the wall and force a smile. "Hey, Cooper. Neither. Just having a minute."

He gives me a knowing look. "Kas giving you a hard time again?"

Is Kas giving me a hard time? Well, he was definitely hard a few minutes ago.

Before he realized whom he was getting hard for.

That douses cold water on the memory.

"No more than usual." I wrap my arms around my chest. "What are you doing up here?" I ask him.

"Ran out of milk." He grins.

"You're always running out of milk. Do you guys just live on cups of tea?"

"And biscuits."

"Can't forget the biscuits. You ran out of them as well?"

His grin deepens.

"Lucky for you, there's milk in the fridge and plenty of biscuits in the larder. I'll grab them for you."

"Before you do"—he stops me with a hand on my arm, which he quickly removes—"I, um…I wanted to ask you…" He shifts on his feet, running a hand through his hair, avoiding my eyes. "Well, I wondered if you'd want to have a drink on Thursday night?"

"With all the guys? Sure." I smile at the thought of being invited to one of their outings.

"Actually…" He lifts his eyes to mine. "I meant, just you and me."

"Oh." *Oh.*

"I mean, it's cool if you don't want to—"

"No, it's fine." *It is?* "I mean, sure. Yes." *Daisy…what are you doing?*

"Yes?" His eyes light up, his lips lifting into a big smile.

Shit, what am I doing? I like Cooper…but Kas…and I've already said yes.

"Yes," I repeat with a smile.

His grin deepens. "Cool. Well, how about you give me your number, and I can text you to arrange it?"

"Sure. But, first, let me get you the milk and biscuits." *And bang my head against the wall while I'm at it.*

I usher him to go inside first. Watching him round the corner, I let out a low groan.

Jesus Christ, Daisy, what the hell are you playing at?

UNSUITABLE

Get kissed by Kas, and then get asked out on a date by Cooper—all in the space of twenty minutes.

Great going, Daisy. Really, well done.

I think I hear movement on Kas's balcony. My head snaps up. I move back to get a clear view, but no one is there, and the sliding door to his bedroom is shut.

Must have been a bird or the breeze or something.

"Daisy? You coming or what?" Cooper's high voice comes from the back of the house, snapping me back to the now.

On a sigh, I say, "Yeah, I'm coming."

TWENTY-ONE

"SIT STILL, WILL YOU? Honestly, Daisy, you're worse than some of the kids whose hair I have to cut."

"I'm sorry. I just don't know if it's a good idea to make such an effort with my hair when I'm not really sure that I should be going out with Cooper. I don't want to get all dressed up and give him the wrong idea."

Cece lowers the curling iron from my hair, and she pins me with a stare in the mirror. "One, it's your first date since getting out of"—she hesitates—"that place."

Cece doesn't refer to it as prison. I think she thinks that it will upset me if she brings prison up, but it doesn't. Honestly, I think it upsets her more—the fact that I was in there and she couldn't do anything to help me.

"It's not a date, Ce. We're just two friends and work colleagues who are going out for a drink."

She gives me a look. "He asked you out. It's a date. And why do you think you shouldn't be going out with him?"

I blow out a breath. "Because he asked me literally minutes after I had my tongue down my boss's throat, and I wasn't exactly thinking straight."

My stomach twists in pleasure and pain at the memory.

I haven't seen Kas since he walked away from me yesterday.

After I came in the house with Cooper, after disastrously accepting his offer to go for a drink, we were in the kitchen, and I heard the front door slam loudly. Then, Kas's car revved loudly before pulling away.

He didn't come home for the rest of the day. And he wasn't at the house at all yesterday or today.

I don't know where he's been. But I do know for sure that he's avoiding me.

I know this because his bed was clearly slept in for both nights. I had the pleasure of making them both mornings.

Obviously, he got up early and left before I arrived for work, and he stayed out until I was gone.

At first, I was relieved because it saved me from an awkward conversation. But, once the relief was gone, absence started to hurt. And all it served to do was remind me of why he'd stopped kissing me in the first place.

And this going out for drinks with Cooper is stupid. I've got enough problems with one guy at work without mixing myself up with another.

"I'm going to cancel on Cooper," I say decisively, making a grab for my phone, which is sitting on the dressing table where I'm seated.

"Don't you bloody dare, Daisy May Smith."

My hand stops over the phone, my fingers curled around it.

"Hand off the phone, Mayday." There's a no-brokering tone to her voice.

Giving her the stink eye, I slowly lift my hand off the phone.

"No, you listen to me. Above anyone, you deserve a night out. After everything you've been through, you're owed a night out with a good guy who's also hot. And Australian. So, you know, accent." She grins.

"Granted, I'll give you the accent. But I said good-looking. Not hot."

"Same thing."

UNSUITABLE

"Jason was hot."

She frowns at me.

"And I thought he was a good guy," I continue. "Look where that got me."

Her scowl quickly softens. "Jason is a plague on society. A waste of perfectly good air. I hate that scum and will wish him well in hell when I send him there. But he's not all men, babe. I don't want what happened with that wankstain to sour you on all men. And I'm not suggesting that you have to have a relationship with Cooper or even trust him right away. But I just want you to go out and have some fun. Let someone wine and dine you—or, in this case, just wine you. You deserve it, Dais."

"I know." I sigh. "But it just feels wrong."

"Because of Kas?"

Cece knows everything that has happened between Kas and me. I've kept her up to speed on all current events in my life. I mean, she's my best friend. I tell her everything.

Funny thing is, when I told her that Kas and I kissed, she didn't seem at all surprised.

When I asked her why, she said—and I quote—"I'm not surprised because I've never seen you so riled up over a guy before, so it was obvious that you fancied him. And, well, you're *you*. So, of course, he was gonna want to bone you."

So, apparently, I'm obvious and boneable.

Just not boneable to Kas.

I'm beneath him. And not in a good way.

Sigh.

"Yeah. I mean, we kissed, and then I immediately said yes to going out with Cooper. It just feels wrong."

"Kas blew you off. Sorry," she adds at my wince. "But he acted like an arsehole. You don't owe him a thing. And you definitely don't have anything to feel weird about."

"I know you're right, but I still feel weird. And I know he's avoiding me." My shoulders slump.

She puts the curling iron down on the dressing table and rests her hands on my shoulders, giving them a gentle squeeze. "Babe, if Kas can't see what he'd be getting in you, then he's a dick. A massive dick." She sizes her hands out before landing them back on my shoulders. "You're awesome, Mayday. Funny and smart and beautiful."

"And an ex-con."

"Hush." She frowns at me. "You're gorgeous, and obviously, Cooper thinks so because he asked you out. And tonight is just drinks with a good-looking, nice guy. It doesn't have to be anything more. But you will go tonight, looking your absolute best because I'm awesome at hair, and I'm an awesome friend." She gives me a grin and fluffs my hair with her hand.

Staring gratefully at her in the mirror, I reach back and take ahold of her hand, giving it a squeeze. "You are awesome, Ce. You're the best."

"I know." She grins again. Then, she picks up the curling iron and wraps another section of my hair around it.

My phone starts to ring on my dressing table. I glance at the display and see that it's Cooper.

My stomach tightens with nerves.

"Hey," I answer. "I'm just getting ready. I shouldn't be much longer."

"Daisy"—he sounds flustered and a little out of breath—"I am so sorry to do this to you at the last minute, but I'm going to have to cancel our night out."

A huge amount of relief and also a little disappointment run through me at the same time. "It's okay. Don't worry."

"No, it's not okay." His tone is frustrated. "I was really looking forward to tonight with you, but now, I'm in my car, on my way back to work. Somehow, all the horses got out and are running amok around the estate." He sighs loudly. "I'm gonna have to round them up and then fix wherever they got through in the fence. It's gonna take all bloody night."

"Do you want me to come help?"

"Don't worry." His tone softens. "But thank you for offering." There's a brief pause before he says, "Rain check for tomorrow night? Same time?"

This is my out. I can say no...but I feel bad because the guy seems to really want to go out for a drink with me. So, I hear myself saying, "Sure."

"Great." I can practically hear his smile down the phone. "So, I guess I'll see you tomorrow."

"See you then."

I hang the phone up with Cooper and put it back down on the dressing table.

"That was Cooper. He had to cancel, so I'm not going out tonight after all."

"Bastard," she says in a mock-angry voice.

"You heard the whole conversation?"

"Yeah, sorry. I didn't mean to listen in, but it was kinda hard not to hear. But he asked you out again for tomorrow night, right?"

I give her a sly smile. "You know he did. And you also know that I said yes."

Grinning, she says, "Attagirl." Then, she winds another section of my hair around the curling iron. "And screw not going out tonight. We're having a girls' night out. It's been way too long since you and I hit up the town. So, I'll finish up doing your hair, then give me half an hour to put my face on, and we'll go out. We can go to this new club in town. What do you say?"

A night out on the town with my girl...sounds perfect.

I smile at her in the mirror. "I say...hell yeah."

TWENTY-TWO

ZAYN'S "LIKE I WOULD" is pumping through the club. I have a drink in my hand. And I'm totally feeling out of my element.

I've never really been a party girl. Having a younger brother to care for meant nights out were a rarity for me.

Honestly, I'm kind of ready to go home. My feet ache, and I'm tired. Plus, I've got work in the morning. But Cece's enjoying herself, and I don't want to be a party pooper.

We went to a few bars before coming to this club, which I've totally forgotten the name of.

Cece's just at the bar, getting more drinks. I tip my head back, checking on her, and see she's chatting with some guy who's in line next to her.

He looks cute.

I finish the last of my drink and put the glass down on a nearby table.

Then, I get this weird prickly feeling on the back of my neck, like someone's watching me. It's been happening to me all night.

I spin my head around, looking, but I can't spot anything—or should I say, *anyone* watching me. Not that I could tell in this place anyway. It's packed. I rub a hand over the back of my neck, easing the sensation away.

Honestly, I'm starting to think I'm going mad.

I glance back at Cece. She looks to be in deep conversation with the cute guy.

Deciding I need the toilet, I catch her eye and mouth, *Restroom break*, to her.

She points to the floor, telling me she'll be there when I get back.

I give her a thumbs-up and then head in the direction of the ladies' toilets.

I make my way through the throng of people and head down the corridor to the restroom. The sign at the end of the hallway points an arrow to the left for men and right for women and disabled.

It's kind of eerie here. The lighting is shitty, and the bass is thumping off the walls, making it feel like a scene out of a Z-list horror movie.

Reaching the end of the hall, I turn right, and my steps falter as my heart picks up pace.

Kas.

He's standing near the disabled restroom, his shoulder leaning up against the wall.

He's wearing blue jeans and a white shirt. His shirtsleeves are rolled up, showing his gorgeous forearms—I might have a thing with his arms—and his hair is loose and tucked behind his ears.

He looks amazing.

But, whatever, I don't care.

What I do care about is what he's doing here.

"What are you doing here?" I echo my thoughts.

He pushes off the wall, so he's standing upright. "Hello to you, too."

I give him a look. "Hello. Now, what are you doing here?"

He tilts his head to the side. "I needed to use the restroom."

UNSUITABLE

"I meant, the club. But, whatever, the men's room is back that way." I thumb in the direction of it.

A smile tips the corners of his lips up. He folds his arms around his chest. The fabric of his shirt tightens around his biceps, and the veins in his forearms are visible...and looking very lickable.

But I don't care.

Yeah, sure, you don't, Daisy.

"Where's your date?" he asks.

I have a sudden flash of guilt, my heart jumping, but suspicion quickly takes over.

I narrow my gaze on him. "How did you know I had a date tonight?"

He shrugs those amazing shoulders of his. "I'm the boss. I hear things."

"Well then, you should know that my date was canceled because *your* horses got loose, and my date had to go round them all up."

"Yeah. Shame that."

Mother...effer.

"You sound real cut up about it."

The corners of his lips lift, as does his shoulder.

My eyes narrow further. "It was you, wasn't it? You let the horses out." It's not a question. I know he did. I can see it in his eyes.

Bastard.

He gives me an affronted look, but that bastard smile is still on his lips. "And why in the world would I have done that?"

"Who knows?" I throw my hands up. "To ruin my night? To piss me off? Who knows why you do the stuff you do? Probably because you get off on making my life miserable."

Or he was jealous.
Over me?
Not likely.

I let that thought flitter away into the darkness.

He stares at me for a long moment before saying in a low, throaty voice, "Trust me, Daisy, when I say that what gets me off definitely isn't making you miserable."

Oh…wow.

But I don't let his words affect me. I keep my expression fixed and my anger flowing. "No? So, you just like to make me miserable for fun then."

Something changes in his expression, and his eyes drift away from me. "Do I really make you miserable?" His voice is uncharacteristically quiet.

I tighten my arms around myself. "Maybe not miserable…but I wouldn't exactly say that you brighten my day either."

Well, apart from when you were kissing me. But then you went and ruined that.

He shifts on his feet. "I don't mean to be an arsehole to you." His eyes come back to mine, and there's something earnest about his expression.

"So then, don't be," I say softly.

He sighs, his eyes lifting to the ceiling. "It's not that easy."

"It's as easy or as hard as you make it."

His eyes flash back down to mine. "You make it hard."

Fire ignites in my belly. "You know what? Fuck you, Kastor Matis!" The words are out before I can stop them.

"Did you just say that you wanted to fuck me?"

My eyes slice to his. His face is serious, but there's a twinkle in his eyes.

The bastard is making fun of me.

"No." I grit my teeth. "You know exactly what I meant." I drop my arms, putting my hands on my hips. I let out a sound of exasperation. "God, can you just stop being such a twat?"

There's a moment of silence.

UNSUITABLE

Then, in a deadly serious voice, he asks, "Did you just call me a…twat?"

My heart bangs hard against my rib cage. Then, I steel my spine. Defiantly tipping my chin up, I say, "Yes, I did. Because you are acting like a twat."

He stares at me for the longest time. His face is perfectly blank.

Then, I see his lips twitch, and he bursts into laughter.

Full-on belly laughter.

I've heard Kas laugh before but nothing like this. It's a beautiful, infectious sound. Before I know it, I'm laughing, too, and it feels good.

"I can't believe you called me a twat," he says between laughs.

"Well, you deserved it." I chuckle.

He wipes his eyes. "Yeah, you're right; I did."

Our laughter has ceased, and now, we're just staring at each other. Eyes caught on eyes.

Something changes in the air between us. It's like the laughter cleared the anger away, and all that's left behind is pure chemistry and heat. And it seems to be strengthening in its intensity with each passing second, drawing me to him.

My pulse starts to beat in my ears. My skin is tingling. My stomach is coiling and tightening.

Kas's gaze slides down from my eyes to my mouth.

I lick my lips, like an automatic response.

I watch as his eyes heat and flare.

My whole body sets ablaze under his hot stare. If I were ice cream, I'd be melting right now.

Jesus Christ, stop being such a girl, Daisy.

I wrap my arms around my chest. The movement seems to bring him back to the now.

He drops his arms and slides his hands into his front jeans pockets.

"Who are you here with?" I say for want of something to say.

"Friends."

"I didn't realize you had any—aside from Jude, that is." I give a saccharin smile.

"Funny." But he's not smiling. Instead, his eyes are making their way down my body, and he's looking at me like he wants to devour me whole.

I have to suppress the urge to press my thighs together.

His eyes lift back to mine. "You look incredibly beautiful tonight."

His words take me aback. And I resent how happy they make me feel.

I hate how he can lift me up and cut me down so easily.

"Yeah, but just not good enough for you." I immediately want to smack myself in the face. I hate that I said those words and how pathetic and weak they make me sound.

"What?" He rears back, like I hit him.

"Nothing. Forget I said anything. I'm going now. Have a good night, Kas."

I move past him, and he catches my arm, holding me at his side.

"You want me to forget the fact that you think you're not good enough for me?"

"I never said *I* thought I wasn't good enough for you."

His brows crash together so hard that I'm surprised it doesn't give him a headache. "You think *I* think that? That you're not good enough for me?"

Looking away from him, I give a slight lift of my shoulder.

"That's fucking bullshit." His words are so vehement that my gaze swings back to his. "I'm not good enough for you, Daisy. You deserve a good man, a better man…and that's not me."

His words shock me to my core.

UNSUITABLE

I stare into his black eyes—searching for what, I'm not sure—but I must find it because something breaks inside me.

I press my palm to his face. His eyes close against my touch.

"I don't care," I whisper. "I want you."

A shudder runs through him. He tugs me into his side, sliding his arm around my back, holding me close to him. He presses his forehead to mine and exhales a shaky breath. "Fuck, baby." His breath tickles and teases my lips.

I want to kiss him, but I also know what happened last time we did kiss.

His chin dips, bringing his mouth closer to mine.

Our mouths are millimeters apart. All I'd have to do is lean in, and our lips would be touching.

Is that what I want?

Sense tells me, *No.* But my body screams, *Yes!*

"I have to kiss you," he breathes over my lips.

His other hand moves to my head, cradling it, as his body turns into mine.

And then he kisses me.

Soft and gentle at first. Featherlight kisses.

But then his tongue sweeps over my lower lip, and the spark between us ignites like a lit match on gasoline.

His fingers tangle into my hair while he continues to fuck my mouth with his tongue.

He tastes like beer and mints and something so uniquely him, and it turns me on like nothing before.

Breaking from my mouth, he drags his thumb down my lower lip, his eyes fixed on it. "All I've been able to think about for days is this gorgeous mouth."

I shiver with need.

But then that small voice in the back of my head asks, *So, why did you leave the other day? And why have you stayed away since?*

But I don't say the words because I don't want to lose this moment. I want him to keep kissing me. I want him to keep making me feel the way he is. Like no one has ever made me feel before. Like he needs to kiss me more than he needs air.

He captures my lips with his again and sucks on my tongue. A bolt of lust shoots between my legs, making me pant and squirm.

In this moment, I want him like I've never wanted anyone before.

A scream of laughter breaks us apart. My head jerks to the side, and I see a group of giggling girls falling out of the ladies' restroom.

My eyes come back to Kas. His eyes are glazed with lust, his lips swollen from my kiss.

Seeing him like this gives me a sense of satisfaction.

His lip lifts at the corner into the sexiest smile I've ever seen, and then he grabs my hand and yanks me into the disabled restroom. He pushes the door shut and locks it.

I hear the giggling girls pass by, and then it's quiet. Only the thumping sound of the music from the club and our shallow breaths are heard.

Kas is staring at me. The look in his eyes almost undoes me.

No one has ever looked at me like he is right now.

Like I'm all he can see.

I lift a hand to his face, touching my thumb over the corner of his mouth.

His eyes close at my touch.

Then, his eyes flash open. He grabs my wrist, pulling my hand from his face, and pushes me back up against the door. His mouth comes down hard on mine, and he starts to kiss me with even more need and ferocity than before.

There's nothing finesse about this kiss. We're basically fighting each other for space.

UNSUITABLE

His hand cups my shoulder, moving down my side. His fingers lightly graze the curve of my breast, making my nipples harden. Finally, his hand reaches my hip, and he grips ahold of it. His fingers bite into my skin through the thin fabric of my dress.

I snake my arm around his neck, tangling my fingers into the hair at the nape. It's the first time I've touched his hair, and it's as soft as I thought it would be.

Kas jams his other hand into my hair. Pulling back slightly, he stares down at me. His eyes are black and shining with desire. He's never looked more beautiful than he does in this moment.

His teeth drag over his lower lip. It's such a slow and deliberate move that everything inside me clenches. I shiver.

He grins, like he knows exactly the effect he has on me.

Then, he tips my head to the side and covers my mouth with his.

He presses his lower body into mine, and I feel the length and hardness of him against my belly.

I love that I can make him hard from just a kiss.

My other hand moves around his back. I slide my hand lower and slip it into his back pocket. I grip his arse, bringing him in even closer.

He groans into my mouth. The sound is so sexy that I feel like I could come from just hearing it.

He bites on my lower lip, and then his tongue comes out to lick away the sting. It's incredibly hot.

Then, his mouth moves across my jaw to my ear. "I want you so fucking badly, it hurts." His voice is hoarse with excitement, and I feel the sound deep inside.

His lips move down my neck, kissing a sweet path back to my mouth. He stops, his lips hovering over mine.

"So, have me," I whisper.

A flash of something moves through his eyes. If I didn't know better, I'd think it was fear.

He shuts his eyes on a shallow breath, and then his mouth is back on mine.

I feel feverish. Needy and wanting.

It's been a long time since I last had sex. Close to two years. And that was with Jason, the fuckwit, back when I didn't know what a lying, deceitful bastard he was.

But, even then, I never felt this good with him.

It's like Kas is in every part of me, touching all of me, and I still want more.

I suck on his tongue, and he shudders.

Feeling decidedly brave and wanting him like I've never wanted anyone before in my life, I slip my hand from his back pocket and slide it around to his front. I take a deep breath and then move my hand lower, palming the hard length of him through his jeans.

I feel his whole body lock up tight.

His eyes close, and his hands leave me, pressing up against the door above my head, caging me in.

He isn't moving or saying anything. But he isn't moving away either, so I take it that what I'm doing is okay.

Curling my fingers around the length of him, I start to move my hand up and down.

"Fuck…" he groans, sounding almost agonized.

I stare up into his face. His lips are pinched, his brows drawn together.

I stop moving my hand, unsure if he wants this.

His eyes flash open. The heat in them is unmistakable.

He wants this.

I reach up on my tiptoes and press a soft kiss to his lips. His hand drops from the wall and cups my face as his tongue runs along the seam of my lips, asking for entrance. I part them, and he moans low as he slips his tongue into my mouth.

I start moving my hand again, and he deepens the kiss.

His other hand comes down from the wall and cups my shoulder. Fingers moving downward, he brushes the strap of my dress off my shoulder, letting it fall. Then, he tugs the front of my dress down at one side, exposing my bra.

His thumb brushes over my hard nipple, making me shiver.

Needing to feel more of him, I reach for the hem of his shirt. Lifting it, I start to slide my hand underneath.

The next thing I know, the hand that was on my breast is now gripping my wrist, stopping its ascent.

I blink my hazy eyes, confused.

When they lock onto his, I see the same look in them that I saw the last time we kissed, and my body goes cold.

Pushing back from me, Kas drops my arm, like I just burned him.

His hands drive into his hair. His eyes catch mine. There's regret and a whole lot of other emotions in them. None of them are good, and I instantly feel sick.

"I…I…" He's struggling for words, and I'm dying inside. Then, he delivers his final blow. "I can't do this with…*you*."

Before I can get out a word, he's moving me aside, unlocking the door, and striding through it.

Gone in seconds.

Again.

I don't believe this.

"I can't do this with…you."

Tears spring to my eyes.

I pinch the bridge of my nose with my thumb and forefinger.

Don't you dare cry over a man, Daisy. Don't you fucking dare.

I blow out a breath and exhale another, fighting back the tears.

God…I can't even…
How could he do this to me again?
How could I have let him?
What the hell is wrong with him?
Never mind him. What the hell is wrong with me?

I need to have more dignity than this.

I *do* have more dignity than this.

Shame on me for falling for his shit again.

I have no one else to blame but myself.

Kiss me once, shame on you.

Kiss me twice, shame on me.

Dropping my hand from my face, I move over to the mirror.

My bra is showing, my lips are kiss-swollen, my face is flushed, and my hair is messed up from where Kas's hands were in it.

The sight makes me want to cry again.

Biting my lip, I tug my strap up, covering myself.

I can't believe I let him do this to me again.

Jesus. How stupid am I?

I must have *dumb bitch* written all over my face. I mean, Jason saw it written there.

I thought I'd cleaned it off.

But, apparently not, because Kas thinks he can screw with me, too.

I just don't get it.

What does he get from this?

It's not like we've had sex.

Or am I just a game to him?

Is this how he gets his rocks off—messing with the pretty, poor little girl who's so desperate for attention that she'll let her boss feel her up in a public restroom?

Pain lances across my chest. I press my hand to it.

I'm so weak and stupid.

I hate that he can hurt me in this way.

And I hate even more that I let him.

I might be angry with Kas. But I'm angrier with myself for being so stupid.

I was stupid over a man before, and that cost me everything.

I won't be stupid again.

UNSUITABLE

I'm not some toy to be played with.

Screw Kastor Matis and his mind games.

I'm done.

If he ever tries to kiss me again, I'm going to knee him in the balls.

Well, maybe not actually knee him in the balls because that's assault and a surefire way to end up back in prison. But I'll imagine kneeing him in the balls while I give him the middle finger.

Screw Kastor Matis and his screwed up self.

I don't need his crap. I already have problems of my own without him bringing more to the party.

As far as I'm concerned, Kas no longer exists. He's invisible to me.

And Mr. Matis only exists inside my place of work.

He's playing games with me, playing me for a fool. He thinks I'm naive and needy.

Maybe I was. But no more.

I won't let him get away with treating me like an idiot anymore.

He tries to come near me again, and he'll find out just exactly what Daisy Smith is really made of.

And, with my renewed sense of purpose and the realization that I've been gone quite a while and that Cece is probably getting worried, I walk out of the restroom and back into the noise of the club.

TWENTY-THREE

I'M TIRED, and my feet are aching. And, to round it all off, it's raining.

But I came dressed for the weather, so if anyone feels like puddle-splashing me, they can because I have my raincoat on, Cece's wellies on my feet, and an umbrella in my hand.

No way am I getting soaked.

I'm on the train, heading into work. My stomach is churning at the thought of seeing Kas.

I'm praying that he won't be there, like he hasn't been for these past few days.

I'm also not looking forward to telling Cooper that I can't go out with him tonight.

I might be done with Kas-hole, but I'm still hurt over his behavior. I would only be going out with Cooper to get back at him, and that's not fair to Cooper.

And I've decided that men just aren't for me.

From now on, I'm Celibate Daisy.

Men are trouble, pure and simple. One man in particular, who goes by the name of Kas-hole.

But he's no longer my problem.

I see my stop approaching. I get up from my seat, hooking my bag on my shoulder and grabbing my umbrella. I walk to the door.

I wait, watching as the station pulls into view, and I let out a yawn.

Cece and I weren't out too late last night. We left soon after my little incident with Kas.

When I got back from the restroom, Cece was alone with our drinks, but she had gotten the number of the cute guy she was talking to.

But she took one look at my face and knew immediately that something was wrong.

All I had to say was one word—*Kas*. And then we were downing our drinks, heading out of there, and getting a taxi home.

I told her everything in the taxi ride home. The driver must have gotten a good story out of it.

By the time we got home, I was exhausted and emotionally drained, and I just wanted to go to bed.

My alarm went off far too soon for my liking, and I had to haul myself out of bed to get ready for work.

I made coffee, poured it into my to-go cup, and left the apartment to catch my train, cursing Cece and the fact that she's off work today.

The train pulls to a stop. I pull my hood up and press the button, waiting for the doors to open.

People on the other side are waiting for me to get off before they can get on.

Raindrops hit my face as soon as my feet hit the asphalt. The rain is heavier here. I put my umbrella up and start walking out of the station.

I've just exited when my feet skid to a stop.

Kas.

His car is parked here, outside the station, like last time.

God, can't this guy just leave me alone?

I focus on my anger and ignore the little spark I feel at him actually being here.

The passenger window opens, and I see him lean over as he calls my name.

UNSUITABLE

He looks good. And warm and dry inside his car.

Bastard.

I scowl at him. Then, I swivel on my heel and start walking in the direction of the estate.

I'm practically marching, my boots splashing through puddles as I go.

I hear his car pull up alongside me. But I don't look at it. I refuse to.

Kas does not exist to me.

"Daisy."

Nope, not talking to him. I don't care if it is childish.

He's a Kas-hole, and I have every right to be pissed.

He left me in that restroom last night with my bra hanging out of my dress after, yet again, kissing me, and then he disappeared without a word.

"Daisy, get in the car."

Did you hear something?

Nope, me neither.

I start humming Pharrell Williams's "Happy" and pick up my pace.

"Jesus, just get in the car, will you? It's pissing down, and you're getting soaked."

Ignore. Ignore. Ignore.

I hear a huff of frustration and then, "For fuck's sake, Daisy, stop being childish, and just get in the fucking car."

Um...

What. The. Hell?

Anger brings my feet to a stop.

I see in my peripheral that his car has also stopped.

Don't look. Don't do it. Don't give him what he wants. He's just trying to get a rise out of you.

Taking a deep breath in, I blow it out through my nose.

Then, because I can't help myself, I give him the middle finger and then start walking again.

I hear him chuckle, which just pisses me off even more.

Then, his car is back, slowly driving beside me.

I hear a horn blare, and I swivel my head to see a car overtaking Kas and giving him rude hand gestures.

I can't help but smile.

As I move my eyes back around, I catch his stare.

He almost has a smile on his face. "You're going to get me into a fight at this rate."

"Good."

"And she speaks."

I scowl at him before facing forward and getting my march back on.

"Come on, babe, please get in the car."

Babe? Since when am I his babe?

Swiveling my angry eyes back to his, I say, "Don't call me babe."

A look of surprise flickers across his face. "Okay." He lifts a hand in surrender. "I won't call you it ever again, if you'll just please get in the car. You don't even have to talk to me."

Ugh. I can't even ignore him in peace. The bastard.
At this rate, he'll follow me all the way to the estate.
Or I could just get in his car and get this over with quicker.

Decision made, I come to a sudden halt. "Fine," I huff. "But no talking."

Then, I stomp over to his waiting car. I yank the door open, get inside, and slam the door shut. Grabbing the seat belt, I put it on. I'm dripping all over his nice leather seat.

Good.

I lift my eyes, and he's staring at me.

At least he has the decency not to smile, or I might just punch him in his pretty face. I'm that mad.

I turn my face to the passenger window, and a second later, he puts the car into drive.

Limp Bizkit's "Behind Blue Eyes" is playing in the background.

"I'm...sorry." His soft words assault me.

UNSUITABLE

I cut my eyes to him. "You said, if I got in your car, we wouldn't have to talk."

He quickly glances at me. "I said, *you* didn't have to talk. But I didn't say anything about me not talking."

Bastard.

"Let me out of the car." I keep my tone even. But it's really, really hard because all I want to do right now is yell at him.

He sighs. "Daisy—"

"No. I'm not playing games here, Kas."

"Neither am I."

"You're the master of mind games."

There's a brief pause. I'd almost call it regret if I didn't know him better.

"I'm not trying to hurt you," he says quietly.

I scoff and turn my face back to the window.

Silence hits.

He blows out a breath. "Does this reign of silence have an end date?"

"No."

"And what about at work? Are you going to freeze me out there, too?"

I tip my chin in his direction and stare at his hands on the steering wheel. "I can be professional, if you can. We can talk to each other at work, about work. But, outside of that, you and I don't exist to each other."

I dip my chin into my chest. I hear him sigh again. But he doesn't say anything more.

He pulls up to the front of his house, and the second he presses the brake, I'm out of the car.

Fast-walking through the bouncing rain, I shove my hood back once I'm under the safety of the porch. I unzip my raincoat and pull it off, and then I take my wellies off.

Leaving my wellies on the porch, I take my raincoat with me and let myself in the house. Crossing the big hallway, I open the door to the coat closet and hang up my coat along with my bag but not before getting out my phone, which I slip into the pocket of my dress.

Shutting the door, I turn around, and Kas is standing there.

"Jesus!" I jump. I press a hand to my chest to calm the heart he just nearly killed.

But he doesn't say anything. He doesn't smile or say a word. He just stands, staring at me.

I shift uneasily, moving my stare from his, unable to take the intensity in his eyes.

My eyes wash over him. His hair is damp from the rain, and there's a light sheen on his skin. And, for the first time since seeing him, I notice how tired he looks. There are dark circles under his eyes, and his eyes themselves look tired and listless.

Even still, he looks beautiful.

I hate that.

Glancing past him, I spy the trail of water he let in. The water I'll have to clean up.

"You're dripping everywhere," I tell him in a pissed off tone.

He doesn't even give the mess a glance. "Talk to me." There's a pleading edge to his voice, which I ignore.

"About the mess you've made?" I gesture a hand to the water he walked in.

He makes an exasperated sound. "For fuck's sake."

"Don't curse at me." I frown.

He laughs a humorless sound, which raises my hackles. "I want to talk about last night."

"I don't."

"Daisy," he growls my name.

"Mr. Matis," I say in a patronizing tone.

"Talk. To. Me." His words are gritted, like his jaw.

"Is it work-related?"

"No."

"Then, no." I push past him, heading for the kitchen.

I'm being childish, I know, but I don't care because I'm mad as hell.

I hear him growl again, and then heavy footsteps follow me into the kitchen.

"For fuck's sake, Daisy! I said I was sorry!"

I spin on the spot. "Oh, well, that's okay then! Kas says he's sorry, and everything is right in the world again." Letting out a hollow laugh, I throw my hands up in the air.

His brows crash together. "Jesus," he barks. "Just what is it that you want from me?"

"Nothing!" I yell. "I didn't ask for any of this! You were the one who kissed me—both times! Then, you acted like a total head case afterward! And I told you that I wouldn't talk about this with you! So, stop following me!"

I stamp my heel, and then I turn and start to walk away. I make it to the utility doorway when his voice stops me.

"I don't know how to do this."

It's not just the words. It's the way his voice sounded when saying the words—helpless.

It surprises me because *helpless* is never a word I would have thought in relation to Kas. Arrogant, overly confident, and a giant pain in my arse. But never helpless.

I slowly turn back to him. He looks defenseless and lost. It's in the pull of his dark brows. In the tightening around his eyes. The downturn of his lips.

It tugs on something inside my chest, curling around my heart.

"You don't know how to do what?" I ask in a quiet voice.

"This." He gestures at the space between us.

"I don't understand." I gently shake my head.

"Relationships," he says, frustrated, instantly getting my back up. "I don't fucking know how to do relationships."

I let out a disbelieving laugh. "I'm not asking you for a relationship. Jesus Christ! We kissed—*twice*. You went cold and walked out on me—*twice*. End of story."

"I don't want it to be the end." His words are soft with meaning, but I can't feel it right now. I'm too raw.

"I don't care what you want. Just like you didn't care what I wanted both times you walked out on me. There's only so much rejection and humiliation that one person can take, and I've reached my fill. At work, we'll talk when necessary and be cordial. But, aside from that, I'm done, Kas."

Something that looks a lot like unrest and frustration and hurt enters his gaze.

I ignore his pain and focus on my own.

He wraps his arms around his chest, moving his stance. "If that's what you want," he says quietly.

I laugh, and it sounds as empty as I feel.

Yeah, this is what I want. Because I was the one who caused all this—not.

Sighing, I shake my head and pass him to leave the kitchen.

When I reach the door, I stop.

He's facing away from me.

"Oh, and just so you know, I'm going out with Cooper tonight, just in case you wanted to let the horses out again."

I see his shoulders tense before I turn and walk out of there.

My feet hit the stairs, and I'm already regretting my parting shot. It was petty and hurtful, and I shouldn't have said it. But he just gets under my skin like no other. And it's too late now. It's not like I'm going to go downstairs and tell him that I am actually canceling my date with Cooper.

But then I'm sure he'll hear that on the grapevine soon enough.

When I reach the second floor, I realize that all of my cleaning products are downstairs in the utility room that I never made it to.

Bugger.

UNSUITABLE

Well, I'm not going back down there now in case he's still in the kitchen.

I'll strip the beds first, and by the time I'm done and ready to wash the bedding, he should be in his office, and I'll be safe to go downstairs.

I walk into his bedroom and see that his bed is made.

Knowing that Kas never makes his bed, I know that he hasn't slept in it. That leaves an uneasy feeling in my gut.

Maybe he hooked up with someone else at the club after he walked out on me...

Nope. Not even going to go there.

I throw the duvet cover back and pick up a pillow with a little more force than necessary.

Kas's scent is all over it.

Ugh.

I tug off the pillowcase and angrily toss the pillow behind me.

I hear a thud.

Crap.

Turning, I see that I knocked over a glass of water that was on his nightstand.

"Perfect," I mutter angrily to myself.

Water spilling everywhere, I dash into Kas's bathroom and grab a towel before jogging back into his room.

Fortunately, the only other thing on the nightstand is the lamp, so cleaning up the spillage isn't too difficult. I lift the lamp, drying off the base. Then, I wipe down the sides of the nightstand and dry off the water that hit the carpet.

I notice the top drawer is slightly ajar.

Worried water might have gotten inside, I pull it open and dry off the lip of the drawer, eyes checking the contents.

All looks good.

Then, my eyes snag on a photograph that's tucked down the side.

I pick it up. I notice that something is written in cursive on the back.

HALEY HALLIWELL. PROM. 2009.

I turn the photo over in my hands. Staring back at me is a pretty girl.

Really pretty.

She looks young. Maybe eighteen. Long blonde hair that's curled around her shoulders. She's wearing a stunning pink dress that goes to her ankles, and she has silver heels on her feet.

And she's wearing a huge, bright beaming smile on her face, her eyes shining with happiness.

It's a smile of adoration…of love. And it was clearly meant for whomever was standing behind the camera.

Kas.

I know because I recognize the garden she's standing in.

She was smiling for Kas.

I feel a pang in my chest. A pang called jealousy. I press my hand against it, trying to rub it away.

It's ridiculous to feel jealous over a photograph, I know. It just bothers me that Kas cared enough about this Haley girl to make her smile…to make her happy.

Whereas with me, he just seems to want to hurt me—over and over again.

Sighing, I go to put the photo back, but then something stops me. And then—I'm not sure exactly why—I find myself pulling my phone from my pocket and snapping a picture of the photo before putting it back where I found it.

Then, I shut the drawer, tuck my phone into my pocket, and continue on with my task of stripping the bed.

TWENTY-FOUR

I'M HOME ALONE, curled up on the sofa with a glass of wine. The TV's on, but I'm not really watching it.

Cece's working late at the salon; she won't be home until nine p.m.

Seriously, who gets their hair done that late?

Cece said she has lots of women who come in to get their hair done for a night out. I don't know if I could be bothered. But I guess, if they have a man to get all dolled up for, it might be worth it.

I was supposed to be out with Cooper tonight for that drink, but I canceled. I was going to do the chicken thing—avoid him at work and just text him—but I knew it would be the coward's way out, and he deserved better than that. I went down to the stables on my lunch break and told him that I couldn't make it. At first, he thought I just couldn't make it that night and offered to rearrange. So, I had to tell him the truth. Well, the closest version of the truth that I could give. I told him that I just didn't think it was a good idea. That I had a lot going on right now, and that I was also still getting over my last relationship.

It wasn't a total lie. I am still recovering from what Jason did to me—stealing eighteen months of my life and also the prior six months that I spent with him.

And, also, I need to get past these feelings that I have for Kas.

They've come on quick and strong and totally out of the blue, but they're there.

It's weird to me that I can have feelings for a guy who, half of the time, I have the strong urge to punch in the face.

I didn't see Kas at all for the rest of the day yesterday. He stayed holed up in his office. The only reason I knew he was in there was because his car was still outside.

I might have checked.

But it was good that I didn't see him, as I wasn't in the mood for another argument. And, honestly, we don't have anything to argue about anymore because whatever was going on between us is done.

I just don't understand him. Why he's like he is. I mean, I got the impression that he wanted me when he was kissing me—his erection spoke loud and clear—but then, the next minute, he was pushing me away and running, like his arse had just been lit on fire. At first, I thought it was because he thought I wasn't good enough for him. But his emphatic reaction to that was genuine.

"I'm not good enough for you, Daisy. You deserve a good man, a better man...and that's not me."

He thinks he isn't good enough for me. He thinks he isn't a good man.

Why?

"I don't know how to do this...relationships."

Why can't he do relationships?

My thoughts go back to that photograph. The photograph that I have in my phone.

It's been bugging me all day. I just know this photograph is important to him. The fact that he keeps it in his nightstand drawer beside his bed tells me that.

And the curious part of me wants to know who she is to Kas. *Why does he have a seven-year-old photograph of this girl in his nightstand?*

UNSUITABLE

Maybe he loved her. Maybe she broke his heart. Maybe she's why he's a head case when it comes to women.

But it's not like I can ask him because then he'd know that I was snooping in his drawer. Technically, I wasn't. I found it by mistake, but I know what he'd think.

And he probably wouldn't tell me anyway. He doesn't tell me anything. He's locked up so tight. I know nothing about him.

I only know his name and where he lives because I work for him. I know how he takes his coffee and that his best friend is Jude. Oh, and he has a horse called Danger, whom he rescued. But that's it.

I don't know when his birthday is. Or what his favorite food is. If he likes to read. If he has a favorite band he likes to listen to.

It's so frustrating.

But I shouldn't care because I'm done with him. So, it doesn't matter.

Sure, you are, Daisy. That's why you're sitting here, thinking about him.

Ugh!

I hate that he's gotten so easily under my skin.

I want answers from him, but I know I'm not going to get them, so I'll find some out for myself.

Grabbing Cece's laptop off the coffee table, I power it up. I open up Google and type in, *Kastor Matis*.

Not much comes up. Just the Matis Estate's website but no photos of him. He doesn't even have a Facebook profile.

But then again, neither do I.

I used to have one, but I shut it down after I was arrested. I didn't want people writing anything unsavory on my wall.

I tap the keys, frustrated.

Then, I delete Kas's name from the search box and type in, *Haley Halliwell*.

My screen fills with results. The top result is a clinical therapist.

Heart pumping, feeling like I'm doing something really wrong, I click on the link. The picture is of an older woman who looks to be in her fifties.

Definitely not her.

I back out and click on the Images tab. The screen fills with pictures. The first one is of that therapist woman. Then, sitting just below that is the picture I found in Kas's drawer. The picture in my phone.

I grab my phone and pull the picture up, just to compare.

It's definitely her.

I click on the picture, and it enlarges with a caption and a link. Then, my body freezes cold at the words.

Girl, 17, Murdered on Prom Night

Murdered?
She was murdered? Surely not. It can't be the same girl.
I look at the words on the back of the picture.

HALEY HALLIWELL. PROM. 2009.

Prom.
She was murdered after that picture was taken.
Oh God.
Hand trembling, I glide my finger across the trackpad to move the arrow over the link and click.

The screen fills with a news story dated June 7, 2009, headed with the same line as the caption.

Girl, 17, Murdered on Prom Night

To the right is the picture of Haley that I found in Kas's nightstand. Beneath that picture is a caption.

UNSUITABLE

Haley Halliwell, 17, body found in Hyde Park.

I scroll down to the article and start reading.

> *Late Saturday evening, a dog walker discovered the body of Haley Halliwell, 17, along with another unidentified person, who is currently in the hospital in critical condition, sources say. Halliwell had been attending her high school prom at the Marriott Hotel on Park Lane. Reports are not detailing much at the moment, and the police are remaining tight-lipped, but the unofficial report is that Halliwell was sexually assaulted, and the cause of death is assumed to be a result of multiple stab wounds. Police are urging any witnesses to come forward.*

I cover my mouth with my hand, feeling sick. She was sexually assaulted and stabbed to death.

Oh God.

My eyes scan back over the text.

> *Late Saturday evening, a dog walker discovered the body of Haley Halliwell, 17, along with another unidentified person, who is currently in the hospital in critical condition.*

Another unidentified person, who is currently in the hospital in critical condition.

Who was the other person? Who was she with? Did that person die as well?

Desperate to know, I open up a new window and type, *Haley Halliwell, murder, 2009.*

My screen fills with countless news stories. I skip the first link, as it's the one I already read. I click on the next link.

Police reports now state that Haley Halliwell attended her high school prom on the evening of Saturday, June 6, 2009. At approximately eleven p.m., Halliwell and her companion—who will remain unnamed but has been identified to police and is not listed as a suspect in the case—entered Hyde Park to take a stroll after the festivity. Shortly after entering the grounds, Halliwell and her companion were approached by three unidentified males. Halliwell was sexually assaulted by more than one of the assailants. She also suffered from multiple stab wounds, but the actual cause of death was strangulation. Her companion—who was also attacked, suffering from multiple stab wounds to the torso—is currently in the hospital in critical condition.

It is still uncertain if they expect the victim to live.

I swallow back hard. Backing out, I go to another link.

Police are still searching for clues in the Haley Halliwell murder case. Authorities are appealing for anyone with any information to come forward.

All the reports seem to say the same. But there's nothing about the other victim, if he or she survived, or if they caught the bastards who had done it.

Was the other victim Kas?

Bile rises in my throat at the thought.

I open another window and type in, *Kastor Matis, Haley Halliwell, murder, 2009.*

I scan the news stories, but Kas's name isn't mentioned in any. I delete the search and type in, *Haley Halliwell, 2009, murder solved.*

I click on the first link. It's dated June 6, 2010.

UNSUITABLE

> *A year later, police are still appealing for any witnesses in connection to the brutal rape and murder of Haley Halliwell to come forward. Halliwell, 17 at the time, had been attending her high school prom and then left with a friend to take a walk in Hyde Park. Her body was later found by a passerby. She had been raped and murdered. No suspects have been found so far in the horrific crime that has rocked the community.*

They never found them. Her murder went unsolved. It was never mentioned if the other person lived or died. But I'm assuming that person lived; otherwise, they would have named him or her. It wouldn't have just been known as the Haley Halliwell murder.

Kas knew and quite possibly loved a girl who was murdered in such a brutal way. And he might have also been with her on the night she was murdered.

My phone rings, startling me.

I scoop it up to see that it's Jesse calling.

I take a few breaths to make myself sound normal. "Hey you," I answer. "How are you doing?"

Things have been going well between Jesse and me since the shoplifting incident. We talk almost every day, and we text regularly.

"Hey, what are you up to?"

My eyes flicker to the laptop screen. I shut the lid down. "Uh, just watching TV. Cece's working late. What are you up to?"

"Just got back from footy practice."

"Yeah? How did it go?"

"All right." I can just imagine him shrugging as he says it.

"What are your plans for the rest of the night?"

"Just gonna chill. Watch some TV. So...I was wondering...well, I was wondering if you'd fancy doing something tomorrow?"

My heart lifts. "With you?"

"Yeah." He chuckles, and that laugh touches my heart and makes it soar.

"Of course," I say, my voice pitching higher with excitement. "I would love that. What were you thinking?"

"I thought we could catch a train down to Brighton—you know, like we used to. Hang out on the beach, as the weather's supposed to be good tomorrow. And there's a fair on at the moment as well."

"Sounds great." I smile. My heart is close to bursting in my chest. "So, should I pick you up tomorrow? I can get a taxi to yours and then have it take us to the train station."

"Sounds great."

"What time?"

"What time are the trains?"

"Hmm, not sure. How about I check the train times, and then text you to let you know?"

"Cool. Okay, well, I'll get off. See you tomorrow."

"See you then."

I'm beaming when I hang up the phone. I clutch it to my chest, happiness filling me.

Jesse wants to spend the day with me! He actually called me and asked me to spend the day with him!

I can't wait to tell Cece!

Okay, so I need train times for tomorrow.

I open up the lid on the laptop, ready to look up times, and I pause at the sight of Haley's picture alongside the news story I was reading.

My good mood instantly disintegrates.

She was murdered. And Kas might have been the one who was with her the night it happened.

The things he could have witnessed...

The thought makes me sick.

UNSUITABLE

Even if he weren't there, he knew Haley, and she was murdered.

Kas's harsh, abrasive, angry ways are starting to make sense in my mind now. Because, if he witnessed what happened…and was hurt…

I close my eyes against the horrific thoughts.

I should talk to him about this. *But what the hell would I say? I mean, how in the hell do you bring something like that up?*

And, also, I shouldn't know about Haley. That picture was among his private things, and I snooped.

Snooping aside, how in the world would I explain Googling her because I was jealous and curious?

I'd sound like a bloody stalker.

I should just pretend like I don't know.

But how the hell am I supposed to look him in the eye and pretend like I don't know that something terrible happened to someone he cared about?

And, if he were the other person there…then the terrible things happened to him, too.

I can't bear to think of him hurt and in pain.

Opening my eyes, I close out the opened windows, clearing my screen of the news stories.

I can't think about it now.

Right now, I just need to look up the train times for tomorrow. I need to focus on Jesse. He's what matters.

And Kas…he matters, but I just don't know how to handle this.

It's my own fault for snooping, but now, I know, and I don't know what to do.

I should ask Cece for her advice. But I feel like, if I told her, then I'd be betraying his confidence. Technically, I wouldn't be, but I've invaded his privacy enough. I have to keep this to myself.

I'll just have to figure out what to do.

Maybe, when I see him next, I'll just know.

But, right now, keeping it to myself seems like the safest option.

I type in the train website and start to look up the train times. I focus my mind on that and the fun I'll have with Jesse tomorrow, keeping my thoughts off of anything related to Kastor Matis.

TWENTY-FIVE

KAS IS HERE AGAIN, outside the station, waiting for me. I don't even bother to fight it. I just walk over to his car and get inside.

"Hi," I say quietly as I click my seat belt in.

"How was your weekend?" he asks, pulling the car away from the curb.

"I saw Jesse." I chance a glance at him.

He meets my eyes, a softness in his. "How did it go?"

"It was good." I smile at the memory of my day spent with Jesse. It was the best day I'd had in a long time. "We went to Brighton for the day. Hung out on the beach, ate ice cream, rode rides at the fair."

"Sounds fun."

"It really was."

"I'm glad for you, Daisy."

"Thanks." I swallow. "How was your weekend?" I ask, looking away.

"It was okay."

He offers nothing more. I could ask to know more about what he did, but I don't.

My mind is feeling all jumbled up from being here with him.

I had a great weekend. I spent all of Saturday with Jesse. And I spent Sunday with Cece. We went shopping and caught a film at the cinema.

I didn't allow myself to think about Kas…or Haley. But, now, sitting here with him, it's all I can think about.

I'm filled with empathy and compassion for this man sitting beside me. All the anger and resentment I felt last week are now gone.

But I still feel confused and guilty over what I know. I feel like I've somehow betrayed him with my curiosity and snooping into his life.

We don't talk for the rest of the short ride to the estate.

He parks outside the house.

"Thanks for the ride." I take off my seat belt and let myself out of the car.

I walk toward the front door. Kas is behind me.

Inside the house, I take my shoes off and hang my coat in the closet.

When I turn around, Kas is standing in the middle of the hallway, his hands in his trouser pockets. He looks unsure.

And I hate this animosity between us.

"Do you want me to get you a coffee?" I ask, offering an olive branch.

He seems surprised at that. "Coffee would be great. Thanks."

I give him a brief smile and then head for the kitchen. I smile again when I hear him following behind me. I thought for sure that he would go straight to his office.

I busy myself with making the coffee. Kas takes a seat on a stool at the kitchen island.

When the coffee is ready, I take his over to him.

"Thanks." He offers a smile.

Still standing, I lean my hip against the island and take a sip of my coffee.

UNSUITABLE

Kas wraps his hands around the mug and stares down into it. "I've thought a lot this weekend."

"About?" I ask quietly.

"You." He lifts his eyes to mine, and the look in them makes my heart beat faster.

"I can't change the way I behaved, and I can't explain why I walked out on you. It was the truth when I said I didn't know how to do this kind of thing, how to treat someone I like. Because I do like you, Daisy. A hell of a lot. I think you're smart and strong and challenging—"

"Challenging?" I lift a brow.

"I mean it in a good way." His lips tip up. "I like that you don't take my shit. You're a fighter, and I fucking love that. And the way you love your brother and have sacrificed so much for him…it's inspiring. You're compassionate and loyal and beautiful. So very fucking beautiful."

He thinks I'm beautiful. And he sees me in this crappy work uniform, stinking of cleaning products.

My cheeks flush at his compliment.

"And I know you said that you were done, but I'm asking you to reconsider. To give me another chance. I'll beg if I have to."

He grins, and I smile.

"Give me a chance, and I promise, I won't fuck it up."

My smile turns skeptical, and I lift my brow again.

"Okay." He chuckles, holding up his hands in surrender. "I can't promise I won't fuck it up because this is me that we're talking about. But I do promise that I will try my very best not to fuck it up." He lowers his hands to the countertop. "I know I'm difficult and a total arsehole at times—"

My brow lifts higher, and he laughs.

"Okay, I'm an arsehole most of the time. But that doesn't mean that I don't want you…because I do. I want you like you wouldn't fucking believe."

He wants me.

"Just give me another chance. Let me take you out on a date. I want to spend time with you, away from this place. So, what do you say? Go out with me, please."

Now that I know what he had to deal with when he was younger—well, I don't know for sure exactly what happened, but from what I've put together, it was bad—it makes him a hell of a lot easier to understand.

And I do want him.

So much more than I ever thought possible.

But I still wait a moment before answering. He deserves to sweat a little.

"Okay," I finally say.

A smile breaks out across his face. "Okay?"

I can't help but smile in return, but I fight to keep it modest. "Okay. You've got your chance. But this is your *last* chance, Kas, so try your hardest not to screw it up." I smile.

His smile turns into a cheeky grin. It melts me.

"I'll try really, really hard." His voice accentuates the word *hard*, and my mind instantly goes in the gutter.

I feel my face heat, so I bring the coffee cup up to my lips and take a sip, trying to cover it up.

Kas puts his cup down and stands. He walks around the island to me. He takes the cup from my hand and puts it down.

Then, he takes my face in his hands, and my heart bumps clumsily in my chest.

"What are you doing tomorrow?" he asks softly. His thumb brushes over the corner of my lips.

"I'm working." I give him a knowing smile.

His brow lifts. "And what about after work?"

I wait a beat and then say, "I'm free."

He grins. "Good." Then, he leans in and kisses me in the spot where his thumb just touched.

My whole body responds instantly. My legs turn to jelly from that one small touch of his lips against mine. I have to grip ahold of his waist to keep upright.

UNSUITABLE

He moves back, smiling, like he's fully aware of what he does to me.

"I'll take you out straight after work. Bring some gym clothes and comfortable shoes with you."

"You're taking me to a gym on our first date?" I squint.

I mean, I like to run and keep fit, but sweating in a gym, in front of Kas, is not my idea of a fun first date.

"No." He laughs softly. "I said, bring gym clothes, not that I was taking you to the gym."

"Okay. So, where are you taking me then?"

He leans in and brushes his lips over mine, making me shiver. "You'll find out tomorrow," he whispers.

Then, he releases me and walks around the island. Picking his coffee up, he walks out of the kitchen.

I'm going on a date with Kas.
Oh my God…I'm going on a date with Kas!

TWENTY-SIX

SUPERHUMANS.

This is what the sign reads on the building where Kas is pulling into the car park.

"We're here." He turns off the engine and takes the key out of the ignition.

We're in Brixton. I'm not sure whereabouts exactly, but aside from this nondescript building and a few factories we just passed, there's nothing here.

"And where is here?"

His lips shift up into a panty-melting smile. "You'll see in a few minutes." Then, he opens his door and climbs out.

Following suit, I hang my bag on my shoulder and exit the car.

Kas has been in a really good mood the whole way here. I'm not complaining; it's just not something I'm used to. But I really could get used to it.

He comes around the car. His tall, strong body is agile as he moves closer to me. He moves so quietly, considering the size and strength of him. Almost catlike. It's almost as if Kas walks on different air than the rest of us.

He's wearing black trackpants, a black T-shirt, and white trainers. He looks really hot.

So much hotter than me. I'm in yoga pants, my favorite pink running tank top, and my trainers. My hair is tied back into a ponytail. I have a little makeup on—mascara, blush, and gloss on my lips, which I quickly applied before we left the house to come here.

Stopping in front of me, Kas tucks some stray strands of my hair behind my ear. His fingers skim over my cheek, making me shiver.

He smiles as he takes ahold of my hand, lacing his fingers with mine, and starts to lead me over to Superhumans.

Butterflies start to riot in my tummy. Crazy how one small act can make such a big impact.

Kas opens the door, holding it for me to go through.

We walk up to the reception counter. The guy behind the counter looks up at our approach. I'd say he's in his mid-thirties. He's combated a receding hairline by shaving his hair off.

He grins when he sees Kas. "Hey, man, how are you doing?" he greets with enthusiasm.

Kas lets go of my hand as the guy stands and leans over the counter. They do that manly handshake thing that guys do.

"Yeah, I'm good. How are things with you?" Kas asks him.

"Ah, you know, life is always bright." He smiles.

I watch with interest. I've never seen Kas interact with people in this way before.

And, by that, I mean, friendly.

"Alex, this is Daisy. Daisy, Alex," Kas introduces us.

Kas steps back to me, and he takes ahold of my hand.

I see Alex's eyes go to our joined hands.

He grins, lifting his eyes to me. "Nice to meet you, Daisy."

"Likewise." I smile, suddenly feeling conscious.

"So, are you here for business or pleasure today?" Alex asks Kas.

Kas does business here?

UNSUITABLE

"Pleasure," Kas answers.

"Cool. Well, let me buzz you in." Alex presses a button behind the desk, and a door buzzes.

Kas holds the door open, letting me through first.

"Have a good session," Alex calls after us.

Session? Where the hell has Kas brought me?

I'm standing in a hallway. The first thing I notice is the music that's playing. It's dance music, like what you'd here in a club. And it's loud.

Kas grabs my hand again and leads me down the short hallway.

On my right, I see a door marked *Men's Changing Room*. The next door along is marked for the ladies' changing area.

Kas pushes through the double doors at the end of the hallway, and then I find myself in…well, I'm not really sure what it is.

It's a huge room.

And it's filled with people doing what I can only describe as something like gymnastics.

The far back wall is covered with this amazing graffiti. To my right is an elevated area, and above that is a mezzanine-style balcony that runs right around the room. To the side of the mezzanine is a climbing wall. Directly above the elevated area, hanging from the ceiling, are gymnastic rings. Beneath the stage is a pit filled with cubes of blue foam. It reminds me of those ball pools at children's play centers.

Directly in front of me is an area with a wooden floor, a ramp running down the side of it, and a mirror covering the whole of the left side. Above it is scaffolding suspended from the ceiling. Beyond the wooden floor is safety flooring, and to the right of that is a trampoline set up with a safety net. There's also some wooden fixtures set over to the left of the safety flooring that remind me a lot of pommel horses.

"So…what do you think?" Kas's voice comes from beside me. He sounds a little unsure, as if he's nervous and anticipating my response.

I lift my eyes to his. "It's great."

"You have no clue what it is, do you?"

"No," I admit, laughing.

He chuckles. "It's a parkour academy."

"The stuff you did when you jumped from your balcony and nearly gave me a heart attack?"

He chuckles again. "Yeah."

"Wow," I say, letting my eyes drift around.

I see a guy, about my age, standing on the edge of the elevated area. He backs up before running at full speed, and then he leaps from it and catches hold of the scaffolding bar with both hands.

I audibly gasp.

Kas chuckles. "Don't worry; he knows what he's doing."

He lets go of my hand and moves to stand behind me. His chest is so close to my back that I can feel the heat emanating from him.

His fingertips lightly touch my waist. That barely there touch sends my body into overdrive.

He's not even touching skin, but I can feel his touch like he's burned through my clothes.

I'm watching this guy move over the equipment like he's some kind of acrobat. But his acrobatics aren't the reason why my heart is beating faster or why my body feels like it's breaking out in fever.

It's because of Kas. His nearness.

The guy jumps from a high board, about fifteen feet up, and I tense.

"You see how he evens his body weight out by spreading his arms?" Kas's fingertips press a little harder against my waist. "That helps him keep his balance," he explains.

UNSUITABLE

The guy lands on his feet with only a slight stumble.

"It's amazing," I say, turning slightly to look at him. "And you do this?"

He nods.

"For how long?"

"Six years now."

I feel like there's so much I don't know about him.

"So, I know you practice parkour, and you do MMA. Anything else I need to know about you? Crime-fighting superhero by night?" I laugh.

He does, too, but it doesn't quite reach his eyes. "No. I'm just me."

"I like you," I whisper.

His eyes darken. "I like you, too."

Then, I hear him start to vibrate. Or I'm guessing that it's his phone.

He lets out a sigh. "Sorry." He pulls his phone from his trackpants pocket and looks at the display. There's a shift in his expression. He looks uncomfortable. He swipes the screen and then puts the phone back in his pocket. "It was my mother. I'll call her back later."

"You could have answered," I say.

"Once she gets on the phone, it takes ages to get her off." He offers a smile. "I'm spending time with you. I don't want any interruptions."

He steps closer, and my breath catches.

Then, over his shoulder, I see a familiar face approaching us.

"Jude," I say.

Kas turns.

"Hey, man." Jude greets him. They do the manly handshake-hug thing. "Wasn't expecting to see you here today."

"I brought Daisy."

"I can see that." He gives Kas a look. "Good to see you again, Daisy." Jude leans over. Placing his hand on my upper arm, he kisses my cheek.

"Oh, hi," I say shyly, a little surprised at his friendly greeting.

Jude is really open and friendly—the total opposite of Kas. Makes me wonder how they became friends.

"So, Kas brought you to see our place," Jude says to me.

"Your place?" I glance at Kas, confused.

"You didn't tell her." Jude makes a tsking sound. "Kas and I own this place."

"You do?" My eyes are still on Kas, but he's glaring at Jude. I see the skin around his eyes tighten.

Finally, he brings his stare to mine.

"You own this place?" I ask again.

"Joint ownership with this idiot. And we have government funding." Kas jerks his head in Jude's direction. "Jude runs the place."

"And what do you do?"

"He's the money man," Jude interjects.

"I handle the financial side of things," Kas says, giving Jude a hard look.

Jude laughs, seemingly unaffected by Kas's glare.

"How long have you had this place?" I ask them.

"Going on nearly three years now," Jude answers.

"Well, I'm impressed. It's amazing." I let my eyes wander around the place again.

When I look back to them, Jude is smiling, and Kas is staring at him with a pissed off expression on his face.

He's pissed off?

Happy Kas didn't last long.

Honestly, if he didn't want me to know he owned this place, then why bring me here?

I start to feel a little irked myself.

UNSUITABLE

"Well, I should get back to it. I've got a class starting soon." Jude starts to back away. "Nice to see you, Daisy."

"You, too." I smile.

"I'll catch you later," he says to Kas before turning and leaving.

And, now, we're standing here in this awkward silence that wasn't there before Jude showed up.

"I'm getting the impression that you're pissed off because I know you own this place," I say quietly.

"I'm not pissed off—"

"You're not exactly happy."

He turns to face me and reaches for my hand, which I let him take. "I just didn't want you to think that I brought you here to show off."

"The last thing I would ever think is that you're a show-off. A pain in the arse? Yes. But a show-off? No."

He chuckles. "You see me surrounded by my parents' wealth every day. I guess I just…" He sighs. "I didn't want you to think I was pushing this in your face as well."

"I don't. I'm seriously impressed. And you should be really proud of this place and what you've achieved."

For the first time ever, I see a little color in his cheeks.

"I am."

"Good." I smile.

He moves in closer.

"So…" I say.

"So…" he echoes.

"Well, you brought me here. Whatever do you plan to do with me now?"

He grins and leans his mouth to my ear. His lips brush my skin as he speaks, "Teach you parkour, of course."

Oh.

Oh, shit.

I lean back, staring into his eyes, my own wide with worry. "I'm not sure about that. There is no way I'm jumping off from a high height."

A laugh rumbles in his chest. "That's the advanced stuff. I just meant, I'll teach you the basics."

"Oh. Okay. And what do the basics involve?"

"Let's go outside, and I'll show you."

I walk beside Kas through the academy. He doesn't take my hand this time. I'll admit that I'm a little disappointed.

As we walk, he explains to me the different structures and what they're used for, and he introduces me to the people training here.

When we reach the back of the gym, I stop at the wall, touching my fingers to it. "I love this graffiti."

"Jude did it."

"Really?" I look back at him.

He nods.

"Wow. He's really talented."

Kas nods again in agreement. "Yeah, he is. He does abstract art as well."

"Does he do it as a job? As well as running this place?" I ask.

Kas shakes his head. "Just a hobby."

"Shame," I muse.

"Yeah. It's a real waste of his talent. But he won't pursue it."

There's something in his expression that I can't quite decipher. But whatever it is, I get that it is not something good and quite possibly has something to do with Jude's past.

I've pried into Kas's past enough without him knowing. I'm not going to pry into Jude's personal business as well.

"Come on." Kas tips his head in the direction of the exit door.

I follow him outside. I thought the inside was impressive, but out here is just as awesome, if not more so.

It's like one huge park yet so much more.

UNSUITABLE

There are climbing frames and a children's playground, complete with a swing set, slide, monkey bars, and a seesaw. And what looks like an obstacle course is set out across the area. There are also all different kinds of structures that I wouldn't even know how to describe.

"This is amazing," I say, walking past Kas, taking it all in. I turn back to face him. "Did you build all of this?"

"Not with my bare hands." His lips curve into a smile. "But Jude and I did design it. Well, actually, Jude did all the drawings, and all I did was give my input every now and then. We hired contractors to build it all."

"It really is fantastic."

"Yeah." He smiles again, and this one reaches all the way to his eyes. "Come on." He walks over and takes my hand, leading me toward one of the metal climbing frames.

Attached to the climbing frame are two platforms facing each other, about three feet of space between them.

Kas stands up on one of the low platforms. "Climb up here, beside me," he says.

Taking my bag from my shoulder, I put it on the ground by the climbing frame. Beside him, I step up onto the platform.

He glances down at me. "Okay, so we're just going to do some precision jumps to get you started."

I give him a dubious look.

"You'll be fine. It's just about balance."

"Of which, I have none."

He laughs. "Just watch what I do."

Kas moves so that his feet are at the edge of the platform. Then, he jumps forward with both feet landing easily on the other platform.

He turns around. "See? Easy. Your turn."

"Oh, yeah, really easy." I roll my eyes, giving him a look.

He folds his arms, giving me a no-nonsense stare.

"Fine," I huff.

I step up to the edge, exactly as he did.

My heart starts to beat a little faster as I look down at the three-foot gap, which doesn't sound like much, but it is.

"I don't think I can do it." Taking a step back, I look up at Kas.

He takes in my wide eyes, and his expression softens, his arms dropping from around his chest. "You can do it, Daisy. You're strong. You're not afraid of anything."

"I'm afraid of falling down there." I grimace, pointing at the space between the platforms, which is only about a four-foot fall, but it's four feet more than I want to fall.

"I won't let you fall." The pledge in his voice lifts my eyes to his.

I stare into his warm eyes. "Promise?"

"I promise."

I take a deep breath and step back up to the edge.

"Okay, bend your knees, and use your arms for balance," Kas guides me, showing me exactly what he means.

I copy his stance.

"Now, just push off the platform with your feet, and propel yourself forward."

I meet his eyes.

"You can do it," he whispers. "Trust me."

Something happens in this moment as I stare into those eyes that I once thought were so cold. I realize that I do trust him.

Then, I just do it. I push off the platform, and I jump.

My feet land soundly on the other platform.

"I did it." I beam.

"Yeah, you did." He smiles.

"No, *I told you so*?" I grin up at him.

"As if I would be so arrogant as to say something like that."

He chuckles, and I laugh.

"Do you want to go again?" he asks.

UNSUITABLE

"Okay." I nod.

We spend a good few minutes with me jumping from one platform to the other, and Kas watches.

Honestly, I'm really enjoying myself.

This is the best date I've ever been on, and it's only just started.

"You up for trying anything a bit harder?" Kas asks.

That stops me in my tracks. "Harder? Like how?"

He gives me a secret smile. "I'll show you."

"How about you show me what you can do, and then I'll do something harder?"

He stares at me, a panty-melting grin appearing on his face. "Okay. Deal."

He moves off the platform we're on and walks over to another climbing frame. I pick up my bag and follow him over.

He climbs up the frame until he's about ten to fifteen feet high. Then, he gets up onto a platform and stands at the edge. He front-flips off the platform, landing on his feet, into a crouch, his hands touching the floor. He pushes up and takes off running toward a pommel horse. With his hands on it, he does an almost cartwheel-like movement. He lands on his feet on the other side where he proceeds to do a couple of backflips in succession, and then he lands on his feet, stopping.

"Show-off." I smile, walking over to him.

He smirks at me.

I stop a few inches away from his body. He's barely out of breath.

"That was seriously impressive," I say.

The smirk vanishes, and a smile touches his eyes as he lifts a shoulder.

I love how modest he is about this.

He reaches out, taking ahold of my hand, and pulls me into his body. He wraps his arms around me and brings his lips down to mine.

He softly kisses me, brushing his lips back and forth over mine. It's a teasing kiss. A kiss with a promise of more. He gives a gentle sweep of his tongue over my lower lip, eliciting a soft moan from me. My hands grip his waist. He grazes his teeth over that same bottom lip, and then all too soon, he's moving his lips from mine. I almost grumble in displeasure.

"Your turn," he says, a husky lilt to his voice.

"For what? More kisses? Because I could totally go for that."

He laughs softly and rubs his nose over mine. "More parkour."

"Oh, that." I give an exaggerated groan. "You sure you don't want to kiss some more?"

He presses his lips to mine again. "If I kissed you as often as I wanted to, I'd never get anything done," he murmurs against my mouth.

"I could live with that."

His laughter rumbles against my lips. I smile, loving the sound and feel.

"Come on." He gives my butt a light slap, making me jump, before he releases me.

"So, what am I doing?" I ask, following him over to the pommel horse.

"I want you to jump this." He taps the pommel horse with his knuckles.

"Um"—my eyes go to the pommel horse and then back to him—"are you insane?"

He laughs. "Not certifiably but quite possibly borderline."

"Funny," I deadpan. "But no bloody way am I jumping that thing."

"Why not?"

"Because I like breathing. And I'd like to see Jesse finish school and go to university and graduate, at the very least."

UNSUITABLE

He laughs again, and it rumbles through his chest. "You won't kill yourself from jumping this, Daisy."

I fold my arms over my chest. "Maybe not kill myself but very likely break my neck."

The laughter starts back up again, his whole body shaking with it.

And, now, I'm fighting a smile because of the infectious sound of it.

Bastard.

His shining eyes meet mine, and he walks over to me. "You won't hurt yourself, gorgeous, I promise."

He called me gorgeous.

I puddle.

Yeah, I'm *that* girl right now.

I clear the simpering girl out of me and stare up at him with a slight frown on my face. "Well, if I do break my neck, I'll expect sick pay for the rest of my paralyzed life."

I can see he's fighting a smile.

"Deal."

"Fine. Let's get this over with then."

I drop my bag onto the grass and walk toward the pommel horse. Kas follows behind me.

"What do I need to do?" I ask him.

"Just take a good run at it. Then, when you reach it, put your hands on the top, and vault yourself over."

I glance over my shoulder at him, giving him a skeptical look. "That easy?"

"Yeah." He smiles. "That easy."

I take a deep breath and walk backward, putting plenty of space between the pommel horse and myself.

Kas steps off to the side, smartly not saying a word.

I stare at the pommel horse like it's Mount Everest. My heart has stepped up its tempo, and my pulse is beating in my neck. I can feel my hands starting to sweat.

I clench my fists in and out, and then I press them to my pants to dry them. I take a deep breath and set off running. I make good speed, but too quickly, the pommel horse is on me, and I can't do it.

I skid to a stop in front of it, hands pressing to the top.

"For God's sake!" I grumble, annoyed with myself.

I glance back at Kas, who is standing, watching me.

"You can do it," he encourages.

Turning away, I take another deep breath. Then, I jog back to my previous starting point.

Come on, Daisy. You've faced worse than this stupid pommel horse. You can do this. Just imagine it's Jason; you're running at him, and you get to smack your hands on his head and jump over the bastard.

And then maybe go back and kick him in the nuts.

My little pep talk seems to have ignited something in me. I start running, like I did before, but this time, a determination builds in me as I go. When I reach the pommel horse, instead of wimping out, I plant my hands on it and vault myself over, landing safely on the other side.

I did it.

I bloody did it!

I spin back to Kas. "I did it!" I throw my hands up in the air, doing a little victory dance.

Smiling wide, he walks over to me. "I knew you could."

I stop my victory dance. "Yeah, you did." I smile softly at him.

Something shifts in my chest, and warmth spreads throughout my body, making me tingle.

"Want to try it again?" he asks.

"Yeah." I smile. "But will you film it for me on my phone?" I walk over to my bag and pull my phone out. "I want to show Jesse. I think he'll be impressed."

"Sure." He smiles, taking my phone from me.

"You need me to set the camera up?" I ask.

"No, I got it."

He walks over to the spot where he watched from before, and I put myself in place, ready to run.

UNSUITABLE

"Let me know when you're ready to film," I tell him, eyes fixed on the pommel horse.

He doesn't respond, so I glance over to him, and something in his expression makes my heart pause.

He's staring down at my phone. Confusion and anger and pain are all clearly etched on his face.

What's wrong with him?

Then, a thought slams into my brain.

Oh, fuck... no...

TWENTY-SEVEN

I'M MOVING QUICKLY toward Kas.

He seems to sense my approach, and I watch with bated breath while his eyes lift slowly to mine.

And then our eyes meet and hold, and I see it there in his agonized eyes.

He's seen it.

The picture of Haley. It was still in my phone.

Why the hell didn't I delete it? I'm so fucking stupid.

I stop a few feet away, unsure of what to do. "Kas," I say his name softly, tentatively.

"Why…" He pauses.

I see his jaw work angrily. His body is locked up tight, like he's fighting to control himself.

A chill runs through me. I wrap my arms around myself.

"Why do you have this in your phone?" His voice is like granite. He lifts the phone to me.

The photo I took of Haley's picture is there for me to see.

I pale. "I-I can explain."

"Then, fucking explain!" he roars.

I jump back a step.

I've seen Kas angry before, but this is a whole new level of anger. He's livid. And he has a right to be.

"I-I..." I can't stop the stammer. My whole body is trembling with nerves. I take a deep breath, trying to calm myself. "I found the picture—by accident. It was last week after we kissed in the club and argued about it. After I left you, I went upstairs and started stripping your bed. I knocked over a glass of water on the nightstand. I cleaned it up with a towel and saw the top drawer was open slightly. I was worried water had gotten inside. I saw the picture in there. And I..." I helplessly lift my shoulders.

"You saw the photograph," he says, his tone low and deadly. "It doesn't explain to me why the fuck you have a picture of it in your phone."

My eyes fill with tears. I've fucked up so very badly.

"I don't know." My lips tremble. "I was just curious...and jealous, and I—"

"Jealous?" he yells, making me jump again. "Why the fuck would you be jealous?"

"I...she—I mean, Haley—"

"You know her name." His voice is quiet but dangerous.

I nod, and a tear falls down my cheek. I free my hand and brush it away.

Kas is staring at me, but it's like he doesn't even see me right now. "What else do you know?"

I bite my lip, afraid to speak.

"What do you know?" he repeats, yelling.

I jump to attention. "I looked Haley up on the Internet."

The silence that hits is like a bulldozer hitting brick, and the look Kas gives me makes me want to curl up and die.

"You know." It's not a question.

But I'm quick to reply, "O-only what was in the articles." My voice is wobbling all over the place. "Th-that Haley was...that she was mu-murdered, and..." I pause, meeting his fiery stare. "That someone else was there with her that night, someone who was also...injured."

UNSUITABLE

His eyes close, as if he's in actual pain. Anguish distorts his beautiful face.

I feel sick to my stomach.

"I'm so sorry," I whisper, more tears sliding down my face.

It's so quiet. Only my pathetic whimpers and Kas's labored breathing can be heard.

"Fuck!" he roars, throwing his head back.

The sound is so feral that it rips at my heart like claws.

Tormented black eyes swing back my way.

Then, without a word, he throws my phone to the ground at my feet, and he's moving…leaving. He strides away from me, his long legs quickly eating up the distance.

Fear seizes me. *What do I do?*

Go after him.

I scoop up my phone off the ground—my stupid phone that caused this problem in the first place—and I run for my bag. I drop the phone inside, and then I start running in the direction of Kas.

I just need to apologize…explain.

Tears are drying on my face as I run. I finally catch up with him in the car park, near his car.

"Kas, wait, please," I pant, out of breath.

He ignores me and keeps moving toward his car. So, I pick up my speed, sprinting to him. I catch up with him just as he's opening his car door. I curl my hand around his arm, stopping him.

He swings back to me, his eyes staring down at my hand like he wants to break it off.

I quickly drop my hand. "Please, just let me explain," I plead.

"No."

"*Please*, Kas."

Hard eyes bore into me. "You need to stay the fuck away from me."

Agony seizes my chest.

He climbs into his car.

Panic-stricken, I move between the driver's door and the car to stop him from closing it.

"Move out of the fucking way," he grinds out.

"No."

His eyes burn up at me. "Don't make me move you, Daisy."

Nerves make me swallow hard. "Please, Kas, just hear me out, and then you can leave."

He glares at me. The hatred in his eyes makes my body start to tremble. "I don't have to do a fucking thing. And you have *nothing* that I want to hear. Now, move the fuck away from my car!"

Ignoring his anger, I fight back, "I at least deserve a chance to explain! When you screwed up—twice—I gave you a chance!"

He pins me with a dead stare. "Then, you were a fool." Cold contemplation quickly enters his eyes. "Or is that me, for thinking you were someone you clearly aren't?"

Those words hit like a knife between my shoulder blades.

I gulp back. My throat burns, like I'm swallowing acid. I swipe a hand at the tears sliding down my face.

"And you can stop with the tears. They don't affect me. Now, move the hell away from my car, or I *will* move you, and it won't be pretty," he says low with meaning.

Fear shakes me to the core. I've never heard him sound that way before. Like he actually means me harm.

Knowing that there is nothing I can do or say to get him to listen to me, I take a defeated step away.

The second I move, he slams the car door shut, and then he's revving the engine and pulling away a second later, his tires kicking up against the gravel, leaving me in a cloud of dust.

As I watch his car leave, a sob hitches in my throat. Covering my mouth with my hand, I swallow it back.

UNSUITABLE

I've screwed up badly. He's never going to forgive me.

I look around me. Thankfully, the car park is empty of people.

Taking a shaky breath in, I dry my face with my hands, and then I get my phone from my bag and press the last number in my Call History, calling the only person I've ever been able to rely on.

Hand trembling, I put my phone to my ear.

"Hey," Cece sings down the line. "How's the date going?"

"Ce…can you come pick me up?" My voice wobbles.

"Daisy, what's wrong?" Her tone is instantly protective.

"I-I…screwed up, Ce. Real bad. And I need you to come get me."

"Okay. I got you, Mayday. Just tell me where you are."

"I-I'm at a place called Superhumans. It's on an industrial estate in Brixton. It…it's Kas's place."

"I'll find it."

"Please be quick," I plead, tears filling my voice.

"Okay. Just stay on the phone with me, Daisy. Don't hang up."

"Okay."

I hear her moving around. Keys rattling. A door slamming. A lock turning. Then, I hear her shoes slapping against concrete as she runs down the stairs of our building.

"I'm sorry to be a bother, Ce."

"Shut up," she chides softly. "You will never be a bother to me. You're my family, Daisy."

"You're my family, too," I whisper, brushing away a tear.

I hear a door slam. Then, a car engine comes to life.

"I'm putting you on speaker," she tells me. The line goes silent for a moment, and then it comes back to life with an echo. "Can you hear me?" she asks.

"I got you," I tell her.

"Good. Now, tell me, do I need to put out a hit on this motherfucker?"

I let out a sad chuckle as I wipe away another tear. "No," I say somberly. "He hasn't done anything wrong." And it's the truth; he hasn't. "This was all me. My fault entirely." And it is.

I've screwed up everything. Yet again.

TWENTY-EIGHT

IT'S LATE. CLOSE TO MIDNIGHT. I'm in my pajamas, ready for bed, and I'm in the bathroom, brushing my teeth. My eyes are puffy from all the crying I've done, and I'm feeling emotionally drained.

Cece is already in bed. She turned in about half an hour ago. She spent all night trying to make me feel better. Not that much is going to make me feel better, apart from Kas, and it's not likely that's going to happen.

I haven't heard from him.

I tried to ring him once I got home after Cece picked me up, but the call went unanswered. When I tried calling again, I got voice mail, telling me that he'd turned off his phone.

I left a voice mail, apologizing again and asking him to call me—well, I might have pleaded for him to call me.

I also sent a text, just in case he decided to ignore the voice mail. Of course, he can also ignore the text, but at least I'll know when he's read it.

Not that he's read it yet. I might have checked once or twice…or a hundred times.

I spit out into the sink and rinse my brush under the running tap. I've just put my toothbrush into the holder when someone starts banging on our front door.

Cece comes out of her room, and at the same time, I exit the bathroom. She's all wide-eyed. I think my expression mirrors hers.

"Who the hell is that?" she asks.

"I have no clue."

"Daisy!" a voice hollers through the front door.

My body jolts in shock, and my heart starts to hammer in my chest.

"It's Kas," I whisper to Cece. Why I'm whispering, I have no clue. "What do you think he wants?"

And how the hell did he get in the building without being buzzed in? So much for building security.

"I'd suggest opening the door and finding out."

"Funny." I give her an unamused stare.

Maybe he's come here to yell at me some more—or worse, fire me.

He bangs on the door again. "Daisy, open the door!" His words are slurred. He sounds drunk.

"You'd better answer the door before he wakes the whole building up," Cece says with a grin in her eyes.

"Shit," I mutter. Then, I quickly make my way through our apartment and to the front door.

Reaching it, I inch up onto my tiptoes and look through the peephole just to be sure. And, yep, Kas is on the other side of my door.

Bracing myself, I unlock the door and pull it open.

I smell the alcohol on him first. Then, I notice he's still in the clothes he was wearing earlier.

"Daisy," he slurs. It comes out sounding like *Duh-easy*. He steps through the open doorway and practically falls on top of me.

"Jesus, Kas." It takes all my strength to hold him up.

His hands grab around my waist as he buries his nose in my hair. "You smell so fucking good," he murmurs into my hair. "I don't deserve you, but you smell so fucking good."

UNSUITABLE

He's really drunk. Reaching out my leg, I kick the front door shut.

Taking ahold of his hands on my waist, I peel them off and step back, still holding his hands because I'm worried he might fall over. I stare into his face. His eyes are half-shut and glazed.

"Let's get you to sit down, and I'll make coffee."

"Don't want coffee." He frowns. "Just want you."

He wants me.

My heart lurches.

He's drunk, Daisy. Drunk people often say things they don't mean.

He lurches forward again, and I catch hold of him. His head falls to my shoulder, his forehead pressing to my bare skin. I feel his body tremble.

"I never wanted you to know." His words are soft but choked.

Then, I feel wetness on my skin.

Tears.

Jesus, fuck.

I feel sick.

"I'm so sorry, Kas. So sorry." Tears blur my eyes. I press my hand to the back of his head, holding him to me, as I wrap my other arm around him.

His face slides into the hollow of my neck, his even breaths hot against my skin.

"It was my fault," he mumbles. "If I'd been stronger…fought harder…she'd still be alive."

Haley.

Pain clamps down on my chest and twists my gut.

I squeeze my eyes shut, fighting tears. "Shh…" I soothe, running my hand over his head. "It's going to be okay, Kas. Everything's going to be okay."

"It's already too late," he says, his lips brushing against my skin.

"Too late?" I whisper.

"For Haley...and for me."

What do I say?

You're still here. She's gone. But you are still here, and I care about you.

I can't say that, so instead, I say, "It wasn't your fault, Kas."

He draws in a shuddering breath. "You don't know anything."

"So, tell me. You can talk to me."

Pulling from my hold, he lifts his eyes to mine. They're still glazed with alcohol. "You don't want to know."

"If you want to tell me, then I want to know."

He turns from me, eyes on the wall, and his body sways. "You don't want to get involved with me. I'm not a good man, Daisy."

He's said that to me before.

"Yes, you are," I argue.

"No, I'm not." His voice sounds so sure. He turns his head to look at me. "I'm a fucking monster, Daisy. Not like those bastards, but a monster all the same. The things I've done..."

The things he's done?

Something cold and hard settles in my stomach. "What have you done?" My voice wavers.

He holds my stare for a moment longer, and then he looks away, back to the wall. "Nothing. Forget I said anything. I don't even fucking know why I came here." He stumbles back a step, his back hitting the wall.

I try not to let his words hurt me.

I try...with no success. They sting like a bitch.

Breathing through the hurt, I focus on him. "Let me help you," I say softly, taking a step closer.

His eyes turn to mine. I can see fissures of pain in them, and they crack me wide open.

"No one can help me," he whispers, broken. "I was lost a long time ago."

UNSUITABLE

Tears start to swim in his dark eyes, and I nearly start bawling.

"Fuck," he mutters angrily. Then, he tips his head back against the wall, hitting it with a thud. He shuts his eyes and begins breathing in and out deeply.

I see movement from the corner of my eye and turn to see Cece standing in the doorway of her bedroom.

"All okay?" she asks, concerned.

"He's just drunk," I answer.

"I'm not drunk. I'm just happy," Kas mutters.

My eyes flash to him. His are still closed.

I remember saying those very words to him when I was drunk.

"Do you want me to make coffee?" Cece asks.

I shake my head. "I'll just put him to bed. Let him sleep it off."

"I don't wanna go to bed," Kas mumbles.

"You're going to bed," I tell him.

"You need a hand?" Cece asks.

"I think I've got it. He can walk." I nudge his chin with my hand. "Can't you?"

Sleepy eyes open to half-mast. "Huh?"

"Can you walk?"

"Of course I can," he slurs, drunkenly sleepy.

I reach over and lock the door. Then, I put my arm around his waist. Gripping ahold of him, I move him off the wall. He starts to walk with me, but he's leaning a lot of his weight on me.

God, he weighs a lot.

I consider myself to be quite strong for my size, but I'm buckling under his weight.

I keep moving, trying to get him to pick up the pace before I fall over. We pass by Cece.

"See you in the morning," I tell her. "And sorry about...you know." I tip my head in Kas's direction.

"Don't worry about it. And he came to see you, so all is not lost," she whispers that last part.

My eyes flash up to Kas, whose eyes are firmly shut, but I'm sure he heard her.

I give Cece an annoyed look.

She just grins at me and then disappears back into her room.

Sighing, I maneuver Kas into my bedroom and then onto my bed, which he hits with a thud and nearly takes me down with him.

Righting myself, I walk over and switch on the bedside lamp. The light illuminates his gorgeous face.

He's sprawled out on my bed, eyes shut, breathing deeply, with one leg hanging off the edge.

Of all the ways I imagined Kas being in my bed, this was not one of them. Drunk and passed out.

He's going to have one hell of a hangover in the morning.

I unlace his trainers and pull them off. Then, I stare at his trackpants and T-shirt.

Should I undress him?

Maybe not the pants, but I'll just take his T-shirt off, so he doesn't get too hot.

I lean over and grab the hem of his T-shirt to lift it.

His hand whips out and catches my wrist, stopping me. "Don't." His low voice is a warning.

I swallow back my surprise, feeling like I was just caught doing something wrong. "I was just trying to make you comfortable."

"Don't...want you to...see me," he mumbles. Then, his tight grip on my wrist loosens, and he rolls over.

He doesn't want me to see him? What the hell is that supposed to mean?

I retreat back, rubbing at my wrist. Leaving the room, I go to the kitchen and get a glass of water and some aspirin for the morning.

UNSUITABLE

I go back to my bedroom, and he looks fast asleep, his breaths deep and even. I put the water and pills on the nightstand, and then I pull the duvet over him, covering him.

Staring down at him, emotion grips my chest.

I reach over and brush his hair back from his face. "Sleep well," I whisper. Then, I lean in and press my lips to his forehead.

"You've made me feel again, Daisy," he murmurs, surprising me.

I shift back and stare at his face. His eyes are still closed.

Then, he lets out a shallow breath. "You've made me feel…and I fucking hate that."

Sadness engulfs me at his words.

I move back and watch him for a long moment.

Finally, I switch off the lamp. On quiet feet, I move through my room and close the door, leaving him alone.

"You've made me feel."

His words haunt me all the way back to the living room.

I grab the blanket off the back of the armchair and turn off the light.

I could sleep in Jesse's unused room, but I don't think I'll be getting much sleep tonight. So, I lie down on the sofa, cover myself with the blanket, and stare up at the darkened ceiling.

TWENTY-NINE

MY EYES BLINK OPEN. The room is at the point where light is just entering dark, casting an eerie glow.

And I'm not alone.

I push myself up to a seated position.

Kas is in the armchair. He's leaning forward, his forearms resting on his thighs, his hands clasped together, his eyes watching me. I see that his shoes are on his feet, like he's not staying.

My heart sinks.

"How are you...feeling?" I ask tentatively. My throat is dry, my voice croaky from sleep—or lack of.

When our eyes meet, I see a heavy mixture of pain and regret in his. Those feelings clamp down on my heart, like a vise.

He exhales a tired-sounding breath and looks away from me.

"Haley was my girlfriend," he says in a quiet voice. "We were together for two years, ever since we were both fifteen. She was my childhood sweetheart, so to speak. She was pretty and sweet and smart and kind. She was just *good*, Daisy. And I loved her for all those reasons.

"We went to the same high school. We'd just finished our A Levels, and we were going to be heading off to university. We'd both gotten places at Birmingham. We had it all planned. We'd go to university, graduate, get jobs, and then move in together. It was supposed to be the start of our lives. It turned out to be the end of our lives...well, the end of hers."

I slowly slide my legs off the sofa and put my feet on the floor, so I'm sitting upright. Kas doesn't even seem to notice I've moved. Right now, he's in a whole other place, and it's not here with me.

It's somewhere bad and haunting.

"It was a Saturday night. Our school was hosting a prom at the Marriott Hotel in central London. Haley was so excited to go. She had spent the entire day getting ready. She'd gone to the beauty salon to have her nails, hair, and makeup done."

His eyes drift across the room, like he's seeing something else, someone else in another time and place. A soft expression enters his eyes. "She looked beautiful."

A sad smile touches his lips and quickly clears. "At prom, Haley wasn't drinking anything, but I had some whiskey with my friends in the restroom. One of them had snuck in a bottle, but I wasn't drunk, by any means. Prom was coming to a close. We had a limo to take us home, but it was a really great night, and I wasn't ready for it to be over. So, I suggested to Haley that we take a walk. I thought it'd be romantic, like in the movies." He lets out a sad-sounding laugh. "So, I told the limo driver to wait. We started walking around the outside of Hyde Park. I suggested we go in. Haley wasn't sure, but I assured her that we'd be fine." He lets out a hollow laugh.

"We'd been walking in the park for only about five minutes when I heard footsteps behind us. I hadn't even known there was anyone else in the park. We hadn't seen another soul the whole time we were in there. I didn't think anything was wrong off the bat...until the footsteps got closer and heavier.

UNSUITABLE

"When I glanced back, I saw two guys—older than us, early twenties—and I just knew. I whispered to Haley to walk faster and then to run when we hit the corner. She told me she was afraid. And I told her not to be, that I wouldn't let anything happen to her."

His eyes lift to mine, and the pain in them is palpable. Looking away, he starts wringing his hands together.

"When we hit that corner, ready to run, we walked straight into another guy…and he had a knife in his hand. It didn't take a genius to figure out that they'd cornered us." He blows out a breath. "I just thought they were going to mug us. Take our stuff and go. But that wasn't just what they were there for.

"They forced us off the main path, deep into the foliage. I tried to fight back. I'd always been tall for my age, but I wasn't built like I am now. I wasn't as strong. And they were older, stronger, and armed. All three of them were carrying knives. I didn't stand a chance against them. They took turns kicking the shit out of me. I remember hearing Haley screaming, begging them to stop, and then her screams became muffled until they were just soft whimpers."

His brows draw together in pain, and more than anything, I want to go to him, comfort him. But unsure of if he wants me to, I stay in my seat, feeling helpless.

"I was on the ground, beaten up pretty bad. My nose was broken, and my eyebrow was split and bleeding into my eye. I could hear them laughing about it…me. They were talking, but I couldn't make out what was being said. Then, I was rolled over onto my back. Two of them held me down. One with a knife to my throat, and the other bastard sat down on me, straddling me, as he hovered his knife over my stomach." He drags a hand over his face, clearing all emotion from it.

I feel sick at the thought of what's to come.

"The guy with the knife at my throat leaned in and laughed in my face. I can still remember exactly how he smelled...rotten breath that stank of cheap alcohol and cigarette smoke." He draws in a breath. "He laughed and said, 'Now, you get to watch while we take turns fucking your pretty girlfriend.' Then, he grabbed my face"—Kas puts his hands to his face, holding his cheeks, in what seems to be a subconscious movement—"and turned it to the side. Haley was..."

He stops, swallowing back his grief.

The pain I'm feeling for him is indescribable. I've never hurt for someone like I'm hurting for him right now.

He exhales a harsh breath. "Haley was on the ground a few feet from me. Something had been tied over her mouth, so she couldn't scream. And the other guy...he was on top of her...raping her."

Oh God, no. My eyes briefly close in anguish.

"He was raping her, and I couldn't do a goddamn thing to help her. She was looking at me with fear and pleading in her eyes, and I...couldn't watch." His words catch in his throat. He presses his fist to his mouth before dropping it.

"I shut my eyes, Daisy. I left her there, alone. I shut my fucking eyes, like the coward I was, because I couldn't bear to see them hurting her.

"A second later, I felt a hot pain in my stomach. The guy sitting on me had stabbed me in the stomach for shutting my eyes. They'd meant it when they said they wanted me to watch. It was just a fucking game to them. *We* were a game to them. The bastard told me, if I shut my eyes again, then he'd kill me. And he meant it." His glistening eyes stare at the floor.

"So, I watched while they took turns raping her. I watched them hurt her over and over again." He swallows hard.

"The leader of the gang knelt on top of me, holding me down. I knew he was in charge, as he'd been the one giving all the orders…and he was the first one of those bastards to rape Haley. He'd made it clear to them that he was going first.

"They were all sick fucks, but he was a special brand of sick, all on his own. He really got off on it. He taunted me, telling me what a good fuck she was. He—" He breaks off at his own words, his breathing heavier, angrier. "He even thanked me for sharing her with him and his boys." The sound of disbelief that escapes him is filled with agony.

Bile rises in my throat at the thought of what he and Haley went through that night.

I wrap my arms around my stomach, trying to hold myself together.

"Then, he told me that, even though I'd been good to him by letting him have my girl, he couldn't let me live. He drove his knife into my chest, and then he just kept on stabbing. He was smiling the whole fucking time.

"I must've blacked out from the pain because I eventually came to, and when I did, they were gone. Maybe they had thought I was dead, or maybe they just hadn't cared to check. But Haley…she was dead. They'd stabbed her multiple times in the chest while I was blacked out, and as I found out later, they'd finally strangled her to death.

"She died alone and in pain."

He's silent for a long moment before he speaks again, "Not long after I awoke, we were found by a passerby who was out late, walking his dog. Somehow, I survived. Some days, I wish I hadn't."

His eyes come to me. His expression is unreadable. "So, now, you know everything."

He stands abruptly.

I shakily get to my feet. "Kas—"

"Don't." He lifts a hand, stopping me from going further, even though I have no clue what to say. "You don't need to say anything, Daisy. I didn't tell you to be a bastard or hurt you or have you feel sorry for me. You wanted to know, and now, you do. You know the very worst part of me."

Then, he walks out of my living room and out of my apartment.

And I let him go.

THIRTY

I DIDN'T GO INTO WORK today. After what Kas had told me before leaving the way he had, I wasn't sure he would want me to be there. I thought he would need some time to himself. I'll make today's hours up this weekend. I just wanted to give him space away from me, and honestly, I needed some time to process.

Kas's words have been haunting me all day, conjuring up the images of what he must have lived through that night. What he still lives with every day.

"Somehow, I survived. Some days, I wish I hadn't."

Those words have stuck with me and affected me most.

I want him to be happy. I want to be the one to make him happy.

He's so quietly strong about everything that happened to him. He calls me strong, but he's the one who is. He's so brave.

Knowing all this has made me realize just what he truly means to me. It's put everything into perspective.

I knew I cared about Kas. I just didn't realize the extent.

I'm falling for him.

Listening to him this morning, finding out what had happened to him…I ached for him. I felt every pain that he felt. And I wanted to kill those bastards with my bare hands for what they had done to him…to her.

The depths of the way it wrecked me wasn't just empathy for another human being. It's because I'm falling for this beautiful, broken, complex man.

That is why I find myself taking the train to Westcott at six thirty p.m.

I just need to see him. Talk to him.

Exiting the train at my stop, I walk the twenty minutes to the Matis Estate.

And then I'm standing outside the gates before I know it.

I key in the code on the keypad, and as soon as the gates part, I slip between them and walk up the long driveway to the house.

When I reach the house, I see that Kas's car is parked out front, so I know for sure that he's home. I don't know what I was planning to do if he wasn't. Probably wait here until he showed up.

I walk up to the front door and knock. Then, I wait.

It's not long before I hear his footsteps approaching, and the door swings open.

"Daisy." He doesn't look surprised to see me.

As far as I know, they don't have cameras on the Matis Estate, so he couldn't have seen me coming.

Weird.

"Hi." I smile tentatively.

He's dressed in black lounge pants and a white T-shirt. His feet are bare.

He looks beautiful. Tired but beautiful.

My beautiful, broken man.

He stands aside to let me in and closes the door once I'm inside.

"Can I get you something to drink?" he asks softly.

"Coffee would be great."

UNSUITABLE

Kas heads off to the kitchen. I take my shoes off and hang my coat up before following after him.

When I get there, he's making our coffees. I lean my hip against the center island, watching him move around the kitchen.

He walks toward me with a cup in each hand and hands one to me.

"Thanks." I smile.

"Do you want to sit in the lounge?" he asks.

"Sure."

I follow him through to the lounge in silence.

There's a clear discomfort between us, for obvious reasons. I just hope that I can clear that away and put us back on a good path. Hopefully, together.

Kas sits down on the two-seater at the far side of the room. He places himself in the center of the sofa.

I get the distinct impression that he doesn't want me sitting next to him. So, I take a seat on the sofa opposite him.

He leans forward. Elbows on knees, cup cradled in both hands, he looks at me.

Leaning over, I put my cup on the coffee table that sits between us.

"I'm sorry to just turn up," I start. "But I wanted to talk to you, and I didn't want to do it over the phone."

"It's fine." He reaches over and puts his cup down on the coffee table without taking a drink. "Look, Daisy, I know you came here to talk, but there's something I want to get off my chest first."

"Okay..." I say hesitantly, biting my lip.

"Well, this morning, I didn't get to say this, but I am sorry for turning up drunk at your place last night."

"Kas, it's fine." I offer a smile. "It was my turn to take care of drunk you anyway." I'm trying to lighten the mood, referring back to my drunken state when he took care of me, but it clearly doesn't work, as his expression remains stoic.

He pulls his eyes from my face and stares down at his hands, which are now clasped tightly together. "I also want to say that I'm sorry for leaving you at Superhumans. It was wrong of me to just abandon you like I did."

"You hardly abandoned me. And you were upset. It was understandable."

"That might be, but it doesn't make it okay."

"Kas, it's fine. Honestly, I was fine."

His eyes lift back to mine. "But you might not have been, and I know that better than anyone. I left you alone and crying on an industrial estate. I just fucking drove away and left you. Anything could've happened to you."

"But it didn't," I say softly. "I'm fine. I was at your building. Nothing was going to happen to me."

He nods, but I can see that he's not going to forgive himself for that. And I understand why he thinks the way he does. After what happened to him, I don't think I'd be able to leave the house, let alone allowing people I care about to move about the world alone.

"How did you get home?" he asks quietly.

"Cece came and picked me up."

"God." He laughs a humorless sound. "I bet she thinks I'm a real fucking winner. Stranding you alone on our date and then showing up drunk at your apartment."

I frown at his dressing-down of himself. "Cece doesn't think badly of you, Kas."

Black eyes flash to mine. I see the panic in them.

"She knows what happened to me?"

"No." I vehemently shake my head. "I might be a snoop, but I would never tell anyone else what you told me. It's your story to tell...not mine. All Cece knows is that I crossed a line, and I upset you."

He nods his head in acceptance of what I said.

UNSUITABLE

"Kas, can I ask…or should I assume that no one else here knows?"

He shakes his head. "After it happened and I was released from the hospital and came back home, it was…hard for me. My parents made the decision to move out of London and start fresh. My dad had a really good job; it paid him well. He and my mum were never big spenders, so they had a lot in savings. They sold the house in London, and it left them with a substantial amount of money. So, they bought this place. They wanted me to be somewhere I could feel safe…or where they wouldn't worry about my safety."

"Your parents sound really great." I give him a gentle smile.

"Yeah, they are. What happened affected them, too. My mother won't go into London anymore…" He trails off. "It's only been recently that they've started going over to Greece for extended periods of time without me. Even though they both call me every day to check in." Shaking his head, he laughs lightly.

"I'm glad you have them," I tell him.

He stares at me, and for a moment, I get lost in his gaze.

"So, um…I came here to talk…well, tell you some things." I shift to the edge of the sofa, curling my hands around the cushion. "Firstly, just to get it out of the way, I didn't come in to work today, as I thought you might need some time and space. And, honestly, I needed to process everything."

"I don't care about work, Daisy."

"Well, I do. And I want you to know, I'll make the time up this weekend."

Knowing what I have to say next, my mouth is suddenly very dry, so I pick my coffee up and take a sip.

He's still watching me when I put the cup down.

My heart starts to beat a hard tune in my chest. I hold my hands together in my lap. "But, work aside, that wasn't why I came to see you. I just wanted to tell you that...well, no, not tell you." *I'm rambling. Stop rambling, Daisy.* "I want you to *know* what you mean to me. And I, um...well..."

I'm twisting my hands in my lap. I lick my dry lips and take a fortifying breath.

"I...care about you." *I'm falling for you.* "And I wanted you to know that." *And, clearly, I'm too chickenshit to tell you that I'm falling for you.* "And I know I broke your trust, prying into your life like I did, and I am beyond sorry for that. And I just wanted you to know how much you mean to me...and that I want to be with you...more than anything."

He's not speaking. He's just staring at me, expressionless.

And my heart sinks. "Okay...well, I guess I should go." I shoot to my feet and start walking quickly to the door.

"Wait."

Stupid hope makes my heart pause.

I turn back to him. He's standing now.

"I don't want you to go," he whispers.

"You don't?"

"No."

My body trembles as I watch him slowly walk toward me.

My heart is trying its best to climb out of my throat.

I nervously swallow down.

Kas stops in front of me and cups my face in his hands.

His scent surrounds me. His breath blowing gently on my skin.

"Daisy...I haven't felt anything for a long time. I was dead inside. I guess, to a large degree, I still am. But that moment you came into my life, it was like...taking a breath for the first time in seven years." He presses his forehead to mine, closing his eyes. "I didn't want to feel anything for you, so I fought my feelings and pushed you away, but all the pushing and fighting didn't change the fact that I wanted you more than I'd ever wanted anyone." Looking at me, he inhales softly. "I...I care about you, too. I don't want to lose you."

"I'm here, and I'm not going anywhere."

I press my hands to his chest, and he inhales sharply. Almost like my touch has burned him. And I know how he feels because my whole body is burning for him.

"It's selfish, and I know I don't deserve you...but I want you so fucking much."

"Kas..." I whisper, closing my eyes. "I want you, too. So much."

He takes a shallow breath. I feel his face leave mine.

I blink open my eyes and stare up at him. The look in his eyes causes me to pause. My pulse starts to thrum.

"There's something you need to know."

"Okay..." I say, my voice betraying my nerves.

"Daisy, after what happened that night...I wasn't able to..." His eyes slide away from mine. Looking past me, he takes a deep breath. "I haven't been with a woman in over seven years."

Oh. Wow.

"Haley was the last person I..." He lets his words drift. "After that night, what they did to Haley...what I saw...it haunted me. I was screwed up for a long time. And I had issues...with the scarring on my body. I still do. But, as the years have gone on and with the help of therapy...well, for a few years now, it's not that I don't want to have sex. It's more that I've wanted it to be with someone who mattered, and no one has mattered...until you."

I matter.

My heart fills with joy.

Moving a hand from his chest, I press it to his cheek. I stare into his eyes. "We don't have to have sex, Kas. We can take this as slow as you need to. So long as we're together, that's all I care about."

His dark eyes bore into mine. "But that's just it. I don't want to wait anymore. I've already waited so fucking long for you, Daisy. I want you now—tonight." He pulls me closer, gently brushing his lips over mine. "Spend the night with me."

THIRTY-ONE

"Yes."

It's one simple word, but saying it means everything is about to change between Kas and me.

And it's what I want. More than anything.

But sex has always been a big thing for me. I've never been the type to sleep around, and I haven't slept with many people. Two, to be exact.

And, obviously, sex is a big deal for Kas, which makes it a bigger deal for me.

He hasn't had sex in seven years, and the last person he slept with was Haley. I'm close to two years with no sex.

Christ, it's like we're both virgins.

No pressure there then.

Nerves twist in my stomach. But they're quickly erased when Kas smiles against my lips before kissing me harder, his tongue gliding over my lips, seeking entrance. I part my lips, letting him in, and his tongue sweeps over mine, making me shiver.

His large hands go to my bum. Cupping it, he lifts me, like I weigh nothing. I like the way that makes me feel. I wrap my legs around his waist and my arms around his neck.

He kisses a path over my cheek. "I want you in my bed," he whispers in my ear.

"Yes."

Then, we're moving. He's carrying me from the lounge to his bedroom upstairs.

It's dark when we enter his bedroom. He gently puts me to my feet in the middle of his room, and he walks over and turns on the lamp on his nightstand. It illuminates a soft glow around the room.

His eyes don't leave mine as he walks toward me.

My body starts to tremble with nerves and need.

Reaching me, he takes my face in his hands and stares down at me. "I've never wanted anyone the way I want you, Daisy."

An involuntary shiver runs through me. I know he feels it because his mouth kicks up at the corner.

He runs his thumb over my lips, his eyes following the movement. Then, he puts his mouth where his thumb just was and kisses me.

It's deep and wet and dirty, and it is the hottest kiss I've ever had in my life.

My hands wind into his hair as his hands roam my body, like he doesn't know which part of me to touch first.

His blatant need for me makes me feel sexy and confident.

Breaking from our kiss, I step back from him.

Lustful, hazy eyes stare back at me.

Lifting the hem of my top, I pull it over my head, leaving me in my white bra. Not very sexy, but then I wasn't expecting to have sex tonight.

Heat flares in those dark eyes of his. So clearly, he appreciates the sight. But he doesn't make a move to touch me.

He's turned on though. His erection is visible behind the thin material of his pants.

That bolsters my confidence to keep going.

Bringing my eyes back to his face, I drag my teeth over my lip. Then, I unbutton my jeans and pull the zipper down. The sound is loud in our breathy silence. I hook my thumbs into the waistband and shimmy them down over my hips until they hit the floor.

And then I'm standing before him in just my bra and knickers.

My body is vibrating with excitement and nerves.

From the exercise I do, I know I'm physically in good shape, but that doesn't stop me from feeling trepidation over what Kas thinks about me…about my body.

I kick my jeans aside and glance down.

Oh dear God.

I'm wearing my Minnie Mouse knickers. I literally have Minnie covering my mini.

I thought it was funny when I bought them. Not feeling so funny now.

"Oh God," I groan. "Ignore the knickers. So not sexy."

"You're wearing knickers?" He steps closer. "I didn't notice. All I can see is you."

"Smooth." I tip my head back.

"Yeah, but I meant every fucking word. You are all I see."

He tugs me into his arms, and his lips come down on mine.

I melt into his kiss. Wrapping my arms around him, I curl my fingers into the fabric of his T-shirt, now very aware of the fact that I'm almost naked and he's fully clothed.

I know he said he has issues with the scarring on his body, and his prior behavior when I tried to touch his body or remove his T-shirt makes an awful lot more sense now.

I don't want to push him on it, but I also want his skin on mine, and he kind of has to be naked for us to be able to actually have sex.

So, I decide the best course of action is not to try to remove his clothes but to ask.

"I want to see you," I say against his lips.

He freezes, so I move my head back a touch, staring into his eyes. I can see a hint of panic in his.

"I want to feel your skin against mine, Kas. I want to feel you."

He holds my stare, and then he seems to make a decision. He steps back from me.

I see his throat work nervously, and I feel bad for him.

"Just pants, if that's easier? You can keep the shirt on."

"No." The fierce tone in his voice surprises me.

Then, I watch as he reaches back with his hand and pulls his shirt over his head.

He stops, holding it against his chest, his arms still through the armholes.

I can see he's visibly trembling, so I stare him in the eye. "You don't have to do this, if you're not ready," I whisper.

His infinite pools of blackness stare back at me. I see the determination rise in them. Then, he's pulling his T-shirt the rest of the way off, and he drops it to the floor.

My eyes move over him. "You're beautiful, Kas."

And he is.

Yes, there's extensive scarring on his body. The remnants of that night. But I don't see the scars. I only see the man I love. The beautiful golden skin that covers his body, the ripple of muscles that lead down to his very lickable-looking V with the happy trail that disappears into his pants.

He works out, and it shows on his body. In his shoulders and arms...dear God, don't get me started. But I'll tell you this...my tongue plans on spending a lot of time getting acquainted with those veins that run through his strong forearms.

I lift my eyes back to his, and the emotion in them nearly slays me.

"Can I touch you?" I ask softly.

UNSUITABLE

I watch his Adam's apple bob up and down as he swallows roughly. He slightly nods his head.

I step forward, lifting my hand. I press my fingertips to his chest.

He sucks in a breath.

His skin is hot to the touch. I run my fingertips over his chest, over the scars and the unmarked skin, tracing down to his six-pack.

"Beautiful," I whisper. I stare up into his eyes.

Something breaks and then roars to life in his gaze.

He grabs my head between his hands and slams his mouth down on mine, kissing me—no, devouring me—and I willingly let him take me.

Because I'm his.

And he is mine.

I slide my hands up his arms and to his shoulders. I hold him, my nails digging into his skin, needing more of him...all of him.

His erection is pressed up against my stomach, and it's a tease. I want to see him...*feel* him.

Lowering a hand between us, I tug on the waistband of his lounge pants. "Pants, too," I breathe against his lips.

A low chuckle escapes his lips, and the sound thrills me.

"Bossy," he murmurs.

"Get used to it." I smile.

His hands leave my head and remove his lounge pants.

It's in this moment that I discover that Kas doesn't wear boxer shorts.

"Oh...wow," I whisper, swallowing nervously.

I've known average. But never big.

Kas is big.

His hot gaze meets mine. I see the spark of a grin in his eyes.

Then, he glances down at his impressively sized cock. "Acceptable for you?"

I nearly swallow my tongue at his blatant words. "Mmhmm," I squeak.

His mouth smiles, and he chuckles. But, very quickly, that laugh disappears when I take my bra off.

"Acceptable?" I dip my chin down at my cleavage, playing him at his own game.

I see his throat work on a swallow.

"Yeah, you could say that." His words come out on a breath, his voice lined with gravel.

It makes me laugh.

That laughter quickly disappears when Kas moves so quickly that he startles me. He picks me up and tosses me onto his bed.

He climbs up onto the bed and kneels between my parted legs. I rest up onto my elbows and stare up at him.

He's magnificent. Like a god.

He reaches forward and hooks his fingers into my knickers.

I might not deserve him, but I get to have him. And, selfishly, I'm keeping him.

I lean back, lifting my hips, giving him better purchase to remove my undies.

I watch, nerves swimming in my stomach, as he slowly pulls my knickers down my legs.

His eyes are ablaze and fixed solely on the spot between my legs. He tosses my knickers to the floor, never once looking away from me.

His eyes graze up my stomach, over my breasts, and finally rest on my face. "You're so fucking beautiful. I don't deserve you, Daisy."

His words grip a tight hold of my heart.

"Yes, you do." My words come out gravelly with emotion.

Leaning forward, he plants his hands on the bed, surrounding either side of my hips, and he presses a kiss to my stomach. My hands go on his head, fingers sliding into his hair. He licks and kisses and nibbles a path upward until he reaches my breasts. He rests his chin between the valley of my breasts and looks at me.

I bite my lip, my chest heaving with excitement.

His lips lift at the corner. Then, he cups a hand around my breast and takes my nipple into his mouth.

"Oh God." A bolt of lust shoots between my legs, and my hips buck up off the bed, needing contact with him, my clit throbbing with need.

His hand comes off my breast and slides downward between my legs.

With my nipple still in his mouth, his eyes lift to mine. Dark and dangerous and so full of want for me.

It makes my stomach flip.

His fingers slip between me, running over my clit. I'm crazy wet, and I'm not even embarrassed about it. I want him to know what he does to me. How much I want him.

His eyes flare at the feel of me. He releases my nipple from his mouth. "You're soaked," he rasps out.

My mouth kicks up. "Well, you're kinda hot, and you turn me on."

A deep chuckle rumbles in his chest. "Right back at ya, babe."

Then, he slips a finger inside me, and all humor between us is gone.

"You're so hot and tight." His voice sounds ravaged with need.

"Kas…" I whimper, my nails digging into his arm.

Reading what I need, he starts to move his finger in and out, moving faster, fucking me with it. His thumb presses down on my clit, rubbing in circles over it. He licks his tongue over my nipple before sucking it back into his mouth, hollowing out his cheeks.

I'm writhing and panting, needing this and him and more, so much more.

Then, he's leaving my breast and kissing his way down my body, shifting lower. His finger lodged inside me, he stills it and puts his mouth on me. His tongue sweeps over my clit, and I cry out.

My legs widen shamelessly. My fingers glide into his hair again, and I push the strands behind his ears.

His eyes momentarily lift to mine, and the look in them almost brings the orgasm out of me. I've never seen such a look of pure need and desire and want.

He licks and sucks on my clit, and he starts fucking me with his finger again, driving me higher and higher.

I'm clawing at the duvet, my toes curled in, my eyes closing, as I move my hips in rhythm with his tongue, and then…

"I'm coming!" I cry out, my hips lifting off the bed.

Kas pins me down with his hands, his tongue mercilessly licking at my clit, until I'm wrung dry and begging for him to stop because I can't take any more.

I blink my heavy eyes open, seeing Kas lift up from me. He pushes himself upright and rocks back onto his heels.

His mouth glistens with me. Eyes still on me, he runs his tongue over his lips before pressing the back of his hand to his mouth.

It's the hottest thing I've ever seen. He's the hottest thing I've ever seen.

He looks so commanding up there, staring down at me with lust-filled black eyes.

"You taste better than I imagined," he tells me in a gravelly voice.

"You imagined this?"

"Every damn night since the first day you stepped through my front door."

"Well, you don't need to imagine anymore. You can have me. I'm yours."

UNSUITABLE

I expect him to smile, but he doesn't. His eyes just stay pinned to mine as his hand goes to his cock, and he starts stroking over it.

Okay, I take back what I said before. *This* is the hottest thing I've ever seen.

He slowly jacks his hand up and down his cock, and I'm riveted.

I swallow roughly. "Is this what you did while imagining?"

"Yes."

"And, in your imagination, what were you doing to me?"

"Fucking you hard while you screamed my name."

Holy shit.

I think I just came again.

I love this side of him—confident and commanding. I wasn't sure how things were going to be, but holy hell, Kas is full of surprises. Sexual surprises.

And I'm a lucky, lucky, girl.

Shivers erupt all over my skin, standing my hairs on end.

I drag my eyes up to his face and give him a cocky grin. "So, why are you all the way over there when you could be here"—I place my hand over myself—"fucking me hard and making me scream your name?"

I see his eyes flash, and then he's on top of me. He grabs my hands and pins them over my head. His mouth is on mine, his erection pressed between my legs. I sigh against his lips.

This is what heaven feels like.

A sexy heaven. And a heaven I really want to be in. Or have his heaven inside me.

Jesus, Daisy, could you be any cornier right now?

His kisses are hot and dirty, and he's practically fucking my mouth with his tongue.

Lifting my hips, I press myself against his cock, wanting his cock to be fucking me. At the angle, his cock slides between the lips of my pussy.

"Fuck," he chokes out. "I can't wait any longer. I need to be inside you."

I press my hand to his cheek. "I don't want you to wait. I need you, baby."

His eyes flare at my endearment. Then, he's moving away, off of me.

"Where are you going?" I stop him with my hand on his arm.

"Just getting a condom."

"You have some?" I lift a brow.

His cheeks redden. "I bought some when you and I…" He meets my gaze head-on. "I wasn't being presumptuous. Just…hopeful."

His lips lift into a boyish grin, and I giggle.

Then, I hesitate, biting my lip. "I have the contraceptive implant. I had it done two years ago. It lasts for three years in total. I haven't had sex for nearly two years. I'm clean. I'd used condoms before, but after, I got checked. So, you don't have to use one, if you don't want to. But I understand if you do."

His gaze softens on me.

"I trust you." He brushes his lips over mine. "And I'm clean, as you've probably guessed."

"So, we're going to—"

"Yeah, baby, we are."

He moves his hand between our bodies and lines his cock up with my entrance, pushing against me. Then, he takes ahold of my hands, fingers linking with mine, pressing them into the pillow. Our eyes locked, he applies more pressure and slowly starts to push inside me.

"Oh God," I breathe as he stretches and fills me.

His features are stretched, tightening, and his jaw is clenched so hard that it might shatter.

UNSUITABLE

Then, when he's all the way inside to the hilt, he pauses. He squeezes his eyes shut, like he's in pain, and I worry that this is too hard for him, that bad memories are invading and taking over. He brings his face down and rests his forehead against mine, breathing deeply.

I need him to move so badly, but I need him to be okay more.

I squeeze my fingers around his. "Kas," I breathe.

His eyes open. I search his gaze, looking for anything to tell me that he's okay.

"I'm not going to last. It's been too long, and you feel too fucking good. I daren't move."

I laugh with relief.

His brows draw together.

And I'm quick to say, "I'm not laughing because of that. I'm relieved. I thought that maybe you were…struggling…" I allude.

Understanding flashes through his eyes. "I'm struggling not to come because you're so fucking amazing."

My smile widens. "I want you—whether it's for two seconds—"

"I can last longer than two seconds," he growls. "Give me some fucking credit."

"You know what I meant. And stop arguing with me when you're inside me." I lift my face to his, softly pressing my lips over his. "Just move, Kas. Be with me, for however long that is. Then, be with me again. And again. I'm here. I'm not going anywhere."

He stares down at me, emotion lining his eyes, lust filling them.

"Fuck me, Kas," I whisper.

Those words seem to push him over the edge because he's moving, pulling out to the hilt and slamming back in. Quick, short thrusts, getting faster and more intense. His hands grip mine to the point of almost pain.

"Daisy...I...Jesus...I...you wreck me. It's you...it will only ever be you."

Emotion clamps down hard on my chest. "You wreck me, too," I whisper.

One of his hands leaves mine and cups my bum, lifting and tilting me. He starts to move with wild abandon, thrusting in and out of me. Fucking me. Taking what he needs.

"Jesus, Daisy...fuck...I'm coming..." His mouth crashes back to mine. "I'm coming," he breathes into me, his hips coming to rest against mine, jerking, as he comes inside me.

THIRTY-TWO

KAS STAYS INSIDE ME, his body trembling against mine. I run my hand over his back, tracing lazy patterns with my fingers, as he breathes heavily against my neck.

He lifts his head, looking me in the eyes.

"You okay?" I whisper.

He smiles, and I feel that smile everywhere.

"More than okay." He presses a sweet kiss to my lips. "Are you okay? I didn't hurt you, did I?"

"No. I'll probably be a little sore, as it's been a while, but it was totally worth it." I press my hand to his cheek.

Taking ahold of my hand, he turns his face in and kisses my palm. "It was…amazing." When he brings his eyes back to mine, the look in them is reverent.

"You sure?"

"Are you unsure?" he challenges, teasing in his eyes.

"No. I just…you haven't since…" I trail off, leaving the words I don't want to say hanging. "And I haven't in two years, and I was never exactly a porn star in bed before that."

Laughter bursts from him.

Even though I love the sound, it's pissing me off right now.

"Hey!" I slap him on the arm.

"Sorry." He gives me a sober laugh.

Then, he brushes his lips over mine. I keep them stubbornly closed for about two seconds before caving and kissing him back.

"This…you and me, together…is incredible. I've never known anything like what I just felt with you."

I want to ask, *Not even with Haley?*

But I don't want to bring her up and kill the mood, so I say nothing.

He must read something in my eyes because he says, "Haley and I were just kids. Sure, she wasn't my first. I'd lost my virginity when I was fourteen with a girl who was a few years older than me, and I'd slept with a few girls that year before Haley and I got together. So, yeah, I had a little experience, but we were still young and didn't have a clue what we were doing. I still don't. And I should be the one worrying if I was good enough for you. I've never been in bed with a woman before you, Daisy." His hand caresses my hip.

"Trust me"—I lift my head and brush my lips over his—"you definitely know what you're doing."

"I guess all those years of watching porn have finally paid off."

It's my turn to have laughter burst from me.

Kas wraps his arms around me and kisses me. "Let me just go clean up, and I'll be back." He brushes his nose over mine before kissing the tip of it, and then he pulls out of me.

I wince a little at the soreness, but I hate the loss of him inside me more.

"Could you bring me a cloth to clean up?" I ask.

"Sure."

I watch him walk to the bathroom and sigh. *He has a great butt. Really tight and firm. And those shoulders…drool.*

Kas disappears inside. I hear running water. He's not gone for long before he's coming back with a washcloth in his hand.

UNSUITABLE

I reach to take it from him, but he moves his hand away.

"Let me." He presses the warm, damp cloth between my legs, gently cleaning me.

I watch him, amazed at the depths of my feelings for this man I referred to as Kas-hole.

"The first time I met you...I never thought we'd be here."

He stops cleaning me and looks at me with tender eyes. "I'm glad we are."

"Yeah, me, too," I whisper as my heart bumps clumsily around in my chest.

"All clean?" He checks.

I nod.

He takes the cloth back to the bathroom. I climb in under the duvet. Kas returns and climbs into bed beside me. He wraps me in his arms, so we're face-to-face.

He softly kisses me. I press my hand to his chest, touching his scars. I feel him tense.

"I don't see them," I whisper. "I don't look at you and those scars independently. I just see you."

"I see them," he murmurs. "And I hate them."

I slide my hand over his chest and around to his back. "Can I ask you something?"

"Sure," he says, but his eyes don't look sure.

But I have to ask, so I take a breath and start talking, "I mean, I think I understand why you didn't want me to see the scars. Because of the way they make you feel about yourself, and you hate them. But then I remembered that day when I walked in on you and Jude sparring. Your back was to me, and you didn't have a shirt on that day. You went and put one on before I saw anything, but obviously, you had been shirtless around Jude. So, why do you feel okay with him seeing them?"

His eyes close briefly before reopening. "Well, I didn't want to have sex with Jude, for starters." He gives me a slight smile. "And Jude knows everything that happened. He's the only other person who does—aside from my parents and, of course, you."

"How long have you known him?"

"We met at group therapy when we were eighteen. I was seeing a therapist, but he also ran a group session for people who were suffering with various types of PTSD. He thought it would be good for me to join his group. Jude was also a patient at the group session. We got to talking and just clicked. He was the one who got me into parkour."

"What about MMA?"

"That was me. I wanted to be able to"—his eyes skim away from me—"defend myself and the people I care about. Jude came along with me and found that he liked it, too."

"You're a team." I smile softly.

"Yeah." His eyes find mine again. "He's a good friend."

I don't ask why Jude was in therapy because it's none of my business. I'm just glad that Kas has him in his life.

He's silent for a moment, and then he says in a quiet voice, "I was afraid…for you to see me. I thought, if you saw the real me…then you wouldn't want me."

I press my hand to his face. "I really like the *real* you. It was Kas-hole that I wasn't so keen on."

He gives me a look of shock. I fight to hold back my laughter.

The next thing I know, I'm flat on my back, and Kas is between my legs with his hands on my stomach, tickling me.

"No! Stop!" I squeal, trying but failing to wriggle out of his hold. "I'm really ticklish!" I gasp.

"Yeah, I can see that."

He tickles me again, and I scream.

"Stop!" I'm panting for air because I'm laughing so hard.

UNSUITABLE

And he's laughing. The sound is beautiful, and it's weaving itself around my thudding heart.

"I'm sorry!"

He pauses and looks up at me.

"I said, I'm sorry," I pant.

"For?" He hovers a threatening hand over my stomach.

"For calling you Kas-hole." I can't help but grin when I say the name.

His smile mirrors mine. "You're not really sorry, are you?"

Pressing my lips together, sealing my smile, I shake my head.

His eyes glitter with mischief.

In a flash, my arms are pinned at my sides, and his mouth is on my stomach.

Then, the bastard blows a raspberry.

"Argh!" I scream with laughter. "I'm sorry! I'll never call you Kas-hole again!"

But, as soon as I say the name, the raspberry assault gets worse.

"Stop! I'll pee myself!" I laugh, tears in my eyes.

I'm wriggling, trying to get free, but he's so bloody strong.

"Okay!" I gasp. "I yield! I'll never say the *K-hole* word again, I swear!"

He stops and lifts his head. "You yield?"

Something dark and dirty flashes in his eyes, making my belly flip. And that's when I feel something long and hard pressing up against my leg.

He's hard for me again.

"I yield," I whisper breathily.

"So, that means you're mine to do what I want with."

I hold his eyes. Biting my lip, I nod my head.

He grazes his teeth over his lower lip. I shift restlessly.

"What do you want to do with me?" I ask on a hot whisper.

He moves lower, keeping my hands pinned by my sides, and he doesn't answer with words. He answers by means of his tongue, pressing it against me, making me cry out in pleasure.

THIRTY-THREE

I CAN HEAR BUZZING. For a moment, I think I'm back in prison, hearing the morning buzz that came right before my cell door would open, giving me that momentary freedom. The buzzing stops, but the click never comes.

And then I register the warm, hard body pressed against my back.

Kas.

Memories of last night flood my mind.

We had sex. Lots of sex. Insatiable, crazy, hot sex until we passed out in each other's arms.

And, now, I'm here with his chest pressed up against my back. His legs tangled with mine. His arm slung around my waist. His hand possessively pressed against my stomach.

A smile lifts my lips. Happiness that I never thought I would ever feel spreads through me.

Then, I hear the buzzing again.

What is that?

Reluctantly, I move, turning in Kas's arms, rousing him slightly. He lets out a sleepy groan as he rolls onto his back, pulling his arm from me.

I see his phone flashing and vibrating on the nightstand. I peer over a little further to see who's calling. The display reads, *Gate.*

Gate?

It takes me a good few seconds to realize that it's not someone called *Gate*, but that it's actually someone buzzing at the main gates of the house.

Duh.

Instead of waking him, I decide to answer the call. I reach over and sweep up his phone. Pressing Accept, I say, "Hello?"

"Daisy, is that you? It's Toby. I'm here for our appointment."

Uh…Toby? Appointment!

Holy shit!

He rescheduled our appointment last week because he couldn't make our usual day.

My probation officer is here. And I'm naked and in bed with Kas.

I'm so done for.

"Yes." The word comes out sounding strangled. I clear my throat. "I'll-I'll buzz you in. Just give me a sex—I mean, sec! Give me a second." I hang up the phone. "Kas!" I shake him.

His eyes flick open, startled and wide-awake. "Wha—"

"Toby is here for my appointment."

He's blinking rapidly, as though trying to process this information. I try not to get caught up on how adorable he looks in this moment with his hair all disheveled and this cute furrow of confusion on his brow.

I somehow don't think Kas would appreciate being called adorable.

"My probation officer," I say to speed up the process even though he knows who Toby is.

"I thought he came on—"

"He does normally," I cut him off. "But he changed the day, and I forgot! Crap! We're naked, and he's out there."

Kas's eyes flash to the closed door of his bedroom, as though he expects Toby to be waiting on the other side.

UNSUITABLE

"Outside the main gate," I clarify.

He pushes himself up to sit. "Have you let him in?"

I find myself momentarily distracted by his bare chest and the muscles rippling over his pecs.

God, he's hot.

"Daisy?"

"Mmhmm?"

"Have you buzzed him in?"

My eyes lift to his grinning ones. "Um…shit, no." I blink. "Your phone was vibrating, and when I saw it was the gate, I answered. I need to go downstairs and buzz him in."

"No need." Kas takes his phone from my hand. He swipes the screen and then does something. "Gates are open," he tells me.

"You let him in? But I'm naked!" I jump out of bed.

A low chuckle rumbles from him. "I can see that."

I flush as his eyes slowly move over the length of me, making me blush.

"Stop it." I can't help the smile that forms on my mouth.

Kas's lips tip up into a sexy grin. "I'm not doing anything. *Yet*."

He reaches out and trails his index finger up my thigh, making me shiver.

I swat his hand away. "Behave. I have to get dressed. He'll be at the front door in less than five minutes."

He gives me a disgruntled look, which I choose to ignore.

I start running around, picking up my clothes and pulling on my underwear.

Kas is just sitting in bed, watching me, hands behind his head, like he doesn't have a care in the world.

But then I guess he doesn't. It's not his probation officer who's currently walking down the driveway and toward the front door.

Clothes on, I run into his bathroom.

Jesus, I have sex hair! It's all mussed up.

I run my hands through it, trying to smooth it down. When I spy one of Kas's hair ties on the sink, I borrow it and fasten my hair up into a messy bun.

I grab his toothpaste, squeeze some onto my index finger, and rub it over my teeth. Not the best way to clean my teeth but needs must.

"You could have used my toothbrush." Kas comes up behind me, pressing his still very naked body against mine. His hands slide around my stomach.

Leaning forward, I spit in the sink, pushing my bum back against him. I feel him press up nice and hard against me, and my lady parts wake up to say hello.

Down, girl. My probation officer is on his way.

I grab the mouthwash and take a swig. I swish it around my mouth and spit it out. Finally, I respond to him, "I'm not going to use your toothbrush." I run the tap, clearing the sink out.

"Why not?"

Meeting his eyes in the mirror, I say, "Um, because that'd be gross."

"You've had this mouth"—he points a finger to his sexy and incredibly talented mouth—"and tongue"—he sticks it out, making me shiver—"on and inside your pussy, tasting you and making you come, for the best part of the night. You've had my cock in your gorgeous mouth. But using my toothbrush would be gross? Sure, that makes sense, babe." He cocks a brow.

Holy Jesus.

I'm practically on fire. Burning up, I'm ready to drop to my knees and take him back in my suddenly watering mouth.

"Toothbrushes clean teeth." My voice catches, and I clear my throat. "Tongues—"

UNSUITABLE

"Lick," he whispers. He gives me a good demonstration of what that magical tongue of his can do when he runs it over the pulse on my neck, sending my nerve endings screaming and making my knickers wet. Then, his teeth start to nip at my neck.

"Kas," I say, but it comes out more like a moan. "We can't…"

"He can wait. I can't. I want you now." One arm tightens around me while his other hand finds my face and turns it to the side. He kisses me. Lush and wet and deep.

I start to fall into him and the moment. He's so goddamn addictive. I can't get enough.

Okay, maybe Toby can wait.

His hand slides down my stomach and to the button on my jeans.

That's when the piercing sound of the doorbell breaks the moment.

He sighs into my mouth.

I tip my head back. "Rain check?"

He rumbles out a sound of assent. Then, he releases me.

His hand swats my bum on the way out. I flash him a grin over my shoulder.

Then, I bolt down the stairs to answer the door. I swing it open. "Hey. Sorry. I was upstairs…cleaning…the toilet."

Cleaning the toilet? Why couldn't I have said I was cleaning the bath or shower? I guess the saving grace is that I didn't say I was just cleaning the inside of Kas's mouth with my tongue.

"Hi, Daisy." Toby smiles at me.

Returning his smile, I step aside, letting him in. I close the door behind us.

I lead the way to the kitchen where we usually have our appointment.

"Coffee?" I ask.

Toby takes his usual seat at the kitchen table. "Please."

I set about making coffee, wondering if Kas will want some.

He'll probably come down. But he might be showering right now.

Wet Kas. Naked, wet Kas.

And, now, my mind is running wild with a naked Kas and all the things we did last night and all the things he did to me.

I can feel my skin start to burn up.

Stop thinking sex thoughts about Kas, or Toby will notice that something is off.

"So, how is everything?" Toby asks me.

"Great!" The word squeaks out, so I go for a quick subject change. "Biscuits?" I ask him.

"You know me"—he chuckles—"can't say no to a biscuit."

Yeah, just like I can't say no to a very hot Greek man upstairs. Not that I'd ever want to say no to Kas. God, the things that man can do with his tongue.

As if conjuring him up, he appears in the kitchen. Barefoot, wearing light-blue jeans and a gray V-neck sweater, his hair damp from the shower. He looks seriously hot.

"Good morning, Kas." Toby smiles at him.

"Morning." The deep timbre of his voice ripples through me.

This man was inside me only hours ago.

Jesus.

I grab the biscuits tin and carry it over to the table, trying to avoid all eye contact with Kas. I'm fairly sure that, if I look at him, I'll give the game away, and Toby will know that we've had sex.

"No uniform today?" Toby says as I put the biscuit tin on the table.

"Um, what?" I glance down at my clothes.

Fuckity fucking shit.

UNSUITABLE

I have on the jeans and top I came in last night. I always have my uniform on when Toby sees me.

Oh God.

"Casual Friday," I blurt out.

Casual Friday? What the hell, Daisy? I'm a maid. Do maids even have casual Fridays?

"Casual Friday?" Toby echoes.

"The staff all put in a little money to wear casual clothes today, and we're donating the money to charity," Kas says calmly.

My eyes flick to his. I see the grin in them. I quickly look back at Toby.

"Sounds like a great idea. Which charity?" Toby asks me.

My mouth goes dry.

"RSPCA," Kas answers for me.

"We've never done that in my office. I'm going to suggest it at the next meeting." Toby smiles, looking suitably happy with himself. He opens the biscuit tin and helps himself to one.

I turn, catching Kas's eyes, which are still grinning at me but filled with heat, too. So much heat.

Crap.

Looking away, I nervously swallow down.

"Coffee?" I ask Kas as I move across the kitchen, heading back to the coffee machine.

"Sure," he answers, his voice molten.

I grab three cups from the cupboard.

"So, how is everything with you, Kas?" Toby asks him.

"Good."

"Business going well?"

"Yep. Daisy?"

I pause what I'm doing and glance back at him over my shoulder.

His face is impassive, but memories of last night are clear in his eyes. My stomach flips.

"Bring my coffee to me in my office."

If you didn't know him as well as I do, then you'd miss the suggestive curl of his lip and the sexual intent in his voice. But I do know him, and I know why he's telling me to come to his office.

Heat surfaces in my face and my lady parts. "Okay." I swallow.

I don't watch him leave the kitchen because I'm too busy trying to control my raging hormones.

Somehow keeping composure, I finish making the coffees and carry them over to the table. I put Toby's cup down in front of him.

"I'll just take this to Kas." I lift Kas's coffee cup in gesture.

Toby lifts his eyes from the papers in front of him, and then he smiles and nods.

Seeing my case notes laid out on the table reminds me why I'm here.

I'm not here because I'm Kas's girlfriend. Well, I'm not actually his girlfriend.

Look at me, getting ahead of myself. We've had one failed date and sex.

But, ultimately, I'm his employee, and I'm here because my probation deems it so.

Excitement dampened, I head to Kas's office, coffee in hand. Reaching his closed office door, I knock.

I haven't been in his office since he barred me from here, which was also the first time we ever kissed.

God, that feels like forever ago.

The memory of that kiss tingles through me, lighting me up, and so does the sound of his deep timbre when he tells me to come in. I open the door before shutting it behind me.

Kas is sitting in his chair behind his desk.

"Your coffee, sir." I grin as I walk over to his desk and place the steaming cup down in front of him. "Is that all?

UNSUITABLE

Or do you need anything else from me?" My tone comes out sounding seductive even though I didn't mean it to. Or maybe I did.

"There is something else I need." He pushes to his feet and rounds the desk, heading for me.

Heat unfurls in my belly at his approach.

Curling his hand around the nape of my neck, he hauls me in for a kiss. His tongue runs along mine, and he hums a delicious sound in his mouth that sends shivers right down to my toes.

He tastes of mint and something so seductively him.

Kas's kisses always send my body haywire, but being in here, with him, knowing that Toby is just down the hall in the kitchen, makes it feel naughty and dangerous, and it heats me up even more.

God, I want him right now.

Guess this girl likes her men with a side of danger.

My hands move over his broad chest, feeling the firm ridges. Going around to his back, I clutch on to him.

His free arm bands around my back, pulling me closer to him. He turns, so he's leaning up against his desk, and I'm pressed up against all of his delicious hotness.

His kisses move from my mouth to my jaw until his mouth is on my ear. "The second Toby's gone, I want you to go straight upstairs, take off all your clothes, and wait for me on my bed."

Holy…shiver.

"Is that an order?" My voice is hoarse with excitement. *But, seriously, who wouldn't be excited after hearing that?*

He kisses my jaw, and his teeth graze over my skin, making me shudder. "Do you want it to be?"

Hell yes. I tip my head back and stare into his lust-fogged eyes. "Only if it results in me coming."

"Multiple times," he promises.

"Then, yes, please."

He growls. He actually growls, and then he's kissing me again, devouring my mouth, and it's hot as fuck.

But I'm also aware that time is ticking by, and Toby is in the other room.

I break from the kiss. "I have to go."

I try to step away, but Kas keeps me there.

"Sooner I'm done with Toby, the sooner I'll be upstairs, waiting on your bed—*naked*," I whisper that last word.

His hand slips from around my neck and cups my chin. He firmly presses his lips to mine, gently sucking on my lower lip. "You drive me crazy," he murmurs.

I take that as a good thing because he wraps his arms around me, holding me tight.

I love it when he hugs me.

I inch up onto my toes and rest my chin on his shoulder, and something very hard pokes me in the stomach. I giggle.

"What?" His questioning voice is a rumble.

I push my belly against his erection, and he chuckles deep and low.

"If it helps, my knickers are completely soaked."

He groans. "No, that doesn't fucking help at all."

I laugh. "Sorry." I press a kiss to the skin at the base of his neck.

As I lift my head, I notice something. "Hey, where's the door gone?"

I feel Kas's body instantly lock up beneath me, his whole demeanor changing. Gone is the warmth, and I feel a chill emit from him that I can't explain.

But that chill has me moving away from him.

When I look at his face, it's blank.

"What door?" His voice is as empty as his expression.

"The door that was there." I point over his shoulder to the place where the door used to be, but now, it is a full wall-to-ceiling bookcase.

UNSUITABLE

Curling his hands around the edge of his desk, he says, "There was never a door there."

"Um..." I let out an unsure laugh. "Are you kidding right now?"

"Babe, no, I'm not kidding. Honestly, I'm not sure what you're talking about."

I rub my head. "The door." I point at the spot again. "It was right there, where that bookcase is. We had an argument about that door. Well, kind of. I came in here to leave you coffee and muffins, and you were coming in through that door." I point at it again. "You tore me a new one about coming in your office. I asked if I should clean that room. You bit my head off again, telling me no. It was also the first day we kissed."

The look on his face is like he thinks I've lost my mind.
Have I?
No, there was definitely a door there.

"I don't know what to tell you, babe, but there's never been a door there. It's always been a bookcase."

"I..." I rub my head, confused.

He reaches out, pulling me back to him, and he softly brushes his lips over mine. "Maybe you're confusing it with something else. The library maybe."

No.

I want to argue that I'm not confusing it with the library. I remember that day clearly because it's the day he kissed me.

Okay, the shitty before and after weren't great, but it was the first time he kissed me, and I will always remember it.

I might not be the smartest person in the room, but I have a good memory. I remember details. Usually because I like to relay them back to Cece. But whatever. I specifically remember the disagreement Kas and I had, his reaction to my asking about the room behind that door, him banning me from his office, and then seeing him lock the door with a key.

There was a goddamn door there, not a fucking bookcase.

But I'm not going to argue with him because sense tells me that he'll keep lying, and I've got Toby waiting for me in the kitchen.

"Yeah, you're probably right." I press my hand to his chest before stepping back. "I should go. Toby's waiting."

His eyes stay trained on me. I try to read them, but as usual, I get nothing.

I hate that I can never get a read on what's going on in his head. He can so easily school his features and hide whatever lies behind his eyes.

Well, he can hide whatever he likes. But I do know for a fact that he just flat-out lied to me, and I don't like that one bit.

The realization that Kas has just lied to me hits me, and my stomach sinks.

"Hey, you okay?" He smiles. It's a gleaming smile, but something about it feels off.

Everything about this moment feels off.

Oh, how quickly things can change. I was happy a moment ago, and now, I'm trying to figure out why the man I'm crazy about is lying to me—over a door, of all things.

"Of course." I give him a manufactured smile. "See you upstairs in an hour." I pivot on my toes and walk out of his office with a bounce in my step, so he won't know anything is off with me.

The second I shut his office door behind me, my smile drops from my face, and that sinking feeling in my stomach comes back full force.

Kas lied to me.

I can't believe this.

He barefaced lied to me and made it seem like I was losing my marbles, and I want to know why.

UNSUITABLE

I fell for a liar before. It didn't turn out so well for me.

Fool Daisy once, stupid Daisy. Fool Daisy twice…yeah, not going to happen.

I won't be so dumb to let that happen again.

So, I'm going to find out exactly what Kas is hiding from me because I won't be anybody's fool ever again.

THIRTY-FOUR

HAVING SEX WITH KAS after knowing that he'd lied to me just wasn't an option. So, I did a little lying of my own and told him that I'd started my period.

Nothing deters a man from sex quicker than hearing that Aunt Flo has come to visit.

Not ideal, but the guy had just lied to me, and I was pissed off. He took it fine. Didn't seem suspicious at all. He just kissed me—really sweetly in fact—and then he disappeared back into his office.

I spent a good few minutes eyeballing his office door before I started on with work of my own.

I was so caught up in it all that I didn't even ring Cece to tell her that Kas and I had actually slept together.

But I think that's what stung most of all. I had given all of myself to him last night, and I thought he'd given me the same in return.

How wrong was I?

I'd spent the night in his arms, and the very next morning, he looked me straight in the eyes and lied to me.

I could've confronted him about the lie, but I knew it would be pointless. He wouldn't have lied to me and tried to make it like I was losing my marbles if he'd ever planned on telling me the truth.

I just don't get it. *Why lie about the existence of a door—a door that I know was there?*

That's only made me curious, which isn't necessarily a good thing. Now, I want to know what's behind that door—or bookcase, as it now is. My curiosity is burning, and I am going to find out.

There might be nothing there, and my search might be fruitless. But he lied about it for a reason, and I want to know that reason.

With frustration and restless energy burning through me, I bend down and tie the laces on my trainers before letting myself out of my apartment. I'm heading out for my early-morning run before work. I need to clear my head, and running is the only way to do it.

I jog down the stairs of my building and let myself out the main door. The cool morning air hits my face, nipping at my cheeks.

Letting the door close behind me, I stand there for a moment. Hands on hips, I tip my head back to face the sky, watching the clouds drift over, as I take some deep breaths of fresh air.

Steady breaths in and out.

See? I'm starting to feel better already.

"Daisy."

My body freezes at the sound of that voice. I *know* that voice. I know it well.

And there goes my good feeling.

Heart pounding, I lower my head, and my eyes meet with the one person I never wanted to see again. "Jason."

He's standing a few feet away, and I'm glad to say he looks terrible. His eyes are bloodshot, dark rings circling them. His hair looks like it hasn't been washed or cut since I last saw him, and his clothes are crumpled. He looks a mess.

"What are you doing here?" I'm not surprised at the level of anger in my voice.

UNSUITABLE

"Daisy." He takes a step forward.

Everything inside me screams to step away, but hatred and pride have my feet firmly set in place.

The breeze blows between us, and I get a strong whiff of alcohol.

"Are you drunk right now?" I scowl.

He lets out a low laugh. It sounds pitiful. Unsurprisingly, I can't find a shred of sympathy for him.

"If you drink constantly, does that constitute as being drunk, or is it just your normal state?"

"I'm not in the mood for games, Jason. Why the fuck are you here?"

"That's the first time I've ever heard you swear."

"Yeah, well, prison will change a girl. Now. What. Do. You. Want?" My hands are clenched into fists at my sides.

"I just..." He softly shakes his head. "I just heard you were out, and I needed to see you. Needed to see that you were okay."

I slap him. Hard.

The sound rings out in the silence surrounding us. And my hand stings like a bitch.

That is the first time I have ever hit anyone.

I don't feel better for it.

My adrenaline spiked, my body is shaking, and my chest is heaving with heavy breaths, like I've just run a marathon.

I want to cry. And scream.

Seriously, it never rains, but it fucking pours. I fall for Kas, and he lies to me. And, the very next morning, my lying bastard of an ex turns up on my doorstep.

I have the worst luck of anyone ever.

Unfocused eyes come back to mine. "I deserved that." His words are soft.

"You deserve more," I grit out.

He gently nods his head, eyes unfocused.

Everything in me starts to hurt from the bad memories of what he put me through, everything I had to endure, and everything I lost because of him.

"Why, Jason?" I don't even realize I'm crying until a tear drips off my chin. I swipe it away with the back of my hand. "I lost everything. I lost Jesse, the most important thing in my life, and he was put in a group home! A fucking group home!" My voice is rising with each enraging word I speak. "And I can't even have him back now. I get to see him on weekends while I prove to Social Services that I'm fit to care for him. And that is all because of you!"

I shove my hands into his chest, and he stumbles back a step.

"You set me up! I went to prison because of you! And I know it was you because there was no one else it could've been. And seeing you here now just confirms it! And you have the fucking audacity to come here because *you* need to know that I'm okay? Well, no, I'm not okay!" I scream that last part. And I don't care if I wake the whole goddamn building up. I've earned the right to scream.

His eyes nervously dart around.

It serves to remind me that Cece is only a few floors up, and she might hear. I don't want to pull her into this. If she finds out Jason is here...God help him. And I don't want Cece going to prison for murder.

Looking at the pavement, I pull in a few calming breaths, clenching my fists in and out.

I look up and stare at his pitiful face.

I can't see the Jason I knew.

God, I used to care about this man. I trusted him. And, right now, I can't see one single reason why that ever was.

"I shouldn't have come," he whispers. "It was a mistake."

"No shit, Sherlock," I snap.

"I'm sorry," he mumbles as he starts to back away.

"Yeah, and I'm sorry I ever met you."

UNSUITABLE

He pauses, lifting guilt-ridden eyes to mine. "I'm sorry you met me, too, Daisy. You were the best thing that ever happened to me—"

"So, why?" I bang my hand to my chest. "You ruined my life, Jason. I went to prison because of you."

"I'm sorry—"

"You keep saying that, but you're not sorry. If you were, then you'd tell me the truth. You'd admit that you set me up. You'd tell me who else was involved."

"I...Jesus..." He drives his hands into his hair, gripping the strands. "I didn't have a choice, okay? I never wanted to hurt you."

He didn't have a choice?

"What do you mean, you didn't have a choice?"

His eyes dart away from me. "Nothing. Forget I said anything."

"No." I step closer to him. "Who?" He says nothing, so I decide to push further. "Was it...*Damien*?"

I know I've hit the nail on the head because haunted, panicked eyes flash to mine.

Anger floods my veins.

I always knew it was the both of them, and seeing the confirmation on Jason's face...it makes me want to slap him again and again and again. And then haul his drunken, pathetic arse to the police station and force him to tell them the truth.

"I'm right, aren't I?" I take another step closer, fury urging me on. "It was Damien. He had you take that key from my bag while I was sleeping, and you gave it to him. He robbed the jewelry store, and then he brought the key back to you. You put it back in my bag and planted the jewelry in my apartment, so the cops would find it. God, I'm right, aren't I? Just admit it, Jason. For once in your miserable little life, tell the truth!"

I know I've pushed too far and too hard when I see the fury hit his eyes. A look passes over his face that makes my heart putter to a stop.

Jason's not built like Kas. He's actually a lot skinnier than he was when we were together, but he's still a hell of a lot bigger than me.

And, now, I'm quickly calculating the distance to see if I can make it back into my building before he can catch me.

He's drunk. I might make it.

And it's like he's read my mind because he catches hold of my upper arm, gripping tightly, his fingers biting into my skin.

He was never violent with me while we were together, but I'm not feeling so sure that he wouldn't be that way now.

He steps up into my space, so close that I can smell the rank stench of the alcohol he drank on his breath.

"Let me go," I grind out, teeth clenched.

But he doesn't let go. I try to pull my arm free, but it doesn't work. It's like he doesn't even feel me right now.

"God, I loved you, Daisy. So much. You were so good. So pure. Too good for the likes of me, but I wanted you anyway. And the way you used to look at me…"

"Love?" I give a bitter laugh. "You don't know the meaning of the word. And, honestly, I'd have rather had your hate because look what your so-called love gave me—a six-by-eight room in a prison block."

Guilt flashes in his eyes. He draws his gaze away from me. "I did the best I could for you."

I laugh another hollow laugh. "Screw you, Jason. You did the best for yourself." I run my eyes up and down him. "God, you're pathetic. A drunk, pathetic excuse for a man."

I know I shouldn't keep pushing his buttons, but I can't stop myself.

"You and your bastard of a brother stole my freedom from me!" I bite. "You set me up for that robbery and then just walked away clean. And you came here for, what? To say you're sorry? Well, fuck you. If you're as sorry as you say you are, then you'll go to the police station, and you'll tell them the truth. Go to the police right now, and tell them that it was you and Damien. That you both set me up. That you robbed the store."

His eyes flare with danger, and his grip on my arm increases, making me whimper in pain.

He leans in close to my face. "I don't know what you're talking about, Daisy." His voice is low but calm and steady. "My brother and I had nothing to do with what happened that night. All I know is what everyone else knows—that you did the robbery. Your access card was used to get in the store. You were the one who had some of the stolen jewelry found in your apartment."

Finding strength, I push him away from me, shoving him back. "Fuck you!" I seethe. "I fucking hate you, you bastard!"

"You should hate me," he says calmly. "And you should be afraid, too. Fear keeps people quiet, and you should be quiet, Daisy."

I wrap shaking arms around myself. "Is that a threat?" I somehow manage to keep my voice steady. God knows how because my insides are rattling.

"No," he says softly, giving a slow shake of his head, like the thought is inconceivable. "I love you, Daisy. I would never hurt you. This is me trying to keep you safe."

"Safe from who? *Damien*?"

Jason holds my stare for a long moment before he looks away. "Take care, Daisy. And, remember, silence is golden." He pushes his hands into his pockets, turns on his heel, and strides away.

THIRTY-FIVE

I STILL WENT FOR MY RUN after Jason left. It took me a good few minutes to calm my racing heart and trembling limbs before I was steady enough to move. But I needed the run. I needed to clear my head of everything that had happened.

When my run was over and I was showered and ready for work, I sat across from Cece at the kitchen table, having breakfast. I didn't tell her about Jason's visit or that I'd slept with Kas or that he'd lied to me afterward.

I was sitting there with it all on the tip of my tongue, but something stopped me from telling her.

Maybe because I know how she worries about me, and I don't want her to worry more than she already does.

Jason's visit has rattled me. Especially the warning he gave me.

And, really, nothing has changed. He hasn't outright admitted that it was him and Damien who framed me. So, it's not like I'm going to go running my mouth off to the police because I have nothing concrete to give them.

And I'm still bugging over Kas and his lying ways. And, now, more than ever, I want to know the truth.

Maybe Jason's visit has increased my need to know. Seeing the reason of why my life was upended and changed forever makes me want to be surer than ever that I'm not making a mistake by being with Kas.

I won't let anything risk me getting Jesse back.

And that's why I find myself in Kas's office right now.

He's with Cooper in the paddocks. Something is wrong with one of the horses. A vet's been called out.

And I'm snooping.

Not my finest moment but needs must.

I have my cleaning stuff with me, and I am technically cleaning his office. I'm just having a nosy look around while I do so.

Specifically, around the bookshelf.

I'm dusting it while looking for anything out of the ordinary.

I know I must look like something out of a bad detective movie, but this is my first rodeo.

So far, I'm not getting much. There are just rows and rows of books and dust.

Not exactly exciting.

Honestly, I didn't even know Kas read. I've never seen him pick up a book.

Reaching up to my tiptoes, I run the duster along the higher shelves, my eyes trailing over them, looking for anything. Any indication that there's a door behind here.

But nothing. Just a wooden panel behind the books.

I wonder if there's a book that you pull out, and the bookcase magically opens.

Okay, I've been watching too many movies. But I'm not really sure what I'm looking for here.

Oh, I do remember seeing in one movie where they literally just pushed against the bookcase to open it, and behind it was a door leading to a secret room.

But would Kas really have a secret room? It seems a little farfetched, even for me.

He could have just sealed off the door for whatever reason and built a bookcase in front of it.

UNSUITABLE

And if he had just told me that, then I wouldn't be in here, snooping, right now.

He lied for a reason. And I want to know why.

Thinking I hear a noise, I glance behind me at the half-open door. Pausing, I hold my breath.

I left the door open, so it wouldn't look suspicious if Kas came back, and I was in here with the door closed.

I wait a few seconds, but there's nothing. Nothing but silence.

Looking back to the shelves, I sigh in frustration. There has to be something behind here. Something he's hiding.

I put the duster down on his desk. Turning back to the bookcase, I run my hand over the shelves. Stopping at the end one, I firmly press my hand against it, seeing if there's any movement.

But it doesn't budge.

I move to the next stack and do the same. And I get the same result.

Frustration furrows my brow.

Am I being crazy here?

No, something is behind here. Something he doesn't want me to see. I just know it in my gut.

And there are only two stacks left to check.

I move to the next bookcase, my heart picking up pace from the fear of being caught. Taking a deep breath, I press my palms flat to each side of the stack, and I push firmly.

Holy shit! It moved.

Only a little, but there was a definite give to the left.

My heart rate sets off like a racehorse, and my pulse starts to thrum in my ears.

I swallow nervously as I press my hands to the left side of the stack.

Okay, here goes nothing.

I give it a strong push.

And it clicks. Then, it opens.

Holy fucking fuck a duck! I was right!

I quickly glance over my shoulder, checking if I'm still alone.

Then, hands trembling, I curl my fingers around the edge of the now unlocked bookcase, and I ease it open.

And there it is.

The door.

The mothereffing door.

I fricking knew it!

Lying bastard Kas-hole.

I grind my teeth together in anger and contemplation.

My fingers are itching as I stare at the door.

Should I open it?

Yes.

No.

Yes.

I've come this far. Might as well go the whole way.

Flexing my fingers, my breathing hitched, I reach out and curl my hand around the doorknob.

I turn it, and…it's locked.

Bugger.

I give it another turn, as though that will magically open the door, but it doesn't open because it's clearly locked.

I'm such a knobhead.

Bending at the waist, I stare at the doorknob. It needs a key to unlock it. One of those Yale keys that fits in the middle of the handle.

Closing my eyes in thought, I try to think if I've seen a Yale key anywhere, but I don't recall anything.

Sighing, I open my eyes. All I remember is Kas locking this door with a key and putting it in his pocket.

He must keep it somewhere.

But where?

My eyes drift over to his desk.

I wonder if…

The back door opens and quickly slams shut, and my heart nearly leaps out of my chest.

UNSUITABLE

Shit!

I quickly push the bookcase back in place, hearing the click, knowing I've locked it. Then, I dash over to Kas's desk and pick up the duster. I start running over his desk and computer, like I've been cleaning it all along.

This is so obvious. I'm so obvious. I might as well have a sign on my forehead saying, *Snoop.*

I'm only dusting his computer, but I've broken out in a sweat, and I'm breathing like I've just run a marathon.

I need to calm down.

Ditching the duster, I grab the furniture polish and cloth. I spray some polish onto his desk and start rubbing at it as I force myself to calm down, taking slow deep breaths.

"Hey."

I look up to see Kas standing in the doorway.

Liar.

"Hi." I give him a bright smile, stopping what I'm doing.

His eyes drift over the room, like he's checking it.

Looking for something, Kas-hole? Or worried I was?

Bastard.

"Is this okay?" I gesture to the cloth in my hand. "I thought I'd give your office a clean while you were out. I didn't think it was still off-limits, but if—"

"Of course it's fine." His eyes smile warmly at me.

I stare back at him, and I can't see anything off in his expression—not that I can usually tell what he's thinking. He's so closed off.

But his warm demeanor is telling me that he doesn't suspect anything.

Maybe he just thinks I'm not smart enough to have seen through his lies.

Fucker.

Knowing that he underestimates how smart I am actually stings. And it pisses me off even more.

"I can't believe I told you not to come in here. I was such a dick." He walks over to me.

I put the cloth down and turn to meet him. He wraps his arms around my waist.

I hide my anger and try to act natural.

I'm not taking him to court over this until I know what's behind that door.

Once I know, I'm going to kick his arse over lying to me. Depending on what I find, of course.

"Well, I'm not disagreeing with you. You were a dick."

He grins down at me, and it leaves a warm feeling in my chest.

He's a liar, Daisy. A big, fat liar. There's a door behind that bookcase to prove it.

"I promise never to be a dick to you again." He leans down and brushes his lips over mine. "Only to use my dick for pleasurable purposes when it comes to you."

My vagina stands to attention.

Down, girl. We have a trickster in our midst.

"How's the horse?" I ask. My words come out hoarse and husky. I might be pissed off at Kas, but my body likes him a lot, and apparently, all it takes is the mention of his cock to send me off to Sexville.

"It's got laminitis. Cooper caught it early, which is good. The vet prescribed an anti-inflammatory. That's why I came back—to grab my wallet. I'm heading to the vet's office to pick up the prescription. Cooper's going to stay with the horse. Do you want to come with me?"

"To the vet's?" My lips purse. "But I'm working."

"And I'm the boss, and the boss wants his girl to come with him." He takes ahold of my ponytail and gives it a gentle tug.

His girl.

Crap. That totally would have melted me faster than ice in hot water if he'd said it to me pre-lie.

UNSUITABLE

Okay, truthfully, I have melted a little. But I'm still mad.

Hopping mad in fact.

It's just hard not to want him or warm to him, especially when I'm in his arms and he's being all lovely and sweet.

Then, it suddenly occurs to me.

I could lose him. I might have to walk away from him. Because whatever it is that he's hiding from me, it might be a game changer.

Do I really want to lose Kas?

No.

But I also don't want to be a blind fool.

I have to know the truth, and the only way I'll find out is of my own accord.

I'm doing this to protect myself. And Jesse.

I let him down due to a man once before. It won't happen again.

"Well then, I guess the boss gets what he wants."

"Good girl," he murmurs.

He kisses me again. He starts to suck on my lower lip as his hands find my butt, and my body comes to life. My hands find their way around his neck, and I kiss him back, sucking on his tongue. He groans into my mouth.

I wind my fingers into the hair at the back of his head. He pulls me tighter into his body. And the kiss goes from sweet to molten in seconds.

My brain is sending out rapid bat signals, but my body's totally ignoring them.

"God, I want you." He breathes heavily. "Stay with me tonight. I missed you in my bed last night."

His words make my heart skip a beat.

He missed me.

"But...I'm on my period, remember?" I surprise myself with my quickness to remember to lie. But then it's not like I could say I had my period for a day, and it was done.

"Babe...I might want to fuck you right now—I always want to fuck you—but that's not why I want you in my bed." *Kiss.* "I want to *sleep* with you. Hold you. Wake up with you."

Oh God.

I'm dying here. He's being so goddamn sweet. It's confusing me. He's confusing me.

Why did you have to lie to me? I want to yell at him.

Of course I don't say that.

He wants me to stay the night, and that means I'll be here when he's sleeping.

It was a rare chance that I got to be in Kas's office without him here today. I don't know when I'll get that chance again.

But, if I'm here and he's fast asleep...that would give a girl plenty of time to look around, for say, maybe a key that'd open a door hidden behind a bookcase.

God, when did I get so devious?

Probably around the time I found myself serving eighteen months for a crime I hadn't committed.

Smiling up at him, I bite my lip. "Well, when you put it like that, how can a girl refuse?"

He smiles big, and it lights up his eyes. "So, you'll stay the night?"

He looks so happy and boyish in this moment. I feel a stab of guilt.

Stop. I have nothing to feel guilty about. He did this. Not me.

If he'd been truthful with me from the start, then we wouldn't be where we are right now. I wouldn't be preparing to sneak around my man's house in the dead of night, looking for a secret key to unlock a secret door.

Reaching up on my tiptoes, I press my lips to his, hiding my own deceit, and I whisper, "Yes."

THIRTY-SIX

I GLANCE AT KAS sleeping beside me.

My heart is racing. My mouth is dry. My breaths are quick.

I'm really going to do this. I'm really going to climb out of his bed and sneak downstairs to find out what's really behind that door.

My palms are sweating.

I press them to the bed, trying to dry them on the bedsheet.

Then, he moves, and I nearly shit my pants.

Turning in his sleep, he turns to his side, facing away from me.

Holy fuck!

Holy fucking fuck.

I press my trembling hand to my chest, applying pressure, trying to ease the race in my heart. It's beating so hard and loud that I'm afraid it will actually wake him.

I can't wake him now. Not when I've just spent the last few minutes easing myself out of his arms.

It didn't take long for him to fall asleep after we finished making out.

Yes, we made out.

He made me dinner. He actually cooked for me. A guy has never done that before. He lit candles and everything. It was really romantic. Then, we curled up on the sofa with our glasses of wine and watched TV together. Well, the TV-watching didn't last very long before we started making out like teenagers.

Kas suggested we go to bed. I agreed.

And we carried on with our make-out session in here. Obviously, we didn't have sex because I'm supposed to be on my period. But, God, I wanted to.

I wanted him so badly. I still do.

After we finished making out, he wrapped me up in his arms and held me like he never wanted to let me go.

And I didn't want him to.

But I have to.

I have to know the truth.

Taking a quiet, shallow breath, I slide out of bed, my bare feet touching the thick carpet.

I cast a nervous glance back at Kas. Holding my breath, I watch the silhouette of his strong back. His breaths are deep and even. He's fast asleep.

And I'm doing this.

Eyes on the half-open door, I tiptoe out of his bedroom.

I descend the stairs on silent feet. The light on the outside porch is casting a small glow in the large hallway.

Feeling a chill, I shiver, wrapping my arms around myself. I only have on one of Kas's T-shirts and my undies. I feel like I should be wearing a black cat suit or something equally badass. Not an old band T-shirt of Kas's that carries his scent. And it's really distracting because I love the way he smells. It brings warmth and hot memories to mind, and that makes me feel like a total bitch for sneaking around his house like this.

Then, I remind myself that I wouldn't be doing this if it weren't for him and his lying ways. I would have been lying upstairs in his arms, probably having sex right now, if he'd chosen honesty.

UNSUITABLE

But he didn't, and here we are.

Well, here I am.

I tiptoe across the floor and into his office.

I quietly close the door behind me, and then I make my way across the room and turn on his desk lamp.

I don't waste any time. I start searching through his desk drawers, looking for a key.

I find one key, but it's small and looks like it's for a padlock or something. But, aside from that, there's no key that would fit that door.

Hands on hips, I survey the room.

If I were Kas, where would I keep a key for a secret door?

I'd keep it with me.

I do a quick mental run-through of what he was wearing when we went upstairs. Jeans and a shirt, and he put those in the laundry basket, so there definitely isn't a key there.

My eyes snag on his jacket, which is hanging on the back of the door. He wore that earlier when we went to the vet's to get the medication for the horse.

I walk over to the jacket. I slip my hands in both pockets. My hand curls around a set of keys in the right pocket.

I pull them out. His car keys. I stare down at them in my hand. There's his car key, a fob—which is for the garage, I think—a Range Rover key ring...and another key.

A Yale key.

Holy shit.

Blood starts to pump through my veins.

Oh my God. This is the key. I bet this is the key!

I rush over to the bookcase, keys in hand.

I open up the stack, revealing the door. I single out the Yale key, and with my hand shaking, I slot the key in the door. I turn and...

Click.

Shit. I'm in.

I'm actually in.

Leaving the key in the door, I grab the handle and turn it.

But I pause before opening.

Am I sure I want to do this? Am I sure I want to know what's behind this door?

I'm not sure of anything anymore. But I do know that I need to know what he's hiding.

On a deep breath, I push open the door.

A light flickers on, making me jump. It must be one of those sensor lights. My eyes adjust to the light, and I see I'm standing in the doorway of a closet-sized room.

And in this closet-sized room are…photographs.

Of me.

"What…the hell?" I whisper.

My heart starts to beat faster as I step further into the room.

There's a photo of me. From the day I left prison. I'm standing outside the prison, a bag in hand.

Why does Kas have a photograph of me?

My eyes start moving over the other photos pinned to the wall.

Me and Cece hugging from the same day.

Me out running.

Me and Cece out together, the night of the club.

Me at the Matis Estate, talking to Cooper.

Me on the train.

One of me with Jesse when we went to the beach.

And…

Jesus Christ.

My hand reaches up to the photo.

It's of me with Jason. But this isn't from the other day. This is an old photograph—from when we were together, not long before I was arrested.

The picture was definitely taken from afar and without our knowledge.

UNSUITABLE

Jason and I are in an embrace. I'm smiling up into his face, and he's grinning down at me.

"Oh God," I whisper.

I turn in the room, eyes scanning. Every wall is covered with something—photographs, news cuttings about my arrest, trial, and imprisonment.

Jesus, he even has my prison mug shot.

Stepping up close, I run my fingers over the picture.

I move over, and there's a map with marked locations.

One is of my apartment.

What the hell?

I don't understand. *Why does Kas have these?*

I move along, and my hip bumps into a table.

No, it's a desk and—

"Oh, fuck," I breathe, pressing a hand to my chest, as my heart climbs out of my throat, leaving me gasping.

On the desk is a gun. And lined up beside the gun are four knives in various sizes. Each one looks as deadly as the other.

Oh God. Oh God. Oh God.

Fingers on the edge of the desk, I sidle around it, staring down at the weapons, like they're going to come alive and attack me.

Once I'm around the desk, I turn to the last wall. I see pictures of Haley.

I focus in on one of the pictures. It's of Haley and Kas. He looks so much younger.

He looks happy.

Pain ruptures in my chest.

I step back, taking in the photos of Haley along with the news cuttings about her murder.

I don't understand what all of this is. What it means.

Why does he have pictures of me and of Jason in here with pictures of Haley?

Standing in the center of the room, I turn slowly, trying to take it all in, piece it all together, and my eyes catch on a photo. I didn't spot it before because my eyes were pinned on the weapons on the table.

But, now, I'm looking, and I'm looking hard.

Because there's a picture of Damien Doyle.

And on either side of the picture of Damien are pictures of two men I don't recognize.

I step closer to the photos, and my stomach empties.

The photos of the men I don't recognize have a big red X marked over their faces.

Damien's is the only photo that doesn't have an X.

Why would—

Oh God.

Oh, holy fuck no.

Just like a blow to the head, it hits me.

A sick, hollow feeling starts to form in my gut.

Three men.

Haley. Kas.

Rape. Murder.

Red crosses mean…are they…dead?

Oh, fuck.

Damien's alive.

Jesus. Fucking. Christ.

God. No.

I turn, more than ready to leave this room, and my heart practically falls out of my chest.

Kas is standing in the doorway.

His chest is bare, and he's wearing the black pajama bottoms he went to bed in.

"Is there *any* room I can keep you out of?" He doesn't smile.

And I nearly piss my pants.

His eyes run over the room, and he sighs. He folds his arms over his chest and leans his shoulder against the doorjamb.

His impenetrable eyes meet with mine. Then, he parts his lips and says calmly, "So, I guess you have questions."

THIRTY-SEVEN

QUESTIONS?
Do I have questions?
Of course I have fucking questions!
But, right now, I'm trying not to piss my pants, and I need to restart my heart to normal function because it's decided to stop working properly.

I part my lips. My mouth is dry, like I've been out in the desert for days.

I...I don't even know where to start.

Kas is staring at me with those beautiful, impenetrable dark eyes of his, giving me nothing.

But he doesn't need to give me anything because I'm pretty sure I've figured it all out by myself.

Damien Doyle was part of the gang that...
And Kas has been...

Jesus, I can't even say the words.

I lick my lips, trying to give aid to speech. "I..." I wrap my arms over my stomach, my eyes flickering around the room.

He has pictures of me from before we even knew each other.

Or maybe Kas knew me a long time before I knew him.

Oh, fuck.

"I...you..." I stammer. "Wh-why do you have photos of me? An-and Damien Doyle?"

"I think you know why."

"Oh God," I whisper, trembling.

He sighs again. "I didn't ever want you to find out, Daisy."

No fucking kidding! I wish to God I hadn't found out.

Me and my snooping fucking nose.

"Y-you...th-the pictures of those men."

"Evan Foster, Levi Betts, and of course, you know Damien Doyle."

"Ar-are they..." I lift a shaking, helpless hand to his scarred torso. His eyes squeeze shut. "Are they the men who did that to you and Haley?"

He breathes deeply through his nose. His eyes open. "Yes."

"Jesus Christ," I whisper. "An-and what do the crosses on Evan's and Levi's faces mean?"

"It means they're dead, Daisy."

Holy fuck.

I want to cry. And run. Far, far away.

I swallow past the bricks lodged in my throat. "Ho-how did they die?"

He adjusts his stance, lifting his hands to the doorframe above his head. His big body fills the doorway. His muscles are stretched out, showing the definition and strength of him.

I'm trapped in here, and if he wants to hurt me, he can.

The only things I have to my advantage are the selection of knives behind me and the gun, but I don't know if it's loaded.

And...I can't believe I'm considering having to defend myself with a weapon against the man I've been sleeping with.

Just when I thought my life couldn't get any worse, I open a door and find Dexter's secret lair.

UNSUITABLE

Kas lets out another sigh. This one sounds tired.

"Evan Foster slit his own throat. He bled to death in his bathtub. And Levi Betts was stabbed to death in an alleyway. Drug deal gone wrong apparently." His steady black eyes stay carefully on mine.

Swallowing nervously, I glance back at the knives on the table.

Did one of those knives…

Fuck. Fuck. Fuck.

My pulse is pounding in my ears, my skin prickling with nerves and, most of all, disbelief. I can't believe we're having this conversation.

I never really thought about what was behind that door. But, in my wildest imagination, I never thought it was this.

"An-and…" I carefully bring my eyes back to him. My stare catches on his scars. I never normally see them; they don't stand out to me because they're a part of him.

But, now, I'm seeing them.

I lift my eyes to his and gulp. "Di-did you…have anything to do with their…deaths?"

His eyes flicker with something…fear maybe?

He blows out a breath. It sounds resigned.

When he looks back at me, the look in his eyes is wary. "I think you know the answer to that as well."

"Oh, Jesus." I back up a step and bump into the desk, making the knives and gun rattle.

Kas's eyes go straight to them and then back to me.

I sidestep the desk, moving away but not too far away that I can't grab a weapon if I need to. "You killed them both."

"Yes."

Oh God.

"And you're going to kill Damien."

He doesn't answer. He just stares steadily back at me, like he's weighing up how to answer.

But he doesn't need to answer because I already know.

Damien's picture wouldn't be pinned up on that wall next to theirs if Kas weren't planning on killing him.

"How will Damien die?" I whisper.

"Painfully."

"Oh God. Are you going to kill me, too?"

"What?" He looks stunned, like I just punched him in his face.

His whole demeanor changes. His arms drop from the doorframe, and he steps forward, eyes wide with shock. "Jesus. No. Of course not. Why would you ever think that?"

And it's this moment that my brain chooses to explode out through my mouth. "Because you have guns and knives in here! And you've killed two men already—who, of course, deserved it—and you are planning to kill another man—who also deserves it! But you've killed people, and you have my picture all over your goddamn wall!" I slice a hand in the direction of the pictures. My chest heaves with fearful, angry breaths as the echo of my words silently reverberate around the room.

Kas drags a hand through his hair, his other hand crossing his chest to cover his heart. "I would never hurt you, Daisy. *Never,*" he states emphatically. "This"—he moves a hand, gesturing to his wall of fame—"is just a part of my life that I never wanted you to find out about."

"Jesus fucking Christ!" I pinch the bridge of my nose, taking deep breaths in and out. "I'm in love with a killer. Only I could fall in love with a killer. God, what the hell is wrong with me?"

"What did you say?"

Dropping my hand, I scowl over at him. "Sorry, should I not call you a killer?"

"You're…" He blinks. Shaking his head, he takes another step forward. "You're in love with me."

Oh. Shit.

Did I just tell him that I was in love with him?

UNSUITABLE

Am I in love with him?
Oh God. I am.
I'm in love with Norman Bates.

Well, he's not exactly a psycho. He's a man out for revenge. But he's killed people. And it's not exactly the ideal time to tell the man you're dating that you're in love with him moments after finding out he's the real-life version of The Punisher.

"I...I...it's not really the point right now," I utter dismissively.

"It's the only point."

When I look into his face, I see tenderness. It curls around my heart and squeezes tight.

I shut my eyes against the feeling. "I don't even know you," I whisper. "I can't be in love with a man I don't know."

I feel him move closer.

"You know me, Daisy. You're the only person who truly knows me."

I open my eyes and stare up into his soulful eyes. The hope in his gaze makes me ache.

I shake my head. "No, I don't. You've lied to me from the second I met you. You knew me before I even knew you." I point at the picture of me and Jason on the wall, but his eyes don't leave mine. "How did I end up working for you, Kas?" My words are quiet.

His eyes close briefly, his brows drawing together, as if I just yelled at him. "I made it so that you would come work for me."

A sick feeling unfurls in my stomach.

"Why would you do that?" I think I already know, but I need him to tell me. I need to hear this from him.

He takes a step back, putting much-needed distance between us. "Because I've been trying to pin down Damien Doyle for a long time. But he has this fucking amazing ability to disappear. And, when he disappears, he goes completely off the grid, and there's just no finding him. Believe me, I've tried.

"I just needed an in with him. That's how I get close enough to kill them. They don't remember me. I look very different to the kid they tortured in that park seven years ago. I get in, and then I kill them.

"Damien had only just reappeared back in London after being gone for a long time, and that was when I found out he had a brother. I saw my way in to get close to Damien. But Jason was skittish. He was afraid of his brother, but he was loyal as fuck to him. Then…I found out that Jason had a girlfriend."

"You know Jason." I wrap my arms over my chest, rubbing my suddenly chilled arms with my hands.

"I'd watched him for a while. Then, one night, I followed him to a bar. Started talking to him. He talked easy with a few beers in him, but he clammed up at the mention of his brother. He liked to talk about you though. A lot."

I squeeze my eyes shut, fists clenching at my sides.

"I watched you…and, fuck, Daisy, you were so beautiful. I had never seen someone so beautiful. Watching you, parts of me started to awaken. But I wanted to hate you because I thought you were one of them. I thought you had to know the kind of people you were involved with. And then, a few weeks later, you were arrested, and I was proven right—or so I thought.

"I knew Jason wasn't capable of orchestrating anything; the guy's a fucking flake. I got that after just spending a few hours talking to him. I knew, in my gut, that it was something to do with Damien. It had him written all over it. And, if you were involved, then that meant you were close to Damien. I saw you as my in. I was going to use you to get close to him. Then, I was going to kill him.

"Of course, Damien disappeared right after you were arrested. So, I waited. Then, when your release came up, I got in touch with a friend of Jude's who works in probation

UNSUITABLE

service. I told him I wanted to help out with the Back to Work program they have for felons. I said I was looking for a maid because my last one had left unexpectedly. He put me in touch with Toby—"

"Tania," I breathe out her name. "Did she leave voluntarily? Or did you make her leave?"

His eyes flash with hurt. "Tania was an illegal immigrant. She was deported back to Poland. I kept it quiet, as I didn't want negative attention brought to the estate."

"Convenient timing for you."

Jaw gritted, he says, "Tania was gone for two months before you started working here. I didn't fucking hurt her, Daisy. I don't go around killing people for fun. Tania's alive and well and living in Poland with her family. I can prove it to you—"

"Were you and she…"

"No." Disappointment flickers in his eyes. "There has been no one but you. You know that."

"Yeah, well, forgive me for not believing a word you've ever said."

"I've never lied to you, Daisy. I've kept things from you, but I've never lied."

"Bullshit!" I jab a finger in the direction of his office. "You stared into my eyes and barefaced lied to me the other day! You stood there and told me that fucking door never existed!"

Anger flashes across his face. "Clearly, that was a mistake. And I might have lied about that—*hidden* that from you, but it was with good reason. But I have never lied about anything to do with you and me."

"All of this has to do with you and me!" I throw my arms around. "You kept this from me!"

"How was I supposed to tell you? *By the way, Daisy, I'm taking out the men who raped and murdered my childhood sweetheart—the men who did this to me and left me for dead!*" He slams a hand against his scarred chest. "That getting my revenge is the only thing that's kept me breathing for the last seven years!" He breaks off, panting, his eyes wild and wide on me.

The worst thing is...I get it.

I get why he's done what he's done. If they'd done that to me or Cece or Jesse—what they'd done to him and Haley—I'd want to kill them, too.

But that doesn't mean I would. I would let the law do its job.

"Why kill them? Why not turn them over to the police?"

He barks out a laugh, but there's not a shred of humor in it. He steps back, leaning against the wall, and folds his arms over his chest, staring straight ahead at the wall that is covered with the news cuttings and pictures of Haley.

"Because the police don't do shit. I gave them descriptions. The best I could. They put out photofits on the news. Canvased the area. Brought in a few suspects. Never the right ones though. Time passed. Interest in the case dwindled.

"So, I decided to do something about it myself. It was the least I could do for Haley and her family. She died because I took her in there that night. So, I was going to do the only thing I could. Wipe those three pieces of scum from the earth. It took me a long time to find them. But when I did..." Pained eyes come over to me.

"When I killed Foster...I threw up afterward." He lets out a sad-sounding, derogatory laugh. "But I also felt good. Like I was finally doing something right for Haley. Killing Betts...I wouldn't say it was easier, but to know I was ridding the world of those motherfuckers felt good. But Doyle...he's the one I want more than anything. He was the driving force in what happened that night."

"He's the one who raped Haley first? The one who thanked you for letting him...it was him who stabbed you over and over?"

He nods slowly. "I just need to kill him...and then everything will be right."

I feel like he's not even talking to me right now.

"I kill Doyle, and I'll have paid my debt back to Haley."

I take a tentative step toward him. "Haley wouldn't have wanted you to do this."

He looks at me, and the pain in his expression cuts right through me. "I owe her, Daisy." He looks away from me and to her picture. Tenderness spreads through his expression. "She was mine to protect, and I failed her. I won't fail her again. I will kill Doyle. I'll get my revenge for her...if it's the last thing I do."

Something inside me breaks.

Watching him stare at her picture, I feel like a voyeur. And I realize in this moment that whatever Kas feels for me will never be anything compared to what he felt for Haley...still feels for her.

I can't even be jealous because she deserved to be loved. And, after what he lived through, he deserves his revenge.

But I can't be a party to it. I have too much to lose.

"I understand your need for revenge, Kas. For what he did to you and Haley—"

"And you." His eyes snap to mine, anger flaring in them. "He put you in prison. He stole eighteen months of your life. Because of him, you lost Jesse. This isn't just about Haley anymore, Daisy. It's about you, too."

My heart constricts painfully.

I take a step toward him. "I don't want you to do anything for me. I made my peace with what had happened to me a long time ago."

But I do want that bastard to die for what he did to Kas. I just don't want Kas to be the one to do it. Kas has endured and suffered enough. More than anyone ever should. I don't want him to suffer anymore. I want him to be free of this.

"I don't want you to go after Damien. I want you to stay here with me. I want you safe." I wrap my arms around myself. "I understand your need to do this, but I can't be a part of it. I won't stand in your way, and I won't ask you to choose. *But*"—I pull in a strengthening breath—"if you keep on your path of revenge, then...this is where we end. I can't risk Jesse. I love you. I honestly do. But I love Jesse more. He will always come first. I have to protect myself to protect him. I need him back home with me, and I can't...I *won't* let anything jeopardize that. I'll keep your secret. You can trust me on that. But I can't be here anymore. I can't be with you."

"Jesus." He squeezes his eyes closed, tipping his head back.

He stays that way for what seems like forever when, in reality, it's seconds. Jaw clenched, eyes tightly shut, his body is so still that I'm not even sure if he's breathing right now.

Please, Kas. Don't go after him. Let it go. Stay with me.

He exhales a breath that sounds a lot like a decision made. And I watch as he opens his eyes and lowers them to mine. I read his answer there, and my heart sinks.

"I never should have started anything with you. I knew it was wrong. I'm sorry—"

I cut him off with my hand. "Don't..."

His eyes stare at the floor. "I have to finish what I started...what *they* had started seven years ago. I have to put Doyle in the ground for what he did. I'm sorry, Daisy."

He looks back up to me, and the apology in his eyes guts me.

And that's when it hits me.

This is it.

Kas and I are over.

Over before we really got a chance to begin.

Pain, the likes of nothing I've ever felt before, lances through me.

UNSUITABLE

If I had ever questioned how much Kas meant to me, I just got my answer.

More than I knew possible.

"Okay." I blow out a fortifying breath, holding myself together when all I want to do is fall apart. "I guess there's nothing left to say. Except for…good-bye."

His eyes flicker with regret. "Good-bye, Daisy."

Those softly spoken words splinter my heart, gutting me.

Putting steel in my back, I curl my fingers into my palms until my nails bite into my skin. I start to walk away.

As I pass him, I breathe him in, and the scent of him is almost enough to stop me in my tracks.

Almost but not quite enough. Because there's someone out there who needs me more.

"Daisy…"

Kas's voice touches my back, and it's agony, stopping me in my tracks. Misery lodges in my throat.

I suck in a breath, closing my eyes.

It takes an age before I find the strength to turn back to him, and when I do, he's still leaning against the wall, not looking at me, eyes on the ground, his arms wrapped around himself.

Summoning his own strength, he turns my way and lifts his eyes to mine, and for the first time, I see Kas.

The real Kas.

He's wide open and bleeding for me.

God, it hurts. It hurts so fucking much.

Tears fill my eyes. I bite my lip to keep the pain in.

"I'm sorry I couldn't be a better man for you. The man you deserve." His voice is rough with emotion.

And the tears spill down over my cheeks.

I know they affect him. I see his hand flex, like he wants to reach out and touch me. But he stays where he is.

"I don't think I'm capable of love anymore," he speaks softly. "I haven't been for a long time. But I do know what I feel for you, and it's…"

He gently shakes his head, his eyes briefly looking away before coming back to me. I see the shine in them, and it makes me cry harder.

"What I feel for you is debilitating and terrifying and exhilarating…and the best thing to ever happen to me. *You* are the best thing to ever happen to me. And, if you only ever believe one thing I've told you, then believe this; if I could love someone, then it would be you, Daisy. A million times over, it would be you."

THIRTY-EIGHT

"IF I COULD LOVE SOMEONE, then it would be you, Daisy. A million times over, it would be you."

Those words have been on repeat in my head all day.

I tip my head against the window, the vibration of the train running on the tracks beating against my head, as Kelly Clarkson sings "Beautiful Disaster" in my ears.

After that night when I walked away from Kas, he didn't come after me. He offered to drive me home, but the pain and confusion and atmosphere between us was bad enough, and I couldn't endure a car ride home with him. So, he called me a taxi.

I'll still have to see him in a handful of hours. Even though I might not be able to have a relationship with Kas, I still need my job. It's one of the things that ensures I'll get Jesse back.

When I got home, I let myself quietly into our apartment. I got in bed and spent the rest of the night staring at my darkened ceiling.

I got up early and went for a run.

When I got back, Cece was up. She was surprised to see me, as she'd thought I was at Kas's. I told her that Kas and I weren't going to work out.

Then, I surprised myself by bursting into tears.

Of course, I couldn't tell her the real reason. So, I just told her that he wasn't right for me.

I knew she knew there was more to it, but she didn't push. She was just awesome, like always. She hugged me and then told me it was girls' night tonight—takeout, wine, and a chick flick.

I dreaded going to work and having to see him. But I put my big-girl panties on and went to work.

He wasn't there.

His car was gone.

And then I started to get worried. Worried that he'd gone after Damien.

I broke down and called him. I got his voice mail, which only made me feel worse. I didn't bother leaving a message.

What could I say? *Please don't kill him.*

I did text him later in the day, just asking him to let me know he was okay.

So far, I haven't heard back.

I'm scared for Kas.

And you know what? The scariest thing is that I don't care that a man is soon going to lose his life. Or that Kas has taken the life of two other men. Because they deserved it. Damien deserves it.

And if thinking that makes me a bad person, then so be it.

Those bastards raped and murdered a seventeen-year-old girl. They forced Kas to watch that brutality, and then they stabbed him and left him for dead.

When I think of Kas killing them, I can't feel anything but justice for Haley.

And Damien put me in prison for eighteen months. I'm not a girl out for revenge, but I can't help but feel it right now.

UNSUITABLE

I know some people would say, *Turn him over to the police.* But slippery fuckers like Damien always manage to get away.

And, honestly, jail wouldn't be enough of a punishment for him. Trust me, I've spent time inside, and the punishment Damien deserves for what he did on that night seven years ago isn't sitting pretty in a jail cell. He deserves to suffer.

An eye for an eye and all that.

Kas lost everything because of Damien. I lost everything because of Damien.

I guess we'll always be tied in that way.

So, between compulsively checking the news for reports of a murder—or worse, of Kas being hurt—I've been aching over losing him.

My day has been a complete mindfuck.

I just need to hear from Kas. I need to know he's okay.

My phone vibrates on the table in front of me. My eyes flash to it, heart racing, hoping it's Kas. I deflate when I see it's Anne calling, which shows how bad things are, but then my heart picks back up when I realize that it's *Anne* calling.

Jesse.

I yank the earphones from my ears and connect the call. "Hello?" I rush out, worry prickling me, as it always does when it comes to Jesse.

"Hi, Daisy. It's Anne." Her voice sounds upbeat, which relaxes me some.

"Hi," I say.

"I'm not interrupting anything, am I?" she asks.

"No, not at all." *Well, aside from me sitting here, obsessing over the fact that the man I'm in love with is out for revenge and will soon kill the man who ruined his life. Other than that, no, you're not interrupting anything.* "I'm just on the train on my way home from work."

"Oh, good. Well, I have some news…some good news."

That makes me sit up straighter. "Good news?"

"Yes. I've been talking with my superior, and we've been looking at Jesse's progress since your release. It's all been positive. Especially since your visits began. He's doing better in school, he's actively seeking to partake in activities, and his overall attitude is better. He seems happy."

That makes me glow, knowing that Jesse is happy because of me.

"And I talked with your probation officer, Toby, and he has nothing but positive things to say, as does your employer."

"Kas?" I breathe his name.

"Yes, Kastor Matis. Lovely man. He had wonderful things to say about you. That you're a hard worker. You're always on time. He said it's clear to him that your sole focus is on rebuilding your life and getting Jesse back living with you."

Tears spring to my eyes. I bite my lip.

"When did you speak to Kas?" I fight to keep my voice normal. I need to know if she's spoken to him since he went off the grid.

"Oh, it was the day before yesterday. Why?"

My hope sinks. "Oh, he never mentioned it, is all." I try to brush off my curiosity, worrying that I might have tipped her off to the fact that Kas and I were once more than just employer and employee.

"Oh, right," she says with a casualness that puts me at ease. "Anyway, we would normally wait a little longer before allowing this, but I don't think that's necessary in this case. I think, if anything, it will benefit Jesse more. And I've spoken to Jesse, and he was more than eager for it to begin."

"For what to begin?"

"Overnight visits. We're going to allow you to have weekend access with Jesse. He can come to you on Saturday mornings. Stay over Saturday nights, and then you return him back on Sundays by teatime. I will, of course, need to come and do a check of your home to make sure everything is up to a satisfactory condition for him, but I can't see there being a problem from what I remember of your place the last time I was there."

"Are you being serious?" My heart is beating faster. "I can really have Jesse for the weekends?"

I feel her smile down the line.

"Yes, Daisy, I'm serious. You've earned this. I'm proud of you. Keep up the good work, and you'll have Jesse living back with you sooner than originally anticipated."

Tears start to run down my face. "Thank you. So much. I...I can't...God, thank you. I won't let you or Jesse down, I swear."

"Just keep doing what you're doing, and you'll have your family back together before you know it."

We say our good-byes after setting a date and time for Anne to do her home visit early next week so that I can begin Jesse's overnight stays the next weekend.

I can't believe it. I'm one step away from getting Jesse back.

The other part of my life might be going to shit, but the most important part of my life is heading in the right direction. And it only confirms that I made the right decision in walking away from Kas because I can't let anything jeopardize getting Jesse back home with me.

Tears are still leaking from my eyes, and I don't care that other passengers can see me because I'm so fucking happy about these weekend visits.

I fire off a text to Jesse, telling him that I just heard from Anne and how happy I am.

My phone beeps a second later.

> *It's cool, right? I can't wait to see your place. Can I decorate my room how I want it?*

God, he can paint it black if he wants.
I type back.

> *Of course you can! We can go shopping for paint tomorrow if you want.*

He responds.

> *Bring your credit card.* ☺

I laugh out loud, and it feels good.

> *You got it, kiddo. Love you.* xx

Love you, too, Mayday.

And that sets me off crying even more.
I turn my face to the window and wipe away the tears.
I feel so conflicted with my happiness over Jesse and my hurt over Kas.
I never knew I could feel so happy yet so sad at the same time.
The train pulls into my station. I get off the train and start the walk home. I know Cece said she was getting wine for our girlie night, but I stop off at the supermarket and get a bottle of champagne to celebrate my news. It's only the cheap stuff, but it's still champagne, and we are going to celebrate big time. I cannot bloody wait to see her face when I tell her that I'm getting Jesse for the weekends.
I forgo the five-pence carrier bag, and with a champagne bottle in hand, I head home.
I let myself in my apartment building and jog up the steps. I put my key in the front door, letting myself in. The place is quiet.
"Ce, I'm home," I call out, smiling. I kick my shoes off. Dropping my bag in the hallway, I head to the living room.

UNSUITABLE

"I've got amazing news—" My words cut off at the scene set out before me.

Oh God. No.

THIRTY-NINE

THE BOTTLE OF CHAMPAGNE falls from my hand, hitting the floor with a thud.

"*Ce.*" My voice trembles.

She's sitting on the sofa. Her wrists are bound in front of her, and her ankles are tied, too. Over her mouth is a piece of duct tape. Her eyes are wide with fear, her cheeks stained with old and new tears.

And, standing behind her, with a gun casually resting on top of the sofa beside her, is Damien Doyle.

"Hi, Daisy."

The bastard smiles. He fucking smiles.

Fear and rage unfurl in the pit of my stomach.

"Damien." I try to keep my voice steady, but it trembles, and he hears it.

I know because his grin widens.

"Been a while," he says.

"Not long enough," I grit out.

He laughs. "See? And here I was, thinking you'd missed me."

Like a hole in the head, motherfucker.

"About as much as I'd miss genital herpes."

He laughs again. Louder. "This is why I've always liked you, Daisy. Never afraid to say what's on your mind." He rubs the side of his face with his gun. My eyes track the movement. "And I'm sorry to drop in out of the blue like this, but I've been hearing things…"

My stomach hollows. "Such as?"

"These wild, crazy ideas that you have about me being the reason you went to prison." He's still smiling, but his gray eyes have hardened like granite.

Jason.

"And where have you been hearing those things?"

The smile widens. "Come on, Daisy. You know Jason never could keep his mouth shut. Some beers in him, and it was like fucking confession time." He laughs a low, cruel sound. "I mean, Jason coming to see you, I should've seen that coming the moment I heard you were out. He always did have a weak spot when it came to you. Had to smack him around a bit for that. I mean, I can't exactly let him off for fucking up. Fucking idiot, that he is. But then he did kinda do me a favor by coming to see me, as I got to hear all about what you've been saying."

I feel a sharp sting of betrayal. But then it's not like I could have expected more from Jason. He's a bastard and a coward, just like his brother.

"I haven't said a word to anyone else," I rush out. "And, even if I did, who would believe me anyway?"

"True." He nods, running a tattooed hand over his shaved head. "But, hearing that stuff, it makes me feel uncomfortable. Like I've left a loose thread. And I don't like feeling uncomfortable, Daisy."

Fuck.

I swallow fearfully, trying to hold myself together.

I see Damien's eyes go to the bottle of champagne on the floor by my feet.

He nods at it. "Celebrating something?"

Fists clenched by my sides, I shake my head. "No."

"Drink champagne every day, do you?"

My eyes meet with his. "Yeah. I live a champagne lifestyle nowadays, didn't you know? I mean, with all that money I got from the jewelry heist—oh, wait. No, that was you." I'm pushing it. I know I shouldn't, but my anger is getting the better of me.

He laughs. The sound scrapes through me like rough nails over soft skin.

"Hmm, I think I'll have that champagne for myself when I'm done here. Do a little celebrating myself."

"Done here."

Fuck.

"And...what are you doing here?"

"Cleaning up a mess."

I just had to ask, didn't I?

Fear twists my gut into knots. It takes everything in me not to cry. I bite the inside of my mouth—hard.

I have to get us out of here. I can't just let him kill us.

I need a plan.

What would Kas do?

Kill him. Without a second thought.

God, Kas, where are you? I need you.

But he's not coming. There's only me.

I need to keep Damien talking until I can figure out how to get us out of here.

My eyes move to Cece. Tears are swimming in her eyes. She looks so afraid. I silently try to convey to her that everything's going to be okay.

Then, I force myself to look at Damien, and I bolster myself with false bravado. "I'm really good at cleaning up messes. Did you know that?" I tell him. "Maybe I can help you with your mess."

He chuckles. "Honey, *you* are my mess." He lifts his gun and scratches his temple with the barrel of it.

I silently wish for it to go off.

No such luck.

He lowers the gun and rests it on Cece's shoulder, making her flinch and me dig my nails into my palm.

"This has nothing to do with Cece," I grit out. "It's between you and me. Let her go and—"

"You don't get to make demands. Hello? I'm the one holding the gun here." He waves the gun around, laughing.

He's laughing like it's a fucking game.

It probably is to him.

He presses the barrel of the gun to Cece's temple.

"No!" I cry.

Cece squeezes her eyes shut, tears running down her cheeks, as her body shakes.

"I'm in charge here, Daisy. And I'm not letting you or your pretty friend go anywhere. I want to have some fun first." He trails the barrel of the gun down Cece's cheek and her neck before moving it across her chest.

My body is shaking with fear and rage. I have never felt as helpless as I do right now.

He hurts her, and I swear to God...

Damien leans his face down to the side of Cece's, and he presses his nose into her hair. She flinches, trying to move away from him.

"I'm gonna fuck you good and hard, honey, and you're gonna love every second of it," he says to her.

"You touch her, and I will kill you." The words are out of my mouth before I can stop them.

But I don't regret them.

Sick, evil grinning eyes lift to mine. "Are you and she...fucking?" The grin reaches his disgusting mouth. "Because I'm down for some girl-on-girl before I fuck the both of you."

Bile rises in my throat, acid flooding my mouth, and I force it down. "You won't touch Cece or me. The only one who'll be getting fucked anytime soon is you. Fucked up by my boyfriend when he gets his hands on you."

His eyes flicker with interest. "Is that so? Jason never mentioned a boyfriend."

UNSUITABLE

"Jason doesn't know a thing about me. But my boyfriend...well, he knows *everything* about you, Damien."

He straightens up and takes the gun off Cece, resting it on the sofa but keeping a tight hold on it. "And just exactly who is your boyfriend?"

I smirk. It takes everything in me to do it, but I have to keep this going. I need to scare him. "He's someone you should be very fucking afraid of."

He holds my stare for what feels like forever, and then he lets out a mocking laugh. "You're so full of shit! You don't have a fucking boyfriend. And even if you did, Damien Doyle ain't afraid of no fucker." He taps the gun to his puffed out chest.

"Well, you should be. You should be fucking terrified, Damien. Ask Evan Foster and Levi Betts. Oh, yeah, that's right. You can't, can you? Because they're dead."

"So? What the fuck do they have to do with anything?" he snaps.

And I know I'm getting to him.

I take a bold step forward. "Who do you think killed them?"

"You're talking shit, little girl. Evan killed himself, the fucking coward that he was, and Levi was stabbed by a dealer."

"Did they ever catch that dealer who did Levi in?" I tip my head to the side in contemplation. "And, you know, come to think of it...Evan slitting his own throat?" I give a shudder, pulling a face. "I mean, it isn't exactly the usual way someone chooses to kill themselves, is it?"

He can't hide the shock that ripples over his features, and through his transparent eyes, I can see his mind working quickly.

"Seven years ago, you and your two little besties decided to rape and murder a seventeen-year-old girl in Hyde Park on the night of her prom. Her boyfriend was with her. You beat him, tortured him, and made him watch

341

while you defiled his girlfriend in the worst possible way. Then, you stabbed him over and over until you thought he was dead. Only…he wasn't dead. He survived. And he's been coming for you motherfuckers, one by one, and it's your turn, Damien."

His face pales, and his voice wavers. "What the fuck do you know about that?"

"Everything. When you're sleeping with a man, he tends to tell you things—pillow talk, you know. And he told me about every bad thing you did and how badly he's going to fuck you up, just like he did Evan and Levi."

"You're a fucking liar!" he snaps, his face turning red. "That kid was dead! I made sure of it."

"Did you not check the news after that night? Or were you just too fucking arrogant? Or did you just not care enough about the fact that you stole the lives of two fucking innocent kids? Well, whatever it was, you fucked up big time, Damien. Because he survived. And he grew up with a lot of rage and hatred, every ounce of it directed at you. You created a killer, Damien, and he's coming for you."

"You're fucking lying!" he yells, losing his cool.

I laugh. "God, I can't wait to prove you wrong. I'm going to really enjoy watching Kas cut you wide open."

"What did you say?" He steps to the side of the sofa, away from Cece.

Shit. I told him Kas's name.

Holding my face steady, I say, "What? That he's going to cut you wide open? Because he will. He'll gut you like a fish—"

"No, bitch. His fucking name." He takes a menacing step toward me. "Say his fucking name again."

Saliva floods my mouth. I swallow it down, lift my chin, and hold my bravado. "Kas."

That's when I see it. It's only a brief flicker. If I had blinked, I would have missed it. But he knows Kas's name.

UNSUITABLE

I smirk, triumphant. "You've already met him, haven't you? Well, I mean, met him again. 'Cause you already knew him, right? From seven years ago. But he's changed a lot since then. This is what he does, you know." I lean forward and lower my voice, like I'm telling him a secret. "He gets close and then"—I draw my index finger across my neck, making a slicing sound in my throat—"next thing you know, you're drowning in your own blood."

My words hang in the air between us. He looks afraid, and I feel strong.

Then, his face suddenly changes, and he laughs loudly, clutching his stomach with his hand.

And my stomach sinks.

"I fucking had you there, didn't I?" he crows. "God, you dumb bitch! Did you really think I would give a fuck about your little boyfriend? Do you know how many bitches I've raped? How many people I've killed? That little cunt and her pansy-ass boyfriend were two in a big-ass pool of people. Let him come. I want him to. It'll give me a chance to finish what I didn't get to finish all those years ago." His eyes narrow and darken on me. "Because I do hate a loose end, Daisy."

He walks slowly toward me, and I fight against the urge to run. Balling my hands into fists, I bite my lip hard to stop from trembling.

Reaching me, he stops inches away. I can smell the stench of cigarette smoke and cheap aftershave, and I want to gag.

He presses the gun to my chest, pushing the barrel in between my breasts. My legs start to shake.

"You know, the first time I saw you, when Jason brought you around, I noticed how fucking pretty you were. But you always looked so uptight, like you needed a good fucking. And I know how to fuck real good, Daisy. You want that, huh? Me to give it to you good?"

I spit in his face. And he laughs.

Eyes fixed on mine, he slowly wipes my spit from his face and then gives me a sick, twisted smile. "I'll let you have that one. But you pull any more of that shit, and I'll put a bullet between your pretty friend's eyes before you can scream for me to stop."

I can hear muffled sounds coming from Cece, like she's trying to shout behind her gag.

I force my eyes to stare back at his. "You pull that trigger, and the neighbors will call the cops faster than your inefficient, small dick can get an erection."

He grins, excitement flaring in his eyes. "Silencer, baby."

He taps the gun against my chest, drawing my eyes down to it, and that's when I register the silencer attached to it.

Fuck. I'm done for. There's no getting out of this.

I squeeze my eyes shut in defeat, and he chuckles softly.

I feel the gun move from my chest, and he comes closer.

He presses his mouth to my ear and licks the shell of it.

I shudder in disgust. A tear runs down my face.

"So, don't worry, baby; no one will hear a thing. Not even the sound of you screaming while I fuck you."

He steps back, and then he grabs the top of my dress and yanks it down, ripping it open, exposing my bra. His eyes flash with excitement, and my stomach revolts, sick with fear.

"If you're a good girl and do as I say, I'll kill you and your girlfriend quickly. You fuck with me, and I'll kill you slowly. I'll fuck you and your girlfriend six ways to Sunday, and then I'll make you watch while I cut her open before doing the same to you. You hear me, Daisy? Play nice, and this will all be over real soon."

Body quaking, I swallow roughly, my throat like sandpaper.

UNSUITABLE

His hand comes up and roughly grabs my breast. "So fucking pretty. I'm going to enjoy every fucking minute with you."

He rips my dress the rest of the way off, leaving me in only my underwear. His eyes run a sick appraisal over my body. An evil-sounding chuckle comes from his mouth. Then, he leans forward, and his disgusting tongue licks the top of my breast.

Tears running down my face, I lock eyes with Cece. She's crying behind her gag, her eyes wide with fear.

I shut my eyes, so I don't have to see her. As though that will stop her from having to see this.

This must have been how it was for Haley and Kas that night.

Something inside me suddenly snaps.

No.

I won't let this happen. I won't be this sick fuck's victim anymore. He's taken enough from me already. He's not robbing me of this as well.

He's never doing this to anyone ever again.

And, if I have to die while stopping him, then so be it.

Because I'd rather be dead than be his victim for one second longer.

Then, I stop thinking and just act.

I tightly grab ahold of his balls, squeezing harder than I ever have in my life.

He cries out in pain and shock. His head jolts up, and he head-butts my chin. I bite my tongue, and blood floods my mouth. But I don't let go. I keep a tight hold of that motherfucker's balls.

"Get the fuck off me, you fucking cunt!"

He hits me with the butt of his gun. Pain explodes in my eye, and I lose my hold on him as I stumble back, clutching my eye.

"You're gonna fucking get it now, you little bitch."

He punches me in the face. I fall backward, hitting the floor.

He's on top of me, and I'm fighting him with everything I have.

But he's too strong.

He grabs one of my flailing arms, forcing it to the floor and pinning it there. I see the bottle of champagne lying on the floor beside me, only inches away.

If I could just grab it...

He presses the gun to my forehead. "What did I fucking tell you?" he snarls. "I told you to behave. But you just don't fucking listen, do you? Do you want me to put a bullet in your girlfriend's head right now? Or maybe I should just put a bullet in yours."

He pushes the gun harder against my head, and I know there'll be a bruise there—if I live through this, that is.

"Because you are becoming more trouble than you're worth. And, honestly, Daisy, I have no problem with fucking your still-warm corpse."

A laugh bubbles up out of me, and it sounds maniacal. I *feel* maniacal.

I stare up at him. "Do your worst, Doyle. I got a feel of your tiny cock, and I'd be surprised if I'd even be able to feel it anyway."

Anger tightens his features. The gun pulls away from my forehead, and then he punches me in the face.

Holy fuck.

The pain is excruciating.

Choking on the blood filling my mouth, I start laughing again. The sound is like a gurgle. I open one eye, staring up at him. "Jesus, Doyle, I can hit harder than you. Hits like a girl and has a tiny cock. That's why you have to rape women, isn't it? To make you feel like more than you are."

"Shut the fuck up, you fucking bitch!" he yells, face bright red, as his hand rears back to hit me again.

UNSUITABLE

That's when I make a grab for the champagne bottle. I get ahold of it, but he catches my hand, trying to wrestle it from my grip.

"Get off me!" I scream, fighting with everything I have.

"I'd do as she says, if I were you."

Kas.

He's here. Thank you, God.

Twisting my head back, my eyes connect with his.

He's standing in the doorway. Pure rage covers his face, contorting his beautiful features. His black eyes look like they're on fire. Every single inch of him screams danger.

He's never looked more beautiful to me than he does now. And I've never felt relief like I do now.

Damien yanks the champagne bottle from my hand and tosses it to the floor behind him. Eyes on Kas, he sits on my stomach, pinning me to the floor. "Well, if this isn't just fucking peachy. The boyfriend's here. Come on in, Kas. Join the party." He waves his gun in Kas's direction. "You know the rules. You've been to one of my parties before. You get to sit and watch while I fuck your girlfriend. And, when I'm done with her, I get to finish you off, like I should've done seven years ago."

An animalistic sound tears from Kas.

And then everything goes crazy.

Kas lunges the short distance across the room, toward Damien. He moves so fast that Damien doesn't even get a chance to lift his gun to point it at Kas.

Kas's body connects with Damien's with a loud thud. The gun flies from Damien's hand. They both hit the floor.

Now free, I don't waste a second. I scramble up to my knees, wildly scanning the floor for the gun, while Kas fights Damien, barely a foot away from me.

My eyes lock on the gun. It's on the floor, by the foot of the armchair.

I dive for it. Hand curling around the barrel, I pick it up. Swinging around to face them, I push up to my knees, and in my trembling hand, I hold the gun properly. I raise it and point the gun at the men fighting on the floor.

I curl my finger around the trigger. "Kas," I rasp out, my voice hoarse.

He doesn't hear me. He's too busy punching Damien in the face.

"Kas! Move!" I scream.

Kas's head jerks back and around, eyes swinging to mine.

It's a mistake on my part because Damien takes full advantage of his distraction and punches Kas in the side of his head, his fist connecting with Kas's temple.

Kas slumps to the floor.

"No!" I cry out.

Damien's eyes come to me. And that's when he sees I have the gun in my hand.

Slowly, Damien gets to his feet. "And what do you think you're going to do with that, little girl?" he mocks.

My heart is pounding. Panic and fear and adrenaline are burning through me like jet fuel, making my hands shake.

Damien tips his head to the side, his eyes appraising me.

I know he's weighing whether or not I have the guts to pull the trigger.

Can I? Can I really do it?

I pull this trigger, and it's game over for me. I will never get Jesse back. I'll go back to prison.

Damien's lips curl up into a sick, twisted smile, and I know he's made his decision.

The choice is no longer mine.

I'm so sorry, Jesse.

Damien lunges for me.

And I pull the trigger.

FORTY

I'D NEVER PUT MUCH THOUGHT into what it would be like to shoot someone.

I mean, it's not like you ever think you're going to be faced with the day when you have a gun in your hand, and a homicidal maniac is trying to kill you, so it's going to be either him or you.

So, of course, it's going to be you.

But pulling that trigger is nothing like you'd think it would be.

It's not all glory where the bad guy flies backward, and I stand here, like a badass.

No. I'm the one who ends up on my ass. The kickback from the gun sends me flying backward.

And then, for what seems like the longest time, everything just stops.

The world goes kind of hazy, and it's like the sound has been switched off.

The only thing I can hear is the sound of my own racing heart, pounding against my chest.

Then, it's like the world slowly comes back into focus. And the volume is turned back up to loud. Every noise is being picked up by my ears. The sounds of traffic outside. The rattling of the windows as the wind blows against it.

Time restarts.

I'm on the floor with a gun in my hand.

And Damien Doyle is still on his feet, staring down at me in shock.

His hand is pressed to his stomach, blood seeping from the hole I just put in him.

"You fucking shot me," he says the words like he can't actually believe that I shot him.

Honestly, neither can I.

Body shaking, I manage to get to my feet. The whole time, I keep my eyes fixed on Damien and keep the gun pointed in his direction.

When I'm on my feet, I quickly glance at Kas on the floor and see that he's slowly coming around.

Eyes moving back over, past Damien, I look at Cece.

She's on the floor, sitting awkwardly against the base of the sofa, like she's wriggled her way off the sofa to try to get to us. But she's okay.

I exhale with relief.

My eyes come back to Damien, whose eyes are fixed on his blood-soaked hands.

I take a step closer to him, and his eyes lift to mine. He looks afraid.

Power and adrenaline surge through me, the likes of nothing I've ever felt before.

It's like someone else has stepped into my body and taken me over.

Gun raised and pointed at Damien, I take another step closer, putting only a few feet between us.

Fear fills his eyes. "You-you don't have to do this," he stammers, stumbling back a step. "We-we can figure something out. I have mo-money."

"Fuck you, Damien Doyle, you murderous sick fuck. Fuck you to hell and back." I take a step closer and brace my feet apart.

I take aim.

UNSUITABLE

"That first bullet was for me," I say in a voice that I barely recognize. "This one is for Haley."

Then, I pull the trigger.

The bullet rips from the gun and slams into his chest.

He falls back this time, staggering. His eyes lock with mine.

I stop breathing.

Then, he drops to the floor.

Silence. For what seems like forever.

"Daisy."

My wide eyes swing to Kas.

And reality hits me.

I killed him.

I killed Damien.

The gun drops from my hand, hitting the floor with a soft thud.

"Oh God. I-I ki-killed him. I killed him…I *fucking* killed him!"

I don't even realize I'm backing away until Kas grabs me, taking ahold of my upper arms. "Stop." His voice is hard but calm.

I still in his grasp.

"Cece needs you." He stares hard into my eyes. "Go help her."

My eyes dart to Cece.

I race over to her and pull the tape from her mouth. She winces.

"Sorry. God, I'm sorry. Are you okay?"

She nods. "Yeah. I think so. Are you?" Her eyes go to Damien's body on the floor.

I can't look.

"Yeah. Jesus, Ce, I'm sorry." Trembling hands fumble at her binds, untying them.

"I'm sorry," she counters. "I let him in. I didn't know, Dais."

"No. Stop now." I take her face in my hands. "This wasn't your fault."

Tears fill her wide eyes, and my heart ruptures open.

"I thought he was..." Her lip trembles. "I thought he was gonna...and I couldn't do anything."

I get the ties on her wrist undone.

She throws her arms around me. "I couldn't have handled it, Dais. If he'd..."

"Shh...it's okay." I smooth a hand over her hair. "It's okay." I ease out of her arms and untie her ankles.

She gets to her feet and hugs me again. Her body is shaking. Mine, too.

I'm afraid to turn around because I know, if I do, I'll see Damien's body again.

"Daisy." Kas's soft voice carries to me, turning me around.

I look at him, but my eyes instantly track to the body on the floor.

I killed a man.

My whole body starts to shake. "I killed him...Kas," I whisper. "I shot him and—"

"No." He grabs my upper arms again and lowers his head, so we're at eye-level. Black eyes stare deep into mine. "You didn't kill him, Daisy. Do you hear me? It was me that pulled that trigger. I was the one who shot Damien. Not you. Me."

My head starts to shake. Tears fill my eyes at the enormity of what he's saying. "No," I choke out.

"Yes."

"Please, Kas. I can't—"

"Yes, you can, and you will. You'll let me do this because there's a kid out there who needs you. *Jesse* needs you." He drives the point home with his eyes. "*I* killed Doyle. I'd come here to see you. Had heard your screams through the door and burst in to find Doyle trying to rape you. Cece was bound and gagged on the sofa. I lunged for

Doyle. We fought. I managed to wrestle his gun off him. I got to my feet and pointed the gun at him, but he came for me again. So, I shot him. But he didn't go down with that first bullet. He came again, so I pulled the trigger a second time, and he went down. All the time, you were on the floor, unmoving, in shock."

"Kas, I can't—"

"Yes, you can. And you will." Releasing my arms, he takes my face in his hands. "You'll do this because it's the right thing to do. It's the right thing for Jesse. God, I'm sorry I didn't get here earlier. Jesus, Daisy, just coming in here and finding him and you—I could have lost you." His eyes close, as though the pain of remembrance is too much for him to bear.

I lift a trembling hand and press it to his cheek.

He opens his eyes. The shine of tears in them nearly kills me.

He gently brushes his thumb over my swelling eye from where Damien hit me.

His eyes lower. Rage flares in his face as he takes in my half-naked state.

"Jesus." The word is an agonized sound coming from him. "Did he?"

"No."

"Thank God." He pulls me into his arms.

I bury my face in his chest. His hand grips the back of my head, holding me to him.

Unwanted images flash through my mind. I shiver in his arms.

"You're cold." He releases me and takes off his shirt.

He holds it up for me to put on. I slip my arms into the sleeves. I don't bother to button it up. I wrap it around me, keeping it in place with my arms, and I just breathe in his scent surrounding me.

He steps close to me and cradles my face in his hands, handling me like I'm precious goods.

He tilts my face up to his. "I love you," he says.

I blink, surprised, my heart stilling in my chest.

"What I said last night—that it wasn't in me to love anyone—I was wrong. So fucking wrong, babe." He leans in and kisses my lips. "I love you like I didn't know possible."

I feel him move away a fraction.

I open my eyes. His are on mine, soulful and filled with so many other emotions that I almost can't take it.

"I couldn't save Haley that night," he whispers. "But I can save you now. Let me take the blame for killing him. Let me do this one last thing for you, babe."

I feel overwhelmed. My chest is so full with my feelings for him that I can barely breathe.

"You don't have to—"

"I want to. I *need* to, Daisy."

I stare into his eyes, understanding what he's saying to me.

"Okay," I whisper. "Okay, Kas."

FORTY-ONE

SEVEN DAYS.

Seven days since I shot and killed Damien Doyle in my living room.

Seven days since Kas told the police that he was the one who had killed Damien.

Him.

Not me.

And it's been seven days since I last saw him.

After Kas convinced me to let him take the blame, I guess I was in some form of shock.

I mean, I had just killed a man. I guess it would have been weird if I hadn't gone into shock.

Kas sat me on the sofa with Cece. Then, he went about setting his scene.

I sat there with Cece on the sofa, holding her in my arms, while she sobbed quietly. And I watched, almost abstractly, as Kas wiped down the gun, removing my prints from it. Then, he put it in Damien's hands, putting his prints back on it. Then, Kas held the gun in his own hand, putting his fingerprint on the trigger, incriminating himself.

He came over and knelt in front of Cece, and he recounted the story to her, the one we were to tell the police.

After he was sure we both had it straight, he called the police.

And we sat there, Cece and me on the sofa, while Kas stood, leaning against the wall across from us, his eyes never swaying from me. And Damien's body was on the floor between us.

Then, there was a hammering at the front door. A voice yelling that it was the police.

Kas pushed off the wall and calmly walked to the front door.

And that was when all hell broke loose.

The instant the policeman saw the gun on the floor where Kas had placed it, he started yelling at us to get on the floor.

Kas was pushed to the floor by one of the officers, hands behind his head.

Cece and I slid off the sofa and got to our stomachs on the floor.

Then, we were handcuffed and separated.

As if we hadn't been through enough already.

But I got that the police didn't know the facts of what had happened. All they knew was that a dead man was in our living room.

They had to be cautious.

Kas was taken from the apartment. I saw him being led away. Our eyes connected for the briefest moment, and I said a hundred things to him in my mind.

Then, he was gone.

I was taken into the kitchen and put in the chair where I sat every morning to have my breakfast. Cece was kept in the living room.

The officer took one look at me, with my beaten-up face, wearing only Kas's shirt, and he removed the handcuffs. He sat opposite me and started asking questions.

I answered every one.

UNSUITABLE

For the most part, it was the truth. About how I'd come home and Damien was here, and he had Cece tied up with a gun pointed to her. I told the police everything.

The only difference was the ending.

I told them it was Kas holding that gun.

I felt sick about lying. My body shook. The policeman thought I was just in shock.

I was. But I was also a liar.

I am a liar.

Clearly believing me and feeling sympathy for me, he then made me a cup of tea.

"For the shock," he said.

I didn't bother to tell him that I didn't drink tea. When he put it in front of me, I just held the cup in my hands and lifted it to my face, letting the steam warm me.

A paramedic was brought into the kitchen to check me over. She cleaned up my eye, which was swelling up big time.

She asked me if I'd been raped. I glanced down at Kas's shirt that I was still wearing.

I shook my head. Then, I remembered how close it had come to happening.

If Kas hadn't come when he did, I'd have been raped…or dead by now.

Cece, too.

He saved us.

I might have pulled the trigger that killed Damien, but Kas was the one who charged a guy with a gun in his hand.

He saved me. Twice now.

After the paramedic finished with me, Cece was brought into the kitchen, a female officer with her.

Cece looked ashen and shook up.

Our eyes met, and a silent conversation passed between us.

She'd lied, too.

I'd made her an accomplice.

I hated myself in that moment.

The female police officer told us that our apartment was now an official crime scene.

We couldn't stay there. Not that I would have wanted to anyway.

She told us to pack clothes to last us a few days. That we wouldn't be allowed back until the forensics were done.

Cece and I walked out of our kitchen and into the hall. Our apartment was swarming with police.

I felt her reach for my hand, and she squeezed it.

"It's going to be okay," she whispered.

She didn't sound like she believed her own words. But I bit my lip and nodded my head.

Then, we silently walked to our bedrooms.

I didn't want to take Kas's shirt off. So, I buttoned it up properly and pulled on a pair of jeans. I quickly packed my bag and met Cece back out in the hallway.

Then, the nice policeman who had made me a cup of tea drove us to a hotel. He checked us in and then told us that they'd be in touch in the morning, as we would have to go into the station to give our official statements.

Up in our shared room, I lay in the bed with Cece lying beside me—both of us not even pretending to sleep, but neither of us wanting to speak.

I was still wearing Kas's shirt. I couldn't bring myself to take it off. Just having his scent around me was a comfort.

And I thought about Kas. He was all I thought about.

I couldn't think about what I'd done…killing Damien. I knew I'd break if I did.

So, I pushed that away, and I thought about what Kas had done for me. He'd saved me. Put me before himself. He'd protected me.

No one had ever done anything like that for me before.

And he'd told me that he loved me.

He loves me.

I couldn't stop the tears after that.

UNSUITABLE

Cece rolled over in bed and wrapped her arms around me. I cried harder. Then, she started to cry, too.

We stayed there, crying together, holding each other, until we fell asleep.

When we woke in the morning, it was to the sound of a knock on the hotel door.

Bleary-eyed, I stumbled out of bed and answered it. It was the policeman who'd driven us here last night. He told me he was there to take us to the station.

He waited in the lobby while Cece and I dressed. I just threw on some yoga pants and a T-shirt. I didn't bother to shower. I ran a brush through my hair and went to the bathroom to brush my teeth.

I saw my face in the mirror. My eye was black and swollen. On my chin was another large dark bruise from where Damien had head-butted me.

Tears swam in my eyes as images of the night before filled my head. I started to shake uncontrollably. I had to sit on the edge of the bathtub to steady myself.

I forced the tears to stop. Then, I got to my feet. Eyes avoiding the mirror, I brushed my teeth.

When I came out of the bathroom, Cece was sitting on the bed, waiting for me. Her efforts to dress were about the same as mine.

She stood up, came over, and wrapped her arms around me, hugging me. "I'm sorry," she whispered.

I jerked back, staring at her face. "You have nothing to be sorry for," I told her firmly.

"I let him in," she said. "I didn't know it was him."

Cece had never met Damien.

"How would you have known? It's not your fault. It's mine."

"No." It was her turn to be firm. "The only person to blame is that sick fucker, Damien. You saved us, Daisy. You saved my life." A tear rolled down her face.

I brushed it away. "You lied for me," I whispered. "You're going to have to lie again at the station. You shouldn't have to do that."

"You're not going back to prison. I will do anything to keep you out of that place. You're my best friend. My family. I protect my family."

I bit my quivering lip. "Kas...he's in prison...he took the blame."

"He loves you," she said.

It was all she said. All that needed to be said.

We left our hotel room and headed downstairs to the lobby where the officer was waiting.

He drove us to the police station.

We were taken into separate interview rooms, and I spent the next few hours telling the same story that I'd told them last night. One officer listened while the other made notes.

I wasn't even afraid that I might make a mistake and trip myself up. By that point, I was too weary to care.

All I wanted was to see Kas, to know how he was, but no one was telling me anything.

Every time I asked, the answer would be the same. "He's with our other officers, being questioned, as you are."

After I finished giving my statement, I was offered some food. I accepted a sandwich even though the thought of eating was the furthest thing from my mind.

I was taken aback when I saw who was bringing my sandwich to me. It was the detective who had arrested me all those years ago.

He took the seat across from me and handed me the sandwich. Then, he proceeded to tell me that Jason Doyle had been found dead in his home early that morning. His body had been there for a day before anyone had found him.

"Suicide," he said. "Jason slit his wrists," he said.

UNSUITABLE

And, also, a letter had been found on him, tucked inside his jeans pocket.

It was a confession about the robbery. He said that Jason had detailed everything about the night of the robbery. How it was him and Damien who had planned it. Jason had given him my access card while I was sleeping. Damien had used my key to gain access and rob the place. Then, he'd returned to my place and given Jason the key back along with some jewelry to plant in my apartment.

Just as I had believed it had happened all along.

My name was cleared. After all this time, that black mark against my name was gone.

I wasn't sure how I felt about Jason being dead.

Relief, I guessed. It was hard to feel anything else.

The detective led me out of the interview room. Cece was waiting for me in the waiting room along with the nice officer who'd driven us here.

He offered to take us back to the hotel. Exhausted, I thanked him and took him up on his offer. We sat in the back of the police car as he drove us through the streets of London.

I watched people walking around, living their everyday lives. Nothing had changed for them.

But, for me, everything had changed.

I would never again be the same.

The officer dropped us at the hotel and told us that they would be in touch soon.

Cece and I got out of the car. I had planned to tell her about Jason as soon as we got to our room, but the minute we walked into the hotel lobby, my eyes locked on Jesse.

He was sitting in a chair, waiting for me, his face lined with worry.

And I burst into tears.

He'd seen the news. Seen what had happened to us. I hadn't even called him.

I felt like the worst sister in the world. But he didn't care about that. He just cared that I was okay.

He rushed to me, nearly knocking me off my feet, wrapping his arms around me.

The surge of love I felt for him buckled my knees. So, I clung on to my baby brother and sobbed on his shoulder, telling him how sorry I was.

I was supposed to be the one taking care of him, but there he was, taking care of me.

He hushed me. He told me he was sorry. Sorry for ever doubting me.

That made me cry harder. Then, I heard a sob come from Cece beside us.

Jesse pulled her into our hug, and the three of us stood together, holding each other.

My family.

But there was one person missing.

Kas.

He's still missing.

Well, not *missing* in the real sense of the word. Just missing from my life.

He was released on bail two days after he was arrested.

And I haven't heard from him.

I only know he was released because I read it in the papers.

I've tried to ring him, but all I've gotten is his voice mail. I've left voice mail messages, but he hasn't called. I've texted him. But he hasn't texted back.

I want to go to the estate, but I'm afraid.

He's ignoring me. He doesn't want to speak to me or see me.

So, if I went to see him…forced a confrontation…I'm scared of what he'd say.

On a sigh, I push my key in the door of my apartment and unlock it.

I gingerly push the door open.

UNSUITABLE

We officially have our apartment back. This is my first time being back here since the shooting.

Cece couldn't face coming back. Honestly, I didn't want to either.

But we've both run out of clean clothes, and we're in this mess because of me, so coming here was the least I could do for her.

I step inside the hallway, and I'm instantly catapulted back to that day—when I walked in here, happy with a bottle of champagne in my hand.

Back when I wasn't someone who'd taken another person's life. Even if the bastard did deserve it.

I walk slowly down the hallway. My eyes catch on the living room door.

It's closed.

I stand and stare at it.

"Daisy."

I spin around at the sound of Kas's soft voice.

He's standing in the open doorway.

He looks tired. Darkness circles his eyes. His clothes look wrinkled.

And he's still the most beautiful sight I've ever seen.

I part my dry lips. "I called..."

"I know." He looks away at the wall. "I'm sorry..." He lifts and then drops his shoulder, seemingly at a loss for words.

His eyes come back to mine. There's an almost pleading look to them.

"I-I heard that you'd gotten out on bail."

"Yeah." He pushes his hand through his hair. "My lawyer says I'm looking at self-defense."

"So, you're getting off?" I hold my breath.

"Looks that way."

"Oh, thank God." I press my hand to my chest, a breath rushing out of me. I feel like an enormous weight has been lifted. "I-I don't know how to thank you for what you did."

He holds my eyes, shaking his head, silently telling me to stop.

I bite my lip.

"Is everything going to be all right with Jesse?" he asks. "Are you still allowed to see him?"

"Yes." I nod, a smile touching my lips. "Before…I didn't get to tell you, but right before what happened"—my eyes drift back to the living room door—"Anne had called, said they were giving me weekend visitation rights."

"Were?"

I look back at him. His face is tight with worry.

"Still are." I give him a soft smile. "I spoke to Anne. She was really good about everything. Brilliant in fact. And, with the truth coming out—did you hear about Jason?"

He nods slowly. Something in his eyes makes my stomach shift.

Did he…

Surely not.

"Jason committed suicide," I continue, watching him with hawk-like eyes. "He slit his wrists. He also left a note—a confession—clearing my name."

His eyes move back to the wall. He nods. "I'm glad the truth finally came out."

I bite my lip, fighting against the words that I'm burning to ask him.

The fight doesn't last long.

"Was this you, Kas? Did you force Jason to write that letter and then…kill him, making it look like suicide?"

He exhales a sad-sounding breath. Then, his eyes move slowly back to mine. "There isn't anything I wouldn't do to protect you."

I suck in a breath. Tears fill my eyes. "Thank you," I whisper.

UNSUITABLE

Who is this man? I don't know what I did to deserve him, but I'm glad I found him—or, as the case is, that he found me.

I can't even bring myself to feel any sadness or remorse for Jason. He put me in prison and then sold me out to his brother. He had to have known what Damien was going to do to me.

Blowing out a breath, I press the back of my hand to my eyes, drying away the tears. "And thank you for what you said to Anne about me."

His eyes flash with confusion.

"You spoke to her on the telephone before this all happened."

"I only spoke the truth."

"Regardless, it helped a lot."

He shifts on his feet. "So, things are looking good for Jesse coming home?"

"Yes." I smile. "Even with…what happened. The fact that I'm"—I stall on the word—"*innocent* of the crime I was put in prison for and that my name is in the process of officially being cleared, I guess it holds a lot of clout with Social Services." I bind my hands together in front of me. "They no longer see me as a risk to Jesse…even though what happened…happened. Because Damien and Jason are dead, I guess they see it as being over. I think."

"It is over," his words are spoken softly.

But, for some reason, they hurt.

Almost like he's saying *we* are over…

"Nothing that happened that day was your fault, Daisy. You saved us…you saved *me*. So, don't ever blame yourself for what happened. Don't hold on to it because it will eat you up." He sounds like he's speaking from experience.

I guess he is.

"Damien was always going to die. You just beat me to it." The corner of his lip tips up into a half-smile, making me smile.

Then, it drops when I remember the reason I'm smiling.

I killed a man. Just like Kas has.

I guess we have more in common now than we ever did before.

Mirroring him, I wrap my arms over my chest. "How did you know that Damien was here that day?" I ask him the question that's been plaguing me for a while now.

"I didn't. It was just lucky timing."

"So, why were you here?"

"To see you."

"Why?"

He sighs. "Because being without you just didn't feel like an option."

My heart constricts at his words. But something tells me there's a *but* in those words.

"And now?" I ask quietly.

He blows out a breath, pushing his hands into his pockets, his eyes making friends with the carpet. "And, now…it still doesn't feel like an option, but…"

And there it is.

I tighten my arms around my suddenly cold chest. "But?"

He lifts his eyes to mine, and what I see in them makes my heart break.

"I'm leaving, Daisy. Once the thing is sorted with the police, I'm leaving."

He's leaving.

"Oh." I step back, needing the distance, though wanting to be closer to him now more than ever.

He exhales roughly. Freeing his arm, he shoves a hand through his hair. "You're so close to getting Jesse back, and being with me, it would hinder that. I might be close to getting off with self-defense, but in the eyes of the law, I killed a man. I *have* killed men. In cold blood. There's no coming back from that, Daisy."

UNSUITABLE

"I've killed someone, too."

Fierce black eyes meet with mine. "You need to forget that ever happened."

"You want me to forget when you won't allow yourself to forget?"

"It's different."

"How?"

"Because I fucking deserve to remember everything. You don't."

"Bullshit!" I snap. "This is bullshit! You're leaving me here, and I'm just supposed to accept that? Fuck you, Kas."

"Daisy..." He takes a step toward me. "You know I'm right. If I stay here, you won't get Jesse back. They'll use me as a reason to keep him from you—"

"No, they won't. Anne said—"

"Daisy," he reasons. Taking my face in his hands, he forces my eyes up to his. Tears are filling them. "I don't want to be—I *can't* be the reason you don't get Jesse back. You'd resent me. End up hating me. I couldn't bear it if that happened."

He's right. I know he's right. Just the selfish part of me doesn't want to let him go.

The selfish part of me wants it all.

Wants him and Jesse.

But I know, in the real world, the two things just don't go together.

Jesse has to come first. He will always come first.

Turning, I step away from Kas.

"Your name is clear," he says from behind me. "You can do anything. Go anywhere. Make a better life for yourself and Jesse. You don't need a screwed up fuck like me holding you back."

I spin around, ready to argue, but he holds a hand up, stopping me.

"And I need time, Daisy." His eyes hold mine, a thousand emotions running through them. None of them are good. "I need to find out who I am." His words cut me down. "I've spent the last seven years of my life chasing revenge, being obsessed with it…and, now…" He blows out a breath, looking lost. "I need time," he whispers.

He's leaving. He's really leaving.

I want to curl up into a ball on the floor and cry.

But I don't.

I do what I always do. I hold steady. "Where will you go?" I ask quietly.

"Greece. If you still need the job at the estate, I'm hiring someone to run it—"

I shake my head.

I couldn't go there every day and see that place. See the bed where he once made love to me…

"If you need money," he says.

"I'll be fine."

"Yeah, I know you will be."

I lift my eyes to him to see a sad smile touching his lips.

And I don't look away. I keep staring at him, soaking in every detail of him, knowing it's the last time I'm ever going to see him.

And he stares right back at me.

My heart is beating painfully. I'm slowly dying on the inside.

I have to get away from him. I need to stop feeling this way.

But I'm not ready to leave him yet.

Deep down, I know I'll never be ready.

"So…" I hear myself saying, breaking our quiet.

Kas doesn't speak. He just walks over to me. And, when he reaches me, he takes my face in his hands. His eyes roam my features, like he's drinking me in.

My mouth is dry. There are hot tears behind my eyes, and my throat feels like it's about to crack.

"Daisy…" he whispers my name. He slowly brings his mouth to mine, only closing his eyes when our lips meet.

UNSUITABLE

He softly kisses me, tasting me, letting his tongue slide along mine.

Tears fill my eyes as I memorize the feel of him against me, the way he kisses me.

Then, he deepens the kiss, clutching me to him. And I match him stroke for stroke.

"I love you," he breathes against my lips. "That will never change, no matter where I am."

I love you, too.

Don't leave me, please.

The words are on the tip of my tongue.

But I never say them.

I have to let him go. For his sake. For Jesse's. And for mine.

"Will I ever see you again?" I breathe through the agony.

He tugs me into his arms and hugs me tight. "Thank you," he whispers, answering my question without actually saying the words. "You brought me back to life, Daisy, and for that, I will never be able to repay you."

I'm never going to see him again.

My heart splinters in two.

He removes his arms from around me, leaving me cold. He stares down at me and gives me a sad smile. "Good-bye, Daisy Smith."

I swallow past my tears. "Good-bye, Kastor Matis," I whisper.

He touches my cheek with his hand one last time, and then he turns and walks out of my apartment and out of my life, taking a piece of my broken heart with him.

EPILOGUE

THREE AND A HALF YEARS LATER

SEEING THE LAST CUSTOMER OUT, bidding them goodbye, I shut the door and turn the sign over to read, *Closed*. Walking back around the counter, I drop my tired butt down onto a stool.

It's been a long day.

A hard day.

Jesse's starting university.

I drove him there this morning, so he could get settled in the dorm.

So, we'd packed my car up with his stuff, and I'd tried not to cry the whole time.

Yep, I have a car. I learned how to drive a few years ago. So much easier having a car, and I'm going to need it with Jesse being in Birmingham.

I was so proud of him when he got accepted. I might have wanted him to stay in London, but he'd loved Birmingham when we visited earlier in the year, and they have a really good law school.

Yep, that's right. My boy wants to be a lawyer.

When he told me what he wanted to be, I won't deny that I was surprised. He'd never shown an interest in the law before.

And the law hadn't exactly been a friend to me over the years.

But whatever he wanted to do, I would be happy with it. I'd support him.

Then, he told me why he wanted to be a lawyer.

He said that the law had failed me in so many ways. My lawyer had failed me. He said there were too many shit lawyers out there, and he wanted to be one of the good ones. He wants to make a difference. Make sure that what happened to me doesn't happen to anyone else.

I got a little choked up at that.

Okay, I might have cried.

I'm a weepy bitch nowadays.

So, I got my boy settled in his room and helped him unpack his things. Then, I left him to get to know his roommates.

I might have cried a little bit then too.

Okay, I held on to him for ages and sobbed before managing to pry myself away from him.

Once I got in my car, it took me a good fifteen minutes to be able to drive, as my eyes were blurry from all the crying.

But my boy has grown up. He's a man now.

And I'm…alone.

Well, I have Cece. But it's not the same.

So, with my bird having flown from the nest, I drove back to London and came back to work. I was supposed to have the day off, but I didn't want to go home to an empty house. So, I came in and helped out Jasmine, one of my part-time employees.

That's right. I have employees. I am the proud owner of a little chic coffee shop called Thessa's.

UNSUITABLE

And, yes, I named it after the place where Kas is from. Well, he's from Thessaloníki, but it's not exactly easy to say, so I went with Thessa's, and I think it has a nice ring to it.

After my name was cleared, Cece encouraged me to pursue compensation for wrongful imprisonment.

I wasn't sure. I didn't care about the money. I was just glad to be free of the blame. To have that black mark taken from my name and to be able to apply for jobs without having to tick that box was amazing in itself.

But then Cece pointed out that I could put whatever money I got toward Jesse's future.

So, I got a lawyer, and she pursued a case for wrongful imprisonment.

My case was won, and I nearly fell off my chair when my lawyer sat me down and told me what I would be getting.

It was enough to set Jesse and me up for the future.

The first thing I did was put a deposit down on a house. Cece and I couldn't bear to live in the apartment anymore, and I would never want Jesse living there. There were just too many bad memories in that place.

It wasn't our home anymore. Damien had taken that from us.

So, we moved our things out of there and started afresh in our new home.

And then, a month later, Jesse moved in permanently with us.

It was the best moment of my life.

I had applied for full guardianship, and after jumping through hoops, it was granted.

I remember the first day he moved back home. Just being there with him, seeing how happy he was, made all the bad stuff that I'd had to go through to get to that point worth it.

I wasn't going to look back and wish that things had been different. I could look back and be angry all I wanted, but it wasn't going to change the past.

I had Jesse with me now, and that was all that mattered.

But I was still unemployed. Jesse was at school, and Cece was working. I felt lost. I spent a lot of those days wallowing and missing Kas, wondering how he was doing.

I'd never been a wallower, and I was starting to drive myself crazy.

One day, when I was out for my morning run, things changed for me. As I was running through the town center, I happened to see a For Sale sign in the window of a cute little coffee shop.

Before I knew it, I was stopping, peering in through the window, and then putting the number for the estate agent in my phone. I headed back home and called the estate agent, asking for the price of the place. I also found out they were selling the shop along with the equipment.

It wasn't as expensive as I had expected. Don't get me wrong; it was a lot of money, but it was affordable for me.

I asked if I could view it. The estate agent told me she had a free spot that day.

So, I got showered and changed, and I headed back to the coffee shop where the agent was waiting outside for me.

The minute she let me inside, I just knew. It was meant to be mine. It was perfect. I loved everything about it.

I asked her why the owner was selling and selling so reasonably. She just said they had to leave the country unexpectedly due to a sick relative, and they wouldn't be coming back for some time.

As awful as it sounds, their bad fortune became my good fortune.

So, I told the agent I would think about it. But my mind was already made up.

It would cut into the money, but it would give me a good income to help with Jesse's future. And there would

UNSUITABLE

still be a decent chunk to get him started in whatever he decided to do when he left school.

I put an offer in on the coffee shop the next day. Lower than the actual asking price.

It was accepted an hour later.

I couldn't stop smiling. And I couldn't help but think that Kas would have been proud of me.

He was the first person I wanted to call. But, of course, I couldn't because I didn't know where he was, and I no longer had his phone number.

After he'd left, I'd deleted it, knowing that I would probably break down and call him. And I couldn't do that.

So, I had no way to contact him.

And then I realized that I also knew absolutely nothing about running a business.

It wasn't just about making coffee—even though I do make an awesome cup of coffee. This was running a business. It was huge.

And I thought I would probably fuck it up.

I started to panic, thinking I'd made a mistake, before rationality decided to make an appearance.

Look at everything I'd done...overcome. I could run a fucking coffee shop.

I could do it.

So, I got Cece's laptop out and went searching for business management courses. I found one at my local college. The classes were at night, so it was perfect.

I enrolled and was accepted.

Then, I focused on making the shop mine. I gave the place a lick of paint and put my own stamp on it, and then I renamed the coffee shop to Thessa's. It felt right to call it that. It was because of Kas that my name was cleared. He was the reason I could afford the place.

And I just wanted something of his, some connection to him, to remind myself that he was real. Because, sometimes, it felt almost unreal. Like Kas had never actually existed. Like he'd never really been mine.

But he had.

I'd had him for a brief moment in time, and then I'd had to let him go.

Kas was never meant to be mine forever, and I had to come to terms with that.

And I did.

Kind of.

But then Thessa's was open, and I actually had customers. I was busy, and I got on with life.

After I had Thessa's for six months, I decided to enroll in a baking course. I had a place where I ordered cakes and muffins from for the shop, but I wanted to learn to make my own.

Growing up, I'd always been able to make a mean birthday cake for Jesse, so I reckoned I could do it.

Turned out, I was right. I excelled in baking. And I now make cakes for the shop as well as still buying in. It keeps me busy, but that's the way I prefer it.

It doesn't leave a lot of time for anything else…like dating. Not that I'm actually interested in dating even though Cece nags me about it on a regular basis.

She's back in the dating game; she has been for a while. She's been seeing this guy called Pierre for a couple of months now. He's an out-of-work actor.

He's cute.

He's just kind of…pretentious.

But I think she could do better.

Cece likes him though, and she says he treats her good. That's all that matters to me. She deserves to be happy.

So, I'm nice to the guy whenever he's around.

But, because she's happy, she's been trying to set me up with guys. The latest was one of Pierre's poncy friends called Gerard. Another out-of-work actor.

UNSUITABLE

I told her what I always tell her, "I'm not interested. I'm too busy with work and Jesse." And blah, blah, blah.

But she's not stupid. She knows that I'm not over Kas. That I've never gotten over Kas.

I mean, you'd think I would have gotten over him by now. It has been three and a half years.

But, as I've learned, you don't get over a man like Kastor Matis. You just learn to live without him.

So, I've resigned myself to the fact that this is the way it is. Spinsterhood for Daisy, and I'm totally fine with it.

My life isn't lacking. I have a good life. I have Jesse.

Even though he just left me for university.

I'm not going to cry again.

I have the coffee shop to keep me busy.

My life is as good as it's going to be. And I'm okay with that.

When I look at the way my life was…and how it could've turned out…this life is a dream compared to that.

Of course I get lonely. Especially at night when I look at that empty space in my bed where I wish Kas were lying.

But he's gone.

He's been gone a long time, and there's nothing I can do to change that.

It's just sometimes hard, knowing that he's out there, living his life without me.

I wonder if he's happy.

I hope he's happy. He deserves to be.

I just wish we could have been happy together.

My phone rings on the counter. I smile at the caller display.

"Missing me already?"

Jesse's laugh echoes down the line. "Just checking to make sure you're not still bawling your eyes out."

"I did not bawl."

"There was snot on my T-shirt from where you'd blubbered on me."

"Oh God." I wince. "I'm sorry."

"Don't be. I'm just teasing. It's nice to know you're gonna miss me. I just hate to see you cry and know I'm the reason for it."

"They were happy tears and sad tears and proud tears. I'm gonna miss you so much, but I'm incredibly proud of you, Jesse, for getting into university. You're going to get your degree and become a lawyer. God, I cannot wait until the day I see you in your cap and gown, up on that stage, receiving your degree."

"I haven't even started my courses yet"—he laughs—"and you've already got me graduated."

"Yeah, well, I just know you're gonna rock it."

There's silence on the line that has me asking, "Are... *you* okay?"

He sighs. "Yeah. It's just...I guess it's weird, being here. In a new place. You know, where I just have a bedroom, and the rest is shared facilities with the other guys. It kinda reminds me of the boys home. The first night I spent there after you were arrested."

My throat closes up. "Jesse..."

"I'm not blaming you, Daisy. Jesus, of course I'm not. I hate the fact that I ever doubted you and blamed you. Just sitting here brought back some sad memories for me, and...I guess...I wanted to hear your voice. Just remind myself that we're here now, and it's different. That things are good. And you're fine."

I swallow back tears. "We're here, and it is different. It's amazing. I'm fine, kiddo. And I couldn't be prouder of you."

I feel his smile.

"You already said that."

I smile myself. "And I'm gonna keep saying it, so you'd better get used to it."

I hear a voice in the background, and Jesse says, "Be there in a minute."

UNSUITABLE

"Everything okay?" I ask.

"Yeah, just the guys I live with are going to the pub. They've invited me to go with them."

"Go. Don't let me keep you. And have fun. And don't drink too much. And be safe. And I love you."

He laughs, and the sound washes through me like a sweet melody.

"I will. And I won't. And of course I will. And…I love you, too, Mayday."

He disconnects the call, and I breathe through the emotion.

Don't cry. You've cried enough today.

Blowing out a breath, I get to my feet to start the cleanup before I lock up for the night.

I always like a little music to clean to. Like I used to when I cleaned the Matis Estate. I used to wear my earphones then, so as not to piss off Kas.

He always was easy to piss off.

But this is my place, and I can listen to music as loud as I want. Well, without annoying the neighboring businesses, that is.

Setting my phone on the counter beside the coffee machine, I go to my music and select Zayn's "Like I Would."

This song reminds me of Kas. It was playing that night in the club when he sabotaged my date with Cooper and was waiting for me outside the restroom.

I like to torture myself with it every now and then.

Sad, but I like to think of myself as being the one singing the lyrics to Kas.

I'm telling him that he will never find anyone who will love him like I would love him. *Do* love him.

And, yes, I'm that sad.

In Kas's mind, I'm probably just a bad memory of a time that he'd rather forget.

He walked away. He was right to.

And, now, he's probably moved on to some gorgeous Greek beauty who isn't saddled with a world of emotional baggage and who doesn't remind him of death and other things I choose not to think about because, if I do, my head might explode.

Actually, it's feeling close to explosion now, so I focus on cleaning the coffee machine.

I'm halfway through cleaning it when Zayn has finished, and now, John Legend is singing "All of Me." I'm getting all emotional, singing along to the lyrics, wishing someone—okay, Kas—felt that way about me, thought those things about me, when the door chimes, opening.

Who's that? I put the Closed sign up. Some people just don't pay attention.

Sucking in a breath, blinking my eyes clear, I turn around. "I'm sorry. We're clo—" The words die on my tongue, and my heart falls out of my chest.

"Kas," I breathe his name, like I expect him to disappear in a puff of smoke.

"Hi, Daisy." His words are soft, tentative.

And my brain is failing me.

I don't know how many times I've pictured this scenario in my head. That I'd be here late, and he'd walk in, telling me that he missed me. That he regretted leaving. That he couldn't get over me. That he loved me. And then I would jump into his arms, and he'd kiss me. Then, everything would be like it was.

I watch too many chick flicks, I know.

But he is here. And, now, I can't move or speak or do anything but stare at him.

He looks exactly the same. Like no time has passed at all.

I'm suddenly conscious of how I look.

Dressed in black trousers and a black polo shirt with the coffee shop's logo. My hair is tied back into a messy bun. I have no makeup on because I cried it all off earlier.

UNSUITABLE

I look terrible.

And he looks beautiful.

His hair is shorter than it used to be, and he has some serious stubble going on. I always did love stubble on him. He's wearing a checkered navy-blue suit with a white shirt. Similar to what he was wearing the first day I met him.

And he looks like everything I ever wanted but never got to have. Not really.

I'm still staring at him. I'm afraid to blink in case this is all a mirage conjured up by my desperate imagination, and he won't be here when I open my eyes.

Damn air-conditioning dries my eyes, and I blink.

When my eyes open, he's still here.

"How…where…how?" I'm stammering. I stop and take a deep breath, resting my palm on the counter. The cool top calms me some.

He's here. He's really here.

I blow the breath out and look over at him. "How have you been?" My voice is hoarse.

He lifts a shoulder. His eyes are fixed on mine. "You know…" He trails off, not actually answering my question. "You look great, Daisy. Beautiful. But then you always do. And you look like you're doing well." He gestures to the shop.

I try not to let the *beautiful* comment get to me, and instead, I focus on the fact that I get the distinct impression that he knows it's my coffee shop. How he would know that, I have no clue. But then Kas always did have a way of just knowing things.

"I'm doing okay." *Never got over you. Spent the last three years pining for you. But, aside from that, I'm just peachy.*

He smiles. And my heart ruptures.

"How's Jesse?" he asks.

"Good." I smile. "He starts university on Monday."

"Which university?"

"Birmingham."

"What's he studying?"

"Law," I say proudly.

He smiles. "And how's Cece?"

"She's great. Why are you here?" The words come out sharper than I intended. But I don't regret them.

I do want to know why he's here. Over three years and not a word. And then he just turns up on what has been a hard and emotional day, screwing with my head even more.

There's a momentary look of surprise in his eyes at my blunt question, but he quickly recovers. "I'm here for you."

My heart shimmies in my chest. "For me?" I take a breath. "I don't understand."

"I think you do."

"No, I don't." I shake my head. "So, you're going to have to clarify for me."

And I want him to be specific. *Very* specific. Because I don't want to misunderstand a word he's saying.

My heart broke for him once before, and it never recovered. I don't want to give myself hope, only for my heart to break a second time.

"I left to ensure that you'd get Jesse back. To give you both a chance at the life you deserved. I stayed away because it was the right thing to do. Jesse needed you. And I was fucked up, Daisy. I was fucked up when you met me. And I wasn't getting fixed anytime soon. I'd been that way for so long that it was all I knew. Then, it was over. And I was lost. When you've lived on revenge for so long and then you have it, you think you should feel amazing. And you do for that brief moment. But then that passes, and you just feel lost. There's no purpose anymore, just the memories of everything in the past."

"You had me." The words come out more broken than I wanted. I wrap protective arms around myself.

He rakes a hand through his short hair. "I wasn't good for you. I screwed up. I was sinking into a hole, and I would have only brought you down with me. You needed to focus on Jesse. And, for once in my fucked up life, I wanted to do the right thing. And the right thing was for me to walk away."

"But for three years, Kas…" My words trail off because I don't know what else to say.

"I took a long time to get to where I needed to be."

"And where was that?"

"To becoming a man you deserve."

"And are you?"

His eyes lift to mine. "I don't think I'll ever deserve you, Daisy. No man ever could. But I'm closer to getting there than I was before, and I'm done being without you. I waited until Jesse was a man. Able to stand on his own two feet. Now, he's at university. And I'm back to claim what was always mine."

"And what if I no longer want you?"

There's a flash of panic on his face, but he shuts it down a nanosecond later and is back to his ever-confident self. "Then, I hang around and bug the shit out of you with romantic gestures until you love me again."

"The Kas I knew wasn't romantic."

"The Kas you knew was a dick."

"Kas-hole."

I grin, and he laughs. I love the sound.

"I don't know. I kind of liked the old Kas. What if I don't like this new, improved version?"

"You won't know until you give him a try…give *me* a try." He moves across the shop, coming around the counter, until he's standing in front of me.

He reaches out and takes ahold of my hand, and I let him.

My skin sizzles, my whole body coming back to life after lying dormant for so long.

"Give me a chance to show you how good life can be with me now. Let me love you. Let me take care of you."

A flash of my earlier thoughts—about what he's been doing in all that time he's spent away from me—cuts into my mind, making me feel cold inside.

I take my hand back from him and wrap my arms around myself again, like a protective shield.

And he doesn't bother to hide the hurt on his face.

"What have you been doing all this time?" I ask quietly.

"I was in Greece with my parents for a little while. They've moved out there permanently now. Then, I traveled around a bit."

His dark eyes haven't strayed from mine.

But all I can see is beautiful locations and beautiful women.

Kas with other women.

"There's been no one else," he says softly, as though reading my thoughts. "How could there be when I was in love with you?"

Was.

"*Still* am in love with you."

He steps up close and takes my face in his hands. I blink up at him. My heart somersaults in my chest. My mouth dries, and my skin is on fire where he's touching it.

"I love you, Daisy. I've loved you for the last three years. I want to be with you, and I will do anything to make that happen."

"What if I have someone else?" I step back out of his hold, and his hands drop to his sides. "You just come here, out of the blue, and say you want me back, assuming I have nobody in my life. Well, I could have a boyfriend, for all you know."

I'm pissed that he hasn't even asked. That he assumes that I'm so pathetic that I wouldn't have moved on from him. That I'd still be single.

So what if it's actually true?

The fact that he just assumes pushes my buttons.

And, honestly, I want a reaction. I want to piss him off.

UNSUITABLE

Don't ask me why because the only answer I can give is that it's because I'm a girl. I'm confused and hurt that he's been gone for so long. But I'm happy that he's here. And I'm feeling every other emotion in between.

He doesn't react. He just stares back at me and asks in a calm voice, "Is there anyone else?"

My face instantly heats because, now, I'm going to have to tell him no. He'll know how pathetic I am, and I only have myself to blame.

Then, it registers that he didn't react. The Kas I knew would have reacted.

Maybe he really has changed.

Or maybe…

"You didn't ask if there was anyone else because you already know there isn't and that there hasn't been in all the time you've been gone. Am I right?"

He doesn't even have the dignity to look ashamed.

He just steps back up to me and puts his hands on my face, where they've always belonged, tilting my eyes up to meet his. He stares deep into them.

"When I walked away from you, it was the hardest thing I'd ever had to do. The only thing that made it manageable was knowing that I wasn't letting you go forever. Daisy, I might have let you go then, but I didn't let you go far. And, honestly, if I'd gotten a whiff of another guy sniffing around, then I'd have gone back on my self-imposed promise to stay away until Jesse was eighteen, and I'd have come here, broken the guy's face, then carried you back to my house, and never let you go."

Well…shit.

What am I supposed to say to that? Unsure, I go with what I always go with when I'm stumped. Humor.

"Should I take it that your stalking ways are still going full force then?"

His eyes spark and grin at me.

I shake my head, fighting a smile.

I really shouldn't smile right now. Because it's not funny.

"Honestly, how the hell did you manage to stalk me when you weren't even here, when you were off traveling the world?"

His brows draw together. "I didn't say I was off traveling the world. I said, I was in Greece for a while, and then I traveled a bit."

"And where did you travel to?"

A hint of something I don't quite understand flickers through his eyes.

"Why do you want to know?" he asks.

"Because you're acting like you have something to hide, and I want to know what it is."

"Well"—he clears his throat—"I was in Greece. Then, I wasn't…and I was here…traveling back and forth between Westcott…and London." Even though he cleared his throat, his words still come out gravelly.

And my eyes widen to saucers. "Oh my God! You've been here all this time!" I step back, stunned and also hurt.

I feel like he's betrayed me—although I'm not quite sure how.

He follows me forward, his hands landing on my shoulders. "Not the *whole* time. I did go to Greece. I stayed there for six months. Then, I came back."

"You've been here for three years! Jesus, Kas." I shake my head.

"I stayed away for as long as I could. As long as it took to get my head straight. Then, I came home. I wanted to be closer to you. If I had to wait to have you, then I was going to be close to you while I did so."

"Jesus…" I breathe, staring up at him. "I don't know whether to be freaked out that you've been basically stalking me for the last three years. Or feel bowled over with emotion at the fact that you couldn't stay away from me."

UNSUITABLE

I have the sudden urge to start singing The Police's "Every Breath You Take," but I don't because that would be weird.

And how could he be here for all that time and me not know?

Or maybe, subconsciously, I did know, and that was why I could never get over him.

Kas gives me a sheepish but hopeful look. "Can we just go with bowled over?"

The look on his face is…so boyish that I can't help but smile. "You have serious issues, Matis."

"Just one. And she goes by the name Daisy."

I give him a playful scowl.

And he smiles, but his expression quickly turns serious. "I want you to be my issue. And I want to be yours. I want you to be my everything. And I want to be your everything." His hand lifts to my face, cupping it. "I want a life with you, Daisy. Try again with me, *please*. Just say yes. Just tell me you still love me and say yes."

Pressing my cheek into his hand, I close my eyes, reveling in the feel of him. I already know my decision. I knew it the moment I turned around and saw him standing there.

I open my eyes and smile. "I still love you, Kas. And, yes. Yes, a million times over."

His face breaks out into the biggest and most beautiful smile I've ever seen. Then, his lips are on mine, and he's kissing me. I never want him to stop.

And, now, I know he will never stop. Because he's here to stay.

It wasn't our time before. But it's our time now.

I once thought of Kas and me as totally unsuitable for one another. We were unsuitable.

But, now, we're perfect.

Okay, well, maybe not perfect.

He's killed in revenge. Killed for me. And I shot a man dead.

But we're perfect for each other, and that's all that matters.

He breaks our kiss, breathing heavily. "So, Thessa's." He nods his head toward the front of the shop. "Does that have anything to do with Thessaloníki?" he says with a touch of accent to that sexy voice, making my lady bits perk up. "Or is it just a coincidence?"

A blush covers my face. I lower my eyes. "I just wanted something to remember you by," I whisper. "Something to remind me that you were real."

He tips my chin up with his fingers, bringing my eyes to his. "I'm real, babe. And I'm here to stay. I'm never leaving you again."

And I know he means it.

"I'm never letting you go," I tell him right before his lips fall back to mine.

I slide my hands up into his hair, and he moans a sweet sound.

He wraps his arms around me, pulling me closer to him until there's no space between us at all. And I go willingly.

I fall back into him, back into the only place I was ever meant to be.

In Kas's arms. Where I plan on staying for the rest of my life.

ACKNOWLEDGMENTS

WRITING *UNSUITABLE* has been a hell of a challenge for me.

Two years in the making. Sixty thousand words deleted. The story line reworked, and the book restarted. Two extended editing dates, and finally, I'm here!

I really stepped outside of my comfort zone to write Daisy and Kas's book, and I'm beyond glad I did.

Kas is literally *the* most complex character I have ever written. He broke me and then put me back together with his inner beauty. I adore every complex part of him. I hope you do, too.

As always, the biggest thank you goes to my husband, Craig. Babe, you're my biggest champion and supporter, but more importantly, you're my best friend. I couldn't do it without you.

My children, Riley and Isabella, you are both literally the best thing I have ever done. Even if I fail at everything else in life, I will always know that I got something right—the both of you.

My girls, Sali, Trishy, and Jodi—Who knew long-distance friends would turn out to be the best friends a girl could ask for? I love you all.

My editor, Jovana—We've been working together for a long time now, and you never cease to amaze me with your awesomeness.

My cover designer, Naj—Your ability to pull out the image that I have in my head and make it a reality astounds me every time.

My Wether Girls—I adore you ladies! Thank you so much for your endless support.

My agent, Lauren, the best agent a girl could ask for—Thank you for always supporting my decisions and getting my books out there, all over the world.

Big shout-out and thank you to all the bloggers who work tirelessly to help promote our books—We authors couldn't do it without you.

And, lastly, to you, the reader—I couldn't do this without you. Thank you from the bottom of my heart.

ABOUT THE AUTHOR

SAMANTHA TOWLE is a *New York Times*, *USA Today*, and *Wall Street Journal* bestselling author. She began her first novel in 2008 while on maternity leave. She completed the manuscript five months later and hasn't stopped writing since.

She is the author of contemporary romances, The Storm Series and The Revved Series, and stand-alones, *Trouble*, *When I Was Yours*, *The Ending I Want*, and *Sacking the Quarterback*, which was written with James Patterson. She has also written paranormal romances, *The Bringer* and The Alexandra Jones Series. All of her books are penned to the tunes of The Killers, Kings of Leon, Adele, The Doors, Oasis, Fleetwood Mac, Lana Del Rey, and more of her favorite musicians.

A native of Hull and a graduate of Salford University, she lives with her husband, Craig, in East Yorkshire with their son and daughter.

CPSIA information can be obtained
at www.ICGtesting.com
Printed in the USA
LVHW030710161222
735314LV00002B/56

9 781537 734811